SOUL EYES

WAYNE L. WILSON

Genesis Press Inc.

Obsidian

An imprint of Genesis Press Inc.
Publishing Company

Genesis Press, Inc.
P.O. Box 101
Columbus, MS 39703

ISBN: 1-58571-147-0
Manufactured in the United States of America

First Edition

Visit us at www.genesis-press.com
or call at 1-888-Indigo-1

ACKNOWLEDGMENTS

I would like to send a heartfelt thanks to Niani Colom of Genesis Press for her faith on the impact of Soul Eyes, by requesting two more books before my debut novel was even published. Many thanks to the editors, Angelique Justin and Deatri King-Bey for their tender loving care regarding the novel. I'm going to start referring to Deatri as the Jenny Craig of the editorial world for helping me to get this manuscript into terrific shape! I would also like to thank my agent, Gina Panettieri of Talcott Notch, for her enthusiasm, expertise, insight, and encouragement. As I've repeatedly said of her, she "got it" the first time she read Soul Eyes and has taken this project in the directions it needs to go. I'm blessed to have her in my corner. My final thanks goes to Taylor Barnes who will always hold a more than special place in my heart. She has always envisioned illustrating the cover art for Soul Eyes and it is her outstanding artwork you see on the cover. I think she did a magnificent job of capturing the essence of the story and for that, I will be eternally grateful.

DEDICATION

To my father, Charles, for teaching me the value of a strong work ethic.

To my mother, Shirley, for giving me immeasurable love and support.

To my daughter, India, for filling my life with her joyful spirit and endless inspiration.

Fatalism: A doctrine that events are fixed in advance for all time in such a manner that human beings are powerless to change them.

CHAPTER 1

Sooner or later it had to happen; anytime, anywhere. Had my daughter, Olisa, been in the country during the time of the L.A. riots in 1992, it might have happened then. Instead, it transpired at Venice Beach during a wild July 4th weekend.

It was on a Sunday night, July 6, early evening, and our soul food restaurant was packed. A twenty-minute wait increased to sixty minutes as couples and families with restless hungry children waited for a table.

My sister, Wilma, scolded one of the new waiters in the kitchen about his billing mistakes, while I was absorbed in my own concerns. It didn't look like I had ordered enough chicken for the night. Meanwhile, the phone begged to be answered. Valerie, our hostess, called in late, so we were also shorthanded.

Gently lifting a phone that I wanted to rip out of the wall, I answered affably, "Soul of Venice."

"Unc, is that you? Aw, man, thank goodness you're there."

"Gumbo? What's up? You need to talk to your mother?"

"No, no, Unc, I gotta talk to you."

"You sound like you been running the decathlon. Everything all right?"

"Yeah, well, no… Uh, I mean everything is all right now, except…" he trailed off.

"Alton, I can't understand a word you're saying. Speak louder! What's going on?" Wilma stood next to me, a hand on her hip as she waited for the authorization machine to clear a Visa. She mouthed, "What's wrong?"

I shrugged my shoulders, covered my ear with the other hand, then tried to muffle the cacophony of voices, clanking plates and the plastic money machine that sounded like a deranged typewriter as it happily lapped up another credit card.

"Uncle Joe, you still there?"

"Yeah, Alton, 'cept I can barely hear you. Where are you now?"

"Your house… With Olisa."

"Is she okay?"

"Oh yeah, she's fine, she's asleep."

"At 7:00?

"That's why I called, Uncle Joe. Some stuff went down at the beach today."

"What stuff?"

He sighed. "Uncle Joe, this ain't something I can talk about over the phone. Is there any way you can come back to the house? I know it's crazy in there. Could I try Aunt Grace at the hospital?"

"No, no, you'll be waiting on that phone forever. I'm on the way. Give me about fifteen minutes."

"Hey! Uncle Joe, before you hang up—"

"Yes?"

"Don't talk to anyone."

"Don't talk to anyone?"

"A reporter might try to contact you."

"Reporter?"

"Yeah… Just don't say a word to anybody until you talk to me, okay?"

I hung up the phone, and Wilma immediately handed me the keys.

"I'm sorry. Something's up. Gumbo wants me to come home."

"Then you better leave. My son wouldn't ask unless it's important. We'll be fine. Valerie came in while you were on the phone."

"Okay, thanks. I'll be back as soon as I can."

"Uh-huh. Judging by that frown on your face, it won't be tonight."

I split out the backdoor, pausing for a second before climbing into my dark green Pathfinder. The underbelly of the clouds looked like pink cotton candy as the sun set. Something big was up. Wilma was right. Gumbo's too conscientious to bother me at the restaurant unless it's serious. All I could think about was what Gumbo said, "Some stuff went down…" My hand trembled as I turned the ignition switch and raced the engine. I had been waiting for this. I could sense whatever had happened was going to significantly change the course of our lives. I remember the first time our lives significantly changed. August 13, 1965, the day our daughter Olisa was born. She was born in the midst of one of the worst riots in our nation's history—the week the city of Watts seared its way into international recognition.

Watts doesn't immediately look like a slum, if you come from New York: but it does if you drive from Beverly Hills… Over it hangs a miasma of fury and frustration, a perceptible darkening, as of storm clouds, of rage and despair, and the girls move with a ruthless, defiant dignity, and the boys move against the traffic as though they are moving against the enemy. He is not there, of course, but his soldiers are, in patrol cars.

—James Baldwin's visit to Watts

August 13, 1965

"Hey, Magnificent Montague, I just love your show! KGFJ is the baddest radio station in Los Angeles!"

"Montague loves you, brother, so what you want to tell our listening audience?"

"That my name is Leonard Jackson, and I go to Gomphers Jr. High School, and I just want to tell everybody, burn, baby, burn…"

"Burn, baby," cried the Magnificent Montague, releasing a scream of ecstasy. Then Otis Redding sang: "They call me Mr. Pitiful, that's my name, now…" I could just see Otis rocking and shaking, body twitching and popping, unable to contain the red hot soul erupting from his lungs.

"Junior, turn that damn music off!" my father-in-law James Willis whispered furiously.

Junior only stared out the car window, mesmerized.

"*Hello, Magnificent Montague? My name is Gloria Freeman, and I just want to tell the world, burn, baby, burn!*"

"*Have mercy, baby, it's burning up out there, and I'm on fire! Here's one especially for you from the fabulous Four Tops!*"

"*Somebody shake me, wake me when it's over*
Somebody tell me that I'm dreaming
and wake me when its over…"

A solemn-faced Mr. Willis exasperatedly reached out then turned the off button of the car radio. He nervously clutched the steering wheel as all three of us, bunched together in the front seat of the station wagon, slowly and deliberately drove west down Imperial Boulevard. Carefully, we dodged roving bands of Negro teenagers haphazardly sprinting across the streets, screaming and hollering, smunching sweaty faces against the window shields of cars, obstructing traffic, and stoning every police car whizzing down the street.

It was hot, incredibly hot, and our sticky shirts were plastered against our skin. The acrid smell of smoke in the air was stultifying. It was past 7:00 pm, and Los Angeles was entrenched in a fiery war of the people. There was no call to arms, no propaganda, no draft notices; it was spontaneous, it was instinctual, and an emotional response to the deep frustrations inflicting a community. We found ourselves unwilling participants trapped in a maelstrom of violence, and desperate to navigate our way home. Dense clouds of black smoke billowed into the sky, making it difficult to discern the natural course of nature's sunset.

Cars keeled over like dominoes as we watched brown and black hands rocking them until their resistance weakened. Eventually they succumbed, tumbling over amidst loud triumphant cheers, finally bursting into fire as they were showered by Molotov cocktails.

Darkness moved quickly upon us as we drove with our inside light on. Advice that came courtesy of a teenager peering inside of our car, pistol in the front part of his pants—"Hey man, it's gettin dark… Better turn your inside light on so we know who you are! Burn, baby, burn!"

Shattering glass forced Mr. Willis to slam on his brakes as Junior and I jerked forward like test dummies slapping our hands against the dashboard. "Shit, is everybody all right?" yelled Mr. Willis nervously, rubbing the bald spot on his head. The noise was so loud it sounded like our windows shattered, but they were still intact. It was the vehicle next to us as more bricks smashed its windows and shards of glass prickled our car.

A young Caucasian couple sat trapped in their Cadillac, eyes stricken with terror as they fought off clawing black hands reaching into their car. The man feverishly worked to start his Cadillac again, struggling with the ignition, futilely pumping the peddle of a gasping, flooded car. Derisive laughter accompanied his every effort as several people pounced upon his hood and bumper, furiously beating the automobile with sticks, bats, bricks, cement blocks, and anything else they could lay hold of.

"Kill whitey! Kill Whitey!" came the frenzied cry. "Hey peckerwoods, bet you mutherfuckers ain't going to be coming through here no more, huh?! Get yo asses out the car you ofay mutherfuckers!"

"Oh my God," whispered Mr. Willis as we sat frozen in place.

They yanked the couple from the car and flung them to the ground. The man looked like some kind of account executive. They beat him so bad his clothes shred from his body, their muffled cries stinging my ears as a mob of people engulfed them.

Somehow, by the grace of God, they actually popped out and managed to escape, fleeing down the street toward a police barricade. The mob overturned their car, torched it, and moved forward like a cloud of locusts.

Imperial Boulevard had always been a heavily trafficked street with many whites heading west to Inglewood, Gardena, and Westchester or east to Southgate, Lynwood, or Downey. There had always been latent worries about being attacked when they passed through the black section, but their fears of a stereotypical jungle were never actualized.

Until now…

But these weren't normal times.

In the aftermath, it was poetically referred to as an uprising, a revolution, a rebellion…

Damn that! It was chaos! A world gone mad! I saw cops chasing rioters, rioters chasing cops, citizens raiding stores, and arsonists boldly showcasing their work.

Rebellions can make strange bedfellows. Elderly people exhorted youngsters to perpetrate crimes and wreak havoc; kids they'd ordinarily feared, alone, on a dark street with their purse or wallet. Now they were teammates. I watched young hoods boldly break into stores followed by senior citizens sharing the dividends. In their faces I saw years of pent up emotions, hurt and pain, now relieved by the big payback! Fuck it—burn it up and start all over again seemed to be the agenda.

A world gone mad!

In a surge of panic, I visualized my wife bearing our child alone.

"Mr. Willis! Mr. Willis! Let's go! Come on now, drive! We got to get the hell out of here! There ain't much time left. We've gotta get home and make sure everyone's all right!"

"Yeah, yeah, I know, I know… I just ain't never seen nothing like this, and I was in Korea. Those poor people… What are we doing?"

I thought I'd have to take over the wheel as he sat there, still dressed in his postal uniform, perspiration coagulating and then rolling down his distressed face. Fortunately, his clouded eyes became lucid again as he punched his foot against the accelerator. The car screeched forward, turning right and barreling down Avalon Boulevard, toward home.

The only one of us who seemed to have a sense of calm in this turbulence was my sixteen year old brother-in-law, Junior. He was the picture of cool as his eyes darted back and forth, engrossed in all the action. Though he never said a word, I figured there had to be an emotional wrestling match going on as he watched his peers engaged in total anarchy. Junior wasn't the type to be involved in the violence, but I didn't think he'd mind picking up a little stereo equipment. He probably needed to be sitting between us because I wondered what choice he would have made if we weren't there to keep him psychologically bolted to his seat.

To my right there was all kind of activity at a Union gas station. Attendants had vanished from the victimized station as rioters freely distributed the spoils of war, generously filling Coke bottles, wine bottles, and beer cans with gasoline, stuffing them with rags and charging back into the fray, whooping and hollering like the rodeo had come to town.

We watched scores of fire trucks and police cars fly by, sirens squealing as blazing fire after fire scorched the darkness. Even where there was no actual rioting, hundreds of people lined up in the streets: some out of curiosity, some awaiting their moment. It was safe to assume that what had happened thus far was only the tip of the proverbial iceberg.

The only thing I cared about at this point was getting home to Grace as quickly as possible. We were only half a mile away when cars started bucking and driving haphazardly. One veered onto the sidewalk to avoid whatever was ahead of it while another spun out of control, twirling like a marble as it crashed into a telephone pole, its white inhabitants spilling out the car, scattering in every direction.

Our car screeched to a halt as Mr. Willis uttered, "What the hell."

Up ahead was a group of thugs straddling an older Caucasian man, pinning him to the ground. The voice crying out in the din was painfully familiar as my body shook. Imagine the depths my heart sank when I witnessed my very pregnant wife in the midst of a huge angry crowd, wrestling with all her might to free this man from their grasp. She raced from side to side, pulling at the thrashing arms of this giant spider of bodies unleashed upon him. Grace's mother, Katherine, and her grandmother, Mama Willis, followed closely behind, failing miserably in their attempts to restrain her. Grace was too frantic, periodically holding her stomach as her screaming pleas for sanity were deflected by howls of contemptuous laughter.

"Stop it! Stop it! Leave him alone, he hasn't hurt anybody. Beating him up is not going to solve anything—you're defeating your own purpose! Leave Mr. Kaplan alone! He's always tried to help everyone in this community. He's a good man!"

I propelled myself from the car, wrapping myself around Grace as I pulled her away. I heard Mama Willis say, "Thank you, Jesus."

When Grace realized it was me, she burst into hysterical tears yanking on my arms. "Joseph, stop them, they're going to kill our neighbor, Mr. Kaplan! We were driving home from the drugstore and saw them dragging him out of his motel… like he was some kind of animal. Oh, God, they're going to kill him…"

All at once a team of helmeted law enforcement officers arrived, whipping out their billy clubs as the rioters dissipated into the arms of the crowd who now lashed at the police officers with a flurry of epithets. A dazed Mr. Kaplan struggled to stand up as one of the Negro officers offered him a hand. Recoiling in fear, eyes bulging, he backpedaled like he was being stalked by a monster.

"Mr. Kaplan, Mr. Kaplan, it's all right," Grace yelled as he wheeled around and ran clumsily away. He disappeared inside his motel building.

The demonstrators cackled with laughter as they closed in upon the small band of officers and yelled obscenities. However, they reserved a shit load of venom for the two Negro officers who stood with the other cops.

"Look at them Uncle Toms over there. What you traitors doing here? Fucking pigs! You ought to be ashamed of yourselves! With those uniforms on you ain't no better than those blue-eyed devils! What you need to do is take off those uniforms and stand here with us. This is where you belong, not holding hands with those honkeys! Better recognize!"

While the crowd spewed their vitriol on the police, Mr. Willis signalled to us to head toward the motel.

"Where the hell do you think you people are going?" The white policeman's hand clamped down on Mr. Willis's arm like a steel vise. The other hand held a baton poised to strike as he jerked Mr. Willis's arm. The smirk on his face spread as he became more encouraged by the multitude of officers arriving on the scene. The growing cadre of police officers incensed the crowd even more.

Mr. Willis casually glanced sideways at the hand gripping his arm. "Before you laid your hands on me, I had planned on going to our neighbor's assistance to see if he's all right."

"Your neighbor! That's how you people treat your neighbor?" he snorted. "No I don't think so, why don't you come along with me." The young, naive, and well muscled cop eagerly tried to assert his authority in front of the crowd, mistakenly thinking that this show of force was enough to intimidate the amassing crowd.

"Sir, please let me go. The 'you people' you are referring to are some young thugs who are probably using some other victims as a trampoline right now. We're not all criminals."

"Says who?" he responded sarcastically, staring stone faced at Mr. Willis with a look that spoke volumes about the insensitivity, brutality, and lack of communication that characterized the relationship between the police force and the community. Mr. Willis winced in pain when his other arm was snatched and the officer pinned him against his car, quickly reaching for his handcuffs.

"Dick put those handcuffs away you damn fool and let him go—now!" sternly whispered the veteran officer standing next to him. Dick was oblivious to the mob inching closer and closer to them. They were ten officers facing a hostile crowd that grew exponentially.

"Get your hands off the mailman, pigs! What the fuck did *he* do to you? Let him go! You motherfuckers is always starting shit like this!"

"I'd advise you to take a clear look at your surroundings and let go of me before things get too out of hand," James Willis advised.

However, it was already too late. Rocks, stones, bricks, and pieces of concrete showered the police officers mercilessly. The rookie instantly released Mr. Willis's arms, shielding himself as fear started to shape itself on his formerly smug face.

I instinctively shielded Grace with my body as I pushed her out of the line of fire. Several fire trucks roared by, crying like babies as smoke drifted into the sky and the area was set ablaze. Next, we heard the terrifying sound of gun shots as chunks of cement popped up from the ground. Everyone hit the turf as the police tore off in the direction of the fire engines, followed by cross fire ricocheting from every direction. One officer, hit by a bullet, tumbled to the ground, holding his leg as his partner scooped his arms around his shoulders and helped him get away.

We fled to the Kaplan Motel on the other side of the street for shelter. Mr. Willis and I assisted Grace as she struggled to catch her breath.

"Honey, are you all right?" I held my breath aware of the answer.

"All right as can be considering my labor pains have started."

"What?"

"Yes," she gasped, holding her stomach.

"We've got to get to a hospital now! Where's the car?" I screamed. The horrid sounds of gunfire afflicted my ears.

"What car?" Mr. Willis cried. His mouth hung open in shock.

The rioters had overturned several police cars, smashing them with Molotov cocktails and cheering when they exploded into huge balls of fire. Mr. Willis's car was parked too close to the overbearing heat. Sparks tickled the hood of his car, blowing up into waves of dancing orange flames as they lit ghastly shadows on our dismayed faces.

"Motherfuckers! Motherfuckers! Can you believe these stupid motherfuckers! Shit! These crazy ass fools, mad at the world, not only burn up my fucking car but my goddamn city! What kind of fucking shit is this?"

"What are we going to do?" I asked, completely alarmed as I watched the carnage unfold before my eyes. The rioters looted Dee's liquor store, carting away cases of beer and wine. Kids nine and ten years old chugged beers like it was soda pop.

"We are going to take this girl inside and let her rest before somebody gets hit with a stray bullet. And then we're going to pray this thing blows over soon enough for us to get her to a hospital, that's what we are going to do," Mama Willis answered brusquely, swinging the door open. Katherine Willis shoved past us, whisking Grace into the motel office as we followed sheepishly along.

"If any one comes a step closer, I'm going to shoot!"

Behind the registration desk stood Mr. Kaplan, rifle in hand, pointed at us. His white dress shirt was torn and bloody, and cuts and lacerations marred his face. A huge knot protruded from the side of his forehead. His eyes were completely lifeless and his body shook like a leaf in a Chicago windstorm. His wife and five-year-old son stood behind him.

"Now Mr. Kaplan, put that gun down, buddy, before you hurt someone. You know we don't mean you any harm."

"I said don't come any closer! Who the hell are you?"

"Ron, it's James… James Willis… your next door neighbor. Don't worry, everything is all right… We are your friends."

"Ronald, it's the Willises," his wife said, shakily.

"Judy, I don't care who it is! We have no friends tonight. We're not their brothers and sisters!" he retorted disdainfully. "How do we know they haven't joined up with *their* people out there? How can we trust them? We are their enemies, which makes them ours. I've got to protect my family," he warned, raising the gun to his shoulder. "Now get the hell out of here!"

"Be serious, Ron! You know us better than that, we…"

"And I'm telling you for the last time; get the hell out of here!"

"And I also have family in here to protect, Mr. Kaplan, and if I don't sit down soon, this baby is going to drop down right here on the floor."

"Grace, get back!" But it was too late to grab her. She stepped right in front of him, and my heart did a somersault.

Grace's unexpected move completely stunned him as his eyes flitted back and forth, reflecting the turmoil wracking his brain. Rigidly he held the gun as he tried to blink away the moisture in his eyes.

Suddenly, there was the sound of little feet and his son, Peter, raced around the counter and hugged Grace's legs.

"Peter, what are you doing? You get back here right now!"

Big blue eyes gazed up at Grace.

"Hi, Grace."

"Hi, Peter."

"Are you really going to have a baby?"

"Yes, Peter, I am." She patted his head. "Maybe tonight. You want to touch my stomach?

"Sure…" She guided his tiny hands around her stomach as he grinned broadly, fascination brightening his face. Grabbing her hand, he led her around the counter to his father.

"Hey, Daddy, what's wrong? Do your eyes hurt, again? This is not our enemy. It's Grace. And that's the Willises. Hi, Junior!"

"What's up, little man?"

"See, Daddy, they're not going to hurt us. These are our neighbors and friends. Did you know Grace is going to have a baby? Daddy, are you listening? Daddy?"

Peter clasped Grace's hand, delightedly pressing it against his face.

"Yes, Peter, you're right, that is Grace," he replied, smiling wanly. He laid the rifle on the floor under the counter, weariness etching his bruised face. His wife massaged his shoulders. His head dropped as he covered his face with his hands.

"What am I doing? I'm sorry. I'm so sorry… I don't know what…"

"No apologies, Mr. Kaplan, no apologies necessary," replied Grace tenderly. "After what you've been through, every person here can relate. You're scared, I'm scared, We're all scared. The world's not quite right tonight. The main thing is that you're alive and among friends. We need to get you cleaned up."

She moved toward him but instead staggered and fell into his ready arms as she doubled over in pain. We rushed her like she was carrying a football, but the women had already taken over the offense.

"She needs to lie down!" barked Mama Willis.

"Here, let me take her back here, there's a bed in this back room," responded Mrs. Kaplan as she ushered Grace into the bedroom with Katherine Willis following closely behind. I tried to follow, but Mama Willis blocked the door like a sentry. She may have only been 5'4" but I wasn't about to step past her.

"Joseph, you men stand guard. When the time's right, we'll call you in here. Ain't no doubt, she'll have the baby sometime this evening, but we need you men out front watching for trouble. All hell's breaking loose out there!"

"But don't we need a doctor?"

"It'd be nice if one did riot calls, but I don't think that's going to happen tonight, baby. And with bullets flying around out there, we're not going to try to drive to a hospital. Besides, I don't think we'd make it in time."

"She's that close?"

"She's that close."

"But who's going to…"

"Child, I've been around enough babies in my life to handle this with my eyes closed, don't worry, we're blessed. By the grace of God, Mama Willis is going to take care of everything.

"But…"

The door quietly closed in my face.

I turned and saw Mr. Willis and Mr. Kaplan softly chatting in the corner. I considered how fortunate we were to be able to take shelter in a motel, which wasn't on the top ten lists of places to loot. What were you going to steal, a room? We felt fairly comfortable in our refuge.

Life lessons say there is an exception to every rule. It happened after I had finally gained entrance to the forbidden zone, largely because of the screams erupting from Grace demanding that I be in the room with her.

I held Grace's hand as she harshly inhaled and exhaled, perspiration running down her face. Her thick hair was all helter-skelter. She gripped my hand so tightly I was sure I'd never regain use of it again.

"You just hang in there, Grace. The way I see it, honey, you can bet the farm on that baby arriving in about an hour or so," Mama Willis cooed as she wiped Grace's wet brow with a hand towel. Mrs. Kaplan and Katherine Willis were busily going back and forth, laying towels on her chair and other bathroom items in preparation for the birth.

I tried to be cool, but I was feeling a little light-headed from not eating all day. But I had to stay strong, it wasn't about me—it was about Grace.

Just at that moment it sounded like a bomb exploded in the front office. "Oh my God what was that?" asked Katherine Willis, clutching my arm. Grace's doe eyes widened and then closed as she continued to focus on breathing rhythmically.

"I don't know, but I'll check it out." I kissed Grace on the forehead and raced into the front room.

Junior stepped inside the door, a worried look on his normally placid face. "Daddy! Trouble's heading this way."

"Damn, I wondered how long it would take." James Willis peeked out the curtain, sucking on his lower lip. He picked up one of the bricks surrounded by glass particles that had been thrown through the window and examined it. "Ron, do you trust me?" he asked quietly.

"Sure, James, I mean, what happened earlier has no reflection…"

"If you trust me, Ron, then I need you to get out of sight right now, and let us deal with this." He picked up the rifle and placed it on the registration desk facing the door.

"Ok, James," he said, reluctantly. "James…"

"Yes."

"I think you should know the rifle was never loaded… It doesn't work!"

"Great."

A foot kicked the front door so hard it almost rattled off its hinges. It flew open, causing more glass from the shattered window to tinkle to the floor. They strolled coolly in, glass cracking underneath their feet, bringing with them the smell and sounds of the streets: the smoke, the stifling heat, the musty mix of alcohol and body sweat, and pure undiluted rage. One of them held a new radio, price tag dangling defiantly, while James Brown's raspy voice screamed, "You know you're out of sight!" The funky guitars, horns, and drum made my feet tap involuntarily, even with my life on the line.

"Burn, baby, burn!"

Four shirtless black bodies stood in the middle of the room caustically surveying everything as a couple of them loosely held empty wine bottles in their hand. The tall lanky one with a "doo rag" on his head displayed more teeth than a barracuda. His eyes exhibited primeval madness, wilder than anything Edgar Allen Poe could have ever imagined. He took a final swig from some malt liquor in a silver can and flung it to the floor where it banged flatly. His lone gold front tooth flashed like a radio transmitter when he spoke. "You brothers ought to be glad we came in here first! We was about to blow this muthafucka up till Shorty thought he saw some brothers up in here!"

Shorty was the one who metronomically rocked the full gas can spilling some of it on the floor. Short in height but not in width, he looked like Winnie the Pooh with an attitude. The gassy fumes made my eyes water. Rags hung out the back of his pants pocket. He nodded at Junior with a snarl that I think was supposed to be a grin.

"So where's that stinky Jew muthafucka?" Doo Rag barked. "I'm tired of these assholes comin' here stealing our money and not giving anything back to the community! We gonna give him another ass whoppin' and show him what Smokey the Bear is really all about. Then we goin' burn this mutha to the ground! His gold tooth levitated in the air when he laughed.

"Tell 'em about it, Smokey!"

"Ain't nobody heard what I axed?" He hitched his trousers and menacingly appraised us. His fingers did a spidery crawl across the handle of the pistol hanging out of the belt of his front pocket.

No one responded. The only noise was the sound of sirens, intermittent gunfire, and the wailing of Junior Walker's saxophone on the song, "Shotgun."

"You niggers must be deaf and dumb. Hear what I'm saying? I don't want to have to ax again! You listening?"

"Better listen up!" warned one of his butt kissing sycophants.

"We're listening. Now, I hope you'll extend the same courtesy to me and hear what I have to say." Mr. Willis stood behind the counter tapping the shotgun lying on the table.

Judging by the shock on Doo Rag's face, it was the first time he laid eyes on it. A slight frown creased his forehead as he remarked in a low whisper, "You got the best hand. Play it, Mr. Postman."

"All right, these are the rules. The man you're looking for is here, but there ain't gonna be no sacrifices. He's our neighbor and we don't want to see him hurt. So I'm going to ask y'all to go on about your business and let us be."

Mr. Willis was icy cool except for the trembling hand behind the counter. I bit my lip as I watched Doo Rag glaring at him as if he ought to be gutted.

"Uh, uh… I know you ain't protecting that white devil. So I'm going to ignore what you said, Mr. Postman. I'm sure we ain't communicatin'. Matter of fact, I'm bettin' this is a smart old man who knows one whistle could bring on a hundred muthafuckas."

Mr. Willis nodded slowly, but kept the gun angled on him.

Junior spoke up, "Man, we don't want no trouble, we all down with you."

Doo Rag gave Junior the once over.

"Well if you so down with us, brotha, then bring that Jew muthafucka out here!"

Junior shuffled his feet uneasily. "Man, I can't do that…"

"Then you need to shut the fuck up! Dig? And tell that old man over there to put his shit down and get the fuck out my way so we can take care of *bidness*! See, we don't like nobody Uncle Tommin us for Massa!" Scowling, he jerked his shoulders as he and his boys stepped forward.

Mr. Willis raised the gun. "I told y'all to move on."

I held my breath.

On my right, I saw an arm quickly rise as one punk who wore an apple hat got ready to sling his bottle at Mr. Willis.

"Mr. Willis, look out!" I screamed.

In a flash, Mr. Willis swung around, and there was a blast as the gun fired shattering the wine bottle in apple hat's hand. He bent over in anguish, grabbing his hand and groaning in pain. Then another blast as a second bottle exploded. Mr. Willis looked more shocked than any of us as smoked drifted out of the gun.

"Gimme that, Shorty!" Doo Rag snatched the can from him, splashing gasoline all over the floor.

"You muthafuckas want to protect whitey? Then you can burn in hell with his devil ass! Come on, fellas, let's blow this joint!"

"No! My wife's in the other room!" I screamed as Doo Rag lit a match and set one of the torn rags on fire throwing it in the pool of gasoline.

There was a cobra like hiss as the flame rapidly died. "Fuck this!" Quickly he set another rag on fire, but suddenly, all by itself, one of the counter fans kicked into high gear and a burst of air blew out, reversing the direction of the flame and setting Doo Rag's pants on fire. He tore out the door, belting out a strangled cry as his fellow hoods chased after him. His burning body blazed like a comet as he streaked down the nighttime streets.

Mr. Willis held the gun at arms length, goggling at it like it had leprosy.

The back room door opened, Mr. Kaplan poked his head out and said, "Thank God, everyone's okay."

Mrs. Willis burst through the open door, tears streaming down her cheeks, wringing her hands nervously. "James? Boys? Are you all all right? All that shooting and screaming…"

"It's okay, Katherine. It's okay. We're fine," James answered, embracing her.

"Ron, I'm happy to say you were wrong. The gun was loaded, and it worked fine."

"James, it's not… It couldn't be… That gun hasn't been fired in years. The trigger mechanism doesn't work anymore. Look, see?" He flicked the trigger, which was as limp as a rubber band. "The only reason I kept this gun here was to ward off robbers and burglars. When I heard the gunfire, I thought they were doing the shooting."

"Well, if that don't beat all." Mr. Willis shook his head. "It was like the rifle jumped to life on its own. As I held it, it tugged me along like a big trout on a fishing pole. I just moved in the direction it pulled me."

Mr. Kaplan shrugged his shoulders. "Weirdest thing I ever heard."

"Then I thought we were goners when he poured gasoline on the floor."

Junior kneeled down and dabbed his finger in the gas spill, raising it to his nose. His face crinkled up.

"Daddy, this isn't gasoline, it's just water…"

"What?"

My stomach felt like it had tiny snakes crawling inside. I couldn't breathe. The stress, not eating, thank goodness the front door was open. I felt much better when I stepped outside the door.

Gazing up at the night sky, I spotted high arcing streams of white water gobbled up by hungry black smoke and bright orange flames; flames that formed tiny little crowns of fire on the neighboring telephone pole. If I hadn't been looking up, I never would have noticed the hulking figure perched on top of the high-rise building next door. His back faced me. Either I was seeing an illusion or the smoke was dimming my vision, but I was positive his feet weren't touching the ground! Almost like an act of levitation. But that's impossible!

Nothing is impossible.

His enormous frame glowed as it stood silhouetted against the supernaturally reddened sky created by the burning fires. He deliberately pivoted toward me. Though I couldn't see his face or eyes, I knew he saw me.

A baby's cry pierced my reverie as I turned around and saw heads snap toward the back room. Grace! Oh, Grace. I scrambled back inside the motel. Smiling family members and friends parted as I rushed through. I was welcomed by Grace's tired, but beaming, face as she proudly cradled the most precious, beautiful, and sweetest baby I've ever seen.

Nestled in a world ravaged by violence, anger, weapons, fire, and screams of injustice, existed an oasis of the purest love. Grace tenderly caressed my face as I snuggled beside them in awe of the tiny little person bundled up before me. I kissed her on the forehead.

"Oh, Joseph, I was so worried… Are you okay?"

"Am I okay? You're asking if I'm okay? I'm fine. How are you?"

"Tired, in pain, and happier than I've ever been …"

She grabbed my hand and smashed it against her cheek as tears spilled over my fingers. I can't imagine a single poet, alive or dead who could have accurately described how deeply I loved her.

"Look at her, Joseph, this is your daughter."

"Yeah… she's, she's beautiful, simply beautiful… Look at all that hair on her head. I thought babies were supposed to be bald."

"Not this one, honey. Would you like to hold her?"

"Hold her? With my hands?" Self-consciously, I began brushing the sides of my pants. "I'm filthy, look at me. I mean, are you sure? I'm not going to infect her am I? I don't know how to, you know, she's so small… She won't break will she?"

"Joseph, be quiet. Hold your daughter."

Grace handed her to me as I fumbled awkwardly to position her just right, afraid of harming her—so fragile and so soft. I floated on a cloud as I tiptoed around the room, gazing into her innocent little face. The warmth I felt from holding her against my chest was indescribable.

"See, Joseph, she's already in love with you. She stopped crying."

"Yeah, she did, didn't she… Aww, she's something, isn't she?"

"Very special, Joseph. Very special… You just know it."

For a brief instant, I thought I saw a glimmer of a woman staring in from the open window—then it was gone.

"Did you tell Mama Willis about our decision?" I asked.

Grace grabbed Mama Willis's arm as she said, "You mean this beautiful lady right here? The one who saw me through my delivery? Grandmother, it came to me months ago in a dream that our child would end up a girl, so we already settled upon a name."

"I tried my best to convince her to come up with some boy names, but she was convinced it was going to be a girl," I added.

"We agreed to name her Olisa—a combination of your middle name, Sharlisa, and Grandfather's middle name, Odis. God, I wish he were alive to see her. You're still okay with that, right, Joseph?"

"Are you kidding? I love the name Olisa. How about you, Mama Willis?"

No answer was forthcoming as she cupped her hands over her trembling mouth, her eyes held by wrinkled dark folds transformed into wading pools.

Fortunately, the rest of the night passed without any more incidents. The sun peeping over the San Gabriel Mountains the next morning offered a special treat to some tired and weary people as we gathered our things.

After saying our goodbyes, Mr. Willis was able to retrieve his second car. We drove Grace and the baby safely to the hospital, traveling through a war torn city that was still simmering with anger. Olisa was born in a sea of tumult later known as the Watts Riots. At the time, the significance of that event escaped us, we were so thrilled to have her in our lives; however, we knew she was a very special baby.

My greatest fear for the past thirty-five years has always been that the world would one day know just how special. This is what I contemplated as I got to the house and waited impatiently in the back alley for the electronic garage door to open. A woman leaped out of an obscure blue van parked in the alley like a ninja warrior. My instincts screamed for me to let the garage door close in her face as she made quick strides toward me, but curiosity got the better of me as I clicked the "open" switch.

She was a Latina, in her early twenties, attractive, with short trendy auburn hair, and golden brown eyes that lit up on cue as she waved to me like we were old friends. Behind her trailed a burly white man with a Yankee baseball cap that covered a crow's nest of lifeless red hair. He had a major case of acne on his sun-parched face and tiredly lugged a hand held camera. She held the microphone down to her side as she aggressively thrust her hand into mine, shaking it forcefully.

"Hello, sir, my name is Eva Sanchez from station KLSC. Would you mind talking to me for a minute?" She was already waving the cameraman into position like it was a done deal.

"About what?" I asked coolly.

"Well, first, may I ask what your relationship is with Olisa Carpenter?"

"I'm her father."

Her eyes expanded like a balloon filling up with helium. "Oh, great!" she replied enthusiastically. "Mr. Carpenter, you're just the man I need to speak to! And, if possible, we'd love to talk to your daughter, too."

"She's asleep."

"Oh, I can understand that. She must be quite exhausted. Well, we can talk to her another time. Um, she hasn't spoken to anyone else, has she?"

"Not that I know of. Like I said, she's asleep."

"Of course; no problem. However, would you mind answering just a few questions about your daughter?"

As the red light on the camera glared at me, my curiosity vanished.

"Ms. Sanchez, I need to go inside."

"Absolutely, but can you at least share your thoughts with us about what happened at the beach this afternoon?"

"Can't. Goodnight."

"I don't know if you realize it, but people see your daughter as a hero. What she did out there this afternoon took guts. It was amazing!"

"Look, I don't mean to be rude, but…"

"Oh sure, I understand. Here's my card. Maybe we can talk later tonight or tomorrow? Call me anytime. My pager number's at the bottom. Tell me what you think of the broadcast at 11:00."

"I'll do that."

"Mr. Carpenter, I'd really appreciate it if you'd promise not to talk to anyone else about this. We'd love to keep this as an exclusive, okay?"

"Gotta go, thank you." I pressed the button for the door to close.

"Mr. Carpenter, one more question. Is it true?"

"Is what true?"

"Can she heal people?"

Thankfully, the garage door slammed shut.

Outside of the door I heard, "Please call me, Mr. Carpenter!"

SOUL EYES

Before the door closed, I saw a girlish pout on Eva Sanchez's face that completely belied her granite-eyed determination.

CHAPTER 2

Olisa's studio apartment was dark, but I thought I'd check the house first.

The minute I opened the back door, I smelled the aroma of buttered popcorn as I saw one of Olisa's closest friends, Laura, with her back to me busily moving about the kitchen. Her coal black hair was piled on top of her head, and feathered earrings swung back and forth. She greeted me with a smile that was like a warm embrace.

"Hello, Uncle Joe."

"Hey there, Little Oak. Whatcha up to?"

"Nothing much. Making popcorn, you want some?"

"Not right now, kiddo."

"Just thought I'd make you an offer before Alton inhales it."

"Thanks for thinking about me. Where's everybody?"

"In the living room," she said, sucking her lower lip and patting my arm supportively as I passed by. I'm sure she saw the anxiousness on my face.

"How's she doing?"

"Out like a light."

Olisa was curled up in a fetal position on the couch asleep. I felt her forehead, at least it was cool. As I studied her face, I no longer saw the squirrel cheeked little girl with eyes too big for her face and billowing clouds of curls who let caterpillars crawl up her arms. Now before me lay a quietly beautiful woman who still let caterpillars crawl up her arms. Her thick, dark-brown hair that flowed in large ripples past her shoulders framed a lofty forehead and elegant cheekbones, sheltering her delicately curved indigo eyes. Even asleep, her warm sienna brown skin shined like she was escorted by her own personal sun. An exuberant writer for *Time* magazine would one day write, "If the Gods built a queen from African soil she would look just like Olisa Carpenter."

Alton sat on the floor in a white tank top and sweat bottoms as he watched *Gun Smoke* on cable. Doc Adams rolled his eyes and scratched his chin as Deputy Festus followed behind him, silver spurs clinking angrily. "What in tarnation do you think I'm talkin about you ol' scutter?" Festus barked.

"I love it when those two go at each other."

"Yeah, they're funny…I met your reporter outside, Eva Sanchez?"

"She got to you, huh? Damn. How did she get this address? I didn't see anyone follow us home."

"They got their ways, I guess. Thanks for warning me. She ambushed me the minute I pulled up."

"Sorry, Uncle Joe, I got a feeling she's going to be a major pain."

"Me too. So talk to me."

Alton pointed the remote control toward the television set, killing the sound. Laura walked into the room with the bowl of popcorn. "Thanks, Laura," he said, reaching for it. "You guys want some?"

We both shook our heads as Laura moved protectively to the end of the couch next to Olisa. Laura released her hair from the bun; it tumbled down in waves. Her radiant black hair, so dark it was almost blue, softened a striking face with prominent cheekbones and a strong straight nose. Her face had gained far more mileage than it should have for someone in her mid thirties, but she had lived a tough life. She began twisting her hair into a single braid as she lifted her pensive eyes and stared at the silent TV screen. Matt Dillon outdrew both of the greasy looking villains raising hell in the saloon as Ms. Kitty sighed with relief.

Laura Nelson was half Cherokee and half German, and had lost both of her parents in a car crash when she was only eight years old. She was taken in by her father's family and raised on a reservation in Oklahoma. She remained there until she was sixteen, then moved to the San Francisco area with more family to help her escape the demons that trailed her. She had been on a path of self-destruction, drinking and using hard drugs. She fled to the Bay area because it had been rumored that she was targeted for murder by a couple of drug dealers she had stolen drugs from. Luckily, she found a mentor in an elderly man known as Chief Eaglespeaker who helped her to pull herself together and radically transform her life before the last call.

She first met Olisa at U.C. Santa Cruz, where they immediately became college roommates, forging a fast and lasting friendship. I have seen them in the same room for hours, neither saying a word, absorbed in their own thoughts, writing, reading, doing whatever, but always enjoying each other's company. Then, Laura might depart with just a nod and that would be it. They had an understanding and mutual respect for each other that didn't need to be expressed in words. I admired the depth of their friendship.

Laura was regarded as family even before she and Gumbo hooked up and fell madly in love. They'd been living together for the past two years. Even though we've teased them about getting officially married all the time, I've never seen two happier people. I teasingly nicknamed her Little Oak, because she was originally from Oklahoma, petite, about 5'2", but as tough and as durable as the tree.

As for my nephew, Alton, I nicknamed him "Gumbo" because he ate so much gumbo in one sitting that it made me seasick. He was also 6'5" and 280 pounds of solid, angry muscle. The former USC All American linebacker and 1st year draft choice for the Tampa Bay Buccaneers pro football team had to abandon his football career when he got into a serious car accident while driving drunk in Tampa, Florida after an all night party binge. He broke both legs, injured several ribs, and suffered facial lacerations, but was lucky enough to escape with his life. They had to use the Jaws of Life machine to peel him out of his Jaguar, which looked like a metal jellyfish afterwards. The severity of his accident left him with a subtle limp, but after months of grueling rehabilitation, Alton had focused his attention on becoming a top body builder and now worked part-time as a bouncer at a prestigious night club in Century City.

"I'm waiting, Gumbo," I said firmly.

"I know, Unc. I don't even know where to start, so much has happened."

"The beginning might work."

He took a swig from a huge Evian bottle. "After I did my usual workout at Gold's Gym, I figured I'd head on down to the beach and check on Laura and Olisa. The beach was packed, and it was hot down there, but everything was righteous, man. People were just into their groove—roller skating, biking, jogging, listening to the music, dancing, checking out the vendors, it was smooth. We were just kicking it, you know… But there was something in the air, man. You could feel it about ready to blow."

"Go on…"

"You know how the tensions have been building again between the black and Latino gangs in Venice. There've been some shootings here and there, but so far no major incidents that broke the truce. Then bam! Next thing I know there's like a few dudes taking sides, shouting and taunting each other. Brothas vs. *ese's*, you know. Dawg had been talking to some honey that *mi vato* had been talking to, and one thing lead to another, and everybody started gathering up their boys."

"Where were you guys?"

"Kicking it at the healer's booths. Olisa was giving me a neck massage when the next thing we see is this huge crowd scattering in all directions—they were panicked, man… screaming and running. The gangs are seriously scrapping—fists flying, trash cans, rocks… Anything that could be picked up was thrown. When the dust settled, there's a Mexican guy lying on the ground next to a huge blade with his hands over his stomach and blood comin' outta him. Homeboy was in bad shape. The worst part is, not a police officer was in sight as the gangs got ready to knuckle up again, but this time you knew it was going to be Dodge City."

"So then what?"

"So then I look up and there's Olisa standing right between the two gangs with her hands up, screaming!"

My head got so tight I thought it would implode. I was working overtime to stay cool, but tension had been my partner since the phone call. "Shit, Gumbo, what in the hell were you doing? Big as your ass is and you let her get past you?! She could have gotten killed!"

I recognized my blunder the minute I saw the hurt whip across his face. Alton would have taken a bullet for his cousin, and I knew that.

His face contorted as he dropped his head and said softly, "You're right, Uncle Joseph, I'm sorry, I should have stopped her. Everything happened so fast. You know... I wasn't thinking. I'm really sorry."

"No, no, I'm sorry, Gumbo. Sometimes I get real stupid. Wasn't any call for me to yell at you like that. It wasn't your fault. Olisa is a grown woman. You're not responsible for her decisions."

Laura rapidly twisted the end of her braid. "He couldn't have done anything, Uncle Joseph, even if he had tried. Olisa moved fast. I kept shouting at her to hit the ground, but she didn't listen. But look, she's here, safe and sound, and that's all that matters, right?"

"Yep, yep, you're right."

Olisa shifted positions as she hugged the pillow, eyes shut tight... just an innocent little girl again. I couldn't imagine her in that chaos.

Gumbo continued, "Blew me out, man. When it finally hit me what was going down, I ran after Olisa as fast as I could, but by then she had those dogs at bay—it was a trip! Those little punks froze like their mother had busted them, didn't they, Laura?

"Yeah, and then she just sat on the ground and cradled that poor bleeding boy, placing her hand over his stomach. She held him close, her head pressed against his. The blood running down her arms didn't even faze her. The paramedics and the police finally showed up, begging her to let them handle it. Alton can tell you the rest, she said, clearing her throat."

"He doesn't have to. I can guess that the boy got up and walked away, didn't he? Just like Flash."

"Yeah, Uncle Joe, just like," Alton responded in a faraway voice. I knew what he was thinking. I could still see that image of Alton's Irish setter lying in the street:

Alton was just a chubby seven-year-old at the time that, his cousin, Olisa, absolutely adored. Olisa was around five, and they were outside playing baseball.

It was late afternoon. Katherine Willis had gone to the store to pick up some dessert, and Grace and Wilma were in the house cooking. The smell of short ribs, yams, and cabbage drifted out of the house along with bursts of sporadic laughter. I thought I also heard a few curse words coupled with the name, Lester, who was Alton's absentee father. I don't think Alton had seen his father more than a couple of times in his life.

Mr. Willis and I were stationed on the front porch, keeping an eye on the kids as they played in the front yard, and the other playing a cut-throat game of "bones" as dominoes slammed harder than a jail cell door. We also grooved to Mr. Willis's collection of down home blues—Willie Dixon, Muddy Waters, Sonny Terry and B.B. King. Mr. Willis and I were feeling mighty good as we leisurely sipped wine like two country gents. Mama Willis rocked on the porch swing with Olisa's little brother, Jon, who was three, in her lap while she read him a picture book story about a train. Jonathan's head jerked periodically as he fought to stay awake, but he was losing the battle as his eyes formed tiny slits.

A loud whack made me look up as Alton smacked the ball over Olisa's head, over the fence, over the curb, bouncing between two parked cars and rolling to the other side of the street. Olisa opened the gate and stopped at the curb, realizing the chase was over.

Flash did not as he leaped over the fence, panting excitedly. The dog streaked past her, red fur flying, and scooted between the parked cars and into the street.

Alton hollered, "Flash! No!!!"

Honking cars, screeching tires and a huge gut wrenching thump made all of us freeze. The clatter of Grace and Wilma's footsteps on the front porch broke the spell.

Grace cried out, "My God, Joseph, what happened?"

I didn't answer, but knew we'd find a red furry body prostrate on the street.

"I'm sorry… I'm so sorry. I didn't see him," cried out a heavyset man from inside his blue Cadillac. With great effort, he climbed slowly out of the car as his eyes immediately dropped to the ground. Clearly, he was distressed by the whole incident. He was nicely dressed; shirt and tie, and a fedora that he had taken off and was nervously exchanging from one hand to the other. "I didn't see him… He just ran in front of me… It was an accident… I'm so sorry for your kids… I didn't mean to hit him. I tried to steer my car out the way… ."

"It's okay, mister. It's not your fault. We know it's an accident," I said softly, staring at Flash's body on the street and feeling my throat tighten.

Mr. Willis kneeled down and examined him. Flash's breathing was ragged. Pools of blood swelled concentrically beneath his quivering body. Mr. Willis's lips were tight as he glanced at me and shook his head. I waved at Wilma to keep Alton away, but he struggled to break free of her arms.

"Flash? Please come to me. Please…" Alton cried. The expression on his face ripped a hole in my heart. He shakily balanced himself on the curb while his mother gently wrestled him, tears spilling from both of their eyes. "Please get up… Come here, boy!"

"Come on now, Alton, honey, this is nothing for you to see. Flash is going to heaven."

"No he isn't!" he snapped back, as he clapped his hands, whistled, kissed at him, and begged earnestly for the dog to rise. "Uncle Joe, please do something. Can you fix him, Uncle Joe?? Can you?"

"I'm sorry, partner… If I could do something right now, I wouldn't hesitate—you know that. But, your Mom's right. We can't help ol' Flash, he's…"

Alton bowed his head sobbing, "Flash is okay. He'll get up, you'll see." His body melted into Wilma's arms as she fell back on the grass in her white dress, rocking him back and forth.

Grace rubbed Olisa's shoulders as she stared helplessly at her cousin. "Mommy, can't we make Flash better? He's hurt, but I know we can help him."

"Honey, there's nothing we can do. Flash is on his way to a much better place where he will never feel any pain."

Olisa's face looked very strained to me as she rubbed her cheeks with her fingers and her body swayed from side to side. I really thought that Grace should have taken her inside the house. Olisa's face was taut and her eyes were enormous.

Suddenly the tension in Olisa's face disappeared and she walked over to Alton and rested her hand lightly on his shoulder.

"Please don't cry any more, Alton. Watch. It's going to be all right. I'll make Flash feel better, okay? Just don't cry anymore. I can do magic."

Alton looked at her strangely as he wiped the tears from his eyes. A glimmer of hope dawned on his face, the kind that resides exclusively within children.

Without any trepidation, Olisa knelt down next to Flash and stroked his body, gingerly touching him with her fingertips. Her eyes were riveted to the points she kneaded on his body like a surgeon as her fingers tip-toed delicately along the contours of Flash's body.

Grace crossed her arms tightly together as she stood supportively behind Olisa. There had to be an internal debate going on inside of her as she stymied herself from dragging Olisa away from Flash.

A small crowd of looky-loos drifted in like tumbleweed, many of their faces registering revulsion as they caught sight of Olisa with the dog.

"Isn't that horrible? What kind of mother would let their child get that close to a dead animal, let alone touch the nasty thing? That's the most disgusting thing I've ever seen."

Ignoring the drone, Grace stood stoically behind Olisa. A sentry guarding the royal gates couldn't have been more impassive. Still I feared a more direct confrontation as the anonymous grumblings grew louder.

"Grace, don't let her do this. It's not good. The dog is dying. Think about it. Both of these kids could be traumatized…" whispered Mr. Willis. "Here, let me get her."

"Daddy, don't touch her! She knows what she's doing."

"But, Grace…"

"No, leave her alone."

I felt sorry for Mr. Willis. I think he was shocked and a little hurt by Grace's cutting tone, but it soon washed away as I saw him mouth the words, "What the…"

The crowd gasped unanimously.

Flash's body was rising and falling heavily. Beneath the fur, the skin undulated. It defied logic, but I realized that the bones were actually shifting, changing shapes, reforming. The skin rippled like snakes crawling underneath a blanket.

When it ended, Flash's eyes sprung open, and he struggled to his feet, rising like a newborn colt. Weakly, he braced on all fours. The longer he stayed on his feet, the more strength he seemed to gain. He reticently tapped the pavement with his left front paw, testing for pain. The fur on his right side was matted with blood, but his body showed no signs of injury. Not one whine escaped from his mouth. Alton squealed with happiness as he burst out of his mother's arms flying toward Flash. He kissed and wrapped his arms around Flash's body.

"Alton, you be careful! Wilma yelled protectively, but with an astonished looked that mirrored ours.

"Mama, it's all right. Flash is alive. I told you. I told you he's not dead, but you didn't believe me!" he yelled triumphantly. "Only Oli did!"

Alton wasn't the most affectionate kid in the world, but I'll be damned if he didn't kiss a beaming Olisa on the cheek. The two of them jumped up and down in celebration as all the adults stood speechless.

The driver of the car, who sweated profusely, cast his eyes upward toward the sky and looked about ready to drop down on his knees and shout hallelujah. Relief and shock merged in his face. He didn't even say goodbye as he quietly stole into his car and drove away. He was lucky; no police were around as he zoomed through the red light at the end of the block.

The crowd slowly dispersed like rats in the glare of a flashlight. I heard two elderly women mumbling on the side as they gaped at Olisa, "Baby, that little girl put some hoodoo on that animal to make it get up like that."

"Mavis, don't be ridiculous. That dog was just knocked out. Ain't nobody got no power like that."

"Hmmph. The devil do."

"Oh, please…"

"Girl, I knows what I seen, and that child raised that dog from the dead with some a dat hoodoo voodoo, with her mother standing there right behind her doing some kind of chant. You can bet all them peoples is from Louisiana and they done bought that wicked stuff with them."

"Oh, Mavis how do you know where they're from? Have you ever talked to them?"

"Don't need to. I ain't never talk to Satan either, but I seen his work."

Mama Willis cradled Jon, who slept through the whole event as she stood behind James Willis. "So whatcha think, Son?

"Maybe the dog only had a concussion or something," James Willis replied weakly, staring at the shimmering blood in the street.

"I don't think so, Mr. Willis," I said as Flash trotted up, tail wagging vigorously, baseball comfortably ensconced in his drooling mouth, and whining for someone to throw the ball. I put my arm around Grace's shoulders, and she sighed as she wrapped her arm around my waist.

Wilma leaned against the fence, grass stains marring her white dress. "Hey bro, sis, is there something you forgot to tell me?" Wilma asked with a hard stare.

I grabbed her hand. "Yeah, Wilma, come on in and have a seat. Got a little time to spare?"

"Brother, I got all night."

Gumbo shook his head. "Do you know that BAD ASS gangster trembled from the top of his head to the tip of his toes, then fell to his knees at Olisa's feet and wept like a little baby? And he wasn't the only one messed up. I saw some pretty hard-core *hombres* shaking after witnessing what she did."

"They weren't by themselves, Al, the entire place got real quiet."

"Yeah, that's true, Laura. I even forgot where I was until I spotted that KLSC camera shooting away like crazy."

"Let me guess, Eva Sanchez," I said, vigorously rubbing my temples.

"The one and only, Uncle Joe." Alton shoveled some more popcorn into his mouth. "Before everything got busy, Eva Sanchez had been conducting these goofy ass interviews all day, asking, what does the Fourth of July weekend mean to you? She had the nerve to ask me. I looked at her like she was crazy. Told her it didn't mean diddly-squat to me. Ask me about the Emancipation Proclamation, and I'll give you an answer!"

I just shook my head. "Damn, I thought I recognized her. She's their weekend street reporter. No wonder I saw opportunity printed in her eyes."

"Dig that. The minute Laura pointed out the camera to me, I wrapped my body around Olisa while this other brother acted like a presidential bodyguard and hustled us through the stunned crowd to Byron who waved frantically at us. Laura and I sneaked her into Byron's van, and we got the fuck out. Excuse me, Unc. I mean, we flew out of there before anybody came to their senses."

"Who's Byron?"

"Byron's one of the sunglasses vendors, a Japanese dude. He parks his van behind the booth. I think he and Olisa trade services all the time—he gives her glasses, she gives him a fifteen minute massage—stuff like that. "

"Runs much deeper than that, Alton. Byron's wife suffered from cataracts and was waiting until she could scrounge up the finances to afford an operation. Olisa massaged her eyes, and now she sees with no problems. They were so grateful I think Byron would have driven her to New York if we needed him to."

They waited for my reaction. I needed a moment to absorb it all because it was too overwhelming. I already had a raging headache. Finally, I asked, "So how was Olisa through all this, Gumbo?"

"Spacey."

"Uh, uh, not spacey, Al," Laura interjected. "Did you see her eyes? It was more like someone had lit a candle in them. When I pulled her into the van, her hands were burning. Can you imagine what effect this must have on her body to prevent someone from dying? But she was calm; we were the only ones freaking out."

"Yeah, you got that right, baby. I was so glad you were there. Uncle Joe, Laura was a lot cooler than me. When we got Olisa home, Laura cleaned her up, changed her clothes, and got her to lie down and relax. Two seconds later, she cashed in her ticket to dreamland."

"I owe you, guys. Thank goodness you were there to take care of my girl."

"You don't owe us a thing, Uncle Joe," Laura said, putting her arm around my shoulders. "I'd do anything for her."

"Well, I appreciate it."

Grace burst through the kitchen door in her all white nurses' outfit.

"Who's eating popcorn in here? I'm starving! You don't know what kind of day I had at the hospital!"

"Sit down, Grace. Your day is just beginning."

Breaking News

A Dramatic July the 4th weekend at Venice Beach:

Gang Violence!

A Moment of Courage.

A Miracle? You Decide…

Next on KLSC—The station that takes pride in giving you the full report! Join us tonight at 11:00!

This broadcast appeared during several commercial breaks in the last hour of a television movie that simply provided background for our conversation. In one commercial segment, groups of gang members punched each other mercilessly; in a different segment, Olisa is clearly seen tenderly caressing the severely injured youth whose hands clutched his stomach.

Olisa was awake, but she refused to watch the broadcast. As she and Laura retreated to her studio she said, "Makes no sense to watch history reduced to sound bites."

Rinngggg!!

The phone startled me.

"Hello? Hello? Hello?"

"Hello?"

"Papa Willis? How you doing?"

"Hey, you watching?"

"Yeah."

"Uh?"

"Yeah, I'm watching!" I yelled, pissed that James had probably forgotten to turn his hearing aid up.

We sat on the phone in silence as Papa Willis flipped to other channels. When it sounded like stereo in my ear, I knew he had returned to KLSC. His voice sounded even more gravely than usual. "Saw the commercials; thought maybe some of the other stations might be carrying the report. Guess we knew it might happen someday," he sighed. "Damn!"

"Yep."

"Huh?"

"Yeah, I agree!"

"Give me a call after the news or tomorrow if you want. I'm sure you guys are probably going to want to talk."

"Okay, I will! Call you later!"

"Yeah, it's going to get better. Bye!"

The good news is, the Olisa story failed to make national news. The bad news, KLSC gave it a tremendous amount of coverage. Ms.

Sanchez looked like a million bucks on screen. Her light brown eyes exuded a glow of confidence I had never seen before, and her personable attitude made you feel like she was discussing the news with you in your living room. She rolled those R's subtly enough to express her pride in her Latina heritage without alienating her mainstream viewership.

"Good evening, Los Angeles, I'm Eva Sanchez, and tonight my story begins as another redundant chapter of the gang violence that plagues our city, but ends as an essay on courage, humanity and maybe, a miracle. Tonight, you'll see for yourself what happened this afternoon on the crowded Venice Beach Boardwalk.

"The city of Venice is certainly no stranger to gang violence. Several years ago, the war between Black and Latino youths claimed seventeen lives and fifty-four injuries over a ten-month period— including many innocent people. Eventually, a truce was forged between the two groups, but that was all forgotten today. No one is sure what initiated the conflict, but it escalated into some of the footage you are about to view. I warn you, many of the images you'll see contain very graphic violence," she said, her face stern.

"There they go, look at 'em, Uncle Joe," whispered Alton, shaking his head and leaning over in his chair.

The TV screen displayed muddled scenes of black and brown kids duking it out. My eyes centered on the frightened faces in the crowd as openmouthed people screamed and stampeded in all directions. The jumbled camera visuals made it hard to decipher what was going on; obviously the cameraman got knocked down as sky and rooftops haphazardly appeared. But even that added to the drama.

"Courage is a quality not exclusive to gender, race, nationality, age, or economic status. Tonight you will see a woman that showed more bravery than many of us will see in a lifetime. They say our society has become apathetic—what you see tonight may skew all your perceptions."

Some time later, I heard the film sequences that followed won some sort of news award for their sensational imagery. They showed

Olisa standing defiantly between the two gangs, unbraided hair fanning wildly behind her, arms outspread, a sorceress casting spells to keep the snarling wolves at bay.

"I apologize for the loss of sound… This woman who has placed her life on the line is pleading for them to stop, begging them to respect the precious lives of the innocents as well as themselves. Unfortunately, we have no visual proof, except for eyewitnesses that the young man you see lying on the ground is mortally wounded. However, keep watching…"

Olisa sat cross-legged on the ground huddled over him, his upper body hoisted onto her lap. Our vision was distorted by her masses of hair draped protectively over him like a pulled curtain. All we could make out were her hands massaging gently, rhythmically, deftly crisscrossing his ululating stomach. Each swipe of her hands became more crimson with his blood.

Through a shaky blue sky, we saw police officers and paramedics in the upper corner of the camera bursting through the crowd. Zooming through a gap in the crowd, we found a Latino youth in a blood soaked T-shirt, embracing Olisa like a lost child. Next, we saw Alton's broad back as he quickly hustled Olisa out of the camera's eye view followed by Laura looking warily behind her. They disappeared and all we saw were the beachgoers hovering speechlessly around the boy who was stabbed. The bewildered youth ripped off his shirt and held it in the air like a trophy.

"The kid you see standing up, laughing, and rubbing his stomach with no pain was critically injured only minutes ago. The witnesses we interviewed swear he was stabbed repeatedly. Did this woman, this hero who intervened in the violence, heal him? Have we witnessed a modern day miracle? Or is this some kind of elaborate hoax?"

"You go girl, milk it for everything you got!" I yelled sarcastically, ready to throw up.

"Hey, where's my man?" asked Alton, frowning at the screen.

"Who are you talking about?" Grace asked.

"Brother man. He shielded us when we ran away. Ain't no way you could miss that big boy.

"Why is that?"

"That dude had to be about 6'8, built, brother so black he was blue, with dazzling snow white hair. Had a mean looking trumpet with him. I figured he was just one of the musicians that jammed on the beach."

"Did he say anything to you?" I asked.

"Never said a word, brother man was all about action!"

I swallowed hard as I thought about the huge figure I saw years ago on the rooftop in Watts.

"That's one of the most incredible things I've ever seen, Eva," replied the eternally handsome and suntanned anchorman, Brevin Hightower, eying her appraisingly while shuffling through a pile of papers. "But are you also telling us that this fearless Samaritan healed this young man?"

"Brevin, according to the people we interviewed, that's exactly what happened. Here are several interviews, including one with the boy stabbed in the fight, Ernesto Padilla."

Padilla looked like he had just won the featherweight championship as throngs surrounded him, cheering and patting him heartily on the back. Hundreds of needlepoint hairs teamed to form a dark shadow on his closely shaved head. His thin muscular body boasted a gallery of tattoos. As she held the microphone to his mouth, his eyes danced wildly, his breath came in spurts, and his feet shifted continuously as if searching for steady ground. He clutched the bloody shirt like it was a souvenir.

"With us we have Ernesto Padilla who amazingly has recovered from multiple stab wounds in the chest and stomach. Ernesto, how do you feel? It's hard to believe you're the same person I saw minutes ago lying still on the ground."

"Oh yeah, you know, he got me good, you know. Peep this—these marks, this is where he stuck me. Man, I thought it's all over, you know. All I remember is this black dude sitting on top of me and hammering my chest with a knife, you know. But hey, you know. I'm just happy to still be alive; you know what I'm saying?"

"Uh-huh. So what started the fight?"

"Oh, some stupid (blip) over a woman or something. But that was just some (blip), man. It didn't matter, we was going to get busy anyway. But it's all good. I ain't into that no more—know what I'm saying? God sent me a sign. Gangbanging is dead for me. You know what I'm saying? It's a sign. Somebody's telling me to give it up before I get smoked."

"A sign? So you do believe this woman healed you?"

"You didn't see it? Hell yeah, she healed me. I ain't never been in that much pain in my life. Scared to breathe and stuff. I thought my guts was gonna fall out, you know? And then when she touched me, aw, man it was like somebody giving you a warm bath, you know what I'm saying? My homies is laughing, but I'm serious… You know, my mother will tell you. She always says to me, you keep doing these bad things and you're gonna die soon. I pray that the lord will give you a sign. That was a sign, dude. She saved me.

"I was in total darkness, you know? I couldn't see nothin', and then I saw this bright light, and it was real warm. I see this nasty ass blood all over me, but I'm feeling good. Man, and all this time I thought all the things they said about her was just talk, you know? But it's true, she's got the power. I wouldn't be surprised if the Virgin of Guadalupe worked through her, know what I'm saying? I ain't lying, homie. Look at me."

He proudly pounded his chest, machismo oozing from him, a challenging stare that dared anyone to dispute his claim. He delivered it with the same amount of gusto he'd use to protect his turf. It's a trip, you know. She took care of me just like that," he said, snapping his fingers.

"What did she say to you?"

"I don't remember all that much, you know… I didn't even know home girl spoke Spanish. That's what I'm saying… about the Virgin. I was so out of it, I thought I was a little boy again… It was like I was home in bed with my mother taking care of me or something, you know?"

"Better stop hitting that crack, Chato," one of his buddies joked off camera.

"I'm done with that (blip) forever, homey. Yeah, she kept saying, believe and you'll be all right, believe and I will heal you."

"You act like you know her. Who is she?"

"Aw, everybody that hangs out here knows her, ain't that right, *vato*?" He grabbed one of his buddies plastered beside him who was mugging at the camera and playfully rubbed his bald head.

"Aw yeah, homes. All the locals know her. My mother says she's a *curandera*, someone who can heal people. I didn't really believe in the (blip) until now, you know what I'm saying? Man, she has the gang's *respeto*, you know. We don't bother her or dis her cause everyone knows she knows what's up. If you got problems, drugs, health, they say you can go to her and she'll hook you up. She can tell the future, too, man. You don't mess with people who talk to the *espiritus*, you know what I'm saying?

"So are you quitting the gang, too?"

Chato's homey held his head down for a second, smiling sheepishly. "Naw I didn't say all that, because that's family. You know what I'm saying? But we gonna try hard to keep the truce now, you know?" He shook hands and vigorously hugged one of the black gang members with a watch cap on his head standing nearby.

"Hey, black and brown don't need to be fighting each other, you know. But Chato's free to do what he wants... cause he's been chosen. Usually you can't leave, you know... but ain't nobody gonna mess with my boy now. *Con respeto*."

The camera cut back to the newsroom desk as gang signs were displayed. The crowd cheered enthusiastically behind them.

"And that's our extended story for this Sunday evening, Brevin."

"Wow! Fascinating, Eva. What a way to wrap up a July 4th weekend!" remarked Brevin, a thoughtful expression on his face. "So what do we know about this woman someone called the Good Witch of Venice?" he asked, cocking his head and squinting his blue eyes.

"Not much, Brevin. All we know right now is that she's a regular on the Venice Beach scene, giving massages, readings, and spiritual advice, but the locals swear she's the real thing. I am told she is very humble and not one to seek publicity. However, we're hoping that she'll consent to do an interview with us. I think the public would love to learn more about this enigmatic hero."

"Well, Eva, I for one would love to hear more about this remarkable woman. It's an amazing story! Please follow up on this one for us."

"Absolutely, Brevin."

Black matter exploded onto the screen as I disgustedly punched the remote. But, not quickly enough to escape the specter of Eva's ebullient face.

Afterwards, we all kind of shrugged our shoulders and called it a night. Gumbo left with Laura after decimating our refrigerator, and Grace retired to the bedroom. I chose to take a dip in our Jacuzzi. Nothing could beat soaking in the bubbling tub's soothing heat as I gazed at the blackened sky accosted by a sprinkling of slithering clouds. Soon my solitude was interrupted by the sounds of police sirens whizzing down the street. Overhead a loud chomping "ghetto bird" passed by with its cyclopean eye flashing a wide swath of menacing light over the Oakwood area, once again canvassing the area for the perpetrators of some crime. It was just another night in Venice.

The moist heat was the perfect tonic for the stress that clung to my body. My fingers turned into link sausages from all the soaking, but the weight of the world fell off my shoulders, at least for a little while as I buttoned my pajamas and climbed into bed. Grace was propped up by two huge pillows reading a mystery novel, but put it down as soon as I got into bed.

"Olisa's light is still on, Grace. You think Little Oak's talking some sense into her?"

"I doubt it. What's she going to tell her, Joseph?"

"I don't know. How about, from now on—mind your own business?"

"You're upset because she helped somebody?"

"No, I'm upset because all hell's going to break loose! She helped some stupid shit that probably got what he deserved."

"Olisa can't choose who to help when someone's hurt. You know that."

"I know. I know… I just don't think being under a microscope is going to be a whole lot of fun for her.

"Maybe it won't be as bad as you think, Joseph."

"Grace, did you see the look in Eva what's-her-face's eyes? She's not about to let it rest!"

"Yes, but it was only one incident. If Olisa doesn't do anything else, what can she prove?"

"In our dictionary, 'if' is a five syllable word. You think you could ever convince Olisa to turn away an injured animal?"

"No and I wouldn't want to. She's got her own mind."

"Exactly."

"Okay, Joseph, but even though it's on film, the reporters are still not ready to commit to the idea that she cured him. The Simi Valley jurors refused to believe that Rodney King was beaten by the police—even after they saw it on video. Maybe it will just fade away after awhile."

"Uh, uh, I don't think so. It's just a matter of time. It's always been a matter of time, hon."

"I guess that's true, Joe. We tried for so long to protect her, didn't we? But maybe this is what God wants. Maybe we'll just have to trust."

"Yeah, maybe…" I replied, nodding my head and wrapping my arm around her as she cuddled next to me. "So what time do you think Jon's coming by tomorrow?"

"Grace scooted up in the bed. "Jon never told me he was coming by."

"Grace, please, get real. We're talking about our son. You know— the one we've known and loved for thirty something years."

"Early, very early," she sighed as she laid her head down on the pillow. I squeezed her affectionately and turned off the night light.

No matter how hard I tried, I couldn't get myself to relax and fall asleep. It reminded me of the time I had insomnia a few months after Jonathan was born. Counting sheep didn't do the trick, so I decided to check on the kids. It was about 1:30 A.M., and I figured the baby was on the verge of waking up as he usually did at that hour. He was sound asleep in his crib. Instead, Olisa was awake, and on her knees at the head of her bed peering through the curtains.

"Hey, what are you doing up?" I whispered. "Something outside?"

Not a muscle moved as she continued to gaze out the window. I heard soft sniffling. I quickly went over and picked her up.

"What's wrong, kid? You have a nightmare?" Her head turned and there were tears streaming down her cheeks. Her hands were folded and pressing against her chest. She trembled slightly.

"Daddy, Can we help Mr. Robinson? He's very sick. If he dies, will he go to heaven?"

"Honey, what kind of questions? Did Mr. Robinson tell you he's ill?"

"No."

"Then why are you talking like this?"

"Because… because when I held Mr. Robinson's hand today, he felt sick, Daddy. Maybe we can wrap him in a blanket like when I was a little baby, Dada. Let's take care of him, okay?"

"That's a nice thought honey, but Mr. Robinson is fine. I just saw him this morning, and we talked for a long time about the Dodger's baseball game. Don't you worry your precious little heart about him. Mr. Robinson's going to be around for a long time."

Ethan Robinson lived next door and had been in the neighborhood for over a quarter of a century. If you wanted to know how much Los Angeles had changed over the years, you should have asked Mr. Robinson. He was one of the early Negro pioneers to settle here after World War II and very proud of it. He still had chickens, geese, pigs, cats, dogs, and even a peacock in his yard. Pops told me he had a pony until all the neighbors decided they had grown tired of smelling horse shit.

Also, there was no better watchdog in the world than his black goose, Mr. Midnight, who honked a warning to all intruders. And you didn't dare provoke him. I'll never forget the newsboy who was feeling his oats and decided to challenge him like a matador to a bull. That goose charged him so fast that boy set an unrecorded high jump record as he sailed over the fence.

Mr. Robinson was a character's character shining those pearly whites from his wrinkled ebony face; always joking that he had more lines on his face than a California road map. But he deserved it, and every line told a story. Even when Mrs. Robinson died in her sleep a few years ago, he courageously maintained his sense of humor as difficult as it was.

Olisa loved going over there, it was like being at the circus with all his animals. "What choo doing, girl?" he'd ask with his rapid fire delivery. "You so cute I'm going to eat you up." Crowds of kids hung out at Mr. Robinson's. He was always sharing stories with the kids about his Mississippi childhood and all the odd jobs he held from tanning hides to hopping railroad cars.

Grandpa Harry was his closest friend. Those two old curmudgeons raised the art of argument to its highest plateau, but they loved each other. Sitting around playing dominoes and checkers was their Friday night routine. I don't think a day passed in which Mr. Robinson didn't tell me some story about my Grandpa Harry, wistfulness blanketing his eye.

His hearing had been getting worse over the years, and he didn't hear me as I yelled hello to him one Friday over the hedge. I figured he was just deep in conversation with a friend as I peeked over the bushes. He was playing checkers by himself—but not really—there was an empty seat on the other side of the board, and I heard him yell, "Harry, study long, study wrong. Don't blame me cause you getting your ass whooped!" He slapped his thigh with laughter and then slowly eased back into his chair as puffs of smoke wafted from his pipe and dissipated into the night air.

Friday games were still on.

I was under the impression his health was excellent, even though he was in his eighties. He always took early morning walks around 6:00 A.M. There was a light on in his bedroom, which was no big thing.

"I really think you had a nightmare, honey."

"No, Daddy, the light next door woke me up. It scared me. It's too bright and too hot!" she cried.

It had to be a nightmare, waking up unexpectedly and seeing a light on next door. That must have frightened her, I thought, as I looked out her window at the house. The light glowed dimly behind the curtain as I watched an obscure figure pacing back and forth. Gaping out the window made me feel like a voyeur, so I clapped the curtains closed.

"Aw, honey. Here, let me wipe those tears. I'm sure it was just a bad dream. Lie down and get some sleep. You'll see... In the morning everything will be all right, okay?"

"Okay, Daddy."

"Are you still my little smugly?"

"Yes, Daddy."

"I love you."

"I love you, too, Daddy."

I gave her a peck on the forehead and stayed up with her until she fell asleep.

As I entered our bedroom, there was a huge, startling bang whose echo reverberated into the serene night. Mr. Robinson's dogs were baying like crazy, and the goose was honking.

Baby Jon started crying.

I heard a click and the incandescent table lamp beamed like a spotlight as Grace hurriedly threw on her robe.

"What was that?"

"I don't know. It sounded like it was next door." My stomach slowly curled into a tight fist.

"Are you going to check it out?"

"Yeah, I guess," I said, not moving.

"You don't think it was a prowler at Mr. Robinson's do you? Honey, what's going on? You look so pale. You're shaking. You think everything is okay? Should I call the police?"

"I don't know, Grace, okay? I'm going to check in a minute, I'm just waiting to see if I hear anything else."

Jon's screams rang in our ears. The dog's hacking barks were irritating my ears.

Olisa squeezed past the open bedroom door and stood there in her lavender pajamas, rubbing her eyes. She toddled over and gripped my numbed legs in a bear hug.

Grace looked at me oddly and nervously said, "I'll go check on Jon."

It took awhile for me to rid myself of the temporary paralysis that stalled my system. Prying Olisa's arms from my legs, I gathered her in my arms and took her to Grace and the baby. The dogs howled with the sounds of the approaching sirens.

"I've got a bad feeling, Joseph." Grace rocked Jon in her arms and peeped through the curtains. "Three police cars and now an ambulance just pulled up in front of Mr. Robinson's."

"All right, all right, I'm going to check it out, stay here."

I grabbed my robe and reticently headed out the door, thinking about the silhouetted figure pacing back and forth in front of the window. Squad car lights flashed across the lawn. Mr. Robinson's front door was wide open, and Mr. Midnight, the goose, honked relentlessly in the corner of the yard.

A cop blocked me at the door as I tried to nudge my way in.

"You family?"

"What's wrong? What's going on? Is Mr. Robinson hurt?"

"Are you family?"

"I'm about the only family he's got here. I'm his next-door neighbor. Is he okay?" I asked, receiving my answer the minute he stepped aside. In the back bedroom, a figure slumped in a chair was being examined by a man with a glove. Through moistening eyes, I saw him removing a rifle from between the man's awkwardly splayed legs. There were huge blotches of red behind him on the wall.

"Sir, can we talk to you?"

"Yes," I answered in a child's voice.

Mr. Robinson had committed suicide. The police babbled at me about some scribbled note they found stating he just found out he had cancer. It said how much he missed his wife, Carla, and that he wasn't going to let some strangers in a hospital see him through his last days. He asked for God's forgiveness and told Carla he'd meet her at the gates… and that was that.

After awhile, I turned and walked back to our house, playing repeatedly in my head what I would say to Olisa. Sorry, everything's not all right in the real world. I was wrong—you were right. If I had listened to you and trusted you, maybe I could have saved his life.

All I could think about was we had lost a neighbor and a friend; and our daughter knew it before anyone else.

Olisa knew.

On the day of the funeral as we walked away from the gravesite, Olisa grasped my hand and said, "Daddy, we don't have to be sad anymore, Mr. Robinson told me he's much happier now."

"He told you? When?"

"He just whispered it in my ear," she replied, grinning broadly and giving me a big hug.

"That's great, honey." As she hugged me, I felt the guilt that had been ransacking my body finally begin to wash away.

Olisa then skipped away shouting to Grace who was up ahead pushing Jon in the stroller, "Mommy, Mommy, guess what happened?"

After that, I never again doubted Olisa's words.

Never.

CHAPTER 3

When I finally fell asleep, the rest of the night was haunted by lurking, shadowy monsters who followed me home as I cautiously tiptoed down the streets of my old neighborhood in Compton. Grotesque, distorted figures hiding behind trees, peering over hedges, hunched upon walls, and stalked me everywhere I went. It didn't matter how fast I ran or where I hid, they always managed to find me. Finally, in desperation, I leaped into the air and flew over land and sea to areas I had only read about in travel magazines; warm, exotic, lush, and beautiful hideaways. The sensation of flying, of traveling wherever I wanted made me feel in control. It gave me peace of mind. I knew it was a dream, but I didn't want it to end. I tried to savor every precious moment, but was startled by a loud bang.

"Sorry, honey, I didn't mean to wake you. The cabinet drawer was stuck again." Grace's hair tickled my cheek as I smelled her perfume, followed by a warm wet kiss on my forehead. "Go back to sleep, I'm going to say hi to Jon before I leave for General Hospital. I hear them talking in the kitchen."

A few blinks later, I parted company with my pillow, splashed some ice-cold water on my face and guided myself through half-closed lids down the hallway to the promising smell of the coffee machine.

"Mornin', Dad. Your red eyes match your robe. Can we hook this coffee up to you intravenously?"

"Cute. Why aren't you on channel 4, so I can switch to channel 7?"

"Eh, there's still a spark of life left in the old man." He laughed, patting me on the shoulder as I stumbled to a chair at the kitchen table. "Somebody pull out the Scrabble board."

Olisa poured a big steaming cup of espresso and quietly placed it in front of me.

"You don't want an ass whooping this early in the morning, Son. By the time I finish with you, I'll be wearing that little Armani warm up suit you're wearing and driving your Range Rover! What's the score? I'm at least five games ahead!"

"Only because you come up with all these crazy words you memorized from your little Scrabble player's dictionary that no one would ever bother to use in this universe."

"Hey, whatever works. If you'd stopped trying to hit all home runs with seven letter words for the bonus points, you might be ahead."

"I'm a gambler, Pops, and gamblers take risks!"

"You guys kill me with your games," Olisa groaned. "Testosterone overload. That's why we have wars! Men have to find someone they can physically dominate."

"Oh I wouldn't go that far, Olisa. I think Pops and I are just frustrated nerds who deep down inside were wannabe athletes."

"Speak for yourself, junior flip. I was pretty good in track. Best high jumper in the high school conference."

"Come on, Dad, that's fine. But wouldn't you have liked to experience what it felt like to be a big time college athlete? At least once? And all the money, women, fame, and glory that goes with it?"

"I could care less."

"Is that right? So that's why you've rejected all my suggestions about turning the 'Soul of Venice' into a franchise? We could open up a chain of soul food restaurants. Check it out—Soul of Manhattan, Soul of Hermosa, Soul of Oxnard—just tell me when you're ready, and I'll find the money."

"I told you before, way too much work, and I ain't got it in me. I like my nice little business. Wilma and I are in total control; we pay all our bills, and even make a little bit of money now and then."

"Dad, you're not listening. I'll do all the legwork. You can act as a consultant. Just sit back, enjoy life, and watch the money roll in!"

I grunted and nodded my head as I sipped the hot brew. We'd been through this a hundred times.

"Little brother, you should know by now that Daddy doesn't want to franchise his restaurant. So give it a break and mind your own business."

"Yes, ma'am," replied Jonathan, grinning at his sister.

"Besides, he's not like you—Mr. Ambitious, with an M.B.A. from Stanford University and a corporate position as vice president of the talent and marketing division of RPM Records."

Olisa smiled admiringly as she stroked the smooth shiny waves in his short and fashionable haircut. She leaned over and wrapped her arms around his neck.

"I guess so… I'm just trying to look out for my pops. That's all," he said, patting my hand.

"And it's appreciated," I nodded.

"Anyway, Olisa, I guess to most people what I'm doing looks great! The company is hungry, and we're on a fast track. They give me plenty of autonomy, an expense budget and I travel all over the world. I meet with top recording artists—stars, people would die to meet… But you know what? It ain't mine. If they don't like the way I sneeze, bam! I'm outta there."

"You don't have to worry about that. They love you."

"For now… as long as I'm making them money. But if anything goes wrong, they'll find a new boy wonder."

"But, Jon, there are people who would kill to be where you are. Aren't you happy?"

He squeezed her arms as he cocked his head and gave her a peck on the cheek. "I must sound like some kind of ingrate. I'm sorry. Things could always be better, but when all is said and done, I'm happy enough."

Olisa kissed him on the cheek and rocked him in her arms.

"But forget all that. The main reason I came by here is to see Venice Beach's newest celebrity."

"Oh get out of here!" she laughed, pushing his head down, her face reddening. Quickly switching subjects she said, "I thought we were going to walk down to the beach and get some breakfast at the Fig Tree Cafe? I might even convert you into a vegetarian."

"And lose my membership to Carnivores Anonymous? Not hardly."

"Okay, so I'll start you out with the eggs lulu, which has chicken sausage. At least I can wean you from pork!"

"Let's do it," he said, standing up and snatching his keys off the counter. "Dad, you coming?"

"You two kids are unbelievable. Has it dawned on you the effects of that broadcast last night? And now you want to casually head on down to Venice like nothing happened?"

"Dad, don't make a big deal out of it, it will blow over. Watch. Hardly anyone will be at the beach on a Monday morning anyway."

"Yeah, besides, she'll be with me."

"That's what I'm worried about."

"That's cold."

"Not trying to be. Olisa, I really don't think it's a good idea. Things are too hot after last night."

"Dad, relax. Everything's cool. My guardian angel will take care of me." Her eyebrows lifted and her eyes teasingly widened as she ominously surveyed the room. I wondered if she was half-serious.

Playfully pushing Jon out the kitchen door she said, "The restaurant is closed on Mondays. Come join us."

"You guys go ahead; I need to take a long hot shower. I'll meet you there!"

"Great! See you later!"

I took my shower, grabbed my bicycle out of the garage, and pedaled down to the boardwalk. The booths were being lackadaisicallyset-up by low-lidded people sipping coffee. Cheap stuffed animals, incense stands, Rastafarian hats and sunglasses were all being pulled out of cartons as vendors assembled their displays. A few derelicts stumbled by, muttering to themselves as I zigzagged between them. It was relatively quiet, but my vision centered on a gathering of people in the distance ahead of me on the boardwalk. I rode my bike straight toward the huddled figures. I knew what I'd find.

Olisa sat on a bench, ensconced in conversation with a blond dreadlocked surfer who had tattoos battling for space on his arms. About ten people hung around, literally eavesdropping on their conversation. I was too far away to hear what was said as I leaned my bike against the railing that encircled the Fig Tree Cafe's outdoor patio area. Occasionally, there were sporadic bursts of laughter as he peered sheepishly at the gathering crowd, while Olisa held his hand and continued to talk. A couple of times, his head jerked back dramatically, followed by intermittent giggles from the crowd. I wondered what startling revelation she just dropped on him.

"Why are you frowning, kid?" I asked.

Her face was comically wrinkled up like a little prune. "Daddy, I thought we're not supposed to use bad words?"

"What word are you talking about, Oli?"

"I can't say it, Daddy."

"Go ahead, you can say it this once."

The word "nigger" jumped out of her mouthlike it had been cooped up too long.

I stared straight ahead.

"Did you hear me, Daddy? You want me to say it again?"

"No. No, I heard you."

"That's a bad word, huh, Daddy?"

"Yes, it is."

"So why do all you guys in the barbershop say it over and over?"

"I don't know, honey. We're just joking. It's a way of letting off a little steam."

"But you told me if anybody called me that, it was a bad thing."

"Yeah, I did, honey. But in this case it's a little different. We don't mean it. You know… It's just a way of kidding around. You can't take it serious. It's kind of our way of defusing the term. Look, it's hard to explain. "

The crease in her eyebrows tightened some more. "If it's a joke, why do you feel bad whenever you say it?"

"How do you know that?"

"I don't know." She frowned, kicking one leg. "Cause when I held your hand I felt pain every time you said it."

"You're right. That's not a nice word, and we might not be able to keep the guys in the barbershop from using it, but you won't hear it coming out of my mouth anymore, okay?"

"Ok, Daddy, cause we don't say bad words," she scolded with a finger in the air and a goofy smile on her face. Then she grabbed my hand and brushed it against her cheek, holding it there while my heart got soggy for the umpteenth time.

"Dad, Dad, over here!" Jonathan waved at me from one of the patio tables. As I carefully stepped over the low railing, there was a twinge in the pit of my stomach the moment I spotted the back of a sharply dressed woman with short brown hair glistening from the touch of morning sunlight. Turning in her seat, Eva Sanchez flashed her bright white teeth in my direction.

Proudly, Jonathan introduced his new best friend, "Dad, this is …"

"I know who it is. How you doing, Ms. Sanchez?"

"Fine, Mr. Carpenter. Please call me Eva." Her smile remained steadfastly in place as she ignored my icy demeanor.

"Just coffee, thank you," I told the waitress while I hesitantly sat down.

"Jonathan and I have been having a wonderful chat. I didn't realize your son was so charming."

"Yeah, he's a chip off the old block, isn't he?"

She laughed politely while Jon narrowed his eyes at me.

"So what have y'all been talking about?" I asked, gravity tugging at the corners of my mouth.

"Oh you know me, Dad, I was going on and on about the 'ins' and 'outs' of the record business." He rubbed his chin self-consciously after catching my why-are-you-consorting-with-the-enemy look.

"And it's been absolutely fascinating! I could listen to him all day long. One of these days I am going to have to convince Jon to do an interview."

"Sounds good. Tell you what, why don't you interview Jonathan and leave Olisa alone?"

"Drop me a line any time." He countered quickly, handing Eva his business card.

"Great! Thank you." She took a couple of seconds to study his card then shoveled it inside her coat pocket.

"Well, I'll leave you two gentlemen alone so you can enjoy your breakfast…"

"Ms. Sanchez…"

"Eva."

"Fine, Eva… Just out of curiosity… Have you ever been here before? I mean, I don't ever remember seeing you."

"No, Mr. Carpenter, never. I took a chance coming here this morning, hoping I'd find Olisa. I wanted to personally introduce myself to her and invite her to do an interview with me at the station! But it seems that I'll have to wait in line."

The crowd around Olisa had doubled. Two bicycle cops asked the crowd to clear the walkway. Olisa immediately stood up and greeted the officers warmly. She shepherded the crowd away from the cafe and into the sand on the beach.

"Why are you doing this?" I asked. "Olisa doesn't need the publicity. Her life is very happy right now, and we don't want to see her hurt by this."

The perma-smile disappeared from her face as she empathetically grabbed my shoulder. "Mr. Carpenter, with all due respect, if I thought this was going to hurt anyone, I'd never ask for an interview. Somebody like your daughter needs to be praised and given accolades for her bravery!"

"And you might receive a few accolades yourself, huh? Better ratings, higher salary?"

"Mr. Carpenter, what can I say? Guilty as charged! I'm a reporter and that's what I do. This is newsworthy; Olisa did something extraordinary. She prevented an escalation of gang violence on the beach, and appears to have healed an injured boy on the spot. The public wants to know more."

"Get real, Ms. San... Eva... The truth is, your viewers can only speculate as to whether she actually healed anybody. I don't remember your station making any definitive statements about her healing him. Why? Mainly because it would be embarrassing if it turned out to be a hoax! No station that lives and dies by the ratings is going to put themselves on the line without absolute proof. So why not let it die?"

She tapped her fingers on the table as we watched Olisa giving a reading to a sista who wore a burnt orange Cleopatra wig, gold lamé jumpsuit, and so much jewelry that when she moved it sounded like wind chimes.

"Mr. Carpenter, I can honestly sympathize with what you're asking and ordinarily I'd agree to do it your way, but..."

"But what?"

"But this is *too* big, and I'd be lying because I saw her heal him as easily as Visine clears red eyes. If *I* hadn't seen it then I would have dropped it."

Clasping my hands behind my head, I watched two pigeons battle over a piece of bread crust.

"Ms. Sanchez, you're young, pretty, ambitious, and a complete professional. I believe you're approaching this with all the good intentions in the world, but your naiveté is going to destroy my daughter."

Pain rippled across her face like she'd been slapped. "Mr. Carpenter, I'm truly sorry you feel that way. You're certainly entitled to your feelings, but my story is going to make your daughter famous."

"She could give a shit."

"But the world does, Mr. Carpenter. People want to know about your daughter and her special gifts. If she wasn't your daughter, could you honestly say this story wouldn't interest you?"

I didn't answer as I toyed with my wedding ring.

"Look at her," Eva went on, "within the short time I have been here, people are drawn to her like a magnet. Earlier this morning I watched a woman from El Salvador drag her two teenage boys here, literally by the scruff of their collars. When she plopped them in front of your daughter, they were bug-eyed scared. I'm talking *ese's*, man. You know, too cool to be afraid. Why? Because this was the woman who saved Ernesto 'Chato' Padilla: the 'mad dog' *El Loco*. This woman rescued their idol. In their world, only a witch or the Holy Virgin Mother would demand such deference."

Nonchalantly, I folded my hands and rested them on the table. "So?"

"So, this woman waited stoically all morning, and when Olisa arrived, she approached her with blood shot eyes and cried, 'Can you ask God to keep my boys from dying in the streets? Can you rescue them like the boy you saved last night? Please, *señorita*, ' she pleaded with Olisa, 'no one can do what you do and not know God.'"

The waitress served a plate of fruit salad with a scone on the side to Eva. She immediately grabbed a knife and started brush stroking apple butter on it like she was sculpting clay.

"Hmmm. This is so good… Care for any?"

"No thanks."

Munching away, she said, "I think at first, Olisa was in a quandary about what to do. But then she did the unexpected, falling to her knees and clasping hands with the *señora*. The few restaurant customers and personnel gaped in stunned silence, unsure of what to make of this."

Jon nervously kept fidgeting with his fingers while listening to her story.

"She warned them that God's love means absolutely nothing unless they are willing to accept it in their hearts. She then asked them to hold hands with her in prayer. The boys continued to stand, but they were visibly trembling. Finally, they sank to their knees as if she had twisted their wrists in a deft martial arts maneuver. A short while later, they parted company so quietly I thought it turned out to be a big dud.

Until I saw the youngest rubbing his hand as if he'd been stung by a bee. Before they got too far away, I caught up with them.

"*Señora, Señora*, are you okay? What happened?" I asked. The *Señora's* eyes were glazed. I wondered if she was even aware that I was walking alongside her.

"My boys are going to be fine. We are going to be fine. God is here. God is here," she repeated with such finality I glanced over my shoulder.

"*Yo no comprendo, Señora*. What do you mean?"

Eyes closed, the *Señora's* fingers grazed along the sides of her face as if it had been transformed into gold. "Her hands, God's hands…"

"What are you saying, *Señora*? Are you saying you felt the power of God in her hands? Do you feel like He is working through her?"

A childlike, giddy laughter erupted from her mouth as she grasped my hands. "*Señorita*, did you say *HE*?"

"Yes."

All three laughed euphorically.

"*Señora*," she said, a crazed look in her eyes, "God is not a he, he is a she."

"What?"

"*She* is God."

"I stood transfixed as I watched this person who I pegged earlier as a staunch, old world Catholic woman, dance down the boardwalk with her sons, spinning and weaving as if it were the yellow brick road.

"So as you see, Mr. Carpenter, I can't stop now. It's become more than just a news feature, it's personal. The best-kept secret in the world has been going on at Venice Beach, and eventually my competitors are going to discover this story, too. But it's my story; I want and deserve the exclusive!"

"So it's just a competition. It's not about Olisa's feelings or the effect it may have on our family."

"Sir, I promise you. Work with me, and I will handle this with as much sensitivity as I can under the circumstances. It's more than just a job to me."

"Yeah." I snickered.

Jonathan tapped my elbow. "Dad, listen to me. I think she's right. Now that the story has broken, they're all going to be coming after Olisa and everyone around her. We might as well cooperate with Eva. What choice do we have?"

"Jon, this is your sister we're discussing! Our backs aren't against the wall. We don't have to tell her…"

"Listen. I'm going to leave so the two of you can talk more privately."

"Excuse me, I thought I recognized you, you're that reporter, Maria, Ava…"

So focused on our conversation, I didn't even notice the contingent around us. One of whom had a very familiar face, but it was out of context.

"Eva, Mr. Mayor. Eva Sanchez. How great to see you here, sir. I'm surprised you recognize me!"

"Pretty soon everyone in the country is going to recognize you, young lady. Especially with stories like the one you covered last night. That was quite a report about that Venice woman, the good witch is it? Very impressive."

"Thank you, sir. Ironically, I've been sharing a table with her family. Mayor Kenneth Halpern, I'd like to introduce you to her father, Joseph Carpenter and her brother, Jonathan Carpenter."

Jonathan leaped up from his seat, quickly extending a hand as I begrudgingly offered mine.

"Gentlemen, it is indeed a great pleasure meeting you," he said with an expansive smile, ready-made for those photographic moments that say, "I care." It was coupled with the patented campaigner handshake of grasping one hand warmly in both of his. Mayor "Happy" Halpern, whose ambitions far exceeded his current position, was a consummate charmer and jokester. So much so, that no one really remembered his platform as a mayoral candidate.

Hap's recent campaign was obscured by more mud slinging than the female wrestlers at the Tropicana nightclub. Happy took full advantage of the notoriety accompanying his liberal rival Clarence Kimbrough's alleged action of picking up a fourteen-year-old minor and spending time with her in a West Hollywood motel about ten years ago. The woman, apparently brighter and some speculate richer thanks to some anonymous support, suddenly decided it was her manifest destiny to tell the public about her torrid one night affair with Mr. Kimbrough during the middle of a hotly contested campaign.

"You must be quite proud of your courageous daughter," he said, whacking me on the back.

"Yes I am. Even before last night."

"Uh-huh. Is that her over there in the crowd? I'd consider it a great honor to meet such a fine woman," he said, grabbing my arm with a hand the size of a baseball mitt. There was still a solid grip in the pink knockwurst fingers of this former pro football player who had been a backup right tackle in the late 60's and early 70's with the Los Angeles Rams.

He ushered me through the group like a hostage. His minions scurried close behind, filming while the wide-bodied mayor threaded his way through the crowd like a running back while shaking hands. A sprinkling of boos rifled through the populace, but it didn't faze his leathery hide a bit.

"So this is your daughter, Mr. Carpenter?" he asked, swatting me on the back for my accomplishment. "My, my, my… Well, it's hard for me to believe that such a gorgeous lady took on the vermin that ravage this city. It's a pleasure to meet you, Olisa," he said, shaking her hand and masterfully moving in position next to her for the fusillade of photographs to come. He prolonged the handshake until he was sure the moment had been captured.

"I'm Mayor Halpern, Olisa. When I spotted you over here, I had to ask your father to introduce me to his courageous daughter. "

What introduction? He used me as his prop.

"Thank you, sir."

"I hope you won't mind a few pictures?"

"Uh, no, that's fine," Olisa answered, a little dazed, but amused by the whole proceeding.

"Young lady, I've been talking with some of my associates about you, including the police chief, and I'm pushing through a formal recommendation to issue you a special citation honoring the bravery you demonstrated last night. We'll have a special ceremony and reception. It's to 'thank you' properly."

A smirk played on her lips, but she followed my lead and nodded her head.

"I mean, to face up to those hoodlums like you did was absolutely incredible," he declared loud enough to illicit applause and cheers from the crowd, as he split time between eyeing Olisa, eyeing friendly faces in the crowd, and eyeing the camera. "The only reason I would have stood up to those criminals is because I'm too *big* to run and hide!" This loosed a loud bellicose guffaw that made his stomach roll like an avalanche.

"What in the world inspired you to do that?" asked the mayor.

It seemed like an eternity before she responded, but when she spoke, the crowd was completely silent, except for the mayor's labored breath.

"Love…"

Ol' Hap got sideswiped by a blow he wasn't expecting. His eyes darted around but his head moved up and down like an automaton.

"A love for humanity. I love those people you refer to as criminals. I want to see them hugging instead of harming each other. I want to see them show an appreciation for life… to go hug a child, an elderly person, a tree. I want them to take that pain rotting their hearts and dump it elsewhere. But they can't do it alone. Maybe if we practiced loving them more than fearing them, we could help put an end to the invisible war that rumbles inside of them and then spills into the streets. Now I'm not totally naive, I realize some are lost to the ills of our society, but all of them don't have to be. Isn't that a great agenda for a party platform, Mayor… To love them, not just leave them?"

Two of the so-called criminals in the gathering mass loudly slapped hands as all eyes froze on Mayor Halpern.

"Oh yes, yes, absolutely. We're working on some programs right now," he replied, head still nodding mechanically and eyes glued on her. It amazed me how he still continued to smile despite the scattered boos.

"Wonderful, wonderful," Olisa chimed, clapping her hands and smiling broadly. She then generously hugged him, which started the cameras rolling again and brought on cheers.

"Now you be sure to give your number to my assistant, Maude, over there so she can get in touch with you about the upcoming cere-mony." A prim, but very attractive, strawberry blonde-haired woman who looked to be somewhere in her mid-thirties briefly smiled and half raised her hand at the mention of her name.

"So what exactly is going on here?" he asked good-naturedly.

Before she could answer, someone from the crowd shouted, "She's doing readings for everyone, Mayor! Why don't you get one?"

"Watch out now, Mr. Mayor," said the jewelry lady, lips bunched up with attitude and her orange wigged head bopping from side to side. She touched the mayor's arm with a little too much familiarity and a couple of bodyguards edged in a little closer.

"Mr. Mayor, my name is Cleopatra Pickins, not to be confused with Cleopatra Jones, although people think I'm a dead ringer for her. Been calling myself Cleopatra for twenty years; ever since Wanda Ellis did me a reading and said that I was Cleopatra reincarnated. Been lookin' for my Marc Anthony, too, baby, but I guess he ain't found the right body yet!" She snapped her fingers and sashayed around the amused mayor, while people hooted and hollered.

"But, honey, let's not get into that cause I could go on and on. What I'm saying is; I didn't think anyone could rock ol' Cleo's world until my home girl came along. Child, this is Excedrin headache num-ber twenty-five. You know what I'm saying? Girlfriend told me so many things about myself, I swear! You listening? People better recognize, honey. Shoot, I love sister girl here cause she's keeping it real."

She hugged Olisa and then did a little belly dance swirl and bowed. The crowd roared.

"Well, is that so? Sounds like a load of fun to me. Are you an astrologer, Olisa?" the mayor inquired, not waiting for a response. "I always have fun reading my horoscope, even though I'm not one to go for that day to day malarkey. My wife tells me I'm a Taurus through and through: obstinate, stubborn, doing whatever I want to. Is that true, Maude?"

"Not at all, Mr. Mayor." She flipped her strawberry blonde hair back.

"Let's hear what Olisa has to say about you, Mayor!" Another voice cajoled.

The frown on Maude's face was barely perceptible, as well as the subtle head shake when they exchanged eye contact. Her blue eyes were mashed against the squared lens.

"Mayor Halpern, don't forget your schedule, you've got an appointment across town and then we head to a luncheon with some of your constituents. We're already late."

"Aw, come on Mayor, do a quick reading! It won't hurt!" a voice from the crowd begged.

Maude once again shook her head and vigorously pointed to her appointment book.

Meanwhile the crowd chanted, "Do it, do it, do it, do it…"

The mayor's eyes danced as he surveyed the crowd, waiting for the chanting to crescendo as if he were waiting backstage for an encore.

"Aw, what the heck, let's go for it, it can't hurt. This is all in fun."

A roar of approval emerged from the onlookers.

Buoyed by the support, or baiting, Mayor Halpern carefully sat down in one of the chairs placed before him in the sand.

"Now you tell me what to do, as long as it doesn't involve telling me how to run the city," he chuckled, glancing reassuringly at Maude whose lips were pursed. She dropped her head and angrily shuffled through the appointment book.

"Go ahead, the library is now open for hours, read me like a book," he joked as his crew yucked it up. "What's in my future? Am I going to be elected for another term?"

"Sir, I am not an astrologer. I don't do horoscopes."

"Okay, okay, that's fine with me," he said hurriedly. "Then just do what you do. Should I hold your hand or something? You need to read my palms?"

The insides of my stomach burned as he held out his hand facetiously, hamming it up in front of the cameras like he was participating in a card trick at the Magic Castle.

Olisa was not smiling. "Mayor, perhaps it'd be better if we did this another day in a private session. Readings are very personal."

He pompously spread his arms out. "How personal could it be? Don't worry; I have nothing to hide among my friends here on this beautiful beach."

He clapped his hands. "Now please, go ahead, I'm running out of time, and Maude is about to skin me alive. Don't hold back. I want the truth and nothing but the truth."

Olisa hesitated and then reluctantly sat down, folding her hands around his. A sneer lurked on the tattooed surfer's face as he edged in closer, trying to hear. It wasn't difficult, because it became unbelievably quiet. All you could hear were the waves breaking along the shore

Olisa's dark eyes gazed beseechingly into Mayor Halpern's. "Sir, I'm really uncomfortable about this…"

"Why? Oh, I see, is there a fee or donation or something? Is that it?" He quickly waved at Maude as she rolled her eyes and lethargically stepped forward.

"No, sir, money is not the issue."

He patted her hands encouragingly, and whispered, "I may be mayor, but you can talk to Happy Halpern like you'd do anyone else. Let me tell you, it's never held the press back!"

He winked at Eva Sanchez who politely smiled back. Her eyes, filled with anticipation, were twice their normal size.

"Come on, now, time is wasting, let's hear it."

She sighed resolutely. "Fine, but no cameras."

He shrugged his shoulders and then swept his hand across his neck. Olisa waited patiently while all the cameras clicked off. The mayor continued to play to the crowd, grinning and joking while she clasped his hand again.

"Before I begin, I want you to understand something, sir. This is not a game to me. When I talk to you about your life and who you are, I become a messenger relaying only what I see. Do you understand?"

He nodded his head, and when his eyes connected with hers, I think it finally hit him that he had just stumbled into some quicksand. Now, it was too late. The cloud fell over her eyes. She was there.

"Mr. Mayor, you asked me earlier if you were going to be elected for another term…" Her voice, now a monotone had exiled the warmth from her throat. "Yes, it's a possibility, but only if you get your life in order."

A bemused grin spread across his mouth as he tried to play to a stone-faced audience. "What's ol' Hap got to do?" he asked, eyebrows tilted upwards.

"End the affair you are having with that woman on your staff the minute you leave here."

I thought rigor mortis set in after death. Mayor Halpern went so stiff he resembled an open-eyed corpse. All the color abandoned his face, and the patronizing little glint in his eyes flickered out. Maude pressed the appointment book protectively against her bosom, like her blouse had been stripped away.

"You wonder if your wife knows about it. She does. She's known for a long time. She's a smart woman, but old fashioned in many ways. As long as it's not flagrant and a public embarrassment, she tolerates it. It's because she enjoys the lifestyle too much and isn't emotionally ready to rock the boat. But, that will change soon. Let me see, you have three children, one a teenage boy, about ready to graduate high school…"

"Well anyone who reads the paper knows that," he snorted flippantly.

Olisa ignored the comment. She was into a groove.

"I sense your son is having a very difficult journey through school, experiencing some behavioral problems, acting out, talking abusively to his instructors and skipping classes. Right?"

Redness seeped into the mayor's face as the corners of his mouth twitched.

"You're aware of the problems, but you chalk it up to him being a rebellious teenager; except it's much deeper than that. Your son is experimenting with drugs, and it's worsening. It's okay to shake your head in disbelief, I understand. So go see for yourself. Examine his face; be aware of his mood swings. Does he go way down and then way up? Are his pupils dilated when he comes home late? Check out his room. In fact, ransack his room, Mayor. It's that important if you care about saving him. He's unabashedly left all types of paraphernalia in front of your face, figuring you're too wrapped up in your own career to worry about him.

"He never gets to see you unless you're surrounded by dozens of political constituents. He loathes what you do. He smiles to please you, but his face darkens. He craves your attention, but not through media shoots. You need to get in touch with your son, Mayor. He's confused and doesn't know what he's doing. He desperately needs help; he needs you. If someone doesn't get to him soon he could overdose or maybe even commit suicide."

"Hey, man, I've been there. I could talk to him, man. I know how this stuff can work on you, man," blurted the surfer whose emotions metamorphosed from glee to sympathy.

"Oh come now, this is getting a little ridiculous. I don't have to sit here and listen to this crap! I can go home and watch a soap opera!" The mayor shifted in his seat, but never got up.

"As long as these distractions exist in your life, you'll never make it to a second term because they'll hit so fast you won't have time to recover. Your wife is in complete denial about the drugs, but should something go wrong, and it will, she will resent you. She's just not going to stand for it, nor the unbearable agony she's suffering to make your dreams come true, particularly if the children become sacrificial lambs to your indulgences. It's vital you reconcile with her and close the increasing gap between yourself and your child. If you continue this affair, your candidacy will die a slow death. Maybe this woman means that much to you and it's not important. But when this rises to a head, your wife will file for divorce from you and viciously expose the scandal. Materially, you are a wealthy man, Mayor, and your wife knows your worth better than anyone. She will do everything within her power to drag you through the mud, knowing at least she will be financially compensated."

The mayor's foot tapped nervously in the sand. Olisa paused, tightening her grip around his trembling hands.

"Mayor, you love your wife, you love your family, and you love your reputation, so my guess is you will ultimately end this affair. The question is—will you end it in time? And when it ends, your next issue will be to find a way to establish a comfortable working relationship with your assistant or find her another job or form of compensation. She's ambitious, too, and sometimes we all serve a purpose for each other. If you fire her, she'll sue you for sexual harassment and/or race to the tabloids intent on destroying your future in politics."

Maude's glasses were replaced by shades as one finger dabbed at the corners of each eye.

"One last thing, Mayor… Stop drinking, and now. Do you honestly believe that your son only learned the habit from school? There are people on your staff who know you're a drinker. They are considered your intimates, but how long do you think that will last? If a scandal begins and they realize you have no hope of being elected, the only thing they will think about is ensuring their survival. If that means throwing you to the vultures, then so be it. That's politics, that's life. Like a flea, they'll find another dog to hop onto."

The mayor stared at the ground, shaking his head. She stroked his hand tenderly.

"Mayor, right now you think I'm trying to hurt you and embarrass you in front of these people, but it's not true. I'm only telling you the truth as the images appear to me in my mind's eye. View what I'm saying as an assist. You are a spiritual being like all of us with problems that we can all relate to…"

"Amen. That's right. That's right… Work it, girl!" screamed Cleopatra, jingling like a piggy bank as she clapped her hands.

"Forgo your ego, see the truth, accept what I am saying and seek to change your life before it's too late. I promise you it will save more than your career. Trust me. Any other questions, Mayor? Mayor?"

An image that will forever haunt me was in a documentary I watched long ago. In it, Bushmen of the Kalahari Desert felled a giraffe. Although I understood its role as a part of the ecosystem, it was still painful to observe such a magnificent beast being leveled so humiliatingly from the skies and brought to its knees. Mayor Halpern was this beast. You could see by his expression that he was disoriented. His head whipped from side to side, anxiousness rising as he looked fearfully at the gaping audience.

Maude had already begun the trek back to the limo, leaving the mayor on his own. Olisa released the mayor's hand, and it fell limply in her lap. Finally, it withdrew like a snake sliding back into its hole as he self-consciously rubbed his wrist. The glassy-eyed look on his face only hinted at the wrestling match going on inside him. He had the pallor of a man who had been sentenced to life in prison. Then, the murky film cleared from his zigzagging eyes, and a face full of pathos was beset by righteous indignation.

"H-H-How did you… That was cruel… Did you people enjoy that? What kind of reading… the cameras are off, right!" he snapped, glaring angrily at the camera operators who were already packed and ready to go.

"Been off, sir."

"Oh yeah, yeah, that's right…" He smiled crookedly. "So that's my reading, huh? You might want to try to make it a little more positive in the future. You know a few jokes help."

Olisa reached to embrace him. "I'm truly sorry, Mr. Mayor. I don't know what else to say to you. I…"

He coldly waved her off. "Oh, you've said more than enough, believe me. Okay, so now, how about the real one?" He clasped his hands together in a half-hearted attempt at joviality, but it fluttered with a thud to a silent audience. Even his cronies forgot to laugh.

He had aged twenty years in five minutes, the skin on his face sagging like the folds on a bulldog. He scrambled to his feet.

"All right everybody, let's go." He awkwardly shook Olisa's hand, touching it as if it were a claw. Weakly, he raised his hand into the air, waving goodbye to the murmuring crowd.

Walking unsteadily toward the car he abruptly stopped, alarmed to find Eva Sanchez blocking his path. He trudged toward her as if he were being forced to face a firing squad; eyes hollow, pleading.

"So what did you think of that reading?" he asked casually.

"Interesting... but meaningless unless it can be substantiated, Mr. Mayor. Is what she said true?"

"No. Oh no, of course not!" I'm sure he didn't realize he was yelling.

"I see... Oh well. It would have made for great copy, but since there's no truth in it, there's nothing for me to say," Eva remarked calmly.

"Thank you, Eleanor, for not turning this malarkey into some sort of tabloid sensationalism," he said, patting her on the shoulder. "You know how people want to believe anything these days."

Eva smiled, not bothering to correct him on her name.

"Yeah, but the only thing that matters is what you believe, Mr. Mayor. Isn't that right?" I interjected smugly, arms crossed.

I knew he heard me, his quivering lips gave him away, but he pretended to ignore it. One of the camera operators tapped him on the shoulder. "Mr. Mayor, we really need to be on our way."

"Sure, sure... Nice meeting all of you." He nodded and spun around as the crew blanketed him and herded him toward the limousine. Before stepping inside, he glanced one final time at Olisa, who was being mobbed by people begging for readings. After an interminable amount of time, he ducked his head down, and the chauffeur-driven sedan sped off.

"That was pretty nice of you," I said to Eva.

"What, not kicking the man while he was down? I didn't lie. I really don't have any facts to go on. That's an area for the gossip columnist to explore, not me."

"So you believe my daughter told the truth?"

"Mr. Carpenter, the one thing I know about politicians is that none of them would have sat through a pack of lies as long as he did without a challenge. You could read his face and tell it was the truth. But hearing a perfect stranger accurately detail why you're an adulterer, alcoholic, and a neglectful father to your voting audience is a little much to handle."

"Think he's going to follow her advice?"

"We'll know if he's reelected."

"Hmmm."

"By the way, no one mentioned that Olisa was also psychic."

"You never asked."

"If I had, would you have admitted it?"

"No."

"Oh, Mr. Carpenter?"

"Yes?"

"I hope Olisa doesn't have her heart set on receiving that plaque from the city."

It was the best laugh I'd had all week.

An African gentleman from Cameroon who was also a visiting professor teaching African studies at UCLA used to periodically visit the restaurant Wilma and I opened in Venice. He always asked to be called Chris, which was short for Christofere. Anyway, Olisa occasionally helped out at the restaurant, and I'll always remember Dr. Christofere wiping his glasses and looking at me with a stunned expression on his angular dark chocolate face, his cupped chin shadowed by a pencil line goatee.

"Joseph, is that lovely girl your daughter?"

"Yes," I answered apprehensively. "Why? What did she do? Drop food on you, spill water? Insult you?"

"No, no, Joseph, nothing like that," he responded with the accent of a man who spent the majority of his life educated in the British school systems. He watched Olisa serving the other patrons. "How old is she?

"She just turned thirteen this past month."

"What? Thirteen? Unbelievable!" he stated, sliding his tinted glasses back on his face.

"Why do you say that?"

"She asked me what I did, and I mentioned I was a professor of literature and teaching African Studies at UCLA. Before I knew it, we were engrossed in conversation about ancient African civilizations. Her knowledge of various cultures is amazing for a child her age. Has she been to Africa?"

"No, she's been no further east than Texas."

"Well I am indeed impressed. You have to understand, I don't always have long discourses with thirteen-year-old kids. I would have sworn this young lady had been all over the world. Her questions were more advanced than some of my graduate students."

"She devours books, Chris. She's at the library so much I think they've reserved a spot with a nameplate for her bicycle."

"Incredible. You've got a winner there, Mr. Carpenter. That child is going to go very far. You should be very proud of that remarkable girl."

"I am. Thank you."

"And what is her name?"

"Olisa."

"Olisa? Pardon, did you say Olisa?"

"Yes, sir. Why?"

He pushed his glasses down to the end of his greyhound nose peering over them and suddenly threw his head back laughing loudly. "No wonder she has to know so many things. With a name like that, she can't help herself."

I didn't know if I should laugh with him or throw him out of the restaurant.

"Oh Joseph, please forgive me, I hope I haven't insulted you, because I'm not laughing at her name. The humor comes from the irony of it all. Do you have any idea what the name Olisa means in parts of Africa?"

"No."

"Oh you Americans, I swear, you name your kids whatever sounds good to you as opposed to what it might mean."

I pulled up a chair beside him, curious as to what he was talking about. "All right, doc, so what are you telling me? That we named our kid after an African cockroach or something? My wife created her name from a combination of her grandparent's middle names. She said it came to her in a dream."

He chuckled again. "Well, my friend, your wife is a powerful dreamer, because among the Ibo tribes in Nigeria, Olisa is a most esteemed name. It means God."

"God? You're kidding, professor."

"No, sir, I would never do so in a place that cooks such fine food. What's her middle name?"

"Nothing complicated there. She's named after my great aunt Belle. Olisa Belle Carpenter."

He rubbed his shaven head with a bemused expression. "Either you are incredibly lucky or the gods are having fun with you. Let's play a little."

"Hit me."

"By reversing the name and changing a letter, in the Ibo language it is not uncommon to see Belu Olisa."

"And what does that mean?"

"In English it is roughly translated as, nothing is impossible with God's help…"

This time I rubbed my head. "Okay…"

"So with a name like your daughter's, she can't help but find success in this world. I'm no shaman, but I'd predict it's her destiny to do great things. The best part is, God can't help but be on her side. Isn't that funny?"

"Very," I said, knowing the professor would miss the trace of sarcasm in my voice.

CHAPTER 4

The next time I saw Eva Sanchez was on the television screen.

"Hi. I'm Eva Sanchez, and for a third straight day, sweltering temperatures in the 90's sent a record-breaking number of Angelenos fleeing to the Southland beaches to seek relief from the oppressive heat. As you can see, this reporter has spent her day and afternoon at Venice Beach, enjoying the cool and refreshing ocean breeze and the carnival like atmosphere that makes Venice one of the hippest and most popular beaches in the world. As usual, there are hundreds of people milling about on the boardwalk watching the skate dancers, street performers, and musicians.

"Many of us have hung out on this particular beach today for another reason besides the heat, and that is to possibly catch a glimpse of the heroic woman who captured our hearts in last week's story. Everyone here is eager for the opportunity to meet this person who intervened in a gang war that in all probability would have escalated and potentially harmed innocent bystanders (Brief footage of the fighting was shown again.)

"The dust seems to have settled, but no one has been able to stop talking about this woman who healed Ernesto 'Chato' Padilla with her own hands. A young man that our sources claim was reputedly the leader of one of the most notorious gangs on the Westside." (More footage was shown as we once again saw Chato lying supine in Olisa's arms).

The camera zoomed in tightly on Eva's face.

"I became obsessed with finding a way to meet this incredible superwoman who disappeared after the incident. Was it my imagination, or was it just wishful thinking?

"Like many of the witnesses out there, I began to doubt what I had seen until I reviewed the video over and over. Unblinkingly, the truth kept staring at me. I had to seek her out, find out who she is, and what would possess her to place her life on the line for a gang banger.

"I got lucky. She's here today. The woman the locals have admiringly dubbed 'The Good Witch of Venice.' However, her real name is Olisa Carpenter, and this humble, yet gregarious woman with her amazing gifts is probably about as far removed from being a witch as Hugh Hefner from celibacy. And I'm not the only one fascinated by her…"

Eva plowed through the beach crowd, holding the microphone slightly aloft.

"… As you can see, there are all types of people here, offering their thanks and showing their appreciation to Olisa. There have been Hollywood celebrities, and even the Mayor of L.A. stopped by last week for a brief chat."

Eva positioned herself next to Olisa as we saw a sycophantic circle of beachgoers standing and sitting around her. Her intricately braided hair was pulled back loosely into a ponytail. Her white flowing dress fluttered in the breeze, fanning across her bare feet as she warmly accepted hugs from several people who reverentially approached her on a one-by-one basis.

Her head involuntarily jerked back as Eva thrust the microphone into her face.

"Hi, Ms. Carpenter, my name is Eva Sanchez of *KLSC Evening News: The Special Edition*. Please forgive the interruption, but would you mind speaking with us for a few minutes?"

Olisa paused, eyeing them warily, "No, uh… no, I don't mind."

"Oh thank you so much. Well I must say it is a pleasure meeting you," she gushed, holding the mike pointed at Olisa's face as if she were a prisoner of war.

"It's a pleasure meeting you, too, Eva," Olisa answered reticently, an ill at ease smile on her face.

"First of all, I want to say, thank you, on behalf of all our viewers for averting a possible disaster last weekend. Your courageousness was exceptional, and showed that it is possible for an individual to make a difference."

"You're very kind, thank you." Olisa appeared relieved to hug a small mulatto boy who was suddenly clinging to her legs.

"I think that little boy is symbolic of how this city feels about you. You're an overnight sensation!"

"Not really."

"Not really? Pardon me, but I beg to differ. I think everyone here would disagree. They love you!"

There was a burst of applause from the onlookers as Olisa's face reddened along with the Venice sunset.

"They call you 'The Good Witch,' but I think that's a misnomer; you hardly look like any old hag I've ever seen. You're beautiful."

Self-consciously lowering her eyes she whispered, "Thank you."

"But that's what makes what you did a week ago even more amazing! Why get involved? Why not be like the rest of us and ignore it? Let the police handle it. That's what they're paid for."

Olisa patted the little boy's head as he scooted into the crowd.

"All I saw were members of my family at war; my brothers. I know them and I love them too much to see them hurt themselves or anyone else. This city has been bathed in too much unnecessary bloodshed. But, please don't credit me. It was purely an emotional reaction. Something snapped inside of me, and I suddenly jumped from the backseat to the front. I just wanted them to stop fighting."

Of course, Olisa glossed the surface, not mentioning what she confided to me afterwards. All day long prior to the outbreak of violence she had been troubled by flashing preternatural images. She didn't speak about the salvo of gunshots painfully ringing in her ears when none existed, or the bloodied people crying over unmoving bodies that were strewn around like a Vietnam war zone, or the paramedics carrying away two small children with sheets over their faces who had accidentally been hit by all the gun fire in retaliation to the stabbing.

No, this was never discussed.

"Well, I'd say you achieved that goal and more. Your bravery has captured the hearts of all who witnessed your heroics. I even understand the mayor and city council plan on issuing you a special citation for your valor under fire."

After the bulls-eye that Eva just shot, the mayor had no choice but to follow through on his promise, I laughed to myself.

Olisa rocked back and forth on her heels, arms folded, contemplating what had just been said. When she replied her voice was soft, yet resolute. "Eva… I truly appreciate what you're saying, and I certainly don't want to sound like some type of ingrate. It's wonderful to be appreciated, but I don't want an award or a pat on the back for doing something that we should all be willing to do out of love and concern for our fellow human beings. My reward is knowing that I saved someone's life. That's all that really matters."

Those around her applauded wildly as if it were a political rally. Eva, normally pretty controlled, appeared startled by the intensity of the cheers. The camera briefly panned the faces of the people in the crowd who mugged and waved wildly.

"But Olisa, people want to reward you because this is something you don't see every day."

"Eva, there are far more deserving people out there. People who work in the trenches everyday to prevent the explosions you saw. Give an award to Jorge Valdez and Silas Jenkins who are long time gang prevention specialists. Award Minister Abe Callender who fights the good fight every single minute and hour in these streets from Culver City, Santa Monica to Venice trying to keep our youth involved in positive activities and away from the seductive allure of the streets. Reward Warner Hass over there…"

She pointed to a grizzled man whose gray white hair was super thin on top and pulled back in a shoulder length ponytail. At the mention of his name, his face flushed as he smiled self-consciously at the camera.

"Warner is a homeless artist, with the thickest green thumb you've ever seen. He tries to beautify everything he touches in Venice by planting flowers and trees in vacant, weed infested lots. I know he's mad at me for even mentioning it. That's because he doesn't do it for the publicity, he does it because he loves Venice. And for a man without a house—this is his home."

You would have thought this was an awards show, the way the crowd applauded Warner. He modestly bowed, politely acknowledging the accolades.

"Award a citation to every mother and father who serves as a positive role model to their children and are strong enough to supplant the constant bombardment of negativity from the media."

Eva concurred, "All those people you mentioned certainly deserve to be commended, but how many could have done what you did—heal a young man with only your hands?"

The silence was unnerving.

"There are many eyewitnesses that swear on their bibles that they saw you heal Ernesto, and I'm one of them. This is known in my community as a *milagro,* or miracle. I say this with the knowledge that this telecast may end up being my farewell interview, but you taught me a lot about courage and standing up for what is right. I feel whatever the consequences, I need to share this with our audience."

Eva paused like a person standing on the gallows who's been asked to say her last few words. Her face worked overtime to suppress all emotions. Finally, in an even voice, she said, "I, too, saw Ernesto being stabbed. I was close enough to see the flesh ripped from his body with each downward plunge of the knife. I was sickened by it, but feeling helpless to do anything but my job, I kept shooting and covering the story. I watched you kneel down and hold him, and then he was all right."

She waited for Olisa to respond, but Olisa was distracted by a friend who'd ducked upon seeing the camera. Olisa gestured with her forefinger to the friend to wait one more minute. She reacted apologetically to Eva's suddenly raised voice.

"… But I know what I saw. Maybe we'll get cut off before I finish what I'm going to say, but, those wounds should have been fatal. My eyes didn't betray me. I saw you stop the bleeding with your own hands. You healed him."

"No, I didn't."

"You didn't?" Eva asked, trying to appear detached, but you could see in her eyes that she realized she may have just committed career suicide.

"No. God did. I was simply the instrument through which God chose to act."

Eva's shoulders heaved and sagged in relief. "So you're saying God gave you to power to heal people?"

"No, I'm saying God is the power. I can actually feel the flow of energy coursing through my body."

"Really. How does it feel?"

"I don't know… It's hard to explain… It's almost like a tidal wave of hot, prickly, tiny, little needles and pins rushing through your body. The tingling sensation doesn't stop until the healing ends, but by that point I'm usually so drained I have to have someone explain to me what happened."

"I see… And are you also psychic? Some of the people I spoke with earlier said you have an incredible gift for seeing into someone's future? Is that true?"

"I guess… But it's not me. God pulls the curtain back on the window, and I just describe what I see." Olisa looked as if she regretted saying anything.

An arm scooped around Olisa's shoulders and suddenly Jonathan's face appeared on the screen.

"Sorry, Eva, no more questions. My sister's tired and we've got to go."

"Wait, can she answer a couple of more questions? Olisa?"

But the twosome had already merged into a sea of people.

Even with her body being jostled by overly enthusiastic onlookers, Eva's smile remained triumphantly planted on her face as she proceeded to offer her closing statements.

Blip.

My only sense of power lately was derived from pushing the "off" button on the remote control. Except the effects of the news report lingered like a sinus headache.

The phone rang. I heard Grace's voice in the kitchen.

"Hello? Yes it is. No, this is her mother. She's not available right now. I'm sorry, please hold, I've got another call on the line. Hello? No, I'm afraid she's not available, may I leave a message? That's okay, you'll call back, fine. I'm sorry, you were saying? Yes, she's the one on television… I don't know if she'll do a private reading… You can afford it? I'm sure you can, but, yes, I can take a message…"

And it rang again.

And again.

And again.

Soon it found camaraderie with the faint ring of Olisa's phone in the studio. Eventually we got smart and delegated the responsibility to voice mail.

And now, hopefully, I attempted to make another smart move. Something I *should* have done immediately after the beach incident— call a family "emergency" meeting.

All of the immediate family was present that evening, with the exception of my parents who retired to Las Vegas several years ago: Grace, Jonathan, James and Katherine Willis, Junior, and of course, Olisa.

"Turn her into a star? Tell me you're kidding, Jonathan. I thought the purpose of this meeting was to defuse the whole thing."

"Agreed. But, Dad, I also think we should take a look at this from all angles," answered Jonathan, leaning against the wall with his arms crossed.

"Jon, there are no other angles, except to protect your sister. Olisa's not one of your damn hip-hop artists."

"Maybe not, but she could be one of our motivational artists. I got a stable of rappers who can't sing a lick, but they sure can write their butts off. Lyrics that the kids identify with, that tells their stories."

"Oh, I see, you mean such profound Shakespearean-like prose such as, 'We be all bitches and whores, trying to make a score?'"

"All rap isn't that way, Dad. Yes, the music is raw, and often reflects the reality of the streets: drugs, gratuitous violence, abuse, and sexual braggadocio… But, there are a lot of folks out there trying to do some positive things that aren't getting any headlines. They're not all cop killers and booty mongers."

"Oh, I'm sorry, my bad, so school me on the true integrity of this noble art."

"Okay, besides being a cultural phenomenon, it has bridged the racial divide. According to the Recording industry, 75% of hip-hop consumers are white. The music is such a dominant force in pop culture that it has become a two billion dollar business."

"Bravo! Your point?"

"Dad, come on, right now I'm just trying to get you to understand that the world is offering Olisa a forum which the world could benefit from. I could pair her with some of our top gospel, hip-hop, and R & B acts and it's on!"

"Well, work's drying up on me right now, so if you're lookin' for some slammin' bass lines, who ya gonna call?"

"Uncle Junior!" he laughed, slapping high fives. Junior wore his hair in tiny little dreads. He had a Fu Manchu beard and sported a sleeveless camouflage shirt along with shorts and military boots.

"Hold it! What the hell is wrong with y'all? We're not looking for more publicity, we're looking for less. What I'm hearing now is a bunch of bullshit!"

"Joseph, please… We want this meeting to be constructive," Grace admonished. She sat on our long white couch with her parents then grabbed my wrist to stop me from pacing back and forth.

"Fine, fine, but you know what? We all swore to protect Olisa from this type of stuff, and now we're discussing the feasibility of entering her into *Showtime at the Apollo*. Have we constructed a website yet?"

"Working on it," Jonathan answered, half-serious.

"Olisa, honey, you're the only one who can put a lid on all this crap! They don't seem to realize your services aren't for sale."

Olisa sat in a Preying Mantis position in the corner of the living room quietly absorbing it all. The look on her face was not what I anticipated.

"Dad, the way Jon presented it to me earlier was not quite as superficial as it sounds. Let's at least hear him out."

"Oh, I see, Jonathan, so you already started your campaign dribble to Olisa."

"See what I mean, Oli? He has never listened to me before, so why should he start now?"

"Jon, that's uncalled for," Grace interjected.

"Mom, I'm sorry, but Dad doesn't care about my views. Nothing I say is relevant to him. I've had to deal with that my whole life."

"That's not true, Jon, I think what you're saying has a lot of relevance. I just don't believe in exploiting family for profits."

"See, that's what I'm saying. I've been convicted and sentenced without even a trial." With an air of defeat, Jonathan plopped down on the easy chair, his mouth set in a tight smirk.

"Jon, I think having you as a son for thirty-two years entitles me to know a little bit about you. You're a businessman, and you see a way of making money in this! All I'm trying to do is get my child out of this predicament."

"What you see as a predicament I view as an opportunity to do good things. Yes, I'm an entrepreneur, but not at the costs of screwing my own sister. I love Olisa," he emphasized, clenching his fist and pounding it over his heart. "I'm proud of her, I believe in her, and I would never do *anything* to harm her. But, this thing is bigger than us. And that's what you fail to see!"

"Oh? Well break it down for me."

Jon shook his head and huffed, raking the floor with his eyes. "You know what? Let's agree on one thing—Olisa is an extraordinary human being."

Everyone in the room nodded their heads supportively as Jonathan let this thought sink in while his fingers intersected slowly together and he sat on the edge of the chair.

"This story will make money for everyone in the media before it ends."

"And we're doing our darndest to curtail that, aren't we?" I snapped.

"Joseph, come on now, let the boy speak his piece!" James Willis said loudly, tapping his hearing aid as he sat on the edge of the sofa. "You may not want to hear it, but I do."

"Thanks, gramps. All I'm trying to say is, once the national networks pick this little story up, and they will, it's going to hit us like an AK-47. We won't have a choice. The media is going to make a profit out of this until the well runs dry, so why should Olisa run and hide? She hasn't done anything wrong. We may not be able to control this phenomenon, but we can certainly go with the flow."

"You can't control an ocean, Jonathan."

"No, I can't, but that doesn't mean we can't sail across it."

My laugh sounded like a snort. He had all the answers.

"There are people who look at my sister with the same type of adulation normally reserved for rock stars and celebrities. Some would walk into hell with a full tank of gasoline strapped to their backs if Olisa asked."

"Uh, uh, not Mayor Halpern," Papa Willis chuckled.

Jon laughed. "Probably not, Grandpa… But in this new millennium, people want more meaning in their lives. They search for peace of mind, and science is not adequate enough. Belief over unbelief, faith rather than doubt."

Mr. Willis nodded approvingly, but I could tell he strained to hear as he closely watched Jonathan's lips.

"Currently, there is a spiritual revival and resurgence of faith that is mind boggling. Business magazines state, God has made a comeback. I attended a trade show recently with one of our gospel artists in Denver at the Colorado Convention Center. I think the Christian Booksellers Association or something sponsored it. Man, you want to talk about merchandising and licensing? This guy told me religion is now a $3 billion dollar plus industry!"

"Say what?" Papa Willis asked.

"You heard me G-man. Three billion dollars and growing!"

Mr. Willis's eyebrows rose as he slapped his knees. "Mama told me I needed to invest a little more in religion."

"She meant more time, James, not money," laughed Mrs. Willis, tapping him on the head.

"Come on now woman," James said, rubbing his head.

"If great-grandma Willis were alive today, she could have any bible she wants: rap bibles, sports bibles, singing bibles, bible cookbooks, comic book bibles, women's study bibles, African-American bibles, Asian bibles, whatever. Word is, there is at least one bible in about 90 percent of all American homes."

"Uh, uh, uh," grunted Mr. Willis.

"Ethereal sells. Nothing in American life is unaffected by the God rush: movies, music, politics, business, television, newspapers, magazines, advertising and computers. I read in some magazine that conventional church memberships have increased. For those disillusioned with traditional religion, there are alternatives. Today, just as many people seek psychics as psychiatrists. They attend yoga and meditation centers, participate in channeling institutes, and indulge in holistic medicine. They also check out crystal balls, tarot cards, hypnotists, and even dominoes."

"Dominoes?" asked James, face scrunched up.

"Dominoes. Am I right, sis?"

"He's right, Papa. Dominoes originally came from China and were used more for divination than games. For example, a domino reading involves shuffling the entire deck and picking tiles at random for your fortune."

"Ain't that a trip," chuckled Junior who dragged on a cigarette and blew smoke out an open window.

"So how does Olisa fit into this equation, Jon?" Grace asked.

"Mom, it's very simple. Olisa is one of the chosen, blessed with God-given talents. She doesn't need artificial devices like crystal balls or tarot cards."

Olisa stretched her neck from side to side, a sign that she was tensing up.

"Olisa's not one of the psychic vampires sitting down at a table in Venice Beach who offer a bunch of generalities in their readings and then wait for you to help them fill in the blanks."

"I know some sincere people out there, too, Jon."

"Oh, I'm sure you do, Olisa. But they still need clues from us. Some of them are so good at analyzing body language, they'd put a psychologist to shame. But they're not you! You're the real deal, sis, get used to it," he argued, smiling affectionately.

Olisa's blank face offered no hint to what she was thinking as she moved her head back and dropped her shoulders slowly.

"And don't even get me talking about televangelists. Go down to one of the religious network headquarters in Orange County, and you'll see what that little picture tube can do to keep the faith! I was there with one of my clients who performed on one of the shows, and I thought I had driven into Disneyland by mistake! Billions of dollars are going into that operation. I'm amazed how televangelists have convinced folks to spend their hard-earned dollars and savings for a box office ticket to heaven.

"Some of these characters belong in a Looney Tunes cartoon instead of a church. Yet everyday, people spend boo-coo money on con artists, players, former pimps, convicts, intellectuals, doctors, and new age shamans. Here we sit with a person who is the real thing. What do you think they would do for her if they knew she existed?"

"Be beatin' on her door with more funk than a James Brown drummer," rattled Junior, closing his eyes and rocking his head from side to side.

"That's right, but the beauty of it is, Olisa really does want to help people. Pop, aren't you always saying that you want Olisa to get a decent job?"

"Well, yeah…I'd like to see her get a steady paycheck. There's got to be better ways for her to earn money than doing readings on the beach and in people's homes!"

"Well, here it is, Pops—saving humanity."

I raised my hands angrily, "Jon, please don't take my words out of context to make your point."

"Fine, whatever, but the time is now. If we put Olisa at the helm as our spiritual leader we can form an organization that uses its monies and profits to help people. And with this being the computer age, Olisa could potentially benefit millions of people. Ironically, we'd use the media the same way they're using us."

Jonathan, every ounce the promoter, waved his arms expansively as he talked and walked the room. He was in his element, doing a pitch like it was a boardroom filled with top executives.

However, where Olisa stood in all this still remained a question mark. I could read her face about as well as I could do Japanese arithmetic. Even though her face was tranquil and her eyes closed, I knew every word Jonathan uttered was under grueling scrutiny.

"Nothing's more tragic than people who have spent their last dime on a guru or television preacher who lands in jail with all their money, hopes and dreams depleted. Who cares if a Jimmy Swaggart cries and apologizes for being a sinner? Sucker, you've been had; your money's gone. As Chic Hearn, the voice of the Lakers used to say, '… the butter's hard, the eggs are cooling, the jello's jiggling, and the refrigerator door is closed!'"

"Word!" Junior chuckled.

"We don't have to worry about Oli. She can deliver on her promise."

"God has the power, Jon," Olisa reprimanded. "Not me, only God."

"Absolutely."

"I still don't understand. How is my granddaughter going to manage to do all this by herself?" Katherine Willis asked.

"Olisa doesn't have to do anything, but be herself, Grandmother. I can be her manager and spokesperson. If there's any paperwork to be done, I'll do it, including setting up a partnership or corporation. Her only job is to help rescue this sorry planet from itself. I'm willing to sacrifice everything, quit my job if necessary, to begin the process of helping Olisa do God's work."

"Yes, the supreme sacrifice. To only end up richer than I've ever dreamed." I mockingly folded my hands in a prayerful pose.

"Joseph!" screamed a chorus of voices.

"That's all right… That's all right. Let him get it out of his system."

"I know you makin' a few dollars on your own, boy, judging by that fancy car and clothes, but this sounds like a pretty expensive endeavor. Where you gonna get that kind of money?" James Willis asked, squinting his eyes.

"Don't worry, G-Man. In my business, you meet a lot of people. I can get the money," he answered confidently.

"Good money or bad money?"

"Good money or bad money? Dad, why do you keep hating?"

"Son, I'm not hating! You've got some great ideas, but it's not you I have problems with, it's your carnivorous associates I don't trust."

"You don't think I'm mature enough to determine that? Or is there some other reason why you've always refused to work with me?"

"All right, boys, can I get my two cents in?" Katherine Willis rubbed her cheeks. "I see where you're going, Jon, but maybe Joseph is right. Are we just tumbling into bed with the devil? 'Leave it in the Lord's hands, ' that's what Mama Willis would have said. Whatever happens will happen."

"Donny Hathaway said, 'Everything's everything, '" piped in Junior.

Jonathan stated, "Grandmother, I hear what you're saying, but Olisa's a celebrity whether she wants to be or not. If you let the media go unchecked, she'll come out looking like the Antichrist. But if you trust me, we can both protect her while promoting a positive message and helping millions of people. This is easy. In my job, I've smoothed over some pretty hard-core images. If you knew the real story behind some of these 'musical geniuses, ' it'd give you chill bumps. They ought to be locked up in a jail cell, not a sound booth.

"All right, Jon, it's all well and good that you want to help your sister be a do-gooder. But beyond your new altruism, are you going to make any money?" I struggled to keep the cynicism out of my voice.

"Yes, and my services will be worth every penny, Dad. So what if the framework is business? We live in a capitalistic society. Deepak Chopra's making a killing, but he's also making people feel good in the process with his books, videos, and seminars. What's wrong with that?"

No one spoke while I shook my head in frustration.

He circled the dining room table and walked up to me defiantly, eye to eye. I angrily chewed on my lower lip. The unflinching glare in his eye brought back memories of the weeping sixteen-year-old boy who once threatened to run away after I had grounded him for violating curfew. At that time I told him, "Any time you think you're man enough, get your ass out of here." After awhile, he backed down. This time I knew I wasn't going to be so lucky.

"So what do *you* suggest we do, Dad? Wrap her up in a cocoon? Or, I got it, put a bag over her head like the elephant man? Better yet, let's ship her away for the rest of her life to some remote region so she can be tormented by her own innate gifts. What a great life."

"Don't you get fucking sarcastic with me, kid! I'm still your father no matter who you think you are."

It seemed like we were the only two people in the living room as we stood there, nose-to-nose, loaded with old family war wounds. I noticed a disturbing new expression surfacing upon his face.

"Let's cut all the bull, Dad. Why don't you just admit it."

"Admit what?"

"Admit to everyone here that what this is all about is you're jealous of me. It's not like its some big old secret."

"Jealous of… what in the hell are you talking about?"

Grace interrupted, "All right you two, enough! We're getting way off the subject."

"Uh, uh, Mom, it's bound to come out sooner or later. It might as well be now. Isn't that sad? My own father's jealous of me."

"Gimme a break."

"You're jealous that I was the one to finish college, go to grad school and end up with a six-figure salary. Isn't that what you wanted to do?" he asked derisively, jerking a finger at me. "Look at him, he's got too much pride to ask me for help. He'd rather toll away at his own business and struggle than ask his son for a helping hand. So now, he's making Olisa a victim of his stubbornness."

"Oh get real, that's ridiculous! Ask your mother, ask your aunt, the restaurant's doing fine. You don't know what the hell you're talking about!"

His smug silence pissed me off.

"Sure, there's been a drop-off in business this past year; all businesses go through that, but we made a few alterations and it's picking up again."

Jonathan acted as if I hadn't said a word. "You're always complaining about how you dropped out of school so you could take care of us instead of following your dream. But hey, we didn't ask you to do that. The way I see it, I lived your dream, and you can't handle it!"

"Oh, stop! How did you get this warped idea in your head?"

"Who knows, but one thing I'm sure about, you focused most of your attention on Olisa because she had the gift. But did you ever notice me?"

"Now who sounds jealous?"

"That may be, but I'm the one that earned all A's. I received all the academic awards, including being Phi Beta Kappa at Stanford. I don't remember you offering me any praise while I worked my ass off in college. Mom gave it, but all I got from you was a dissertation on how to do better."

"Oh, please... I complimented you all the time! Yeah, I stayed on your ass because I wanted you to succeed above and beyond me;something wrong with that? You worked harder didn't you? Hear that, everybody? He's a big success in the corporate world, but all the thanks I get is a spoiled, egotistical child who thinks he knows more than anyone else."

"You mean more than you, Dad, don't you? The thought that Olisa might accept my help drives you crazy, doesn't it! That's why you're blocking me. You can't handle the fact that I might be able to do more for her than you..."

How much more this argument may have escalated I'll never know, because Olisa's cry pierced the thick air. I saw Olisa hunched over on her knees, scrunching her face in her hands.

"Stop it! Both of you, please quit before you say the wrong thing and never speak to each other again!" She clamped her hands to her head, her voice settling to a whisper. "God, I wish I had never helped anyone, if all it amounts to is seeing my family fighting over something I've done."

Tears ambled down her face as Grace held her in a fierce embrace. The look my wife shot me made me feel so small. I knew better than to have gotten sucked into such an ignorant confrontation.

"I'm sorry, baby girl. I'm really sorry, we're all a little tense, and I guess we took it too far. Listen, I'm just scared... scared of the predators out there who want to rip innocent people apart. And, I'm an overprotective and sometime obnoxious father who only wants his daughter to be safe and happy."

"We all do, Dad." Jonathan echoed softly. "We're just trying to find the best solution to this whole thing, right?"

I didn't say anything as I sidestepped Jonathan and meandered over to the screen door like a dog with his tail between his legs. I stared at the neighbor's house across the way.

The house was uncomfortably quiet before Papa Willis asked, "Jonathan, what makes you think this will work out the way you envision?"

"The timing is perfect, G-man. If we're really honest with ourselves, doesn't society just want to be mothered? Our society runs contrary to our emotional makeup. We elect a male president to run the country, but even when the father runs a household, the mother rules it emotionally. As kids, no matter how much we love our Dad, when we are sick, we high jump Daddy to get to Mommy. We want Mommy to give us chicken soup, wipe our foreheads, cuddle with us and read us stories. In these troubled times, I'm not sure male energy is what we're looking for. I think we need a woman's touch. This society is begging for a goddess, and her name is Olisa."

"Jon, you can stop right there. I am hardly a goddess."

"Maybe not, Olisa, but wasn't Jesus just a man before men started embellishing his image in the Holy Book? If Jesus were here today, he'd need the same P.R. campaign."

The gasp heard around the world was Katherine Willis. She had been a devout churchgoer, organist and choir director at Faith Baptist Church for over twenty-five years." She gawked at Jonathan as if he held a red trident and grew horns and a triangle tipped tail.

"Look, all I'm trying to say is when I saw Olisa interacting in that crowd with such unshakable energy, it convinced me she has the power and charisma to take us by the hand through the 21st century. I've watched strangers open up to her like they've known her all their lives. The challenge would be finding a way to translate that gift to millions of people."

"So what you're trying to say is, we may have the next Mahatma Ghandi on our hands," James Willis commented, playfully sizing up his niece.

"Yeah, and we know what happened to him." I still had my back to them hands pressed on the screen door like a cat with its claws stuck.

"Naw, Joseph, she's going to be all right, as long as we're around," Junior said admirably. "Hey, y'all know what Olisa means to me… she's helped me through all the stuff I been through. I still regularly attend rehab meetings thanks to my niece. I would have died if Olisa hadn't been there to help me get that mess out of my system. I suppose the world should be given the same opportunity I had." He pointed at her, "Don't worry, baby, I'm still working on that song for you. Just you wait and see. It's gonna be 'fresh.'"

Olisa's eyes greeted him warmly.

"What about you, Papa Willis? What's your take on all this?" Jonathan asked confidently.

"Grandson, you know how I feel about you. I'm so proud of you sometimes, I don't know what to do. You're as smart as they come, and I love to hear you talk. And that's why it hurts to say this, but on this one you don't know your ass from a hole in the ground. You need to listen to your father, because he's right. Don't let this girl get thrown out there to those buzzards."

"But , G-Man, with her gifts she will change so many lives. People love her."

"That's where you're wrong, boy. Granted, my granddaughter has special gifts, but ultimately, they'll never truly care about her. People are only concerned about *numero uno*. They'll run over her and never look back. I don't want to see that happen to my girl. She's too precious for that."

"But, grandfather…"

"No, no… It's my turn… I just don't feel good about it. You get cynical when you get to be this old. I've seen too much bullshit in my lifetime. I've said it before and I'll say it again: Our job is to protect Olisa and keep the wolves away from her door."

Jonathan, obviously disappointed, asked his mother how she felt.

Grace's drawn and red-rimmed eyes were awaiting mine as I slowly turned to face her. "You can end the survey here because we are not entitled to be a judge or jury. It's not up to us, Jonathan. As far as I'm concerned, I'm like your father. The thought of throwing her into the jaws of this wretched society frightens me. Perhaps, I could be more objective about someone else's daughter, but this isn't the case. This is our flesh and blood. No matter who she might be to others, this is and will always be our big little girl," she said, her eyes never leaving mine.

"So you can't go by me," Grace said, resting her eyes upon Jon. "I will be the first one to admit I am being selfish and self-serving, and that's not right, either. But neither is going around the room soliciting everyone else's opinions. This decision is not ours to make. It can only be made by Olisa."

"I was just trying to let her know how her family feels about it," Jon said defensively.

"Bless your heart, Jonathan. I love you and I truly believe you think you are doing the best thing for all concerned. But the truth is, you are just rallying support for your idea. Olisa already knows how we feel about her. She is certainly capable of making her own decisions. So don't ask us—ask her. You're discussing her life. Whatever decision she reaches, we will stand behind it." Grace's voice cracked, but its resoluteness was unwavering as all eyes drifted toward Olisa.

Good, I thought. Another person in my corner. Things were looking much better, until I caught Olisa's eyes.

The second her eyes lifted and locked upon mine, my heart fell. I didn't wait to hear her response as the screen door banged behind me on my way out.

Somebody shouted my name or maybe everyone did, but I was out of there. My tennis shoes squished the pavement as I sprinted down the walk streets toward the beach. Houses on both sides seemed to cave in on me, so I ran faster.

I crossed Abbott Kinney Blvd. after coming off the walk streets and cut up to Venice Boulevard, heading west till I reached Dell Ave. I abruptly turned left and ran up the small rolling hills to the canals. I looked around me at the radically changed landscape. Instead of streets, there were waterways intentionally built by Abbott Kinney like the canals of Venice, Italy, but on a much smaller scale. Pausing to catch my breath, I opened a gate to a place next to the canals that we called "duck park." The sounds of quacking greeted me from the occupants as they paraded around. A couple evaded me and splashed into the water.

When Olisa was a little girl, I'd often take her to duck park so she could play on the swings and playground slide. Then we'd walk down the canals and feed the ducks.

Tonight the park was completely empty.

The humid air didn't help my wheezing as I sat down on one of the swings, struggling to regain my breath. My T-shirt was soaked with sticky perspiration. In the darkness, I watched the interplay of protean shapes and shadows created by the glimmering house lights bordering the park. Except, one of the shadows rose up like a great leviathan. The huge shadowy figure stood ominously in the park on a small raised bridge, looking down at the ducks that clustered around his feet. The man's face was smothered in darkness, but the top of his head glistened like a polar ice cap. A trumpet hung limply in his hand until he raised it majestically to his lips.

The most beautiful and melodic music I have ever heard flowed out of his instrument. His body rhythmically swayed as he cultivated sounds from that horn like he was drilling for oil. Man, it was sweet… So sweet. His unique style defied categorization. I had never heard anyone play like that in my life!

He bent, shaped, and transformed the notes before they even came out of the trumpet's bell, which bloomed as bright as a giant sunflower. There was a special timbre in his playing that could be described at best as almost otherworldly. Every note from his horn proceeded to take on a life of its own; a living breathing wave of intense, unwavering emotions. I was experiencing the melisma of a virtuoso who breathed a lifetime into each musical note.

He wore black shades, a black tie, and a dark single-breasted suit with a white-collar shirt like many of the hipsters when I was growing up. He was an anachronism, but his music was timeless. Mesmerized, I sat motionless in the swing, eyes closed, and ears sopping up every musical note. The soothing ballad momentarily washed away my anxiety. I felt honored to be the only audience privy to this cat. By the time he finished his song there were tears crowding my eyes.

"Hey, bro, that was just 'mad, ' whatever it is, you've got it."

"You think so?" he intoned in a profound and mellifluous basso. He tilted his head in my direction and seemed pleased with my assessment. He blew a few extra notes, and even these made my skin crawl. Every duck in the area seemed intent on cuddling around his feet. They were incredibly calm, some even asleep.

"Yeah, no question," I said dreamily.

"Thank you. It was for you."

"For me? You mean you knew I was listening?"

"Someone is always listening."

"Yeah, okay…"

"Do you mind if I join you?" he asked politely.

"Oh, no, not at all." What else was I going to say. I watched as he walked down from the small bridge. The ducks lethargically parted just enough to allow space for him to walk through. The lone streetlight in the park wrapped its light around his body, forming a dark shadow whose outline radiated energy. I didn't have to stand up to see that although I am six feet tall, he dwarfed me by about a foot. His massive shoulders stretched across his body like the topography of the Grand Canyon.

However, for a man with such an intimidating bulk, there was gentleness in his body language that took precedence over his physical demeanor. But as he approached me, I noticed how he casually sized me up and there was intensity behind those shades that made me appreciate his concealed eyes.

He sat down on a bench next to the swing I was sitting on. That's when I had a chance to truly study him. And, this might sound like a strange comment coming from a heterosexual man, but it's the truth. He was one of the most magnificent creatures I have ever seen. An artist's fantasy. His sculpted face looked like it had been constructed from the finest black marble. Sharp angular cheek bones, high forehead, and a straight nose with wide nostrils flaring out in perfect symmetry. There wasn't a line, blemish, or wrinkle marring his face. It was so smooth and shiny that I imagined to touch it would be like grabbing a wet bar of soap. His closely cropped white hair glistened.

Self-consciously I asked, "So what are you doing out here? Practicing for a gig?"

A half-smile parted his lips. "No, what I'm doing is searching… searching for the one note that will transcend all the others; a note that will be the epiphany for the greatest concert ever."

"Oh," was my intellectual response.

"Let me elaborate," he added. "I just don't do what you refer to as 'gigs' anymore, though I still enjoy listening to the musicians of your time."

I thought, my time? After awhile I said, "So what's a cat as great as you doing sitting out here at night playing a trumpet for free? You ought to be in some club or concert hall somewhere, or something…"

He fiddled around with his trumpet keys for a second, looking as if he were composing a song in his mind. "You're very kind, but I don't play for engagements. I play for God."

"Oh."

"As a humble servant of God, I play for the world with all that I have because what it gives in return is greater than what you could ever imagine. Am I making sense or are my ramblings causing your eyelids to close?"

"Oh no, I hear you…" I uttered, a little too defensively.

Brother man was different, but so were most musicians. He enunciated each word as if it had to be factory tested before departing from his lips. His deep, rumbling bass had a pure refined tone to it: slow, steady, thick, and just as powerful as molten lava. And possibly just as incinerating when angered. It was a worldly-wise voice. You believed this man could be equally comfortable sitting with a beggar or a king.

"I must tell you, my friend, tonight seemed more inspiring than others. I felt compelled to play a tune to ease the pain of a troubled soul. Would that be you?"

He waited for my answer patiently, although I had the uneasy feeling his eyes were like burning coals behind those glasses.

"Yeah, partner, that's me. I'll tell you, man, before I heard you blowing that horn, I didn't know if I was coming or going. But your music calmed me down. I don't feel so out of it now. I can think again."

"Good… good. That's what I want to hear." He seemed genuinely pleased as he cradled and stroked his trumpet.

"So why were you so distressed?"

I studied the ground. The directness of his question caught me off guard. The evening's events hurdled the levee and rushed me like a flood.

Sensing my discomfort, he leaned over and touched my shoulder with his hand, and my skin started tingling. Suddenly, a warm breeze washed over my body, and I was more relaxed than anyone ought to be at night in the park.

Someone playfully poked my shoulder, and I jumped out of the swing, shocked to find my grandfather Harry standing over me, a big glowing smile on his face. He grabbed me in a hearty bear hug, and I giggled like a little kid.

"Look out there, boy, what you doin' with that frown on your face? Tell Big Daddy what's wrong so he can fix you up."

I didn't hesitate because I trusted him more than anyone else in the world. He never laughed at me no matter how many ridiculous things I told him. No one cried harder at his funeral than I did years ago. I told him everything. Grandpa Harry gave me that knowing smile. "Boy, don't you worry about a thing. Everything's going to work out like a charm, trust me, you know I'm right."

And then, Grandpa Harry, his body still roly-poly, lumbered away until he disappeared, leaving me with an enormous grin on my face. I clung to my euphoria until the stranger dropped his hand from my shoulder.

Then I shrank back into the real world, confronted by my own confused expression reflected in the man's black sunglasses. Now I was sitting next to him on the park bench. Flabbergasted, I had just poured my heart out to a complete stranger. He held the horn to his lips, fingering the keys as if he were playing a silent tune.

"You are greatly anguished about your daughter's future, Joseph. Why? This is not a decision you have to wrestle with."

"I'm her father. Why can't I be a part of my daughter's decision making?"

"Your daughter is pursuing her life's calling; her destiny if you prefer. It is not your choice. This is something she must do. Some call it fate."

Like a pouty kid, I kicked sand with my foot. "Wait a minute. You know who I am now, who are you?

"I am a part of your past, your present, and your future. I am sometimes called the messenger… I can see by your downcast expression that this explanation is unsatisfying. Who do you think I am?"

My body involuntarily shook, because it dawned on me who he was. He was the man on the roof top over thirty years ago during the Watts riots, he was the man Gumbo and Laura spoke of, who helped Olisa escape from the beach, and he was the presence I had been feeling around me for so many years…

"I believe you're an angel."

The only response was the rustling of duck wings milling around his feet.

"Okay, so what is our fate, angel? Are Grace and I just pawns in a bigger game? We were just kids when Grace accidentally became pregnant the first time. We didn't know how to be parents, especially to such a gifted child. But we raised her in the best way we knew how. And now you're basically telling us to butt out?"

"No. I am encouraging you to be a part of her journey."

"So why were we chosen?"

"Joseph, does human vanity lead you to believe you were chosen? Did you choose the color of your skin? Did you choose to be born in this country? What is, has always been. Olisa found life through you. She could have been born in a Chinese village, but the essence of who she is would have still existed. Always remember, her birth is as much a part of your path through life as it is part of her own path."

I was having a hard time listening as stinging tears blistered my eyes. I gripped the bridge of my nose with the tips of my forefinger and thumb. "I don't know… To be honest, I've always been in awe of Olisa. I've never felt worthy to have a child like her."

"Your worth is a value only you can determine, my brother. It has been an inner struggle for you and the source of many of your conflicts."

"You mean like with Jonathan?"

"Only you can answer that. We may not always understand what is occurring at a given moment, but eventually time reveals all truths. But, I can tell you this, your son is playing his part, too. He is doing what he must do on his own personal journey. There are many directions, but only one exit, and sometimes it entails starting over again and again till we find it."

"I think I understand. So why are you here?"

"I am here, Joseph, because I have been called."

"What do you mean?" My body shivered, but I was hardly cold.

"Your world may be about to turn in on itself, quickly becoming a planet that no longer values anything. It's a world bent on self-destruction. Your daughter may be its last hope."

Not a muscle on my body moved.

"My daughter? Olisa? Olisa is a single person, how can she…"

"Shhhh…" he said, holding a finger to his lips. "I only know who she is and that she will save all of you from yourselves. Your eyes widen with fear, but fear is your worst enemy, Joseph Carpenter. Trust is your friend. Just be there. Olisa will need you."

"My wife once said the same thing."

"You are fortunate to have married such a wise woman."

The comment brought a smile to my stricken face despite the foreboding words I heard earlier. He stood up and we shook hands, his engulfing mine. And, once again, I experienced that snugly warm feeling. I watched him slowly saunter away into the night. Before he was completely out of my sight, he turned. From that distance, the voice I heard should have been a yell, but it traveled to me as a whisper, "Always remember Joseph, nothing is impossible."

He placed the trumpet to his lips and shockingly, the street lamp's glass casing imploded, shattering into millions of pieces and fluttering dreamlike to the ground. The isolated light bulb hovered unnaturally in the air like a tiny yellow moon. Then, slowly, effortlessly, I saw those same pieces ascend from the cement and reform anew enshrouding the glass bulb. It now shined with a light more brilliant than before.

The horn player disappeared so swiftly, I thought my mind was playing tricks on me.

I went back and rocked in the swing, alone, once again until my solitude was broken by the unexpected crunch of footsteps on gravel. It made me catapult from the swing. The ducks arose from their stupor, briskly flapping their wings and quaking incessantly as they scattered, hopping and waddling toward the canals. Splash after splash filled the night air as battalions of ducks skittered across the water.

"Daddy?"

"Olisa, is that you?"

"It's me. Are you all right?"

"Yeah, kid, I'm fine."

"I had a feeling you might be here."

"Then come over here and give your pitiful old man a hug!"

The reflections from the house lights made the dark, murky waters of the canal sparkle as we strolled alongside of it hand in hand, just like the old days.

"I'm sorry, Daddy."

"Sorry? Sorry about what? I'm the one who should be apologizing, not you!"

"No, Daddy, this whole thing. Every time I try to do something like this, it always falls apart. Just like with grandma…"

"No, don't ever say that, baby. Mama Willis's death wasn't your fault."

We were at the Willis' for a Sunday dinner. Four-something in the afternoon, Mama Willis complained that she needed to take a short nap. This wasn't an unusual request, she usually nodded off on the couch, bible spread out on her lap or retired to her bedroom. A little later, I noticed that Olisa wasn't outside playing with the other kids. I figured she might have been in the room with Mama Willis, probably bugging her to read a story instead of letting her go to sleep.

I poked my head inside the partially opened door and heard a tiny desperate voice pleading, "Please, Grandma, please get up. I want you to read to me, or I can read to you, Grandmama, but you have to get up first. Get up, Grandma Willis. I'm trying to help you. Why are you still sleeping?"

With the building frustration in her voice, I realized something wasn't right. I hurried in and caught her furiously massaging Mama Willis's chest, kneading it and squeezing it just as she did with Flash. Marble sized tears dropped from her eyes and hit Mama Willis's chest like a leaky faucet. Her heavy eyelids opened and closed with each effort, almost as if she were trying to come back, but the ominous dark gray hues lined in Mama Willis's stiff visage where all of life had dissipated told another story. Her right arm hung limply to her side. Her left arm held her bible fused in the crook of her elbow.

"Olisa, Mama Willis is gone." My voice was surprisingly controlled as my trembling hand touched her wrinkled brow. Seeing Olisa's anguish made me delve for psychological resources I never knew existed.

I managed to tug her away as she melted into my arms crying uncontrollably. I opened the door, my drawn face clearly indicating the great tragedy that had befallen us.

Later that evening, Olisa sat alone in the corner of her bedroom in her red wooden chair, tensely rocking back and forth. I felt guilty encroaching upon the territory of this young, but old soul, who lived deeply in the sanctuary of her thoughts like no nine year old I'd ever seen.

"You all right, honey?"

"Daddy, how come I couldn't save her?" She asked this as if it were a human failing."

"There was nothing you could do, Olisa. Your great-grandmother's heart just gave out."

"But God blessed me with the magic. That's what you told me!" Tears invaded her crinkled eyes once again as I saw the reflection of myself, the betrayer, in her pupils.

"I don't know what to tell you, sweetie... Yes, God did bless you with the magic... But you've got to try and understand. It was time for Mama Willis to go to heaven. We have no control over that."

"Why not, Daddy?"

"It was God's will."

Her lip poked out and her feet hammered the floor like car pistons.

"I don't like God anymore."

"Don't you ever say that, Olisa. I know it hurts, but it's not God's fault. You know what? I'll bet you Mama Willis is happier now than she's ever been."

I tried earnestly to sound upbeat, but I had been taking care of Grace, too, who also grieved deeply over her grandmother, and the stress had worn me down. The tears refused to fall anymore as Olisa sat like a miniature image of Rodin's "The Thinker" trying to sort it all out in that little brain of hers.

For many nights thereafter, she continued to wake up in a cold sweat, crying, and pleading in her sleep, still trying desperately to save Mama Willis. It took some time before she comfortably fell asleep in her own bed again. For a while, she had been terrified to even go to sleep, afraid that God might snatch her overnight while she slept. Weeks passed before she slept deeply like a child again, but it was even longer before she made her peace with God.

We stopped in the middle of one of the bridges crossing the canal as Olisa gazed out over the water.

"Daddy, maybe I should have been more patient. The paramedics probably would have arrived in time to save Ernesto."

"No, baby girl. Don't start second-guessing yourself on my account. Ernesto's clock was ticking. He didn't have time to wait for the paramedics."

"But, Daddy, look at the huge mess I created."

"The mess created itself. What if you hadn't done something? What if Chato had died? It would have tormented you forever."

She slowly nodded her head as her tensed body surrendered to my arms closing around her.

"Daddy, what should I do?"

"Bring Los Angeles a football team."

"Besides that."

"To be honest, I thought you had already decided."

"So did I until I saw my father and brother slugging it out over this. That's a little hard to deal with."

"Yeah, I suppose it is. But your father and brother are two ignoramuses who have their own stuff to work out. When I think about it, maybe I haven't been as good a father as I should have been to him."

She locked her arm affectionately around mine. "Now who's second guessing themselves? You've been a great father to both of us."

"Glad you think so."

"Jon does, too."

"Okay, good… Hey, kid, whatever decision you make, know that I'm behind you all the way. Even if it drives me crazy, which you've been known to do."

"Thanks, but I already made my mind up," she laughed, throwing her head back and absorbing the beauty of a night sky salted with twinkling stars.

"I told my brother I couldn't do it."

"Why? I thought… Wait. You're not saying that just because of me, are you?"

"Yes and no. Mainly because I just can't do it. You asked me recently why I returned."

"Yeah, well, mainly I asked because I couldn't understand why you'd return to a home where the water, heating, lighting, and toilets actually work. After all, the Peace Corps offered you such a luxurious existence in West Africa and then Guatemala. I thought you had gone crazy!"

"You're being sarcastic, but the real truth is, I'd have gone crazy if I hadn't come home."

"Why do you say that?"

"It's the voices again."

Ever since childhood, Olisa heard voices in her head: talking, laughing and whispering. The kids thought she was a weird little girl, especially when she'd answer them out loud. They were as much a part of her as the air she breathed. She used to explain that they were like overhearing conversations on a party line.

Olisa didn't learn to find peace of mind with them until she met with a Hopi Medicine Man who was a friend of Little Oak's. He told her she had to stop fighting to hear them. Stop trying to shut the voices out. That it was the voices of the dead spirits trying to connect with her, and that they had found a conduit to help them communicate with the material world. The advice seemed to work because I never heard her complain again. In fact, she told me that once she accepted this, the voices were no longer muddled, but clear and distinct. They became guides for her when she saw things inside of people.

"So what did they tell you, kid?"

"To go home, because you are needed. They were so intense, I thought something happened to you or Mom. But now I understand. It was to save Ernesto's life. That's it. Now I can move on," she said, flipping her braids back.

This is when I should have told her about my conversation with the angel. About how the whole world rested on her delicate little shoulders, but I couldn't.

"It's up to you. But I'd be happy either way," I lied.

"Dad, I really do love my brother. I guess I was leaning in his direction because I wanted to believe he was right. He asked me if I preferred helping one person a day or one million. I didn't honestly have a good response. He kept saying I've got to do it, and that we can always change the structure whenever we want to. For the moment, at least, I was tempted to follow his lead."

"I understand. With Jonathan it's always 'proceed with caution.'"

"Jonathan may be very driven and rambunctious, but I truly believe in his heart he feels he's trying to do a good thing."

"Well, I've never been concerned about your brother's heart. It's the spirituality of his pocketbook that worries me."

"True…"

"So what did Jonathan say when you said no to him?"

"That he understood and that I needed to go find you and let you know my decision."

"That was it?"

"That was it, except I'm not being realistic. I'm still going to have to deal with the fact that they are never going to leave me alone."

We walked the rest of the way home in silence, Olisa's arm interlocked with mine. I remembered how proud I was when we performed the father-daughter waltz during her debutante. She looked so beautiful all dressed up in an elegant white gown, hair up in a chignon. Now her hair was in thick double braids, poking out of one of those floppy "Chamber's Brother's" hats with retro 60's vest, bell-bottoms, and sandals. She was still beautiful.

Nevertheless, even though she said what I wanted to hear, I didn't feel any sense of victory. Jonathan was right. They weren't going to leave her alone.

The house was quiet as we entered the front door, except for…

"Hey, Dad."

"Hey," I said, walking apprehensively into the dining room as Jonathan pulled out a chair for me and then coolly strode to the other side of the table and sat down. I was greeted by a Scrabble board, a pile of neatly turned over letter tiles waiting to be shuffled, and two Cuban cigars. He had a sly smile on his face as he held a pen and pad, motioning for me to sit down while Grace stood behind him, arms crossed and grinning.

I pulled on my earlobe as I studied the empty game board like I was appraising a classical piece of art.

Olisa strutted briskly past Jonathan, lightly cuffing him upside the head.

"Hey, look out now!"

She slid her arm through Grace's and said, "Mom, let's leave these two peacocks alone."

"Gladly," she answered, tickled to see the men in her life preparing to smoke the peace pipe.

"You must be a masochist," I said, leaning over and lighting his stogie as it kissed his lips. I rarely smoked except on special occasions. The first cigar I ever had was when Jonathan was born.

"I guess I am. It hurts when I have to keep whooping you."

"Tell Scotty to beam you up cause you're living in a dream, boy."

"You gonna shuffle, or do I have to do that for you too!"

"Son?"

"Yeah, Pops."

I slowly shuffled the letters, carefully trying not to turn them over. "You know your mother and I love you, right? And we're very proud of you," I said.

"I know that, Dad."

"All right, that's good. I just wanted to make sure. I mean, sometimes people say things in anger, but they don't mean it."

"I don't pay it any mind, Pops. We're all guilty of that."

"Good."

"So would you stop shuffling those letters before I fall asleep!"

"Oh, that's how you gonna act? Now I'm gonna have to put some stuff in the game like Edward G. Robinson did Steve McQueen at the poker table in the movie the *Cincinnati Kid*? You goin' down, baby."

I whipped him by about a hundred points that night. But it's not much fun beating a distracted player who makes amateurish mistakes. Oh, all the bluster was there, but the mental wheels gyrated in other directions. When you got past the long curly eyelashes on that boyishly handsome face, I knew that this wasn't over yet.

CHAPTER 5

Timing is everything.

K.C. Richards, a record distributor and business associate of Jonathan's, desperately needed someone trustworthy to house-sit for two weeks while he and his family were away on vacation in Sydney, Australia. Richard's house was in the picturesque resort town of Santa Barbara, California, which is about 100 miles north of Los Angeles. He also owned a coterie of animals that had to be fed: three dogs, a cat, an iguana, two hamsters, a rabbit, an ostrich, and a scarlet macaw.

Jon asked Olisa if she'd be willing to do it, and she didn't hesitate to say yes. First of all, she loved animals. Secondly, it offered her the opportunity to temporarily escape Venice for a little while until things, hopefully, cooled out.

K.C. lived in a hilly and ritzy area known as Hope Ranch. While there, Olisa discovered a desolate and magnificent stretch of beach. She had to clamber down a cliff to get to the sandy beach, but it was worth it. The privacy gave her peace of mind as she took daily strolls with her roommate, Free.

Freeloader was Olisa's golden retriever. He was a three-month-old pup whom she found barely alive in an alley several blocks away: frail, starved, emaciated, and dehydrated. Of course, Olisa triumphantly nursed him back to life. Freeloader turned out to be a great dog, intelligent and fiercely loyal to his savior, Olisa.

The day Olisa returned home from Santa Barbara with Jon, something had changed about her. Something in the eyes.

They pulled into the garage, ignoring, as usual, the KLSC truck and other assorted vehicles camped out in the alley. Jonathan's tinted windows allowed no one to see inside the car. After so many false alarms, a blasé Eva Sanchez nonchalantly waved instead of engaging in her attention-getting semaphore routine.

Olisa and Jon quietly walked through the door. The perplexed expression on Jon's face totally contrasted Olisa's placidity. He stood at the door for a few seconds, rattling his keys. Finally, he shook his head and muttered a quick goodbye, angrily revving his car and screeching off. Unperturbed, Olisa headed into her studio after a cursory discussion about her stay in Santa Barbara.

I assumed they had a spat. Naturally, I wanted to knock on Olisa's door and press her like a hot iron, but Grace tapped my shoulder. "Leave it alone, she'll come to us when she's ready." Sure enough, just as we were settling for bed and I was about to flip off the switch on the table lamp, there was a soft tap on the door.

In a barely audible voice we heard, "Mom, Dad, are you up? Can I come in?"

"Of course , baby," Grace said.

"I'm sorry. I hope I'm not disturbing you guys."

"Don't worry about it, kid," I replied patting the bed for her to sit down.

"She lay down along the foot of the bed crisscross from us with her head on her hands.

"You can turn on the overhead light if you want to."

"No, no, Mom… I like it better this way with just the lamp on."

I was proud of myself for exercising a little patience and not saying anything while Olisa juggled her thoughts.

"Last night during my meditations on the beach, I thought about our conversation at the park, Dad, and thought, if I'm feeling this stressed out, what in the world will it feel like later. I even made plans in my head to drive down to Ensenada and hide out among some friends until this thing blows over."

"That makes sense to me. If you need some money, all you've got to do is let us know. When did you want to go?"

Olisa folded her hands and lightly pounded them against her chin. Frowning, she stared deeply into the shadows.

"Everything changed last night."

Once again, I wanted to take off running, but this time I expected Grace to match me stride for stride.

"I was on that deserted stretch of beach I told you about, last night…"

She paused as if she weren't sure whether to continue. "I am absolutely sure there were no other people in the vicinity," she blurted out defensively, but not so much to us as to herself. "… If there had been, I know Free would have at least given a warning bark. But yet, I sensed this presence. It made my skin tingle, and Free must have felt it too because his tail beat my arm mercilessly."

Olisa spoke like she was talking in her sleep, trembling and twitching slightly. She continued to gaze into a universe we were not privy to.

"Did you see the full moon last night?" she asked, not waiting for an answer. "The sky was midnight blue and the moon had a supernatural glow. It looked so close I felt like I could scoop it into my arms."

A whimsical smile spread on her lips as she abruptly set on the edge of the bed, her twinkling eyes ballooning. "The sky was so beautiful it was like seeing a living Van Gogh painting… And the sea… It literally sparkled, I mean, wow, it was magnificent. I was so taken in by it all that I failed to notice this woman standing ankle deep in the ocean waters staring at me. I don't know how she got there. She was like a mermaid emerging from the sea. However, after awhile, it occurred to me that she wasn't standing in the water. She stood inches above it.

"I started rubbing my eyes, thinking it was just an illusion from fasting the past couple of days. But I knew I was fooling myself—she was real."

I wiped my clammy hands against the covers as Grace leaned forward.

"I called out 'hello, ' but she didn't answer. Oh, I wish you guys could have seen her. She looked like a shimmering porcelain doll in the moon's light. The vision of her floating just above the water was breathtaking!"

Grace listened intently as she slowly cupped her hands tightly together.

"She wore multiple layers of clothes that twisted and flapped in the breeze. Her olive colored skin gleamed as if a fluorescent light burned beneath her skin. Her hair was loose, flowing, fanning the moon—so long that the tips danced against the edges of the water."

Grace turned toward me, her dark brown eyes misting as she grabbed for my hand.

"Sounds like your lady."

"Yes," Grace sighed nostalgically. "I told Olisa how she used to visit me every night when I was pregnant with her." Grace's eyes grew heavy as I held her face in my hands and kissed her warm, full lips. I stroked the spongy salt and peppercorn rows that crowned her head while she snuggled into my arms.

"It was her, Mom," Olisa confirmed in an ethereal voice, her glazed eyes staring past us. "Sometimes I'd wake up when I was little and there she'd be standing in my room. I always thought it was just a reoccurring dream. As she faced me, I couldn't see her eyes, which appeared to be closed. In her presence, I felt as if every part of my body and mind was exposed. When she finally spoke, I can't say whether her mouth even moved."

"What did she say?" Grace asked softly.

"She began by asking a question."

"Why are you afraid, Olisa? You have nothing to fear. Not when God is by your side."

"Listening to her soothing voice was so comforting and so warm it made me feel like I was soaking in a hot tub. I don't know if I spoke aloud or if it was in my head, but I answered,

'Because I am weak. I can't do this. For me, the blessing has been a curse. I am not the one you want. Let someone else who has more strength and more confidence be the bearer of God's great gift.'"

"Olisa, God is all the strength you will ever need. Weakness and fear are frailties of

being human. Do not lose faith in who you are, for your humanity is a vessel for the greatness that is God."

"'What,' I asked, 'does God want me to do?'"

"To be a child again and open your heart to the world."

"'And how do I do that?'"

"Be a world unto yourself."

"'I don't understand.'"

"It is important for you to be open, to love freely, compassionately, and without restraint like you did as a child. Don't give fear refuge to be your judge and jury. You are here to help people as only you can."

"'I can't.'"

"Yes, you can, baby."

"It was another woman's voice directly behind me, a voice that made my heart beat vigorously. One no longer straddled by age or pain."

Olisa's chest swelled as she paused to gather herself.

"I flinched more from surprise than fear when I unexpectedly felt arms close around me—arms that offered me so much comfort that I wanted to remain in them forever. I recognized the hands except they were smooth now, no longer callused, no longer wrinkled: thick, strong,

welcoming hands, brimming with a new life. 'Grandmama Willis?' I asked."

"Yes, child, but don't you turn around. Just feel how much I love you."

Olisa was up and crouched in the corner of the room holding herself. As much as both of us wanted to go to her, we didn't budge. She was reliving the moment, and the last time we did that she became completely disoriented and chastised us for disturbing her concentration.

"'Oh, Grandma,' I cried as she held my shivering body. 'I miss you so much. Please don't leave me again. I need you, especially now.'"

"Honey, I've never left you. Don't you know that?"

"'Yes, no. I don't know. I just want you to stay.'"

"I can't, baby. I'm only here to tell you that the Creator has special plans

for you. Don't
   be afraid to commit. When you step into the light, you will know and
understand the realities of your life."

"As her hands and arms began to fade, the chill of the night air made me shudder. I cried out, 'You can't leave me now! There is so much more I need to know, Grandmama.'"

"I'm here for you, baby... Just know you are loved more than you'll ever know in this
life..."

"Afterwards, I crumpled into the sand and then became seized by a sudden panic. I thought I was having a full-blown heart attack. My breathing was out of control as I scrambled and clawed madly at the ground like a burrowing sand crab. Grains of sand cut painfully into my eyes and the sudden savagery of salt water crashing against my body forced me to tumble over onto my backside, dragging me into its maw like a piece of flotsam.

"I almost died last night... If not for the powerful hands that wrenched me from the riptides and pulled me ashore. As I lay in the sand, gasping for air and spitting out gallons of salt water, there was a sonic boom of wind so loud that my skin must have turned as white as these walls. A miniature tornado engulfed me with billions of fairy-like particles of light swirling and dancing mischievously around my head."

Olisa's eyes blinked rapidly while her head whipped back and forth.

"It was so weird... My body became limp. I began to levitate above the ground, rising as if I was being toted by a hot air balloon. It was all beyond my control and then it finally dawned on me that this is a test of faith. "

She fixed her eyes on us.

"One of Mama Willis's favorite sayings was, 'You must have faith in things not seen.' Somehow I managed to open my mind and release my fear as an air of serenity settled upon me. I started to trust, and instead of fighting, I surrendered to whatever fate had in store for me."

She unconsciously straightened the covers at the foot of the bed, contemplating all that had transpired in her brain. Though she was only a few feet away, she sounded as if she were speaking from another room.

"A brilliant incandescent light fell from the sky and quickly passed through me like a finger through the flame of a candle, hot but not burning. The sensation coursing through my body filled me with so much joy that it caused spontaneous screams to leapt from my mouth. I laughed loud and hard while floating through a velvety night sky. It didn't even faze me when I began free falling to the earth, which received me like a fluffy pillow.

"When I awoke, I thought it was the warm surf splashing my face, but it was Freeloader licking me. I sat up and was shocked to find myself perched on top of a cliff. Below, a magnificent panorama of beach stretched out before me. Streaks of light rocketed from the ocean followed by the tip of an orange red sun slowly ascending above the water making the sea sparkle like a million gems. It was awesome."

She sat on the edge of the bed, her fingers in a wrestling match with her hair. "Am I crazy or just being overly dramatic? Things like that don't happen to people, right? Was it just a silly old dream?"

I replied, "Olisa, you don't just dream, you experience."

She cocked her head, and through the loose strands of rippling hair offered a mischievous grin.

"Is this what you'd call an epiphany, Dad?"

"For someone else, yes. For you? No. For you I would call it affirmation. You have been subconsciously preparing for this moment all your life. You are the host, not the guest to this party."

There was a long silence before she asked, "Will you guys be all right with my decision?" The question was directed more at Grace whose tears had already soaked through my shirtsleeve.

"Of course, Olisa. I knew it was only a matter of time. I just kept hoping it would never come."

"For what, Mom?"

"For you to fulfill your destiny."

SOUL EYES

It was on.

After hearing about Olisa's change of heart, Jonathan's grin was more widespread than Earvin "Magic" Johnson signing his first Laker basketball contract. But Jon had always been right about one thing. Olisa's decision one way or the other would not affect the media machine, which had whipped itself into a firestorm. A videotape turned in by a beachside resident named Greg Hill who shot another angle of the now infamous gang battle had preceded the heightened activity. Though it was extremely amateurish, it gave an even better glimpse than KLSC of the stabbing. The new one showed hand and knife working like a jackhammer on Ernesto's chest. Once again, we saw Olisa cradling Chato and kneading his bloodied stomach with her fingers.

Still, it was debatable, even with the most recent video, as to whether Olisa actually healed the boy. The latest video argued a pretty strong case for the latter, although most reporters declined an opinion, leaving it to their audience to decide—all except for Eva Sanchez. Eva unflinchingly asserted that Olisa had performed a miracle healing. Consequently, the station's ratings skyrocketed.

Given the green light, Jonathan took over with an air of authority that neither of us had ever seen. He feverishly worked at building a protective structure as this televised struggle continued. He made sure we'd be ready to deal with any fallout that might occur.

"Mom, Dad, I hope you don't mind. I called the phone companies for you and had the telephone numbers changed to a non-published number. Please be selective about who you give your number to."

"Yes, sir."

"In the meantime, anyone calling your former home phone number, including Olisa's phone, has been rerouted to a separate office phone for business. I've already got one of my administrate assistants, Savannah, handling the phones and screening calls for us."

"Okay. So you're still working for the company?"

"Oh yeah… At least for now… Oooh, is that the doorbell?"

Grace opened the door for a short squatty white man dressed in gray uniform overalls with a red Protect-a-watch label on the breast pocket of his uniform.

"Over here, Jeff! Jeff's done a lot of work for me on other homes."

"Hey, hey, how you folks doin'," he replied in a thick Brooklyn accent. His eyes surveyed the room like a guy casing a bank.

"This gentleman here is going to do a thorough inspection of the house and Olisa's studio and see what kind of security system will work best. No offense, Pop, but it's time to trash that antiquated system you been using and get a more sophisticated alarm," Jonathan quickly commented, escorting Jeff past us.

"Whatever you say, Jon," I said, looking at Grace who bemusedly shrugged her shoulders.

And that's the way it was for a couple of weeks—Jonathan ushering a variety of technicians through the house. He also footed all the bills, although I suspect the record company reimbursed him since Olisa was listed as one of RPM's newest motivational artists.

In the beginning, Jon apprised Olisa of everything he was doing. There was a mutual show of respect and adulation between the two of them that was being nurtured. As much as I disagreed with what they were planning, the greatest enjoyment Grace and I received from this was watching our kids work together.

However, business is business. Jonathan knew what he was doing way before I caught on, like a talented chess player ten steps ahead of the game. By keeping Olisa out of the public eye for a couple of weeks, John sprinkled fertilizer on the public's curiosity about this miracle worker who was suddenly nowhere to be found.

Handmade signs cropped up on a daily basis in the city of Venice: *Where are you, Olisa? Olisa, save us, we need your healing before we become normal Angelenos! We want the Big O! Where is the Good Witch of Venice? Oz needs her. Come on back, Mama Venice, outsiders are trying to run the asylum! Where's a good psychic when you need one?*

KLSC continued to fire off clips from the same beach incident and interview, but that was running thin. No other stations had anything else other than the videos. Jonathan's efforts to keep her off the streets and out of the public eye worked successfully. The city had concocted a fever, and the time had come to treat it.

Jonathan made sure all calls from the media and interested parties were handled professionally and diplomatically. Callers were told that Olisa was on a spiritual hiatus and needed time to recharge her energies. And yes, everything that was whispered about her was true.

However, whatever Jonathan's timeline was, Olisa's was far shorter.

One night Grace, Olisa, Jonathan, and I were chowing down on some Indian food from Tandoori restaurant. The three of us were engaged in an animated discussion about the assassination conspiracies of the Kennedy's, King, and Malcolm X when Olisa sedately said, "Jonathan, it's time."

For a minute, I thought he was going to gag on the Baryani rice. "Time for what, Oli?"

Frowning she muttered, "I'm tired of sitting around indefinitely. I need to get out and talk to people before I go crazy. Whatever it is we're doing, let's do it—this is not going to make it. If you can't…"

"Sis, relax. I hear everything you're saying," Jonathan answered reassuringly, hands in the air. "We're not just kicking back. We've been rehearsing for the big event—getting ready, more prepared, you know?"

The expression in her eyes served notice that time had run out.

"I mean, you're right, it's time and you're ready now. You're ready," he said repeatedly. "All right, here we go… Let me make a couple of calls, and I'll get something going. You'll see. I was just kinda hoping you could be patient for…"

"No."

"Hey, cool… No problem, sis. Let's do this. It's gonna happen. Don't worry. Sit tight for a couple of more days and then we're there. Okay?"

She nodded and resumed eating.

Solving the conspiracies would have to wait. Jonathan abruptly hopped out of his chair and headed to the den with a cell phone in one hand and a lamb samosa in the other.

"Meet Jonathan Carpenter, one of the top executives of one of the fastest growing small independent record companies on the west coast—RPM Enterprises. CEO, Roberta P. McMillan, has nothing but praise for this young man, crediting him as a significant factor in their continuing trajectory toward the top of the recording industry. We've asked him to join us this evening; not to talk about the success of RPM, but to discuss a new venture he is starting with his sister, Olisa Carpenter. Carpenter, you'll remember, is a woman who is rapidly ascending her own ladder as a folk hero after her fearless stance during what the station fondly calls the Independence Day Resurrection."

"Jonathan, thank you so much for joining us on the *Special Edition* section of our news program."

"Hey, happy to be here, Eva. Thank you for inviting me."

Eva casually brushed her long bangs with her fingertips even though her carefully groomed style was in little danger of covering her eyes. A fast rising celebrity in her own right, her new hairdo had been mentioned in fashion magazines, particularly because it was a bold and sexy cut for a newscaster. The public liked her willing to risk it all attitude, which was symbolic of her hairstyle. Many were touting her as the Latina version of Diane Sawyer, and of course, she ran with it.

"My first question is, how is Olisa? And where is she? I'm looking at my watch, and there's still time if she wants to make tonight's show."

Jonathan chuckled right along with her as he adjusted his natty deep green silk tie. "Eva, she would love to be here, but she is on a spiritual hiatus at this time. What happened on the weekend of July the 4th forced her to reexamine her role in the world."

"And has she found it?"

"Oh yes. And that is to help people in whatever way she can. "

"Well, on that note I'd say this is the perfect time to tell us about this new organization the two of you have formed."

"My pleasure. We've created a company called O.L.I.S.A., Inc. Naturally, my sister doesn't like the idea that we used her name, but to me it signifies what she personifies. The initials stand for, Only Love can Inspire the Spirit to Awaken."

"Sounds good. So what is the purpose of your organization?"

"Simple. Our mission is to heal the world ."

Eva teasingly smirked at the camera. "Gee, that's a novel idea. I wonder if this is a short-term goal or long-term goal?"She turned back to a grinning Jonathan. "I don't mean to be facetious, but how do you propose to accomplish this?"

Jonathan displayed his most charming smile. "Drop by on Thursday night for our first concert, Ms. Sanchez, and you'll find out."

"Concert? I'll be there. Where is it being held?"

Jonathan faced the camera. "Thursday night, O.L.I.S.A. Inc. is inviting all of you to attend the First Universal Concert of Spiritual Healing, to be held on the Santa Monica Pier. For years, every Thursday, during the summer, the Santa Monica pier has offered the Twilight Dance Series. These are free concerts featuring top-rated entertainment. Fortunately, we've been written in as the final Thursday evening concert for the summer. There's no admission fee, donations only. If you want more information, call... Is it all right to give out the number?" He gave the number. "It's on a first-come first-served basis, and we are anticipating a high turnout. Only a limited number of people are allowed on the pier so come early."

"So if we go, what can we expect?"

"You can expect to have a great time. It's going to be *the* feel good event of the summer. It will be well-organized with loads of entertainment: motivational speakers, and music and bands including the renowned bassist, JJ Willis, who volunteered his services and is assembling some of the hottest studio musicians in the area. Also, expect a couple of surprises if all goes well."

"And what about Olisa?"

"Who do you think is headlining?"

"Olisa?" Eva asked, genuinely surprised by Jonathan's calculated time bomb. "Doing what?"

"Miracles," Jonathan calmly answered.

"Excuse me?"

"Miracles."

Eva waited for him to qualify his answer, but Jonathan's only response was a complacent grin.

"Okay… I can't wait."

"It will be worth it," Jonathan replied, shaking her extended hand.

"And there you have it, folks. Maybe this Thursday some of the questions in your letters, faxes, and emails will finally be answered. Was the healing of Ernesto Padilla a coincidence, hoax or truly a miracle? We'll find out because KLSC will be there."

I wasn't sure what Olisa was thinking. Her face was blasé as she studied the telecast, but the light reflecting from the television made her eyes glow like two copper pennies as my heart beat like dueling tap dancers. After the interview ended, she kissed Grace and I goodnight and headed into her studio. Throughout the night, I periodically awoke to see her bed lamp burning behind her closed blinds.

As D-Day loomed closer, Jonathan moved into high gear as he diligently tried to make sure everything was in place. I had never seen him so crazed. He was the exact opposite of Olisa who was as mellow as Jonathan was super-hyped. If he had managed to sleep over three consecutive hours leading up to the big event, I'm shocked.

"Son, you've got to slow down. If you keep going at this pace, you'll give yourself a heart attack. You look like you got weeks worth of groceries in those bags under your eyes."

"Dad, we got one shot, just one, to make this thing happen, and I'm going to make the best of it. When we get past Thursday, then I promise you, I'll sleep for a week."

"Fat chance, but I'm going to hold you to that," I said to his back as he walked quickly down the hall holding his cellular phone (his third ear) and stuffing a Taco Bell burrito down his throat.

That's why I forced him to go to lunch with me Wednesday afternoon. I wanted him to relax and have a good and healthy lunch.

However, some unexpected problems dethroned my good intentions. I knew I was in trouble when I walked into his posh Century City office and found his lip stuck out so far you could have slipped a CD in it.

"All right, all right, stop pouting. Who took your ball this time! You tell those bad boys that your father… Oops, sorry, I didn't realize you were on the phone." I tiptoed in and eased the door closed.

He dropped his finger from his lips and pointed to the chair. "Hey, Dad, have a seat. They've got me on hold… You won't believe it." He held the phone to his ear like it was a lead weight.

The expression on his face was so sour I thought about running down to the lobby gift shop and buying him a pound of Rolaids.

"Yeah, Savannah… You got her? Good. Hold all the rest of my calls."

He rolled his eyes as he waited for the line to connect.

"Eva, Eva, Eva… how are you? Tell me it isn't so. Wait. Hold on… My father's here. We're going to lunch after we finish… No, no, you don't have to hang up… I'm not about to let you go now that I've got you on the line. Do you mind if I put you on the speakerphone? Just a second. Can you hear me?"

"Yes. Good afternoon, Mr. Carpenter, How are you?"

"Hanging in there, Ms. Sanchez," I answered. "And yourself?"

"Very good, thank you, but please call me Eva. How's that amazing daughter of yours?"

"She's doing all right."

"Great, because I'm looking forward to seeing her Thursday night. Venice Beach has the eighth wonder of the world living there. How could you have kept this a secret for so long?"

"Just lucky, I guess."

"Well, Eva, according to my assistant, KLSC plans on keeping this secret a little longer. What the heck is going on?"

"I'm just trying to be upfront with you, Jon… Management has asked me to pull back on the story temporarily."

"I thought your ratings improved since you began doing the story."

"They did. But the word got handed down that the execs want me to focus on more real news instead of tabloid journalism. Look, they even cut my upcoming new special series report on the paranormal."

Jonathan planted his elbows on his desk and rubbed his forehead. "Tabloid journalism? Come on, Eva. What you're really trying to tell me is management is afraid to bare their ass in public. They don't want to be the laughingstock of the networks if this turns out to be a hoax."

"More or less."

"Uh-huh… Let me get this straight. You coax me to be on your program, I announce our upcoming concert, which is only a day away, and now you're telling me that the network is not going to cover it. That's not right, Eva."

"It's not personal, Jonathan," she answered, lowering her voice surreptitiously. "I'll still be there."

"But not in an official capacity. In other words, without the camera crew."

It was quiet on the other end.

"So what am I supposed to do now?"

"Go on with the show."

"Without any publicity?! You guys screwed me. I could have done other shows, but I trusted you."

"I'm sorry, Jonathan… Look, I know you're upset and probably thinking about going to the other networks, but I can tell you this—they're not going to touch it either. Not until it's all substantiated."

"Substantiated?" Jonathan jumped up and stood spread-eagled over the speaker. "This is bullshit, Eva! You were there, you saw her heal Chato!"

"I know, but Chato refused all medical treatment, never went to a doctor, and disappeared a day later. I personally don't doubt the authenticity. But it looks suspicious and the big boys upstairs are sweating me about it."

"It's documented on film!"

I shook my head to Jonathan's cigar offer as he slammed the cigar case and quickly lit one, acting as if his mental equilibrium would be restored once it touched his lips.

"Some of it. But what certifies these images as being any more credible than the ones you've seen in a pitched tent at a good ol' country revival meeting?"

"Because she really did it!"

"Prove it."

"What about that day with the mayor?"

"I came alone, with no cameras, and even if I had, who's to say what she told him was true. The mayor never confirmed it."

Jonathan took an extra long toke on his cigar as he slumped into an armchair that had enough leather to start a stampede.

"Okay, I get the point. So now you think this is all a fairy tale?"

"I didn't say that. Jonathan, you know how I feel about Olisa. Otherwise, I wouldn't have put my career on the line. There's not a lot of job security for a Latina reporter in this business with all the competition out there. The only thing that saved my ass was the ratings increase. But I can't afford to take that chance again. Everything has to be corroborated. Eventually, I think I can pull enough information together to make this the greatest news story of the century. But that's going to take time, research, and interviews. You understand?"

"Sure, as long as you understand that I can take our story elsewhere. The tabloids are making six figure bids to us everyday."

There was a long pause and a sigh over the speaker.

"That's certainly your option, but do they offer you legitimacy? You want Olisa's story side by side with I met an alien in my backyard with three heads?"

"Then I'll put together my own crew and we'll make something happen."

"It's up to you, Jonathan."

The chair gasped as Jonathan propelled himself forward, trailed by a huge bloom of smoke. He paced back and forth.

"Mr. Carpenter, what about you? How do you feel about all of this?"

"Ms. Sanchez, this is Jonathan's show, but you know where I stand. As far as I am concerned, I hope the whole thing dies out with the eight track tape."

"Eva, I've gotta go and get ready for tomorrow."

"I understand. Well, I wish you the best of luck. I'll be at the show no matter what. Okay?"

"Fine."

"Jonathan, one last thing. If I ever get the green light again to do this show on paranormal phenomenon, do you think Olisa would consent to healing a person on our broadcast if we found someone with a certified medical ailment as part of a segment on healers?"

"Call me when you get it together, and then we'll talk, goodbye," Jonathan replied, in a monotone that masked the outrageous grin spreading on his face as he switched off the speakerphone.

"Pop, a change of plans. How's Italian food sound to you?"

"Boy, if you don't get that shit eating grin off your face.—you haven't stopped smiling since you got off the phone and drove us to Brentwood. Big Joe Turner would say, 'You're acting like a one-eyed cat peeping through a seafood store.' What are you so doggone happy about? I know you said Horacio's is your favorite Italian restaurant but…"

"After today, Pops, Horacio's may be my favorite, period."

"That right? Then deal me in, cause I haven't got a clue to what's going on."

"First, have a taste of some of this proscuitto and cantaloupe, it's kicking." Glancing over his shoulder he whispered, "Lot of studio people hang out in here, you know…"

I nodded my head as I stirred my salad.

"So what did you think of Eva's suggestion?"

"You mean about having Olisa heal someone on her show who has a medically proven illness? It's a good idea if you're trying to get attention."

His grin spread even wider.

"No, not just a good idea. It's a great idea!"

He closed his eyes and held his head back rolling the Merlot in his mouth.

"Now think about this: What if this wasn't just an average person, but a very famous celebrity?"

"Like?"

"Like someone very big, very rich, very popular, and very white."

I chugged my wine.

"What does the color of this person's skin have to do with it?"

"Dad, how do you spell crossover appeal in dollar bills?"

"Very carefully. All right, I'll take a walk with you. If that happened, I'd say the ratings on the show would go through the roof. I can't even imagine…"

"I can. That's why I'm smiling."

He waved to the maitre d', a tanned, very handsome young man who escorted two very attractive and dressed to the nines young women to a table. Once he headed our way, they giggled and appraised his ass as he confidently strolled toward us with a curved grin.

"It sure would be nice to have some decent service in this joint instead of watching the host flirt with all the pretty women!"

"Is that you, Mr. Jon? How did you slip past security again?"

"I told them I was here to kick your behind and they immediately let me through. Oh, by the way, Danny, this is my father, Joseph."

"A pleasure to meet you, sir. I pray you have other children?"

"Yes, I do."

"Danny's a real charmer, isn't he, Dad?"

"We always try to show our best face for the homeless, sir," he joked, rubbing Jonathan's shoulder. "So when are you going to sign me up?"

"Just hang in there kid, your time will come, we just haven't found a spot for a rapper who sings Italian operas."

"Obviously you're not trying hard enough, but how could you when you spend all your time in here."

"You got that right," Jon chuckled, hugging his arm. "Hey, is the chief here tonight?"

"Only for our paying customers."

"Really? Okay, well let's give her some motivation. Tell her that her bastard son is sitting here with her black lover and is about two seconds from doing a lap dance with one of her best paying customers!"

"Why didn't you say so, sir? Let me see if I can find her. Nice meeting you, Father Carpenter," he said, warmly shaking my hand. "Dinner is on me tonight, Jon, but only because your father's here."

"Great, then we'll be back tomorrow."

"That's fine, it's my night off." He squeezed Jon's shoulders. "I'll see you later, buddy."

"Thanks, Dan, we appreciate it."

"Hey that was nice."

"Danielle is a really great kid and one hell of a tenor. If he becomes half as big in the world of opera as his father is to acting, then he's going to live a pretty nice life. And don't think those little honeys flirting with him aren't aware of that."

"Who is his father?"

"Ever hear of Nick Cavaliere?

"Nick Cavaliere. *The* Nick Cavaliere?"

"*The.*"

"You mean the same man who's practically won every stage and film acting award around?

"Yep, that one."

"No kidding? Damn! That's my boy! He's the king!"

"Was."

The comment was so cold it made my blood freeze.

"Oh my God, Jonathan, you can't be thinking…"

"Sure I am. Cavaliere is one of the most revered actors on the entire planet."

I could only agree as I thought about Nicholas Cavaliere who came from a dirt-poor Sicilian background, dug his way out of the trenches and climbed to the top of the ladder. Over the past thirty years, he made so many career comebacks it became passé. Just two years ago, at the age of fifty-eight, he was the top box office draw and his face was plastered on as many magazine covers as any young Hollywood gun. He was paired with leading ladies half his age because of his charm and outrageous good looks. He was one of those unique artists whose sophistication and manliness appealed to both men and women.

Instead of riding peacefully toward the twilight of his career, Cavaliere stampeded to the apex, commanding mondo bucks per picture; that is, until a falling scaffold on a movie set altered the course of his life by crashing into his spine and paralyzing him from the neck down. It was sad to think that someone who brought so much enjoyment to millions of people was struck down like that.

"And, let me guess, you think you got the cure for what ails him?"

"Only if you believe in miracles."

"Ooohhh there he is, my long lost son. And who is this good looking gentleman you have brought with you? Is he for me? You could have at least asked him to take his wedding ring off."

Jonathan rose to greet an impeccably dressed woman in a dark suit with a bright red rose in her hair. Her hair was stretched tight into a bun with one thin white streak that flared boldly in the middle. She was a strikingly handsome woman with an elegance about her that lit up the room. From all the stories I had read about Nick's impoverished beginnings, I couldn't have ever believed that this classy lady had ever been a part of such a poverty stricken environment. But then again, I always believed that true class can never be purchased, it's as much a part of you as the nose on your face. She greeted Jonathan with two wet smacks on each cheek. Eventually, fixing her emerald eyes on me.

"Mama Cavaliere, this is my father, Joseph."

"Oh I have heard so much about you, Joseph. Welcome to our humble little eatery. Please, please sit down. Eat, eat, or your food will get cold." Her flowery voice was strongly peppered by her Italian accent.

"Nice meeting you, Mrs. Cavaliere. Jonathan brags all the time that you have the best Italian food in town.

"That's why I love having your son here, he lays it on thicker than my special marinara sauce." He laughed. "But please, call me Lena,

Joseph. Your son raves all the time about your restaurant, too. Didn't I just read a review about it the other day in the 'Living' section of the *Los Angeles Times*?"

"Yes, we were happy about that."

"Good, good, I hope it brought you lots of business?"

"Definitely. We're grateful for any boost we can get."

"I understand… The economy's been tough on all of us little guys in the restaurant business, especially with all the chains out there waiting to devour us as soon as we take a nap. But we do our best to survive, yes?"

"Yes, ma'am, that's what it's all about."

"Well, you enjoy your food before it gets cold. It loses its taste when you let it sit."

"Well, Lena, you're invited any time to come down our way. We'll fill you up with so much soul food you'll think you were born in the south."

"I'm sure I'll love it, but I'm afraid my stomach and hips will be miserable. However, life is too short, so I accept!" She laughed. Now the two of you enjoy the rest of your afternoon."

"Mama Cavaliere, before you leave there is one more thing, something I would like to discuss with you," he said whisking her hand into his.

"My goodness, Jonathan, don't look so serious, you're scaring me. Are you about to propose marriage again?" She tilted her head and looked querulously from him to me.

"No, Mrs. Cavaliere, not this time. But what I am proposing has everything to do with your husband."

"Nick?"

"Yes. How's he doing?"

"Fine," she said, her smile evaporating.

"No, Mrs. Cavaliere, I mean, how's he really doing?"

Her eyes blinked rapidly. "He's fine, Jon. Why do you ask?"

"I ask because I know someone who can heal him."

At first, I thought the din from the lunch crowd had drowned out his words, until I saw that her jaw was clenched so tightly it made a vein in her temple poke out like a broken bone. She paused and looked away, then patted Jon's hand.

"I appreciate what you're doing, but let us deal with this on our own. Thank God, Nicholas made a lot of money in his career. He's being treated by some of the world's finest doctors and specialists, but with all the money that we've shelled out, he's no better off than the day he suffered the accident."

"That's what I'm trying to tell you, Mrs. Cavaliere you don't have to spend another dime. If you hear me out, Nicholas could be walking tomorrow."

"We both know that would take a miracle."

"Exactly. The person I…"

"Stop, Jon." Her eyes glistened. "I know you mean well, but what you suggest is impossible."

Jonathan started to say something, but she waved for him to be quiet.

"Nick wants to be remembered the way the public saw him two years ago; the confident and heroic man who was wheeled out before the cameras, smiling, and swearing he'd never cease giving up the fight to walk again."

"Mrs. Cavaliere, you talk as if he's not alive."

"The Nick the public knows is not. I didn't know it at the time, but his farewell performance occurred at that press conference. He tried a few voice-overs for commercials and several cable documentaries, but when he realized that sound machines had to enhance and manipulate his voice to make up for the loss of power and control, he took it as a slap in the face and gave it up. Acting is Nicky's life, and it was all stripped away from him. Instead of rehearsing his lines anymore, he only talks about dying. And what hurts the most is knowing I'm not even a good enough draw for him to want to live."

Her shoulders heaved as she put on a game face and smiled at one of the regular patrons.

"I'm sorry, Mrs. Cavaliere"

"Forget it. It's the life I chose."

"Well, I appreciate you sharing this with us, but…"

"Don't. I only told you this so you would honor my wishes and never bring it up again."

She lifted her eyes to the ceiling, battling against the legion of tears.

"Don't you see? He's too fragile. My husband's ego has always been as massive as his insecurity, but his insecurity will no longer make room for the competition. How can I subject him to one more expert? Or one more letdown? All I want is my Nicky back again—positive and loving life. I don't want to hear another doctor say, 'We're doing everything we can, Mrs. Cavaliere, but now we've got to leave it in God's hands.'"

Jonathan quickly pulled a chair out. "Mrs. Cavaliere, you don't look so good, why don't you sit down."

"Yes, I guess you're right. *Grazie*."

"Listen to me, Mrs. Cavaliere, my sister is not a doctor, but she has been blessed with extraordinary gifts. Olisa has the power to heal people."

"Olisa. Olisa? Where have I heard that name before?" Lena frowned, as she repeatedly tossed the name around in her head.

"You probably saw her on the news reports."

"I don't have time for TV, no…aaah… I think I know… Do either of you know a woman named Cecilia Moss?"

Jonathan shrugged his shoulders. "No, never heard of her. You, Dad?"

"Actually, it sounds familiar. Who is she?"

"She is a very old friend of mine, and lately, she's bragged about receiving some amazing readings from this beautiful African-American woman. She claims this woman is the best psychic she has ever been to; high praise coming from Cecilia because she's seen them all."

"That's my sister."

"Lena, does Cecilia lives in Malibu?"

"Yes, Joseph, so you know her?"

The Malibu Ladies, I chuckled to myself.

"Not exactly, but I think my daughter may have mentioned her name on a couple of occasions."

"Cecilia has been begging me to go see her, even though she knows I'm not into that gypsy fortune telling stuff. Now it's finally making sense."

"What is?" I asked.

Well, it was around July. Cecilia left a somewhat disturbing message on my voice mail while I was out of town."

"What did she say?"

"Jonathan, I don't remember exactly. I was in Europe at the time, but she was breathing so hard she was practically hyperventilating. It was something like, call me, no matter what time it is. She said this woman psychic healed some gang kid around July the 4th, and it was all over the news. Then, she got the giggles and said she couldn't stop shaking because she was so excited. It sounded like she was on the verge of a nervous breakdown. Before the voice mail cut her off she said, 'Olisa can cure our Nicholas.'"

"She can," Jonathan replied, rubbing Lena's hand. "I swear to you, Cecilia is right. My sister can heal Nick."

Lena shook her head, pushing back a strand of disobedient hair

"I can't believe I'm still sitting here…"

"Because deep down inside you wonder—can this woman heal my husband? Do I dare to be wrong?"

Her eyes sought out mine. A parent-to-parent thing.

"Is this the truth?"

I felt like a hostile witness subpoenaed to testify.

"Yes."

Jonathan enclosed her hand inside his. "Will you talk to Nick?"

"No, you will. Finish your meal, and I'll drive you over there. It's only five minutes away. I'll call him and let him know we're coming. But don't expect a grand reception."

"We understand."

"I'm probably making the biggest mistake of my life."

"Only if you don't listen to me, Mama Cavaliere."

She walked away, still shaking her head. I kept expecting her to turn around and tell us to forget it, but she returned jingling her car keys.

The plink of Jonathan's fork startled me. His arms were crossed, and he was beaming. It had been a long time since I'd seen him look at me so proudly.

The Los Angeles home of the Cavalieres lies in a very affluent section of northern Santa Monica, toward the end of Ocean Avenue. The road curves upward into a residential area that sits on a cliff facing the hills of Pacific Palisades, which is littered with homes. We passed several joggers at the end of 4th street headed toward the famous steps that all the trendites on the Westside regard a great cardiovascular workout. In fact, Jonathan bragged he ran the steps three to four times a week. Although I'd guess it was more like three to four times a year, judging by the potbelly he steadily nurtured. People trudged up and down the steps, looking like ants spilling in and out of an anthill, but instead of food morsels they carried Walkmans.

The car pulled into a white and expansive Mediterranean style two-story house with a red tiled roof. As we climbed out of her silver blue Mercedes, I noticed a brown hand parting the curtains and then quickly closing them.

Seconds later, the front door swung open and a middle-aged, heavyset Latina woman, huffing and puffing, hair askew on top of her head, smiled cheerily as she held the door open with one hand and fumbled with a pile of laundry in the other.

"Oh, hello, Estella. You didn't have to come down here and open the door, I know you're busy."

"*Esta bien, Señora*. Cavaliere. Mr. Nick is waiting for you in the den."

"Thank you, Estella. This way, gentlemen." We nodded at Estella as we were escorted through a very ornate hallway with marbled floors and Romanesque columns leading to the stairwell. We entered a den that was twice as large as our living room, and a library that contained so many books they looked like wallpaper. Behind a mammoth desk, a staid body sat up in a wheelchair facing us like he had been velcrossed. The only sign of life was his eyes flickering open at our approach.

"Nicholas, these are the two gentlemen I told you about," she said, kissing him on the cheek and standing behind him.

The handsome face that caused millions of hearts to flutter when it hit the big screen now resembled the Pillsbury Dough Boy. His greasy, unwashed hair skittered to his shoulders, and a tangled full-length beard laid flat against his chest. His icy blue "dangerous" eyes were still captivating, and sized us up like a cat on the prowl. When he cleared his throat, it sound like chalk scratching a blackboard.

"How you doin?" he said with little enthusiasm. "Sit down." He smiled as he stared blankly. "Don't let my presence disturb you. Just view me as one of those old movie props they stick in a room." His familiar voice still projected, but sounded like all the bass decibels had been lowered.

"Nicholas, don't…"

"I'm so sorry, dear. I just thought the occasion deserved a dash of humor. I mean, after all, no offense guys, but obviously my loving wife is so frantic she's resorted to seeking witchcraft to cure my little ailment."

His hands were positioned to rest comfortably on his knees. It was hard not to feel something. I honestly could not look at him without picturing the vibrant actor held captive by his own body. It didn't help to see the plethora of awards behind him on the mantle, including his Oscars for Best Actor and Best supporting actor. In every article I ever read about him, the words, "masterful performance" were written so many times he should have hyphenated it as a last name.

Lena ignored him and formally introduced us.

"Mr. Cavaliere, it is truly an honor to meet you. I have admired your career for a long time." Jonathan continued to baste on the compliments with Nicholas flinging thank you's back at him. However, his eyes bounced like basketballs, so it was no surprise when he put an abrupt end to the pleasantries.

"My wife tells me you claim your sister can cure me. So tell me, who is this person planning to rub snake oil all over my body?"

Jonathan chuckled, and, without skipping a beat, immediately launched into his pitch mode, pulling up a chair beside Nick and bragging proudly about Olisa's accomplishments and all that happened recently, including informing him about the upcoming concert, O.L.I.S.A., Inc., and anything else he could think of. I found myself admiring him as I listened to him do his thing. He was articulate, charming, and absolutely fearless. The kid talked to the superstar actor like they had been childhood friends.

Throughout the spiel, Nick's eyes were coldly analytical. Every time he swallowed, it made my throat hurt.

Finally, Jonathan looked him square in the eye and said, "Nick, when you meet my sister, you'll see what I mean. Believe me."

Nick blinked hard, a sneer distorting his lips.

"Believe? A few years ago, I believed I was invincible. Lena and I both come from a long line of Catholics. It's kind of an inherited thing, you know? We're so Catholic, at birth our umbilical cord was a rosary. Now, my wife was never what I'd call a diehard Catholic, but have you missed one Sunday service since my accident, Lena?"

"No," she whispered as she continued to rub his neck.

"When I was paralyzed, I used to think God was finally punishing me for all the bullshit I did in my youth. But then it hit me, God doesn't really give a shit."

He paused to swallow some water. Lena held the bottle for him as he sipped through a straw.

"Everyone's praying for me, and if I could get down on my knees I'd join them. But with all these prayers, cards, letters, and good wishes from around the world, I'm still here. You could set my leg on fire, and I'd never feel a fucking thing. Everyone tells me, Nick, my boy, just have faith. You know what faith got me? My own permanent theater seat."

His gagging laughter was the only sound in the room as I shifted uncomfortably in my chair.

"Even the local archdiocese trumpeted my cause, but here I am. So with all this heavenly blather racking up big fat zeros, how can your sister compete?"

His bitterness reminded me of the first time I saw him on stage. He gave a performance so powerful I left the theater as if I'd been cold-cocked.

"Ask me about that after you've completed your first marathon," Jonathan responded.

"I don't get it," Cavaliere smirked, his blue eyes sizing Jonathan up. "You don't act like one of those wacko religious freaks, but I keep thinking they ought to put you away for what you're saying to me."

"They could put me away for a lot of things, but this isn't one of them."

"I guess being stuck in front of a TV set pays off sometimes. So that was your sister I saw being interviewed by what's her name... Sanchez?"

"Yes, sir."

"Mr. Carpenter, you must be pretty proud of your daughter for standing up to those gangbangers like that."

"Pretty much."

"Okay... Being a father myself, at what point did you want to strangle her and send her to the most isolated region on the planet?"

"Oh, about two seconds after I heard the news."

"I understand, man. I truly understand," he said, laughing with me. "I've got two daughters and a son. The girls are modeling in Europe. If they ever did anything like that, I don't know..."

For the first time since we had been there, the sternness on his face softened as he smiled tenderly at Lena. She kissed him on the forehead.

"Still, I have tremendous admiration for your daughter. She's a courageous woman. It says something about you, too."

"Thank you."

"But all this other stuff... Healing this kid... I don't know. It defies all logic. But, I could be wrong. They say anything's possible. Old ladies lift cars off loved ones when the adrenaline flows, etc. Maybe I'm just too jaded. I know how far the press can run with half-truths."

Lena wiped the perspiration from his brow.

"So tell me… Did she really heal him?"

"Without question," Jon said as he calmly faced Nick's unyielding stare.

"My wife says she knows you guys and that you're sincere as all hell. I figured I'd at least listen to what you had to say. Hell, what choice do I have? I need people these days to blow my damn nose."

Lena massaged his temples and whispered softly in his ear as he visibly tried to slow his breathing.

"Hypothetically, let's say she did heal the kid… Maybe this was a one-time deal. If I let your sister do a number on me, what guarantee do I have that she'll be able to do it again?"

"A better guarantee than you'll get to star in a one hundred million dollar action flick."

I hoped Jonathan had his cell phone with him, because I had a feeling we were going to need a taxi.

Tears were running down Nick's cheeks, but he was laughing, causing Lena to shoot him a double take. Obviously, it had been awhile since laughter had eased into the house.

"Hey, man, I like you, you're all right. And, I hear you're a hell of a businessman. So what's the deal? What do you get out of this?"

"The deal, Mr. Cavaliere, is that I want to see you mesmerizing us once again on the big screen."

"So would I, but there's got to be a catch. If you're so confident about her abilities, why didn't you just bring her here?"

"Because I want you to come down to our concert tomorrow night at the Santa Monica pier and let her heal you on stage. The kind of publicity your healing would generate is worth more…"

"Whoa, you got to be kidding. I've barely left my cocoon in two years, and you actually think I'm going to make a damn fool of myself in front of all those fucking people at some holy rollers revival service?!"

Lena tried to massage his temples again, but he shook his head angrily.

"Here's the deal. You bring her here, alone, and if she raises my body from the dead, I'll call a press conference and squawk like a parrot."

"Mr. Cavaliere, please, just this one time. We need you."

His head rolled back exasperatedly to the side, and the brief interest I saw in his eyes dissipated.

"No. That's my final answer. Actually, just forget the whole thing. I'm not going to be your guinea pig. You think I want to listen to, Sorry, Mr. Cavaliere, this has never happened before, I guess your faith wasn't strong enough?!"

"Oh no, that's not it, Mr. Cavaliere, I…"

"It doesn't matter. My wife means well, but I should have listened to my instincts from the very beginning." He shot Lena an accusatory glance.

"Please, sir, just give Olisa a chance," Jonathan pleaded.

"Olisa is a remarkable person, and I wish her and both of you the best. Thank you. Lena."

Lena's purse was already in her hands as we were quickly shepherded to the library door.

"Gentlemen, I'm sorry, will you please wait in the living room? I just want to say goodbye to Nicholas, and then I'll drive you back to the restaurant."

Before stepping out the door, Jonathan somberly turned and said, "If I have in some way offended you, I apologize, Mr. Cavaliere. That was surely not my intention. All I can say is, I really hope you will come or at least maybe we can set up a time for Olisa to come and visit you. We're talking about your life. I promise you, you won't regret it. At least think about it."

But all we saw was Lena's trademark customer relations smile as she gently closed the double doors of the den in our face.

It was killing Jon not to be able to talk to Lena about what had just happened as she drove us back to the Horacio's, but he knew not to push it any further. On the way back to the restaurant, we babbled with Lena about all kinds of superficial things, like it never happened.

"I blew that one didn't I, Pops?" he disconsolately asked later as we sat inside his car outside the restaurant."

"No, not at all. You were being upfront. It just wasn't meant to be."

"Hmmm."

"What you've got to do now is get ready for the concert tomorrow."

"Yeah, yeah, you're right."

"You gonna stop by the house for dinner tonight?"

"Yeah."

He sat for a second then gunned the engine while reaching for his cell phone.

CHAPTER 6

I drove home cruising west on Palms Boulevard. It was a nice, peaceful drive. As I hit the crest going through Mar Vista Hills, a beautiful, orange-red sunset greeted me.

I stopped off at the Wild Oats market and grabbed a few groceries before heading home. When I got to the house, it sounded like there was a party going on inside. Free cheerfully barked his way into the conversations, and jiggling animated heads were silhouetted in the kitchen.

I dramatically slammed open the backdoor and stepped into the kitchen.

"Uh-huh, caught ya. So this is what y'all been doing while I work my fingers to the bone night after night, huh?"

"Took you long enough." Grace laughed.

"Hi, Dad, guess who just dropped by?"

"Oh-my-God! There's a white man in my house with his arm wrapped around my daughter! What is the world coming to? Aren't people safe in their homes anymore?"

"Daddy's become a comedian since you left, Peter."

"Mr. C. has always made me laugh, Olisa."

I held Peter by the shoulders appraisingly, and gave him a big bear hug. "You're looking good, Petey boy."

"You, too, Mr. Carpenter." His pale blue eyes were as warm as Caribbean waters, but dark circles bordered them.

"Man, look at you! All dressed up like you're on the cover of *GQ Magazine*. Is that how they're styling in the Big Apple these days?"

"Mr. C., in New York I'm just a termite looking for a piece of wood. I can't compete. You know us native Californians; hand me a T-shirt and some jeans and I'll be all right. I don't think I ever really fit in well there. It's just not me."

"Just not me! The way I hear it, you fit in well enough for one of the top public relation firms in the nation to offer you shares in the company!"

"Yeah, but…"

"Doesn't my boy look great?" Grace remarked admiringly. "That cute little boy with the beach ball eyes turned into quite a good-looking man. Still got all this curly hair, too." Grace stood on her tiptoes and ruffled his hair.

"Yeah, buddy. I always used to wonder about you. For a blond dude, you've always had a little color in that skin of yours!" I shot him the ol' fisheye. "Are you one of them Ethiopian Jews or one of those Jefferson-Hemmings castoffs?"

"Neither one, as far as I know." He grinned.

"Can you dance?"

"Enough to get by." Peter offered a little tap dance to the delight of everyone.

"Naaw, if you had any in you, all that white blood swept it away."

"Daddy, stop. I don't believe you sometimes."

"It's okay, Olisa. This is what I miss, being around my second family. When Mr. Carpenter picks on me, I know he loves me."

"See? Mind your own business, girl. Peter knows what's up. So, Pete, how's your parents doing, man? They're in Florida, right?"

"Still in Miami, loving it, never coming back, and living in this retirement community that looks like something straight out of Disney World. Plus, now they have more time to trade guilt on who was responsible for how I turned out."

"Oh, you know your parents love you."

"In their own way—which reminds me, they send their best to everyone."

"Tell them we send them the same."

"Will do."

"Little Oak, you and I are there tonight. How did you know I had a taste for some of your special guacamole?" I swiped the bowl of chips from Alton.

"Because you asked me to, Uncle Joe."

"So, Pete, what y'all doing back in Los Angeles? You here on vacation?"

His blue eyes deepened. "You don't know…"

Heads started dropping like autumn leaves.

"Don't know what? See, around here, sometimes they forget to deliver the mail in my hood."

"I'm staying in Los Angeles indefinitely. I took a leave of absence."

"What?"

"Isn't that great? My boy is back in town," rejoiced Grace, hugging his arm.

"And my big brother." Olisa hugged the other one.

"What? That's a cause for celebration! So you mean I'll finally get a chance to meet your friend—is it Ryan?"

Peter shuffled his feet, eyeing Olisa who offered him a sympathetic smile. "Ryan's gone, Mr. C. He died of a sudden brain aneurysm a few months ago. That's why I needed to get out of New York for awhile."

"Hey, I'm sorry, Pete, I didn't know…"

"It's okay."

Olisa rubbed his arm reassuringly.

"Yeah, but are you okay, man?"

"I'm hanging in there."

He looked so fragile and vulnerable. Even with Grace and Olisa bolstering him up on each side like bookends, for a second, he looked like he wanted to slip between their fingers and collapse to the floor.

"You do that, kid. And whatever I can do, please let me know."

He heaved a deep sigh and nodded his head.

"Just being here with my second family makes it a lot better."

"Peter, I only wish I had known, maybe…"

"Don't, Olisa. You were out of the country at the time, and there's nothing you could have done, anyway. It happened too fast. I just wish I could have told him how much I loved him before he died."

"He knew," Olisa said as she hugged his arm affectionately.

"Thanks, Olisa."

"Peter, it's going to work out fine. You're a good man with a good heart—don't none come any better." Grace kissed him on the cheek."

Peter wrapped his arms around both women. "I love you guys."

Seeing Pete's face reminded me of the little boy that used to follow Grace around like a puppy when she was pregnant with Olisa. He was so fascinated with the idea of a baby living in her stomach. I still see the awe in his eyes as he watched Grace cuddling Olisa as a newborn. Ever since she was born, Peter has always been a big brother to her. They managed to stay in contact even after his parents got the hell out of Watts and moved to the suburbs shortly after the riots. When he got old enough, he'd take the bus to our house.

As teenagers, a two-hour phone call for them was a short conversation. And when phone calls weren't as convenient due to traveling, then they fired off hundreds of letters and postcards to each other. Man, time passes fast. After all these years, the two remained friends. Olisa affectionately described Peter as, "My friend for life."

"So, Pete, if you really want to take your mind off of things, why don't you join us at the concert tomorrow?"

Peter's face flushed with embarrassment. "Man, Mr. C., now I'm really embarrassed."

"Act like I live in the dark ages, Peter, enlighten me."

"Okay, Jonathan called me a couple of weeks ago to seek my advice on doing press releases for O.L.I.S.A., Inc. I told him if he could be patient for a couple of more weeks, I'd be out here and give him some free tips. Of course, Jonathan has already decided that I will handle the P.R. program."

"What? Now Jonathan knows better than to be asking…"

"It's okay, Mrs. C. I really don't mind. It's a good antidote for my depression. It's a no brainer. You know I'd do anything for Miss O." Peter wrapped an arm around our grinning daughter.

"Petey, did you bring an appetite with you? I'm sure eating is far better than being interrogated by my husband," Grace joked, pulling his arm.

"Yes, ma'am."

"Grace, I wasn't interrogating."

"Laura is cooking one of her special dinners tonight, so why don't we go into the dining room."

"Oh, is that right? Little Oak is cooking tonight? Didn't you have to rush me to emergency at Santa Monica Hospital the last time she cooked?"

"Only because you ate too much, Uncle Joe," Laura sassed me as she peered into the oven and ladled sauce over the baked chicken. "Alton doesn't seem to have suffered from my cooking."

"Gumbo eats alien hay in his bread, how can you go by him?"

"Bean sprouts, Unc."

"Whatever."

"I wouldn't push it, Uncle Joe. You know Little Oak knows how to work with those herbs."

"That's right, Uncle Jo, you don't want to find some rare seasoning in your food that doesn't sit real well in your stomach."

"Now I can't believe my Little Oak would ever do anything like that to her Uncle Joe."

She reached for a second dishtowel as she arched an eyebrow.

"Ohhh, let me help you with that chicken, young lady. We don't want you to strain your back or anything. Right, Gumbo?"

"You're on your own, Unc. I ain't got nothin' to do with it," laughed Alton.

"Appreciate your support, Gumbo."

Alton shrugged as he recaptured the bowl of chips while I hauled the chicken out of the oven.

"Thank you, Uncle Joe. Now I see what Aunt Grace sees in you."

"'Bout time."

"It's so great to be home again." Peter chuckled.

Jonathan dropped by midway through our meal with his newest "hottie" whose black miniskirt was practically sanded to her body. The muscles in her calves moved like harp strings as she nimbly stepped across the carpet in her strapped high heels. A sweet perfume wafted through the house assimilating with the spicy aromatic smell of Little Oak's chicken. She smiled like a beauty contestant when she was introduced to the room.

"*Monsieur* Kaplan, did you have a good flight? Man, you don't know how happy I am to see you," he said warmly as he and Peter slapped backs. "Welcome back, brother. I'm sorry about what happened. It's all going to work out."

"It is."

"Hey, I want you to meet La Tisha. She's a singer, andI'm working on securing a label contract for her. She's already shot a couple of videos for us. She's the bomb, isn't she?"

"Yes. Nice meeting you, La Tisha," Peter said, extending his hand.

"You, too." She regally offered Peter a limp hand that somewhere in her mind she conjoined with class.

"Peter is the old friend I was telling you about, and a brilliant public relations expert. Tish, when you hit it, this is the man you want to know."

"Oooh," she remarked, wiggling her shoulders.

"Is someone out front?" Grace asked as she peeped through the slats in the front door.

I heard the front gate clink shut.

"Oh, Mom, that's probably a buddy of mine I asked to stop by. I hope you don't mind. Yeah, that's him. Come on in, man. Looka here, everyone. This is Logan Matthew."

"Oh, no, I'm just Logan, Lo, whatever you want to call me," he said, stuffing his hands inside his baggy jean pockets as he walked into the living room. "It's cool."

Matthew was one of the most laid-back dudes I had ever met. I immediately took a liking to him. He merged into our midst as effortlessly as butter melting on a hot roll. Even Little Oak, who is leery of all strangers until she gets to know them, sported a silly grin on her face. Logan's charms only enhanced his subtle good looks.

Grace put it best. "He's like punch that's been spiked. By the time you realize someone's slipped in the alcohol, you're already drunk. Slender, with cinnamon brown skin, and glistening black hair cut perfunctorily close to his head, Logan's droopy jaguar shaped eyes gave the appearance of nonchalance. But, I could tell by the way he examined his surroundings when he entered the house that he didn't miss a thing.

"Where's my sister? I want her to meet Logan."

"At ease, Jon, don't call the FBI. I'm here."

We were all gathered in the living room when Olisa casually sauntered in from the hallway.

"Olisa, this is…"

"Logan Matthew! What are you doing here?"

He seemed just as taken back as he warmly clasped her hand. "I was going to ask you the same question. You… you're Jonathan's sister?"

"Wait a minute, you guys know each other?" Jonathan questioned.

Neither one answered immediately. Finally Logan broke the silence, "Well kind of…"

"What does that mean? Is that like kind of pregnant? Either you do or you don't!" I was surprised by the hint of irritation in Jonathan's voice.

"We met at a gallery in Santa Monica, but she never told me her name."

"Well, it wasn't just any gallery. It was the very prestigious R.D. Bowles Gallery in Santa Monica. They were hosting a photography exhibit honoring your work. We only talked for a few minutes. There were so many people waiting to talk to you… I didn't want to take up all your time."

"There were other people there?"

"Yes." Olisa blushed.

"You know, after our conversation, I looked all around for you, but you were gone. I even searched for a glass slipper. Wow. I didn't think I'd ever see you again, and here you are. Ha! Jonathan's sister. Boy, what a small world."

"I guess it is." Olisa agreed.

Their hands gradually parted, but Logan's eyes still held hers.

"I'm trying to remember, did you even like my work? Be honest."

The burst of laughter from us startled him.

"It's obvious you really don't know Olisa," chimed Little Oak, laughing.

"I loved your work," Olisa answered quickly. "It's so passionate. Obviously, you love what you do because your photographs show an innate compassion and sensitivity for your subjects."

"Thank you."

"So tell us about your work, Logan," Grace cajoled.

"Well, I love music, particularly jazz, so there are lots of photos of jazz musicians. Same thing with children. I have shots of children from all over the world: Guatemala, Nicaragua, New Guinea, Rwanda, and Sarajevo…"

"But you're playing it down, Logan. These aren't just coffee table photographs. You have managed to capture on an intimate level the quiet, innocent dignity, humanity, and even tragedy of these people. I feel like I know them. After leaving the show, your images found a home inside my brain for weeks."

"Meeting you did the same thing to me."

Whatever else Olisa planned to say disappeared, as her face flushed.

"Jonathan tells me you've also traveled extensively?"

"Yes."

"One of these days we'll have to get together and swap stories."

"I'd like that."

"Olisa, show our guest to his seat in the dining room so he can finally get something to eat," Grace insisted, filling in the awkward silence that suddenly transpired.

Once Olisa escorted Logan to a seat at the table, he exclaimed, "Ooooh, if this taste as good as it looks, then I'm in deep, deep trouble."

"No, you're in trouble if you get up from the table and go to the bathroom. The last time I did that, Gumbo cleaned my plate off."

"Aww, that ain't true, Unc. How you gonna diss me in front of our guest?"

"Excuse me? Did you forget what happened on Labor day, last year? Huh? Oh, you're quiet now? Uh-huh."

"Unc, you still holding that against me? I swear, I didn't know that food was yours. I thought Laura fixed a plate for me."

"Uh-huh, whatever… Just keep your eye on your food, Logan."

"I'll do that." Logan laughed.

But he lied. The only thing he kept his eye on was Olisa. Even while he addressed me, his pupils mirrored Olisa's face.

"Logan, I'm dying to see your work after hearing Olisa describe it. Do you have any pictures with you?" Grace asked sweetly.

"I'm afraid not, Mrs. Carpenter. The only thing I brought with me is my best friend who is resting in the trunk of my car."

"Pardon?"

"My 35 mm camera."

"Ohhh."

"I don't believe you, man," Jon interjected. "Don't you know by now to carry your portfolio around with you?"

"I know, I'm really bad about that. I just feel kinda funny doing that."

"La Tisha, you ought to see some of this man's work. You heard my sister. In my estimation, we're talking genius."

"Thanks, Jon, but let's not go that far. I'm just a photographer."

"Just a photographer? Give me a break. The way you manipulate the lighting in your work, what process do you use in your photographs?"

"Some photos I rework with oils, varnishes, crayons, and other mixed media. My goal is to explore the human condition, so I try to bring the truth of what I see to the surface."

"Outstanding! Man, your images are so arresting, you could get an orangutan a modeling contract. Hear me?! I've worked with hundreds of photographers, and you are not a photographer… You are an artist! Your shots are masterpieces!"

"Hey, man, I appreciate that."

"Do you specialize in any type of photography, Logan?" La Tisha asked, proud to contribute to the conversation as she mechanically rubbed Jonathan's arm.

"Uh, mostly documentary photography, photojournalism, whatever you want to call it."

"Just documentary photography. There he goes again. Logan, you drive me crazy, but I love you. However, you do need to light a fire under your agent's behind. She's not selling your work the way she should."

"She's doing all right, Jon. I'm to blame for some of the delay. I'm probably not as cooperative as she'd like."

"Typical artist. That's why I always say, creative people should never handle business or finances. Remind me to give you the name of another agent you might want to check out."

"Thanks."

"Logan, next time I hope to see your work." La Tisha smiled, glancing sideways at Jonathan like a child seeking approval.

"You may have already seen some of it, Lady T. Logan shot several videos for me including, 'Mookie Moan's, ' 'Tear down the Roof, ' and Holy Cross's 'Gospel Strut,'"

She gasped as she picked at her food. "Wow! You did those videos? Those were hot!" La Tisha exclaimed, jiggling in her seat.

"Thank you. Most of it I shot with my eyes closed. I'm used to doing still photography, but I guess it all worked out."

"Yeah, to the tune of a couple of Grammy nominations and one MTV award on his first go around! When he asked me how to go about filming this I told him to give it the same feel as he did with his photography and women—that seemed to work!" Jonathan guffawed. "Oh, I'm sorry. I hope I'm not embarrassing you, Lo?" Jonathan asked a little too innocently, glancing sidewards at his sister. "You know how it is when you get to talking shop."

Logan scratched the back of his neck, and for the first time, avoided eye contact with Olisa.

"Well anyway, in a matter of days he shot the video like he'd been doing it his whole life. My boy's a natural!"

"Logan, you ready to eat some bread? I'm sure you don't need it buttered anymore." The laughter lifted the tension as I passed him the basket. I could tell he was relieved to see the focus shift as we delved into politics and Washington scandals.

During the first conversational break, Jon asked, "So Lo, what have you got next on the agenda?"

"Uh, nothing right now, you know, I'm just waiting to see if this grant with the Ford Foundation is going to go through."

"What? Hey, that's perfect, well while you're on hold you might want to consider this. I need someone to shoot photos of Olisa at our concert tomorrow. Actually, I need a photographer for an on-call basis. And now that I find out she loves your work as much as me, it could be a great marriage. I mean, only if you're interested."

"Logan, please forgive my son. He knows better than to discuss business at this dinner table."

"Mom's right, Lo. My bad. You haven't even digested your food, yet."

"I'm there. I'd love to do it," Logan said excitedly.

"You sure?"

"Very."

"Cool."

"Hold on, Logan. Jonathan has no business putting you on the spot like that. You don't have to do this," Olisa remarked angrily.

"Olisa, I want to."

"Logan, he hasn't even told you what he's going to pay."

"Olisa, it could be a freebie, I don't care," he replied softly, causing feet to shuffle under the table.

Tiny tics played at the corner of her mouth as she twisted the ends of her hair. "That's very nice of you, but you must have better things to do."

"Like what?"

"Like working on something that will benefit your career."

"Shooting pictures is my career, Olisa." He kept his eyes on her. "However, if what you're really getting at is you'd feel uncomfortable around me, then I can respect that. I won't do it. Don't answer now. You can think about it and let Jon know."

Olisa dabbed at her food, her brown eyes gradually rising. "I'm fine as long as you are."

"You already know my answer."

"Well all right," Jonathan uttered. "Lo, let's meet after dinner and we'll discuss the particulars."

"I can't wait to get started." Logan smiled. "I just hope I don't get on your nerves, Olisa."

"I wouldn't worry about it," Laura said nonchalantly as she collected dinner plates. She made an extra effort to avoid the look Olisa shot her. "Dessert anyone?" Laura asked, barely suppressing a smile as she grabbed Grace's hand and pulled her into the kitchen. Olisa quickly excused herself and trailed right behind them. Faint giggles emanated from the kitchen. Of course, when they came out with plates of chocolate raspberry cake, their faces were passive.

"Hallelujah, I think we've built ourselves one heck of a team," trumpeted Jon as he raised his glass for a group toast.

After the toast, Jon exchanged places with La Tisha and sat next to me, whispering in my ear, "Great photography, cheap labor. He hasn't worked consistently in a year."

He planted a kiss on La Tisha's cheek as she blushed with appreciation. Then he raised his glass of Chardonnay. "Another toast to a great future!"

As the glasses clinked, I thought, Jonathan may not be getting out of this as cheaply as he thinks.

The concert was scheduled for 6:00 p.m. By 5:00, the Santa Monica pier was jam-packed, and the vendors were pleased because everyone was making money. The arcades, restaurants, old-fashioned merry-go-round, and pier rides, including the Ferris wheel and roller coaster, had extremely long lines. There were so many people, the spillage descended to the sand around the pier and swarmed the volleyball pits.

It had been a hot day in the high 80's, but we were blessed by a refreshing ocean breeze, which made us all very grateful. Judging by the excited chatter filling the air, there was an eagerness to get the festivities underway. People anticipated a very interesting evening.

Except for me.

I feared that a giant disaster loomed on the horizon, and my daughter was the sacrificial lamb.

Rather than hang around backstage with family and friends, I chose to be in the audience. I don't know why, really. Probably because I grew tired of hearing my stressed out son marching around like a modern day Napoleon, barking at the crew as they hustled around. I knew if I hung around any longer, we'd just get into an argument. I was just as nervous as him and Olisa didn't need that. She needed support.

However, being a part of the crowd was in itself a little scary.

An elderly white man wearing a beaten old World War II cap and veins crisscrossing his face like a Thomas Guide leaned against my shoulder, his toxic breath numbing me with its potent mixture of alcohol and tobacco.

"Let me ask you something, fella. Whatcha think about all this?" He took a long drag on a cigarette. After each nicotine hit, his face bunched up like a Shar Pei dog.

"I don't know... It's interesting."

"You can say that again, pal. I tell ya. The only reason I'm here is curiosity. Of course, a lot of these damn weirdos you see out here are looking for some kind of religious cult they can join. Suckers! If you ask me, there ain't anything but a bunch of fools waiting to be scalped in this goddamn audience."

Little Oak would have loved him.

"I've lived in Santa Monica for over forty years, my friend… Native Californian, Los Angelean… There ain't many of us my age around. Went to Hollywood High School before it became Hollyweird. Ha, ha, I've seen it all.

"I don't know where you're from, ace, but you should have seen what this beach was like during the 60's and 70's. Fucking hippies shoutin' all that peace and love stuff while the whole city was sliding down the crapper. All you need is love… That was just a big ol' cornball excuse to do drugs and fuck like dogs in the street. Look where it got 'em. People dying from diseases that knock penicillin on its ass. Now all them baby boomers are out there trying to make an honest buck, instead of bucking the system. All that shit their mothers and fathers told them was right," he scoffed.

He flicked his cigarette to the ground, mashing it reflectively as he lit another one. He coughed as if he were gargling snot.

"Then there was a time when all those crazy Jesus freaks were marching all over the place beating drums and chanting shit. Crazy idiots! God bless California, though, this state is a grab bag for every kind of religion. People can't stop lookin' for Jim Jones. Take a look at those young gals over there about 4:00 high…"

I saw three young girls, dressed wildly. One had platinum blond hair, shorn liked it was cut in the midst of a major earthquake. Her black roots seeped out of her scalp like oil from the ground. All three displayed rings and tattoos on virtually every open area of the body, and I'm sure it didn't stop there.

"Ain't that something? What can you say about that shit? Look at 'em, sittin' there ready to light up some incense. How can any self-respecting parents let their daughters step out the house looking like that? Ain't they got mirrors! The morals of this nation lie in a politician's pants. Hmmph."

I crossed my arms and nodded politely.

"Buddy, I don't know how old you are, but you got to be much younger than me. I've been on this planet for seventy odd years," he said proudly, his elbows smacking my ribcage. He cast a weary smile from his yellowed teeth. "There's always some new jerk trying to tear into someone's asshole. And tonight we'll see it again. You'd think after watching all these cock-sucking preachers doing jail time after screwing high-class prostitutes with your money that they might learn something. But people don't learn a goddamn thing!"

He spit out smoke with a sneer. "Man, I been through the depression, fought in World War II, did some time in Korea, and struggled through every kind of hell you can think of, but I ain't never going to let nobody dick me and then piss my money away. You got me?"

"Yeah."

"… But some folks are just begging to part from their fucking money. Hell, you'd stand a better chance playing lotto," he hoarsely cackled. "The only good thing about this is. I hear this girl is quite a looker…"

My subconscious willed his irritating voice to a muted drone as I spotted Alton, the newly designated Chief Security Officer of O.L.I.S.A Inc., speaking into a walkie-talkie. As he spoke I watched security, which included many of his buddies and fellow bodyguards, position themselves around the stage like a wagon train. Others were assimilated into the crowd, but they were easy to spot since the majority had bull necks and horny toad stares. They weren't alone. The police presence in general was heavy duty as two pair of police officers clomped through on horseback.

"When's this goddamn thing going to start! Hell, its starting to get dark! It's damn near 7:00. I thought they were supposed to start on time! Holy cow!"

As if on cue, Jonathan strolled onto the stage, charmingly addressing the crowd. "How's everybody this evening? We thank you for coming. Welcome to the First Annual Universal Concert for Spiritual Healing!" He paused for the modest cheers. "First, I must apologize. We ran into some technical difficulties, but it's okay now!"

Those "technical difficulties" he referred to occurred because we couldn't find Olisa. We were supposed to meet at the house at 4:00. No Olisa. At 5:30, still no Olisa. That's when the real panic set in and poor Jonathan aged so fast he almost passed me.

We scoured the neighborhood in Jonathan's rented limousine. Thanks to Little Oak who knew Olisa's favorite walking routes, we found her seated on a decrepit milk cart in an alley near Palms and Abbott Kinney Boulevard, shooting the breeze with two homeless men. Ignoring a relieved but pissed off Jonathan, she refused to get into the vehicle unless she could bring her friends.

I think Jonathan wished he could shoot her with a taser dart and drag her there, but time was running out. He closed his eyes and held his breath while her honored guests adjusted their tattered clothes and hustled into the limousine. Logan had a fat grin on his face as he snapped their pictures with his camera. It didn't help Jonathan's nerves as Olisa debated him the entire ride to the pier about the makeup and attire he selected for her. Nor did he seem particularly amused by the malodorous air reeking from our unwashed guests as he thumped button after button until all the electric windows had sidled down.

But that was earlier. Jonathan on stage was the essence of cool. He wore an elegant three-piece khaki-colored suit. He was extremely proud of his compromising back-to-earth look, particularly ever since Olisa informed him that the word khaki means earth-colored in Hindi and hailed from the days of the Raj. This was his politically correct contribution to the occasion.

Amid the roar of the cascading roller coaster, he introduced the agenda for the evening and the artists who were going to perform, saving Olisa for last. There was a polite applause as a low buzz circulated throughout the audience.

"Now I've got to tell you, if you're here to have fun, then have fun. If you feel like praying, then go ahead and pray. If you need love, then be prepared to receive more love than you ever bargained for. Stevie Wonder was right when he said, 'Love's in Need of Love today.'"

A smattering of applause rolled forth.

"… And, if you need some spiritual healing, then get ready to be healed."

"Yeah, right," hissed Mr. Skeptical, punching my shoulder.

"I can guarantee you this, you will not be the same person you were prior to coming here this evening. You are going to witness things you never imagined; things that aren't dependent on blind faith or trust. Tonight you will leave here assured that miracles do exist."

"This cat must think he's Rod Serling of the *Twilight Zone*. Listen to him."

"If you think we're going to put the pinch on you for money, or pass the plate around, forget about it. We're handing out pamphlets with our mailing address on them. You can send donations or comments directly to the address at the bottom. This is not a church service. It's a celebration! If you feel inclined to give us a donation by the end of the evening because we've added some value to your lives, then that's your call. If not, hey, that's cool, too. There is no pressure here. You get enough of that in your everyday life. Tonight's gathering is a time for unity. But you didn't come to see me… so without further adieu, let's crank it up and hop on board the love train with JJ Willis and the Studio All Stars!"

Brother-in-law JJ and his ensemble of renowned studio musicians zapped us with some torrid jazz laced with a Latin sound as multicolored stage lights flashed above the band. JJ had rounded up the "crème de la crème" of musicians. They didn't have popular name recognition but were highly respected by everyone in the biz—Francisco Gomez on lead guitar, James "Deacon" Harris on Keyboard, and Melvin "Die Hard" Cooper on drums; all of whom had played with a who's who lineup of stars. The band wore contemporary brightly colored tye dyed shirts with "Olisa" in hip-hop type across the front and "One love" on the back. And they burned the stage up with some hot bossa nova that got the crowd moving and grooving. Dancing broke out in random sections of the crowd. The sheer élan of the music made blood pressure and spirit rise simultaneously.

Performing next was one of the local black high schools choirs, offering a set of rollicking gospel numbers. They met with a rousing ovation from a crowd that unanimously decided, if we get nothing else out of this, let's at least enjoy the music.

It turned out to be kind of a nice break when Ulysses Ferguson, a avant-garde literary poet widely heralded on the college circuit, read some spiritual poetry, backed by Francisco on classical acoustic guitar.

The program flowed along nicely with a crowd that was into it on every level. Occasionally, there were sporadic bursts of, "We want Olisa." Jonathan strolled out again amidst more thundering Olisa screams, giving the crowd a long pause and a look like he was about to unveil the greatest secret in the world. Dramatically, he said, "If you want her so bad, you got her!" A huge roar arose from the crowd. "But first…"

"AAAWWW…" groaned the audience, cracking themselves up at their unanimous response.

Before Jon said another word, the band launched into a scathing rendition of James Brown's "Cold Sweat" and suddenly local boy turned famous—Oakwoods' pride and joy—Rapper Master Mookie X Moan (who just so happened to be a superstar on the RPM label) stormed out on the stage in a furious humping dance. Raising his fist, the band halted on cue as he faced the audience in a stare down, spreading his legs wide in a sexually defiant stance, eyeing the crowd through black geometric shades, mouth curled into a sensuous snarl, bald head glistening like a burnished light bulb.

The youngsters went stone stupid, hands rhythmically pushing toward the skies, mimicking him as he led them in this raucous gesture. In the hip-hop world he was the man: hard, former old G, DJ, dance master, and the Wizard of Rap. He stood menacingly, sizing up the crowd with a playful arrogance on his greyhound face. Mookie snatched the microphone, and the band kicked out more nasty "Cold Sweat" funk as his sandpapery voiced rap sliced through the salty sea air, attacking the song with a staccato rapid fire delivery that blazed wildly all over the song like a deranged uzi come to life. The tone was set off in his usual braggadocio style, but the words paid homage to God and its newfound messenger, Olisa. I vaguely remembered in a cover article in *Rolling Stone* magazine a brief blurb about the rapper finding God—obviously, Jonathan remembered, too.

Before long the hyped up crowd got in on the action voluntarily, chiming in on each chorus, pumped up higher than a helium balloon as the band delivered some serious first class funk.

I loved JJ. He rarely made sense when he opened his mouth, but you understood what he was throwing down when he thumped and stroked the hell out of his bass. His tiny dreads jumped around like Medusan snakes as his head pitched back and forth. Meanwhile, "Die Hard" beat the holy shit out of those drums like it was his last hurrah. Dancing spread through the crowd faster than the flu. They danced on the stage, on the pier, on the beach, everywhere. Age didn't matter; race was a non-issue. The house rocked.

I had to give Jon his props. If his goal was to wake the crowd up, he more than succeeded. They were pumped, revved up for a spiritual revival. The delayed start had long been forgotten.

When the band finished playing, the crowd begged for more. Mookie's gritty voice shouted, "What's up Westside! What's up Oakwood! Peeaaace. Thanks for givin' me some love, y'all. Thank you JJ, y'all is the bomb. Hear what I'm saying? Give 'em some love, people."

A huge enthusiastic cheer went up.

He waited for the screams to subside then said, "Hey, we want to thank y'all for coming to the first Spiritual Healing Concert. Yeah, this is one of them old-fashioned town hall meetings out here on the beach. Cause we're here for a purpose: To celebrate God… Yeah, that's right, give it up… and to celebrate life. We also want to pay tribute to a woman who fought for peace with her life a month ago… That's right, go on and clap. Show her some love, cuz we as a people need to see that this peace and love can continue!"

Screams of support zipped through the audience.

"Did we rock you, dawgs?"

The audience playfully barked, "Woof, woof, woof, woof."

He shook his head, talking to the crowd as if he were just hanging out in the streets. He sat down on the edge of the stage, arms encircling his bent knees as he held the mike up thoughtfully pausing and gazing into the crowd. His voice dropped to a whisper. "Whew! The lady I'm about to introduce to you is going to rock you, too. And, she's going to drop some stuff on you that will last far beyond the music.

"All of you who have invested your time and money in the God-cons and spiritual pimps of the universe are going to be in for a treat. This is the real deal. Hear what I'm saying? Sista's all the way live. It's like dis. When Jonathan came up to me and said would you like to do something for this program, ordinarily I'm all about gettin' paid, you know what I'm saying?"

"Heard that!"

"I did this stuff for free, cuz I want y'all to know about someone who can help you in your life, just like God did mine. I ain't layin' no born again stuff on you or tellin' you how to be saved by going home and reading your bible or Koran or whatever. Don't get me wrong, ain't nothing wrong with that either, but I'm talking about someone who can help us tonight!"

"Amen."

"Yeah I was out there… Just like some of you other hardheads… Bustin' ass, knockin' fools out, taking money, sellin' drugs, doin' drugs, all that stupid crazy ass shit! Until the day I met a gangsta badder than me. Same old story, y'all read it… dude shot my ass five times over some fly lady I was layin' up with. The truth is, I should have been a dead muthafucker—another young black male statistic. I wasn't famous, yet, so what the fuck difference would it have made to find another nigga dead? They'd say he probably got what he deserved!"

"That's right! That's the way shit goes down, homes."

"Ain't it?!" he said, nonchalantly flipping the mike in his hand. "But this nigga wasn't going anywhere! This homeboy lived to see another morning!"

"That's right!"

"Why? Because God didn't punch in my time card. God gave me a second chance, and I did all I knew how to do—rap."

"Uh-huh… Tell it!"

"So there was no way was I going to refuse to be a part of this. When Jon Carpenter asked for my services I was honored, cuz I know this lady can help a whole lot of people out there get a second chance."

He stood up and started strutting as the stage persona returned.

"I opened my heart out to y'all, so the least you can do is join me in welcoming the star of this show! I want everybody, and I mean everybody that wants peace to clap your hands. Don't hold back shit! If you ain't down with peace, then take your sorry butt on outta here! Ain't no room at the inn! Let me hear y'all say PEEAAACE!"

"PEEAACE!!!"

"Act like you're in church! I said, PEEEEAAAACE!"

"PEEEEAAAACE!"

"Talk to me Los Angeles… Say whaaat?"

"PEEAAACE!"

"It don't matter if you black, brown, yellow, red, or white. We need…"

"PEEEEEAAAACCCE!"

"All right then. This wonderful lady wants peace, too… in this city, in this nation, and in this world. But she ain't spoke in front of a crowd this large before, so she's feeling a little shy. I told her we ain't never experienced anybody like her before either, so we even. C'mon now and put your hands together for the flyest lady in the City of Angels. She don't care about mayoral awards and government citations, all she needs is your love."

They began stomping and applauding rhythmically as a sampler of the rock group Queen blared from the speakers, "We will, we will rock you!"

"Meet the one shining soul in all of Los Angeles. Meet Olisa."

There was a huge ovation followed by a chant, "Olisa, Olisa, Olisa," as Mookie conducted the cheers, waving his hands and swaying with the multitude.

How could she sustain this type of energy? The band had done a fantastic job of creating a celebratory urgency to the evening, but I feared the ending was going to be anti-climactic. I had only seen Olisa with small informal groups, how would she interact with an audience this size? Even with a microphone, I couldn't imagine her soft-spoken demeanor penetrating through to this rowdy group.

But my worries eventually suffered a quiet burial.

She stepped onto the stage barefoot, and a hush befell the expectant crowd. All you heard was the isolated rattle of the empty Santa Monica West Coaster Roller coaster.

She paused on the corner of the stage, obviously overwhelmed by the large turnout—people ogling and aahing, fingers pointing toward her as if they were observing the landing of the mother ship. For a second, I didn't think our star attraction was going to take another step forward as she surveyed the audience. At the opposite end of the stage, Jon applauded vigorously, smiling and bidding her to move forward. Only I noticed the nervous tics bouncing on his face piercing the calm veneer. Just when I thought he was about ready to lasso her, she languidly trekked forward, moving into an arena that offered no turning back. Logan swirled around her like a ballerina, his camera snapping like a teething puppy as he attempted to capture life's defining moments in that little box.

Demurely, she reached center stage, keeping her eyes almost entirely on the comforting presence of the band members who were playing a beautiful gospel tinged musical interlude and deferentially bowing one by one as she passed by. Junior stepped forward and kissed his niece on the cheek.

She nodded and pressed her heart with both hands slowly and repeatedly like a mother receiving her favorite sons as thank you's were mouthed to the band members.

The humorous twist of the evening was seeing Mookie Moan, the stud prince of Rap, shyly greeting her like an acolyte to a priest as he handed her the microphone. Noticeably shaking, she set it down on a podium that was hastily set up by one of the stagehands and tenderly caressed the side of his face with one hand as she studied it like an aged map by firelight. I don't think he ever wanted to let go as he held her hand possessively to his face. Suddenly, and without warning, he crumpled into her arms like a deflated balloon. A couple of the stagehands moved forward, but she quickly waved them off massaging the back of his head with her hand.

The superstar rapper changed into a quivering young man, dark glasses askew, and the back of his hands rubbing his eyes. She continued to hold him up, releasing him when his body straightened like a capsized surfboard. The shades fell back over his eyes, but he kept his head down as he inched back gesturing toward the mike.

Olisa was genuinely surprised and touched by the whole affair. Even though the program was masterfully orchestrated by Jonathan, nothing could substitute for the heart and soul that went into it. As she stepped up to the podium, fixing her shy gaze upon us, she looked like the village girl who suddenly discovered that some quirk of fate made her queen of the realm.

She was made up to look the part, too, wearing a resplendent white gown and a high African gele headdress. Her shining high cheekbones naturally endowed her with an air of nobility. She looked gorgeous, but I couldn't find my daughter within the mask. Jonathan's people had slathered on the makeup.

Although she tried to portray a good front, she was uncomfortable. Her confidence and decorum seemed to wane with the dying of applause. Her body continually shifted as she waded through an intimidating stack of notes perched on the podium, staring at them as if they had converted into mocking cartoon faces.

"Oh my God, the band, Mookie Moan, all the performers were so fabulous… I don't know how I can… I just need a minute," she mumbled as she quickly shuffled through the pile of formal notes glaring with intimidation at her. The honeymoon was over, and she was expected to perform as the strain visibly seeped into her face. In a corner of the stage, Jonathan hunched like the ghost of Ed Sullivan.

It was awful watching Olisa's panic take shape. This was not at all what she had imagined for herself, and I didn't know how she was going to handle this humiliating breakdown as the crowd's restless murmurings began to intensify. I blamed myself for not putting my foot down a little harder.

And I blamed Jonathan.

Why did he force her to take on something she wasn't suited for? It just wasn't Olisa. But it didn't matter now. We needed to get her off that stage. Already Jonathan and Rapper Mookie Moan were casually moving toward her like an emergency rescue crew but then froze when a cavernous bass voice thundered from the audience.

"Take your time, girl, no one's rushing you. We'll stay here as long as it takes… All night if we have to. Just say what you feel. It's all good. All we ask you to do is keep it real!"

Suddenly a chorus of encouraging and supportive voices followed.

For the first time that evening, a relaxed smile alighted on Olisa's face as she gazed for a long time in the direction from which the voice emerged. She leaned on the podium, eyeing the audience mischievously. Carefully lifting the pile of papers like a ceremonial rite, she hurled them up into the air with such force that they swirled to the ground, flapping like hundreds of butterflies around her as she raised her hands victoriously.

Meanwhile, Jonathan looked shell-shocked until he heard the crowd screaming like they were watching Pete Townsend smashing his guitar. His grimace coalesced into a grin.

"Would someone please help me remove this podium?" Olisa asked. "We are not going to need it."

Jonathan pounced on it as he clapped his hands and emphatically gestured for the stagehands to get it out of the way!

"Thank you very much. I don't need a prop. I don't need a church to praise God. God is everywhere! It reminds me of how a few years ago, one of my closest friends, Laura, who happens to be backstage, took me to see the redwoods. When I entered that magnificent forest full of trees thousands of years old, I fell to my knees and cried like a little baby. It was one of the most spiritual and humbling sights I have ever beheld. Nothing had been marred by man's hands. Once again it reaffirmed to me that no manmade cathedral could ever bring me to my knees faster than God's green earth!"

Her eyes were closed in earnest, face lifted toward the sky, arms outstretched, one hand gripping the mic, the other hand was palm up with her fingers slowly opening and closing.

"Can you feel it? Can you feel it? Can you feel God's love? OOOHHH, it feels so good so wonderful to know we are blessed by God's presence," she cried out in ecstasy. "The sweet smell of the sea air… The touch of a breeze on our faces, a warm cool night… Wait… Listen to the sound of the waves… Can you hear it? Look at the stars… Oh, these miracles of life surround us each day. Isn't God's love wonderful?"

A chorus of yeses met her. Even if you didn't feel it, her sincerity made up for it. You believed that she believed.

There was sustained applause as she bathed joyously in our adulation, hands clasped prayerfully against her breast. When she finally opened those unfathomable eyes her gaze swept us and she said, "Thank you so much for letting me be a part of your gathering this evening. Sometimes that's all we really need; the knowledge that we're here for each other. This evening, you've made me feel loved and welcomed. Your applause and your giving spirit humble me. I am very grateful."

Her resonating voice was so powerful and engrossing that it sliced into our emotions. Yet, at the same time it was intimate and personal.

"The last couple of weeks, I've been groomed and rehearsed in anticipation of meeting you. I've tried to be all the things I think you want me to be. Aren't you flattered?" she asked, raising her eyebrows coquettishly. As she spoke, she unwrapped her headdress while lithely walking around the stage.

"But what it really comes down to is being yourself—right?"

A resounding "yes" punched the sky.

She pulled the last of the wrap, unfastened a hair clip and with a sharp shake, her hair tumbled down dramatically. Tropical vines of African braids fell into place around her shoulders like rank and file soldiers.

"Well I can try to be myself, but in the end it won't be enough. Anything that happens tonight will be because of us, not me. You didn't think you were going to kick back while I did all the work, did you?"

I was amazed that she could make them laugh at their own expectations.

"It's our faith that will make it possible. We are here to celebrate God, and life, and each other. We are here to build a united wall, a fortress of love that will not offer refuge to hatred or violence."

"No!"

"I am you and you are me. We are all flesh and blood. Our spirits are not grounded by such limitations. Ultimately, it is not our bodies we must nurture, but our spirits. That is the only way we will be able to transcend the vulgarities and inanities of life."

"Tell it."

She stood on the edge of the stage with her hands clasped around the microphone then turned and pointed at Jonathan. "That man over there is my little brother, Jonathan. I love him so much, but every once in awhile, he has this habit of putting his foot in his mouth. He promised you miracles. However, I can't promise that."

She paused weighing her words very carefully.

"Many of you saw or heard that I healed a young man this past summer. I didn't do it—God did. It all came from God. I was simply the vehicle. Miracles are not my promise to give. Only God can dictate that. And if the Creator grants it, then, yes, tonight you will see miracles."

"Yeah, right, here we go… Time for the big cop out," blasted the resurrected voice of my old World War II friend.

Luckily, she couldn't hear him as she hunched down and studied the multitude of eager upturned faces.

"I am so happy to see so many of you here. Even those of you who are trying so hard to put on your 'Joe Daddy Cool' masks, but your eyes give you away. Your eyes tell the truth. They tell me you care. I'm sure some of you only came out curiosity. I don't blame you. Hearing all those bizarre rumors about some witch in Venice would have gotten me to show up."

She waited until the nervous laughter abated.

"Or, maybe I'm being vain and you didn't come to see me at all. Maybe you came to catch a glimpse of the lovely Eva Sanchez."

Olisa acknowledged Eva's presence in the audience by blowing a kiss. Eva was out of my vision, but it was easy to ascertain her vicinity by the way the crowd wadded up.

"Or, maybe you came to view the tightrope act and see if I'd slip and fall on my bottom. It's possible. I'm not real agile. Whatever your reason, I believe you care about the state of our world and want it to change for the better."

Olisa zeroed in on a couple of boys down front. "No one else may be able to see it, but I can, it's there… I know it."

They hid their faces under their caps as she grinned.

Her voice descended to a whisper, yet snapped like a basketball whizzing through a net.

"What happened on July the 4th was an act of spontaneity. It was not planned, despite what some of our friends in the media say." She chuckled. "At that moment I found I cared more for those kids trying to hurt themselves, than my own welfare. Why else would some skinny, little black chick run out there and audition as a carving board for Thanksgiving?"

"Amen, sister."

"And I didn't say that to seek pats on the back, because the next time something breaks out, I might be the one elbowing a few people to get by."

People laughed, but I don't think anyone sincerely believed she would ever abandon anyone.

"That evening taught me something. I learned if we can find a way to put aside our own needs and learn to love, respect, and appreciate each other without expectation, miracles will happen. But it calls for self-sacrifice. I know it's not easy. It's the hardest thing in life to do. But we can try."

"That's why you don't see any miracles coming out of me, cause I love myself too much," joked someone from the audience.

"And that's all right, my brother." Olisa smiled. "You should love yourself, but just try and ration a little bit for us, too."

Smiling, he nodded and displayed the peace sign.

"I heard y'all singing 'one love' earlier. It's not a cliché. One love will set us free. It will shape the future of things to come. You see, love is the fulcrum for spontaneity. When we're in love we don't stop to think, we react. If we can love and forgive each other without restraint, then we will wield true power and together create miracles that will shock the world."

"Tonight, I'm going to ask you to love me as I love you. And, I ask that for just one minute of your lives, you focus on loving the person next to you more than yourself. Don't freak out. Just for a minute."

"JJ, give me the countdown. Now don't cheat! Here we go, repeat after me—I love you more than I love myself. C'mon, look at each other, and say it. Don't stop, you'll see, it feels good! C'mon now—say it! I can't hear you!"

Hundreds chanted, "I love you more than I love myself."

"Oh, see, you don't want to stop, do you?" Olisa laughed, doing a seal clap with her hands. She still held the microphone in her hand, and each clap sounded like thunder. "I love it. You may not want to admit it, but it not only makes you feel good, it makes you feel powerful, huh?"

"This is what we are trying to bring to the formation of our new organization. We entitled it O.L.I.S.A., Inc. mainly because we're not real creative," she replied with self-deprecating humor, which I was glad to see since no one would know that she fought tooth and nail not to have her name included in the title.

"It means, One Love Inspires Spiritual Awakening." She waved off the cheers. "The primary purpose of our organization is to prove that our love will not only heal the world, it will be our salvation."

Her eyes then swept the audience, and she spoke for about twenty more arresting minutes, unlike any preacher I have ever heard.

She didn't rain fire and brimstone on us.

She didn't wage war upon our moral conscience and turpitude.

She didn't dig our graves and make us lie down in it for the shameless sinners we are.

Nor did she shovel heaps of guilt, fear, and self-worthlessness upon our psyches until we begged for forgiveness and redemption.

She only spoke of love.

About how living a life guided by love and compassion is the way to un-complicate our existence. She even quoted Mother Theresa, "A life not lived for others is not a life."

"This is not right, not right at all," she said abruptly. "I shouldn't be standing here above you. I should be among you." And to my chagrin, she passed the microphone to her befuddled brother, signaling for him to follow her as she strode down the stair steps and into the eager arms of the crowd.

At the bottom of the stairs, she was quickly greeted by a concerned Alton who leaned over and whispered something in her ear. Smiling, she stood up on her toes, kissed his cheek and gently pushed him aside as Jonathan held the microphone aloft.

"We are all family tonight. I have nothing to fear from anyone out here, not when I walk with God."

There was fervent applause and cheers as she waded into the mass of onlookers. It looked like a New Orleans parade with Jonathan by her side holding the microphone aloft like a candle, Alton on the other, Logan zipping back and forth holding his camera high and shooting away. A caravan of stern countenanced bodyguards, lumbered behind Olisa as she glided through the crowd.

"We aren't here to promote religion or declare that our belief is the only way to salvation. We are here to seek cooperation among all faiths and build a bridge of change. All we care about tonight are these four letters: L-O-V-E."

"Human beings aren't born violent. As babies, we want to be held, caressed, and loved, but society has taught us how to hate, how to attack, and how to think. The negativity recycles itself, sprouting new arms and legs. Isn't it time to ask yourself how long do you want this vicious cycle to continue?"

Olisa stopped the caravan in front of a young white teenage girl with loping curls of chestnut hair whose hands were clamped to her elbows.

"When do you want it to end, girlfriend?"

"Right now! I just can't deal with it anymore!"

"That's right—now!" Olisa agreed, her eyes sparkling like hot flames. "So you and I will start it off with a hug. How's that sound?"

"Okay," the girl agreed reluctantly, bowing her head. Her jaws tightened as she fought back the tears.

Olisa reached out and gave the girl a prolonged hug. Finally she pulled back, holding her by the shoulders and reading her face.

"Look at that beautiful evening sky. Doesn't it feel magical?"

"Yes…"

"Do you know how vital it is for you to hold that feeling in your heart?" she asked, gently massaging the girl's temples.

The girl nodded as the tears flowed freely.

"You are a very special person. Yet, he condemns you for not being good enough. You aren't listening to him are you?"

The girl shook her head slowly.

"You wonder if he loves you enough. Move on with your life. Don't try to convince him or change him. If he truly loves you, he will figure it all out. I hate to say it, but he may have to experience the pain of losing you before he realizes what he truly has."

"Uh, thanks. Wow," she said smashing her curls with both hands and shaking her head, "That's awesome, that's exactly what…"

Her sentence was lost to infinity. The caravan had moved on.

"I love you more than I love myself. Say it, even if you don't believe it. Even if it feels funny. It gets easier with each repetition."

She stopped in front of a young Filipino male with bright orange hair and an open Hawaiian shirt, displaying his washboard stomach.

"Aww I can't say all that, you know, that's not me, I don't love anyone more than I love me…"

"Do you love your mother?"

"Of course. But that's family."

"Tonight we're your family, too."

"All right. Cool. How about I just say I love the way you look better than me," he said, cutting his eyes flirtatiously at her.

"I'd say you're getting close, but you've got a little more work to do," she laughed, hugging him.

"We are not recruiting religions, but soldiers who will help to create a better place for ourselves and our children…"

"Horseshit!!"

Mr. World War II, pushed his way through the crowd, meeting Olisa face to face. Alton expanded as he slid in front of her, supported by the jeering onlookers.

"I think you've said enough, partner," Alton warned him.

"You don't scare me!"

"That's what makes my job more enjoyable."

Olisa poked Alton's double-barreled biceps.

"We don't need to go there, let him speak, Gumbo." She raised her arms and waved for silence. "What is it you want to say to me, sir?"

"Thank you. My name is Fred Plechas, ma'am, and I take offense to people casually tossing about the word 'soldier.' You are talking about me and all my comrades, alive or dead. I am also a proud American citizen who would have gladly fought in Korea, Vietnam, the Gulf, or wherever this country asked me to go. You'd never find me hiding in some Canadian rat hole like some of the other draft dodgers and cowards roaming around in this country who have now traded in their yellow streaks for white collars…"

A cascade of boos and heckles fell on him, but he was unperturbed, "I've been around long enough to know when someone's playing peek-a-boo behind five dollar words."

"Why do you say that, Mr. Plechas?"

"Because you're a fraud, Miss. You don't have any special powers. You're just like all the rest of them preachers, trying to steal hardworking people's money. You're just prettier to look at. You think all this spiritual garbage and kissin' and huggin' is going to make us forget you're supposed to be some kind of miracle worker? I didn't forget. You can try to fool all these youngsters out here by disguising your failings with all this high-powered music, but it doesn't move me no way. Where are the miracles, lady?"

I felt like whooping his ass with that cane he was leaning on until I caught Olisa's eyes. They were as nebulous as desert sand until she spotted me—suddenly they brightened and there was an easy smile on her face.

"Some of us out here want a miracle so bad we'll probably invent one in our tiny little heads and go screaming to *Hard Copy* or *Nightline* about it. Or, maybe you hired some out of work actors to pretend to be saved at the right moment. Is that what you did with that rapper up there? Does Mr. foul-mouth have a percentage in your new company?"

"No, Mr. Plechas."

"Doesn't matter. The bottom line is, you're just as big a crook as all the rest of them nitwits out there."

"Is that what you believe, Mr. Plechas?"

"Damn right. I call it as I see it. You can't snowball me. I've seen the best, and it ain't gonna to happen to me. Being a soldier in the United States of America is the most noble profession there is."

"What bullshit... read the paper, man... sexual harassment, gay bashing, conspiracy..." yelled a man behind him with a beard twisted into two short pig tails and a long red pigtail trailing down his back and ham hock arms.

"And I'm not going to let you sully it with a lot of malarkey. You couldn't possibly know what being a true patriot is all about!" he scowled. "Look at you, boy! You look like a beached whale. Ain't they told you the war is over? You don't have to piss behind Canadian trees anymore!"

"Fuck you, old man."

"There you go, a prime example of what I'm talking about—ignorant liberal buffoons who are willing to accept anything. I only came here to see how you were going to con people into believing you could do miracles. But it's already the same old hype," he muttered with disdain.

The boo birds in the audience pounced on him, but he persevered, arms belligerently crossed as he glared at Olisa. She raised her hands, patting the air like a quarterback trying to silence the home crowd. "Please, why are you berating this man? He volunteered his opinion. Respect his right to communicate, regardless of whether you agree or disagree with him. You might be surprised. I partly agree with him."

The silence tumbled down like a broken stage curtain. Even Plechas eyed her suspiciously.

"Mr. Plechas, it's true, I've been avoiding the part in the show where the woman performs a miracle. But not for the reasons *you* think. I didn't want the real message to be overshadowed. My plan was to get people to realize that we are all potentially capable of healing one another and performing miracles.

"But it's never enough is it? You saw through my act, Mr. Plechas. Maybe God is calling me through you. I've got a feeling, the time is now."

She took a deep breath, her shoulders rising as she squeezed her hands together.

She stepped forward and Plechas stepped backwards.

"Okay, Mr. Plechas, what do you want me to do?"

He was caught off guard as his eyes flitted nervously, mugged by the angry silence. He rubbed the elbow of the stiff arm that looked soldered to his eagle-headed cane. The knotted nose that had been to a few bar fists in its time faded in and out of its scarlet coloring as he habitually flicked his thumb and pulled on each nostril as if he were going to sneeze.

"Hell, I don't know. You're the so-called expert. Must be some people around here that need your kind of help. Just look around."

"No, I'm more interested in you, Mr. Plechas. How can I help *you*? Do you need a miracle in your life?"

"Huh?"

"Why don't you move closer, Mr. Plechas, so I can give you a hug?"

"Huh? Oh no, I'm not into that type of stuff… Pick somebody else…" He refused to budge, eyeing her warily.

"You're not afraid, are you?"

"Don't be ridiculous!"

"Then let me show you the innocence of a hug."

"Huh? Geez. Sure. If that's what will make you happy… no big deal," he replied, wiping the sweat off his face. He stepped forward with his right leg rising and falling like an accordion.

He reached out to formally shake her hands, but she pulled him inside her arms and held him tightly. His arms dangled limply, helplessly, fingers wiggling.

"How long has your leg been injured?"

"Uh, uh, it's been over forty years, took a couple of bullets on the battlefield," he recounted shakily.

"Did you receive a purple heart?"

"Yes, ma'am."

"That's wonderful. You must be proud."

"Yes, ma'am."

"Relax, Mr. Plechas, stop fighting me. The sensation you feel is God's love flowing through you," she whispered. Jonathan inched the microphone closer to her mouth.

"Mr. Plechas, I can tell you have suffered deep hurt in your lifetime. I wish I could have been there for you. You're a widower, aren't you?"

"Yeah, yeah."

"You lost her several years ago, and you miss her like it was yesterday. I can feel your pain. It's been buried for a long time, huh?"

Olisa's face was skewed in anguish.

"She believed, didn't she… Your wife, that is? She never lost faith that a cure would be available for her one day. She saw doctors, priests, ministers, spiritualists, and psychics. You spent almost all of your savings, but then the cancer spread too fast and she died, leaving you alone to pick up the pieces. I couldn't help you then, but God is here now. And, I can tell you your wife is better than she's ever been. Cappy, she wants you to move on with your life."

Several bystanders shrieked as his body jerked spasmodically like he was being riddled with bullets from ferocious cross fire. Sweat glistened on his face as his hands weakly pushed against her chest. He retreated, moving, stepping, feinting like a boxer, struggling to distance himself from her. Disorientation smothered his face. The scraggly chicken hairs sprouting from his head were no longer protected by the cap that fell off during the convulsions. I doubt if he heard Olisa's gentle entreaties as his eyes guardedly watched her. He tripped over someone's foot and fell to the ground like he had been dropped from the sky.

Olisa bent down and picked up his cap, slipping it back over his head and offering him a hand.

His hands scrambled over hers like crabs as he lowered his eyes deferentially. His lips remained unhinged.

"She's the only one that ever called me Cappy—short for Captain America. How in the hell could you have known that?"

"I'm sorry I couldn't do anything for your leg, Mr. Plechas."

"I guess it was not God's will," he intoned sarcastically, still eyeing her suspiciously.

"I suppose not. It appears God found it more vital to rid you of the cancer wracking your body."

At first I thought Plechas had fallen into some mud as he vigorously wiped at the black substance layered on his arm, but it wasn't mud. It was some kind of black bile oozing from his mouth and settling on his shirt like an oil spill. When he grasped what was happening, his eyes were as wide as tea plates. Gurgling sounds emanated from his throat as the panic made him gag.

"This is not right! Get away from me! You really are some kind of witch, aren't you? What have you done to me?"

"You have been given the chance to breathe again, Mr. Plechas. How does it feel?" The compassion flowing in her eyes was so beautiful it pained me.

"You don't have to be afraid of me, Mr. Plechas. I just wish I could have been a part of your life sooner."

He groaned sickly as the look he gave Olisa vacillated between praise and vilification. A hairy arm plucked his cap, which had fallen to the ground again and torpedoed it through the air.

"Oh my God, oh my God, " shouted Mr. Plechas giddily. "I…feel…great! Do you hear me—great! I *can* feel it… The cancer *is* gone! I don't believe it. No pain! How in God's name did you do it?" he asked, snatching her arm, and then sheepishly releasing her as he was struck by the ignorance of his question.

"Oh, what a big, dumb, fool I've been. I'm… Can you ever forgive me?"

She laid her hand gently on his shoulder. "Mr. Plechas, enjoy your new life."

Crossing his arms and grabbing his shoulders, he dropped to his knees, swaying autistically as cigarettes from his breast pocket spilled lifelessly to the ground. The mixture of laughter and tears coming from him were as incongruent as a snow blizzard in July.

Olisa and I locked eyes for a second, but a mass of bodies sealed the gap. Raucous cheering, whistling, and amen's filled the night air. Someone invoked Olisa's name with the urgency of an ailing child. Cappy's hat flew through the air back and forth like a Frisbee.

To my relief, the next time I saw Olisa, Alton hurriedly marched her back up the stairs to the stage.

"I'm sorry to say that management has informed us that I need to stay up here or they will close the show earlier than expected."

There was a loud groan.

"I agree with you, but we don't want any accidents out here tonight. We are here to heal each other, not hurt each other. Okay?"

"Amen."

"So we're just going to have to bring some folks up here."

Before the evening ended, two more people were escorted up to the stage and successfully healed: a blind East Indian boy and a woman with severe arthritis. Both were filled with such awe and gratitude that they refused to leave the stage until the show was over, as if their departure might break the spell of enchantment, and they'd revert to their former selves.

Glancing at my watch, I was happy to see it was almost 9:00 p.m. The City of Santa Monica required that all events on the pier conclude by 9:30 P.M. Olisa was showing signs of visible exhaustion, so I was happy to see it coasting to a close.

"We are all blessed with the ability to heal each other. It is not all physical. Sometimes it can be as simple as telling a friend how much you love them and assuring them you will always be there. We must truly learn to love ourselves and each other, and to forgive one another for the sins, the hurts we have perpetrated upon each other. Healing the spirit, is the cure to all the world's ills."

But about twenty minutes later, that message whizzed over their heads faster than planes arriving and departing from LAX.

She knelt down on one knee, cuddling the little boy who's effervescent smile was contagious. He constantly touched his eyelids to assure himself it wasn't a dream. He had regained the sight lost to him in a hit and run accident several years ago when he was only five years old. This same accident took the life of his mother, his father tearfully informed us before Olisa laid her soothing hands over his eyes.

Kids, God bless them, they don't prescribe to any body's sense of time or diplomacy. As Olisa was concluding her speech, the little boy had been restlessly moving around in her arms to the point of distraction. Finally he blurted out, "Ms. Olisa, Ms. Olisa look at that man! That's Merlin, the Magician," he exclaimed. "Will you ask him to come up here? He's sitting right over there."

Olisa's eyes skirted around, finally settling.

"I see who you're talking about, Ravi, though I don't think his real name is Merlin. We only have a little time left, maybe we can induce the gentleman to come up here and join us. Sir, would you mind?"

Everyone turned their heads, searching for this Merlin character. It was then that I noticed a very large man in the audience with shoulders as wide as a landing strip. His short icy white hair shimmered in the darkness. How could I have missed him? He towered head and shoulders over everyone else. My heart skyrocketed when he turned his head; even the dark shades couldn't conceal the fact that he saw me, too. He moved aside to let a woman pushing a man in a wheelchair emerge. They proceeded reticently up a ramp on the side of the stage. When they rolled toward center stage, my heart leaped again.

Jonathan gawked like he had seen a ghost.

The woman was Lena Cavaliere.

And the Merlin look-alike was none other than Nick Cavaliere wearing horn rimmed glasses and a black fedora. His dark hair streaked with swaths of gray trickled down to his shoulders, and his beard rested on his chest. I forgot that one of the last roles Nick Cavaliere played before the accident was Merlin in an epic remake of the "Sword and the Stone." And this kid spotted him and made the association. No one else did. No one had seen Nick in two years. Even the tabloids had only captured sketchy pictures of him these past two years.

Glancing back over my shoulder, I was not surprised to see the big fella had vanished.

"Are you Merlin, sir?" Ravi asked innocently.

"I wish I was, son."

"You sure look like him."

I could understand where the child was coming from, but I don't think the movie Merlin ever matched the agony on this one's face.

"Why do you look so sad, Mr. Merlin? Don't you know that Ms. Olisa can help you, too?"

"I certainly hope so, young man." His voice sounded like his throat was jammed by hundreds of cotton balls.

Olisa nodded wearily. "If it is God's will you will be healed."

I don't think Olisa had any idea of who it was, not that it made a difference.

She leaned over him, sandwiching his head in her hands. Her braids obscured his face.

"Do you believe in God, my friend?"

"I used to. I can't honestly say what I believe now."

"Do you believe you can be healed this evening?"

"I-I-I don't know… I hope so… Yes, what do you want me to say?"

"The Creator's love is so powerful that it doesn't really matter. Miracles happen whether you believe in them or not."

The crowd's silence was intense as she laid her head on his shoulder. She locked her arms around his body and pressed him tightly against hers in an almost sensual embrace.

"God loves you and wants you to know that your spirit is far more important than anything else the physical world can offer. You are ready to give up, but like your wife, I won't let you."

Tears rolled down his cheeks, pooling in the creases of her elbow. Hearing his tormented cries made the palms of my hands moisten. His eyes were squeezed shut, cheeks puffing, and the veins in his temples protruded so far out I thought they were going to burst through his skin.

A barrage of unintelligible words streamed out of his mouth as if he were speaking in tongues. His eyes rolled into the back of his head, and he continued to babble, no longer caring about the onlookers. The air was hauntingly still.

His head fell back and no other words came out of his mouth.

"Now you know the power of true love. There are no masks to hide behind here. You are free. You can stand up any time you're ready. Just let go of my arms first." She laughed.

His head sprung forward. He was unaware that he had been clutching her elbows. His euphoric howl glided through the air, louder than the seagulls.

"Lena…" he shouted excitedly. "Look at me, Lena. My hands… Oh sweet Lord… Can you believe it? Do you see what I'm doing?"

"Yes! Yes! I see! I see!" Lena shouted back, her fingers fumbling to unhinge the belt that imprisoned him to the chair.

Gingerly, he rose from his wheelchair.

Lena's eyes were so big I swear I could see the green in her irises from where I stood as she watched in stupefaction. The closer he came to standing completely upright, the more she hopped like a game show contestant.

Some of the youngsters were ecstatically yelling, "Go Merlin, go Merlin, go Merlin…"

Ravi held Nick by the waist as he giddily wrapped one arm around the kid. He looked like a first time rollerblader trying to maintain his balance. Olisa snaked his other arm around Lena's trembling shoulders.

The stage looked like an outtake from a David Lynch film: a Merlin clone supported by a black woman, a white woman, an East Indian kid; surrounded by a bunch of hip looking musicians, and Jonathan "Don King" Carpenter raising Nick's arm high in the air as if he'd just won the greatest title fight in history.

But the Cadillac was just rounding the corner.

Nick Cavaliere wasn't the only one with a flair for drama. Jonathan slowly removed Nick's hat and glasses.

Till this day I still get goose bumps from the scream that became the clarion call for the end of our privacy. I always joked it was Eva Sanchez who squealed because this had truly become the biggest story of the year, decade, maybe even century.

"Isn't that Nick Cavaliere? Yes, yes, that's Nick Cavaliere! No it's not. Yes, it is. Nick Cavaliere!"

Those two words—Nick Cavaliere—whizzed through the crowd faster than e-mail. After awhile it turned into a chant. Heads bobbed up and down clamoring for a better view and jockeying around like hungry seals awaiting raw fish to be thrown.

Nick Cavaliere.

SOUL EYES

You couldn't have scripted a more perfect Hollywood ending as he fought to stay on his feet. I could just hear the epic John Williams score playing in the background as the credits rolled.

People randomly dropped to their hands and knees as if they had been smitten by virulent plague. Others were huddled and wailing at the top of their lungs, faces heavenward as their hands fluttered above their heads. The newly sanctified made a trampoline out of the pier as they exuberantly bounced up and down proclaiming the appearance of the Holy Ghost. Those speaking in Spanish called it *Espiritu Santo* (the Holy Spirit). Many individuals wore solemn expressions and clasped their hands tightly together as they recited the Lord's Prayer, their lips moving slowly and deliberately.

This was about as close to a preview of Judgment Day as I'd ever want to see.

The healing of Nick Cavaliere single-handedly legitimized to all who were present that this was no sleight-of-hand feat, but an authentic honest to God miracle. Nick and his career were resurrected from the grave like a modern day Lazarus.

As I watched Nick standing on his own, hands clasped shakily above his head, Olisa collapsed into Alton's rock solid arms as he rushed her backstage.

I shoved my way through the throngs of people, ignoring the incoherent patter assaulting my ears. But I wasn't the only one. A tidal wave of people, mostly teenagers, rushed the stage. My pronouncements about being Olisa's father were like trying to find a contact lens outside during a blizzard. Instead, I was met by reptilian stares and hands that smacked my chest and knocked me backwards as I collided into other flying bodies. While getting up, I dodged a person rolling past me like a bowling ball. He immediately jumped up and dissolved into the wall of humanity surging forward.

Mass hysteria.

The emotional decibels were turned up so high the pent up energy searched for some type of release. The bodyguards were affected by it, too. Their faces may have been carved in stone, but their eyes were overtaken by fear. Adrenaline rushed through them like rapids as they pushed and strong-armed folks around with far more brute force than necessary. They couldn't help themselves. They were fighting more than just the crowd. They were battling against what our primal ancestors have always feared—the unexplained forces of nature—magic, superstition, God. It was the "fight or flight" syndrome. I think they wanted to run; run as far away as possible till they could sort it all out and place it in a nice tidy compartment in the back of their minds. The same way I had been doing for so many years.

Eventually, the hyped up crowd overwhelmed the meager number of security forces and hurdled on stage victoriously. They wanted the magic to last forever. They danced, gyrated and lustily celebrated, grabbing whatever souvenirs they could get their hands on. Many tussled over the microphone, stand, podium, wheelchair, and notes, anything Olisa had touched. They ripped wood from the stage as if it had been anointed with holy water.

Soon an angry megaphone blasted orders for them to disperse, followed by an aggregation of helmeted riot police marching into the crowd, carrying batons and rifles loaded with rubber bullets. Having been the recipient of a couple of errant batons in my youth, I didn't have any problem heeding the advice. Particularly since the guards had been able to get the performers offstage long before the celebrants had wrested control. I confidently assumed that my family knew better than to wait for me in the limousine. I'd get home fine. I only prayed that they would, too.

Meanwhile, police helicopters flashed their spotlights in a dizzying array of lights, transforming the night into artificial day, accompanied by network news copters just receiving word that a potentially full-scale riot was taking shape on the pier. I saw camera operators and reporters from all the major networks scurrying to the scene and interviewing everyone they could to get some sense of what was going on.

Luckily, things were already beginning to quiet down, and it didn't look like it would be as bad as I originally thought. Yes, a few rambunctious souls got roughed up and carted away, but there were no further skirmishes and the excitement fizzled out. No one really wanted any trouble. This was a riot fueled by people needing to burn off energy, not anger. For all the attendees it was a great night beset by a celebration that got out of hand. Many people aided the officers in calming people down.

As I headed toward the "blue" bus stop, I saw Mr. Plechas holding court in front of the merry-go-round with a group of reporters who poked microphones toward his throat while he talked. He had acquired quite a few new friends since the last time I saw him. They patted him on the back while he spoke animatedly about the evening's experience.

Actually, I was more surprised Eva Sanchez wasn't scurrying around competing for interviews. Knowing her, she was probably already at the station.

"God bless you, brother."

"Yeah. You, too, man," I replied, layering it with a little more bass than usual. A burly biker clad in snatches of black leather drunkenly stumbled into my path with his beefy arm cupped around his Cruella De Ville-haired girlfriend. He swigged beer from a can and splashed most of it on her bony shoulder. However, this didn't even elicit a blink from her droopy eyes.

"Do you accept Jesus in your heart, brother?"

I nodded affirmatively hoping this would prevent a drunken dissertation.

In those murky eyes sheltered under foliage of thick bushy eyebrows, he buckled a little as he sized me up. In another day and time, if he had been with his buds, he might have had more fun trying to kick my ass instead of quoting scripture—but, alas, this was a night reserved for miracles.

"Good," he said, finally patting my shoulder after a couple of intoxicated misses, "because the end is near. Only those who believe in Jesus, our Lord and Savior, will live in our father's kingdom. You must beware of all false prophets—Book of Revelations, man."

"I hear that," I confirmed, nodding. He squeezed my hand like it was a cow's udder, satisfied that we were on the same page.

"God bless you, man," he said, raising his hand for a high five and holding my hand with his greasy hand as he gave me a bleary-eyed, "We Are The World" look. Finally, he swerved clumsily toward another victim as he and his female appendage blocked their path.

I couldn't wait to get home. However, home didn't turn out to be the treat I expected.

CHAPTER 7

Ordinarily, it would have taken about ten minutes, but it took over an hour to get home by bus because of the traffic jam.

Jonathan greeted me at the backdoor, eyes glittering and chest swollen. Behind him I saw Eva Sanchez dashing down our hallway. Noticing me she waved excitedly and then disappeared into our brightly lit living room pursued by her shadow.

"Why is she here? What the hell is going on?"

Jonathan put his arm around my shoulder and touched his forefinger to his lips as he escorted me into my living room and pointed.

While the camera crew tested the lights, seated in the center of the living room and talking on our couch were Eva Sanchez and Nick Cavaliere.

Eva was beaming as the intimate interview started. And why not? She possessed the scoop of the century. While all her rivals were at the pier busily picking up the scraps, she was meeting with the man himself. Nick Cavaliere rarely did interviews, even when he was at the height of his fame, so this was a real coup and she was taking full advantage.

I was more amazed that he agreed to be interviewed so soon after being healed. I assumed he'd want to go home and rest, but he was bristling with energy. His hair was pulled back in a ponytail, and his beard had been brushed out. His eyes may have been blood red, but his face was no longer gaunt. All the color had returned and it was practically shimmering. His distinctive baritone had returned from hiatus; though more humble than I remembered.

"Nick, you mentioned earlier that you almost didn't attend this concert. In lieu of what has happened, I can't imagine that now."

"Thank God, neither can I."

"What finally convinced you?"

"My wife."

"What did she say?"

"Nothing. Her eyes said it all. When the offer was made to me to show up at this concert, I refused. Man, the look on her face… as if I had betrayed all the trust in our marriage. But I deserved it. We had vowed to fight this thing and search for hope wherever we could find it, and I gave up while she kept fighting. An hour before the concert, I told her to get her keys."

"Did you ever think it would all end like this?"

"No." He rubbed his legs, still in disbelief. "But that lovely woman, deservedly asleep in her bedroom, changed all that. I am truly at a loss for words on how to even begin thanking her. With the Carpenter's blessings, I hope they will allow me to stay here until I have a chance to personally express my gratitude to Olisa. I am eternally indebted to her. I owe her my life."

There was a watery veil over his eyes as he motioned for Lena to come and sit beside him. She snuggled into him, gazing at him like she had been reunited with a long lost lover.

"And what about you, Mrs. Cavaliere. How do you feel tonight?"

"Truly blessed. It's all so utterly unbelievable. I haven't been able to absorb it all yet. It's like this great big wonderful dream, and I'm hoping I'll never wake up. I just want to thank my adopted son, Jonathan Carpenter, for bringing us to his sister. Hopefully he's survived all the kisses I smothered him with."

Jonathan grinned from ear to ear.

"Nick, it may be a little difficult for our viewers to see, but we're showing the videotape of Olisa healing you. Can you tell us how you're feeling at that moment?" Eva asked, her gold eyes magnified.

"Out of control. Disoriented. Watching the video feels like an out of body experience. I can barely remember anything. I just remember staring into big brown eyes and feeling these prickly sensations competing inside my body. It tickled, it hurt, and it was like tiny little hands moving things around. Until tonight I never would have believed something like this could have happened."

"You mean a miracle?"

"Yes, a miracle. The fact that I'm sitting in this living room talking to you is a living testament to that. I'm tired, but it's like I was shot with some kind of powerful stimulant. My wife keeps telling me to relax, but I don't want to fall asleep because I'm afraid it will all go away."

"How soon do you think you'll go back to working again?"

"Work? I just want to play." He rocked Lena in his arms.

"I understand what you are saying. But, speaking on behalf of all your loyal fans, now that we have you back, please don't deprive us of seeing you in the movies again."

"Thank you. That's very kind… but all I care about tonight is being with my wife, family, and friends. Besides, maybe they've forgotten all about me. I might be lucky if I ever see another script again."

"Mr. Cavaliere, that's one worry I don't think you'll ever have. No one's ever going to forget about you after this night."

A hand grabbed my hand and led me into the hallway.

"Nola, I told you we can't do this in the house, sooner or later my wife is going to catch us."

"Shut up. Don't you know how worried I've been about you?" Warm and welcome lips pressed against mine.

Quietly we tiptoed out the backdoor.

"Oh, Joseph, thank goodness you're okay. I don't know what I would have done if you had gotten hurt. Do you know how much I love you? I was so worried about you when all the commotion started." Grace's head was in my chest as she squeezed me tightly. A breeze lifted the strands of her hair, tickling my nose.

"What are you talking about? I was the one who started it!"

"Just be quiet and hold me."

We stood in the middle of the courtyard clinging to each other.

"I don't know what I would have done if anything happened to you, Joe."

"Nothing was going to happen to me, Grace. I'll always be around to make your life miserable."

"Promise?"

"Promise."

"Joseph, please don't laugh at me when I say I'm scared."

"Me too."

"You were right, we should have closed the door, now it's too late."

"Sweetheart, the door opened when she was born. We could only avoid it for so long. If not today, then tomorrow. But you already know that."

"Yes, but it doesn't make me feel any better."

"Grace, I promise you, it's all going to work out in the end."

I just wish I could have said it with a little more conviction.

Shortly afterwards, Grace went back inside the house to check on everyone. I decided to stay outside. It was too claustrophobic in there. I had more than my share of people, cameras, reporters, and bright lights. I parked myself on a lounge chair in the patio and took in the warm night air and silence.

"Do you mind if I join you?"

"Hey, Nick, of course not, let me grab a chair for you."

"No, sir, let me!" he announced proudly, hoisting one of the lounge chairs and sliding it next to me on the patio deck.

"Eva Sanchez still here?"

"No, she left awhile ago, back to wherever reporters burrow."

"So you're not real high on them either, huh."

"No, but I've had to carve a peaceful coexistence with them in my business, Joseph. However, I'm sure there are a few that aren't too enamored of actors, either." He laughed. "How's your daughter doing?"

"Sound asleep. And at the rate she's going, she'll wake up sometime in the 22nd century."

"Very good."

"Where's Lena?"

"In the house, blabbing everyone's ears off. Can't you hear her? But I love it. She's having the best time I've seen in, oh, let's see… a couple of years."

He fell silent for a moment as he laid his head back.

Your family and friends are good people. They've been great to us. Your wife insists that we spend the night. She's already preparing the guest room."

"Sounds like her."

"But we'll probably leave, as tempting as it is. I think Lena and I need some quiet time before the circus festivities begin."

"I understand. We'll give you a rain check."

"We'll take it, Mr. Carpenter. I just wish I could have been as hospitable to you as your family has been toward me. I told your son, already, but I need you to know, I'm very sorry, I…"

"Man, please, as much as you've gone through?! If it had been me, I'd have taken a pistol and shot your ass on the way out!"

He laughed. "Still, I should have been a better man. Instead, I was a big, stupid, egocentric jerk. You guys were just trying to help. And I almost blew it."

"If it helps, Nick, it wasn't like that. I came along for the ride. It was solely Jonathan's idea."

"So what you're saying is you didn't suffer any sleepless nights on my account."

"No, sir, not one."

"Thank you, *now* I feel better."

We both laughed.

"So that's why you look so glum on the happiest day of my life!"

"I'm not doing a good job of hiding it, am I?"

"Not at all, my friend, but I understand." He leaned in closer to me, pulling on his beard. "Don't forget, I'm a father, too, and I've got a fairly good idea of what this type of press will do to you and your family. Are you sure you're ready for this?" He rested his hand on my shoulder, concern etched on his face.

"No."

"Even though I promised your son, if you'd like, I can call off the press conference tomorrow. I also have the right to kill the interview with Eva Sanchez. You just say the word."

"No, that's okay. It's not that I don't appreciate what you're trying to do, Nick, but the train was already set in motion back in July. We'll just ride it and see where it goes."

"Joseph, you are aware that reporters have been knocking on your door all evening? The big guy, I think he is your nephew? He has been chasing them away."

"Yeah, I know."

"That's nothing, my friend, not even a fraction of what you are about to encounter. They will attach themselves to your family like leeches. If you ever need help, just ask. I know a lot of people. Okay?"

"Sure, thanks"

"I mean it, Joseph. I will never be able to do enough to reciprocate what your daughter has done for me, but I'll do my best."

"Thanks, Nick."

Wilma stuck her head inside the door.

"Is it on?"

"Yeah, 5:00 on the nose, come on in."

She slipped into the small back office of the restaurant and covertly closed the door as we sat on the edge of the desk while I switched from channel to channel to see how many stations carried it. Damn, all the majors, plus. I turned up the sound so we could hear over the employees bustling around in the kitchen.

The press conference was held at the spot where it all happened— the Santa Monica Pier. I hadn't seen that much media in Santa Monica since the O. J. trials. Nick Cavaliere sparkled like a million bucks. His wavy dark hair was neatly cut and graying in the temples like the edges of sea water caressing the shore. His former Rip Van Winkle beard was trimmed to a full beard, highlighted by painterly strokes of gray. The icy blue eyes that ignited thousands of bedroom fantasies exuded a quiet dignity as he smiled and graciously bowed in acknowledgment of the stupendous ovation he received by the members of the press when he walked on the stage.

He wore a light colored sports coat and brown cotton trousers that matched perfectly with the professorial tones he opened with to address the world press. He started out a little unsteady, but soon his natural grace and charm took over. His supple masculinity also returned, surrounding him like a halo as he patiently answered all the questions about his remarkable recovery.

Nick was flanked by a legion of medical specialists who redundantly shook their heads as each one grabbed the mike and confirmed the unanimous diagnosis that this event was truly a medical phenomenon. Yet, many were reluctant to use the word miracle! The only one that seemed at ease with it was Dr. Shimkin who was a noted homeopathic specialist.

One physician in particular, Dr. Michael P. Rosenthal, one of the top spinal injury specialists in the world, made me want to administer the Heimlich maneuver on him because he appeared to choke every time he acknowledged Nick's miraculous recovery. Of course, we were forced to endure all the rhetoric and warnings that the diagnoses might be a little premature.

Rosenthal also cautioned that we should be careful not to so quickly ascribe any divine powers to Ms. Carpenter without the sufficient amount of testing, "We still don't know the capacity and depth of the human mind and its ability to heal itself. It has been documented in medical literature that in many societies, particularly primitive ones, that a strong enough belief in a shaman, witch doctor, or medicine man can sometimes lead the body to heal itself."

Nick's laughter bordered on derision.

"Doctor, ordinarily I'd defer to your authority because your credentials could fill a phone book, but this time you're wrong. Look at the film. The truth is right there. Zoom in on my face if you must. That pathetic expression you see hardly connotes undying faith. I was scared to death. I went to the concert in desperation, and I wanted to get the hell out of there as soon as I arrived. If not for my wife, I'd have left. So, you can present all the case studies you want. The woman you see in that videotape is the reason I am standing here before you."

The doctor looked like he was about to choke again.

"Mr. Cavaliere, I'm not intimating that what has happened to you is not astounding. It is! It's just that I don't want to mislead the public and say that this woman actually cured you until we've had a chance for further study... I..."

"My being here gives you a fairly good idea of what *this* woman can do. Something your fine team of expert specialists failed to accomplish."

Nick took some more questions from the media as Dr. Rosenthal stepped back from the dais, frustrated and mumbling. As he looked to his medical team for support, the majority averted their eyes.

"Thank you for asking... Yes, I will act again. Thank God, and thank Olisa, but..."

You could hear the whirring noise of the video cameras, but no one said a word as Nick tried to compose his thoughts. "I really don't deserve to be standing here proclaiming how grand my life is. I'm a sniveling coward. Thoughts of suicide crossed my mind every day. I didn't fight the good fight. All I cared about was whether I'd be quote, unquote normal again. But that's bull! There are courageous souls in this world suffering from paralysis who, unlike me, never stop fighting. They have made themselves a functioning part of this society. These are the ones who deserve to be healed. Not me. I just got lucky.

"If I hadn't met with Olisa this morning, I don't think I would have returned to the film business. She's the one who encouraged me to do what I do best and act. She convinced me that, ultimately, I could do more good with my celebrity status than bowing out by helping people who are suffering from paralysis. Consequently, I have started the Nick Cavaliere Foundation to fund research for spinal injuries."

He waited for the applause to abate. "Thank you. Now, although I hate to say it, I'm tired ladies and gentlemen. Two more questions."

"Theo Balanis, *New York Times*! Nick, congratulations! We're glad to have you back."

"Good to be back, Theo."

"I think Americans, correction, the world, shares your enthusiasm. This is all so unbelievable! But I'm sure I'm not alone when I ask, when do we get the chance to meet this miracle worker? I have a list of questions longer than my arm. Why isn't she here? Is she hiding something or what?"

"I may have been gone for two years, but questions from investigative reporters never change. Theo, I thought you already received your degree from Pessimism U.?"

"Still working on my thesis, Nick." He laughed heartily.

"Okay, Theo, then let me tell you this. The lady has nothing to hide. I invited her, no, begged her to stand here with me. She turned it down because she didn't think it would be appropriate."

"Appropriate? If all the rumors flying around are true, she'll be bigger than the pope! She heals one of the greatest actors of our time, and she doesn't want to be a part of the celebration? She ought to be basking in the applause, not avoiding it."

"If she possessed the same ego as you and I, that might be true, Theo. But why celebrate what's second nature to you? She didn't know who I was. She treated me simply because she cared."

"Okay, so let's say I buy that… Then why the big concert and everything?"

Nick paused to measure his words, "You still don't get it, Theo. That ingrained cynicism clouds your brain. She is one of the purest souls you'll ever find on this earth. You don't have to search for hidden messages with her. Her only agenda is love. The concert was the first step toward unifying people. I don't think anyone here can take issue with that."

"You sound like her spokesperson, Nick."

"I'd be her footstool if she asked, Theo. I'm not exaggerating when I say, she is the closest to God I'll ever get in this lifetime."

Wilma scooted off the desk and cracked the door open as a cacophony of loud laughter, frying chicken, and clattering silverware burst into the room. She leaned against the door with her back facing me.

"I guess I better go in and check on things. We are training a new cook this week."

"Yeah, okay." I replied, continuing to work on the daily receipts at my desk.

Wilma turned and faced me. She was pondering something as she rubbed her hands together.

"What's up?" I asked.

"Got a feeling we'll be seeing a whole new crop of customers this week, so I want to get everybody in gear. What do you think?"

"I think that's an excellent idea."

"Yeah, me, too. You gonna stay in here for awhile?"

"Yeah, just a few more minutes."

"Fine. Take your time, there's no rush."

"Thanks, sis."

She walked over to me and placed a hand on my shoulder.

"Hey, did I ever tell you you're my favorite brother?"

"I'm your only brother."

"Yeah, but you turned out to be a pretty good one." She leaned over and kissed me on the forehead.

"Wow! What's that all about?"

"I don't know. Just felt like it."

"Okay…so tell me this, why did you beat me up all the time when we were kids?"

"Bored, I guess."

"Hmmm."

"Hey, if you ever need some time off, don't hesitate to take it. We'll be okay here."

"Wilma, I appreciate it, but I can't let you handle the restaurant all by yourself. You need help."

"No. Your children are going to need you more than me, and you must be accessible. Besides, I don't need you, anyway. You've always been deadweight."

"Too late, Wilma. You already told me how wonderful I am."

"Damn, oh well…"

"Thanks, sis. I love you…"

"You better." She socked me in the shoulder.

"Ow!" I yelled, rubbing it. "Now that's the Wilma I'm used to."

I saw a smile on her face before the door clicked shut, and the kitchen sounds dulled, and the image of Nick Cavaliere continued to glow brightly on the television screen.

"So what did you guys think of the First Universal Healing Concert?" Eva Sanchez asked.

All three girls giggled nervously among themselves. Finally, the one with the purple and green hair and raccoon eye makeup spoke up. "It was the most awesome thing I have ever been to. One big party! It was soooo great. I loved it!"

"Yeah, it was great!" her friends echoed.

"What made it so great?"

"Oh… everything… the weather, the band, the people, and she was soooo cool, man! By the time it was over, I felt like we were all part of one big family. It was beautiful. My mother used to make me go to church every Sunday, but I can't ever remember feeling that good afterwards!"

Eva slightly cocked her head. "But what about the riots afterwards?"

"Riots?" the girls laughed. "That's so exaggerated! The only people who got out of hand were the security guys. A few people got super excited… that's all! It was a celebration, man. God was watching over us last night and partying with us. It was soooo cool. I was one of the ones that jumped on stage and danced with everybody else. The bands and all the music were to die for. "

"And what about Olisa Carpenter? What do you think about her?"

"Oh, she is soooo pretty! She's like a goddess," they sighed. "She's just like real cool. We used to see her on the beach all the time, you know, but I don't think anyone knew she was all that. She makes you feel like you can just be yourself, and that's pretty hip. She's not fake like all those other preachers, you know? You feel like you can talk to her, too… like she would never ignore you."

"Yeah, now if she had a church I'd go every week and listen to what she had to say. She's not one of those church hypocrites. Yeah… I wish she had a church, I'd finally have a reason to go."

"Why?"

"Cause she's someone we can finally relate to. She's one of us. She's the first one who ever really made me believe there is a God. You know what I mean?

"Y'all creating quite a stir over there in California. There used to be a time I didn't see enough of my granddaughter, now all I have to do is turn on the TV set or go down to the newsstand! The news programs show Olisa going in and out of the house so much, I feel like we're neighbors."

"It's something isn't it, Mama?" I said into the telephone as I peeped through the kitchen curtain. There were about twenty reporters camped outside our fence on the walk street.

"Boy, you're not kidding! This past week I think I've seen Olisa's face on practically every magazine cover. Although I kind of like that title in *Centerpiece Magazine*: "The High Priestess of Venice Beach.""

"That's one of Jonathan's favorites, too."

"But she looks tired, how's she holding up?"

"You'd look tired, too, if every time you step out the house your picture is snapped."

Just at that moment, a reporter who was sitting on a tree branch snapped my picture. I quickly drew the curtains closed then plopped down at the kitchen table.

"Lord…"

"But you know… Considering the circumstances, Olisa's handling it pretty well. Better than me. I'm ready to bust somebody in the mouth when they get to bugging."

"That's my boy, just as ornery as his father." My mother laughed. I could hear her juggling the telephone as the steam iron hissed away on the other end. "Billy gives them a pretty good piece of his mind when they call. We even had a couple of reporters at our doorstep the other day asking questions about Olisa."

"They're showing up in Vegas?"

"Yep, but it don't bother us none. It can get boring out here, so it makes life kind of interesting. Your father even fed a couple of them some barbecue ribs he had just made."

"Good. Did he poison them?"

"No, just expanded their waistline a little and gave them a lot of nothing information to take back home. Told them the food had been blessed by Olisa and had all kinds of healing nutrients inside."

"You guys are bad. So now they believe that your rib tips lower cholesterol level, huh."

Food. That reminded me. I scrambled through the box of doughnuts left on the table and found the last jelly doughnut. Yes!

"Uh-huh! But seriously, son, I know I'm not telling you anything you don't already know, but watch your back. Those tabloid fellas have been snooping around a lot. And the offers they're putting out could pay off our mortgage."

"Now I know how you're going to pay for your next Caribbean vacation."

"Hush, now… You're joking, but do you know they actually came to our house and convinced the gardeners that we hired them to do some interior design work on the house and they needed to get inside so they could give us a quote on the work."

"What assholes!" I shook my head as I munched on my doughnut. Why didn't they get more jelly ones?

"Thank goodness, I forgot my purse and came back home just as they were strolling in. I had to threaten them with the police."

"What did they do?"

"First they apologized, then they slipped me their phone number and urged me to call if I wanted to make a financially lucrative deal."

"Man, those suckers don't give up! Mom, if you think it's bad there, imagine what it's like here. Our neighbors aren't real happy with the way the press has invaded our quiet little walk street."

I wiped my hands with a paper towel then peeked out the window again.

"I bet."

"It's been over a month since that beach concert. Olisa hasn't done a single interview since then and the press has come up with more stuff… Things I never even knew about Olisa."

"You and me both."

"It's something how fast they can get information about you when they want to."

I watched Alton and another security guard chase a reporter out of the yard.

"Ain't it? Is Olisa ever going to do another interview?"

"She doesn't have to the way they been coming out of the wood-works to talk about her. Olisa never knew she had so many friends."

"Yeah, I know… Bright lights can bring out the idiots real fast. But I understand, her healing that actor made everything somewhat crazy. Ain't nobody ever seen anything like that before, especially on film. That little Mexican girl on that news program done made a career out of showing that film. I see her all over the place nowadays."

"Not as much as me, particularly now that she's taken KLSC to number one in the area." I closed the curtains again after seeing some Jesus freaks marching down the walk street with a banner that read, "Jesus is Lord, Not Olisa!"

While I was on the phone with my mother, the doorbell rang and Grace received another flower arrangement for Olisa that she would probably take with her the hospital. Hundreds of flowers and gifts were being sent to Olisa, and she had requested that all of them be donated to hospitals and charities.

"Yeah, Mama, Olisa will probably say something sooner or later. *Hard Copy*, *60 Minutes*, *20/20*, *Dateline*, and every news and talk pro-gram around have begged her to do an interview with them. Limousine drivers drop by the house everyday offering to escort her to their pro-grams. I can't believe how much money they are spending to just court her."

"Lord have mercy. So why doesn't Olisa do a couple of interviews?"

"That's what Jonathan keeps asking. Olisa doesn't see the point of rattling endlessly about herself on these shows. She'd rather do the concerts because she feels they are more productive. She finds interviews boring, egocentric, and a waste of time. To tell you the truth, she's really not that comfortable with any of the attention focused on her."

"How is my grandson? Is he still working at the record company, too?"

"He gave his notice the day after the concert."

"He quit that great job? But that's so risky!"

I rummaged through the box to see if there was one more jelly doughnut. No such luck.

"Mom, don't shed any tears for Jonathan—he's fine. The company doubled his salary, which was already pretty fat, just to stay on board as a consultant. Believe me. He keeps himself busy. He's got a new office in Culver City, near the studios, hired a staff, and literally has expanded overnight. There he fields requests and handles more mail than the White House. And, you ought to see the donations."

"Donations?"

"Money, Mama, raining into the company like a monsoon. It's incredible. So trust me, Jonathan ain't crying about quitting his job."

"All right, as long as he's doing fine. By the way, your father yelled you need to cut your grass. He saw your yard on TV."

"Tell him I'll take care of it." I chuckled.

We talked and joked for a while longer. I felt much better talking to my parents after getting off the phone. To say it had been hectic the month following the Santa Monica Concert is the greatest understatement of all time. Every blurry footstep thereafter surged forward at warp speed. I get winded even thinking about it.

"Hey, Joseph!" Grace yelled from the living room.

"Yeah?" I yelled back from the kitchen.

"Come here."

I didn't like the sound of her voice.

"What's wrong?"

"There's nothing wrong. I just thought you might want to see this. Hurry up!"

I stopped working on the ham and cheese sandwich I was making then rushed into the living room.

"What?"

"Shhhh…" she said, putting her forefinger to her lips and then pointing to the TV. She patted the couch for me to sit next to her.

I rolled my eyes as soon as I saw Eva Sanchez with that big cheese-eating smile on her face. Standing beside her was a heavyset black woman who nervously shifted from side to side. Next to them was a sign that read, Thomas Paine Middle School. Grace turned up the volume.

"With me today is Brenda Bennett, who attended the same private school as Olisa Carpenter. Brenda has worked as an administrative assistant at Thomas Paine for the last twenty years." Brenda offered an awkward nod to the cameras. "Brenda, you were in seventh and eighth grade with Olisa, is that correct?"

"Um, yes, Ms. Sanchez."

"Please, just call me, Eva."

"Yes, ma'am."

"So, Brenda, why don't we go inside one of the classrooms and see what it was like for the two of you."

"Sure." Brenda replied, pulling keys out of her purse.

The camera cut to them sitting at desks in the classroom.

"So *this* is where Olisa sat, huh?" Eva asked, tapping the desk.

"Yes, sometimes…" Brenda answered, her eyes flitting around.

"So, Brenda, what was Olisa like? Any stories you can share with us?

"Um, well, to be honest, I really didn't know her that well. She was quiet… stayed to herself a lot. Don't get me wrong, she wasn't snooty or anything… not really even shy… just different…"

"Different?"

"Yeah… It's hard to explain… kinda spacey sometimes… like she wasn't always there. But if Mrs. Richard fired a question at her to see if she was paying attention, she'd give her about five times more than what you asked for. The teacher kind of realized she was different, too. With other kids, Mrs. Richards would jump all over them if they looked like they were daydreaming. Olisa, she usually left alone. I used to sit across from Olisa, and sometimes she'd be talking to herself or rubbing her temples like she had a headache or something. Once she caught me staring at her, and the look she gave me kind of made me nervous."

"Why?"

"It wasn't a mean look or anything. At first her eyes were kinda muddy looking, and her face was all pinched up. Wherever she was, it wasn't in the classroom. Then her eyes grew real large. I instantly felt this tingling sensation in my head, and every nerve in my body felt like it was on fire. As hard as I tried, I couldn't take my eyes off hers. Her eyes were real deep looking... I don't know... you may think this sounds weird."

Brenda paused, unsteadily. She self-consciously folded her arms and rocked slightly back and forth.

"Not at all." Eva touched her shoulder empathetically. "Please continue."

"Well, it's just, to this day, I swear she knew what I was thinking. It kind of made me mad, because all of a sudden I felt real vulnerable. I think she sensed it because she started blinking a lot like she was struggling to wake up. After awhile, she seemed to recognize me and her face became calm, even apologetic. I thought she was going to say something to me, but, instead, she smiled and resumed taking notes. It was strange."

"Talking about strange... Did you ever see her do anything unusual?"

"You mean like healing somebody? No, I didn't know she could do stuff like that until I saw her on the news. But I did see her hypnotize some classmates one night."

"Hypnotize? In eighth grade?" Eva gasped. She seemed sincerely taken aback.

"Oh, yeah!" Brenda piped up animatedly. She appeared a little more trusting of Eva. "It was at a school retreat one weekend at Big Bear Lake. That Saturday night the counselors had a staff meeting, giving us free time to hang out in the recreational center. We were bored to death until this nerdy girl named Natalie, who was one of Olisa's closest friends, mentioned Olisa knew how to hypnotize people. Of course, we jumped all over that and begged her to prove it. No one really believed she could do it. I could tell she was irritated with Natalie for telling us and claimed it was nothing but stuff she read in a book. We didn't go for it and stayed on her.

"After awhile I think she got sick of us bugging her, so she got up and asked for volunteers. That got us all excited, and we were ready for a big laugh. I hate to admit it now, but mostly at her expense. Behind her back, some kids called her a witch because her hair was always loose and wild looking." Brenda emphasized this by gesticulating with her hands. "I always thought she was pretty, but she never did anything special to herself. She never talked about clothes or fashion, hair, make-up, boys, or any of the things girls talked about. It made her an easy target.

"Olisa lowered all the lights and volunteers were asked to lie down on one of the mats in the center of the room. She rubbed their temples and spoke very softly, asking them to focus on her voice. Ten minutes later, they fell into a trance."

Eva looked at her like, "You can't be serious."

"I'm serious." Brenda laughed. "If you had been there you would have seen people answering questions like robots. It was hysterical. She had kids singing, laughing, and flapping their arms like chickens, anything she wanted them to do. Everybody loved it. Olisa was the hit of the party. I think Olisa enjoyed herself, too. It was the first time I had ever seen her relax and not be so serious. When I look back, I think it was her way of fitting in. A lot of times she would go off by herself and draw or read a book. It was good to see her mixing it up with us.

"But it all backfired when Freddie Banks asked for a turn. I remember him cracking jokes and winking to all his buddies. He was a little more of a challenge for her because he refused to take it seriously, acting as ignorant as he could. She warned us it wouldn't work unless we all remained very quiet. And that was a joke considering there were thirty teenagers stuck in the same room with Freddie acting silly and making farting and burping noises."

Eva smiled knowingly.

"It didn't stop her though," Brenda continued. "She kept working on him. I think she was into the challenge. She was down on her knees, steadily massaging his temples, and whispering soothingly to him while he kept mocking her. The thing I remember is the burning intensity in her eyes. I had never seen anything like it before."

"I think everyone noticed it, because after awhile the laughter died down and Freddie's jokes abruptly stopped. We kept expecting him to suddenly burp or fart or do something silly like bounce up and start dancing, but his body was real still. We gathered around them in awe, looking at her with renewed respect. She had taken down the class clown."

"Is he sleep?" someone asked.

"He's in a trance," she answered.

"Can you ask him questions?"

She nodded her head.

"Can you tell us what your name is?" Olisa asked.

"Frederick Douglas Banks," he answered flatly.

"And where do you live?"

"Los Angeles."

"At what address?"

"Uh, uh, on Chelsea Ave."

"Forget all that," someone shouted. "Ask him who he's digging on."

"Is there someone you like in class?"

He got this silly grin on his face, "Yeah."

"Who?"

"Kendra."

Kendra hollered, 'oh no', and we fell out. Olisa raised her hand for us to be quiet.

"Do you want to kiss her?"

He grinned. "Yes."

"She's here right now, show us what you want to do."

"He wrapped his arms around his chest, and his tongue slipped out of his mouth like some nasty little serpent. Kendra ran out the room, shrieking as we cracked up. We shut up the minute Olisa's hand shot up. That's cause this was getting good."

"'Do you like music?"

"Definitely."

"Who is your favorite singer?"

"Nat King Cole."

"Nat King Cole, Huh? Let's hear you sing like Nat King Cole."

"Sure enough, he did his best Nat King Cole impression… I think he sang, 'Route 66' or something snapping his fingers druggily along."

"C'mon," Eva interrupted. "Was he really hypnotized, or was he just pulling your leg?"

"Oh no, Ms. Sanchez," Brenda replied resolutely. "He was hypnotized and everybody was all over him.'Look at that fool!' they said. 'Nat King Cole? That's old folks' music! Oh, man… ain't that a trip? All he talks about to us is Parliaments/Funkadelics, the Commodores, The Isley Brothers, Average White Band—where the hell did Nat King Cole come from? Wait till this fool wakes up."

"'Why do you like Nat King Cole?" Olisa asked.

His eyelids fluttered and he told us, "Cause my parents loved him. He was their favorite singer."

"Oh? And what are your parents doing tonight?"

Freddie frowned and shook his head from side to side; his lower lip loosened and started quivering.

Olisa's face got tight.

And so did Brenda's as she retold the story.

"What's wrong, Freddie?" Olisa asked, cautiously.

"My parents are dead!! They were killed in a robbery when I was five… Oh, I really miss my mommy and daddy. My aunt and uncle told me, you have to live with us now because your parents have gone to heaven. But I don't want to live with you! I want my parents to come back! I don't like being alone! I want Mommy and Daddy! Mommy! Daddy!" He had started yelling in a five-year-old's voice, sniffling and wiping his forearm across his nose. His head rolled from side to side as he moaned like he was being tortured.

"Everybody in the hall freaked out, including Olisa. I think even his closest friends thought that his aunt and uncle were his real parents. Everybody screamed at her to wake him up. It stopped being funny."

Brenda hesitated again, but Eva smiled reassuringly, and nodded at her to keep going.

"Olisa panicked at first, then took a deep breath and got real calm. Oh yeah, before bringing him back, she told him he would remember nothing except how good he felt."

"About a second after she snapped her finger, Freddie leaped up and broke into this dance we used to call the breakdown. He started bragging that stupid stuff like that never works on him. He didn't even know his cheeks were tear stained. He got a clue though when he noticed how quiet it was, and that some of the girls and boys were crying."

"Olisa seemed very disturbed by it all and went back to her cot and started reading her book again. A couple of times I woke up and saw her lying on her cot reading by flashlight." Brenda got quiet and gazed at the desk Eva was sitting in. She looked like she was about to tear up. "I've always felt kind of bad because no one said anything to her afterwards. I wanted to tell her it wasn't her fault, and that we were just stupid kids who got into something way over our heads, but, instead, I just closed my eyes real tight, like everyone else, and tried to go to sleep."

"Well, Brenda, from the little I know about Olisa, I can guarantee you she forgave you a long time ago. She hardly strikes me as the type to hold grudges." Eva smiled at her warmly and then at the camera.

"I hope so," Brenda sighed.

"Do you think any good came out of it?"

"Yeah… Freddie never cracked another joke about her again. Actually, he stayed as far away from her as possible."

Olisa's star blazed through the sky, overshadowing everything in its path. The public hungered for more information about her, and the mass media did their best to oblige. To date, she hadn't done one interview, but it didn't matter. They played off of her mystique. The public was intrigued by the unexpected emergence of this healer who crashed into their lives with the impact of a meteor. Who was she? Where did she come from? Anyone who had a story about Olisa suddenly found themselves on major talk shows and radio programs. They were fascinated by this woman who didn't fit the mold of what people had come to expect from their present day religious icons—mostly men with designer suits, beatific smiles, and condemnatory glares.

Her enigma was further heightened by a timely music video, filmed days before the concert, at least in the public's view. The real deal is, it was shrewdly orchestrated by Jonathan. It was Mookie Moan's "Stairway to the Man," a rap narrative, borrowing musical licks from Led Zeppelin's "Stairway to Heaven." The song was about how a modern day Job suffers through hell on earth—facing drugs, poverty, violence, and racial hatred. Every time he finds himself in deep despair, Olisa's image appears. She is cast as an angel, splendorously adorned in glistening white, with huge wings and mounds of hair add-ons billowing behind her from a heavenly studio breeze. Her ethereal image floats from scene to scene, always there to give the main character support as he encounters and conquers each obstacle.

The video concluded with Mookie as an old man escorted by other fashionable looking angels into a brilliant white light. The video fades out and we see Olisa strumming an ornate African harp inside the slowly closing gates of heaven.

It cost a ton of money to achieve the surrealistic and stupendous special effects that imbued the video with its spiritual ambiance. Apparently, it was worth it. Subsequently upon its release, the song zoomed to number one, toppling long-standing records for song, album, and video sales. Olisa told me later she actually had a great deal of fun doing it, but was shocked by the results. Her presence actually overshadowed Mookie Moan's even though she was only a peripheral character. She received instant certification as the MTV darling of her time among the youth. Her celebrity grew bigger than any of the current crop of divas; all of this without playing an instrument or singing one note.

Even before she became famous, people swarmed around Olisa. However, it went way beyond that on a Sunday afternoon in late September.

"Hey Mom, Pops! What's happening down at the beach this afternoon? I was going down Abbott Kinney, and there were droves of people rushing down there. Is there some kind of special event today or something?"

"I don't know, Son. When you find out let me know" I answered, barely looking up from my newspaper as he walked in the back door and plopped down on the couch next to Grace, plying her with a big smack on the cheek and cuddling her in his arm.

"When I see that grin on your face, I know you been up to no good."

"*Ah contraire*, Mama. It's all good. I've got some great news. Where's Olisa? I'm not saying a word till she's in the room!"

"She's in the studio."

"No she's not. I just got through banging on her door."

"Then where is she?"

"That's what I'm asking you?"

"Uh oh," I said as all of us jumped up yelling her name and combing the house. "She's gone!"

I looked out the window and noticed there were no photographers on the walk street. Usually, their heads popped up like the villains in a video game. Damn, I should have known the peace and quiet was too good to be true.

About that point, Alton and Laura waved as they ambled up the walk. Seeing the concern on our faces Alton said, "Please tell me Olisa's back."

Grace rushed up to him. "Alton, what does that mean? You knew she was gone?"

Alton made some sucking noises and then his eyes slid to Laura's.

Meekly she said, "She's going to kill me. I'm not supposed to say anything, but she promised me she'd be back by now. She called very early this morning and complained she was tired of being cooped up and had to go to the beach to see a sunset and have some breakfast."

"Do you guys think this is some kind of game? This isn't high school!"

Smirking, Laura refused to acknowledge Jonathan's outburst.

"Thank you, Honey. You did the right thing in telling us," Grace said.

"Why did you wait until now to tell us?" Jonathan barked, angrily jingling his car keys.

"Because I made a promise! I thought she'd be back sooner," Laura shot back, blotches of red seeping into her face.

Defending Laura, Grace yelled, "Jon, get off her case! You know as well as I do that when Olisa's in that frame of mind, nobody can stop her from doing what she wants. At least she told somebody. Now, instead of yelling at Laura, let's go find your sister and make sure she's all right!"

"I told her not to go anywhere alone. Sometimes she just doesn't listen!" I grumbled.

"She didn't go alone, Uncle Joseph!" Laura softly replied.

"Huh?"

"She went with Logan."

Jonathan jingled his keys again. "Shit!"

As we followed behind Jonathan to his car, I leaned over and whispered into Grace's ear. "All right… how long I been in the Ice Age this time?"

"Probably about two weeks."

"So how did I miss this? Is something going on between them?"

"If not, then it's only a matter of time."

"How do you know that?"

"Didn't you notice the way they looked at each other when they first met at the house? Or should I say the second time?"

"Probably a father's denial. So what makes you so smart?"

"I'm a woman."

"That's kind of sexist, isn't it?"

"Yeah, maybe… okay, because I'm me."

"That, I can deal with."

CHAPTER 8

There are many ways to God.—Arapaho proverb

Even though the beach was only a few blocks away from the house, we hopped into Jon's Range Rover because we had no idea how far we might have to go to find her. As it turned out, we only had to drive a couple of blocks before we figured out her whereabouts. All you had to do was follow the stampede barreling down Windward Ave toward the beach.

"She's over there! Where the roller skating is. That's her!" kids shouted, some running and others skateboarding past us into a swelling mass of bodies covering the now vacant hill where the former Venice Pavilion stood like ivy on a rampage. At the heart of it all, standing center at the highest point of the incline, was Olisa. The pied piper of Venice was surrounded by people who literally gathered at her feet, some sitting cross-legged. It was unbelievably quiet for such a large group of people. They were consumed by every word she uttered. Logan's camera dangled from his neck as he clandestinely moved through the sea of bodies like a sniper, interweaving among the trees, searching for the best possible shot angle. Peppered throughout the crowd like metal flowers were news cameras. Helicopters roared overhead, whirring past like giant dragonflies.

I heard a police officer behind me speaking breathlessly into his walkie-talkie for backup. Olisa seemed completely unfazed by the whole process. She just went with the flow. She genuinely loved being outside and interacting with people more then being stuck inside a cramped house. Ironically, the graffiti on a side wall read in bold red letters:

Whoever drinks the water I give him will never thirst!

SOUL EYES

Jesus

Although I can't speak for Jonathan, I finally got past my irritation with Olisa. I watched her standing regally at the top of the slope, her hair covered by a scarf, talking, counseling, and preaching to a rapt audience. Logan was only a few feet away from her, crazily snapping pictures of her and the crowd like his camera was an automatic weapon.

Observing the people who made up the Venice circus in awe of Olisa was a sight all by itself. They were all there: gypsies, Rastafarians, healers, folk singers, Michael Jackson derivations in sparkly coats and gloves, roller skaters, body builders, healers, spray painted people in silvers and blues, Ecuadorian musicians, an Iranian harpist, the aboriginal string quartet, flamenco guitarists, the frogman, addicts, prostitutes, surfers, basketballers, the Hip Hop brigade, and more. All circled her in a proprietary and reverential manner. She was Venice's own "Mother Spiritual," the guru supreme of this assortment of eclectic personalities who made up show time at Venice Beach. A writer for *Vanity Fair* wasn't too far off when he dubbed her the "High Priestess of Venice."

Alton managed to get us closer to the front flashing his security badge and intimidating physique, but the closer we got, the more congested it became, so we halted our trek after a point to prevent any further tension from developing.

"We tried, didn't we, Joseph?" Grace waxed nostalgically. But we can't hold her back."

"No we can't, Grace," I replied, stroking her neck. "You can build a basement, but you can't stop a tornado."

Seeing all the people gathered around Olisa caused me to reflect on the church we used to attend in Los Angeles when Olisa and Jonathan were kids. All the elders used to sit around Olisa and play a game with her in which they would call out a book of the Bible and a random verse number—such as, Proverbs 16:16. She had to recite the passage verbatim that corresponded with that numbered verse. They rarely stumped her. I still chuckle, thinking about how they'd shake their heads in amazement as she quoted the text while they scrambled through their bibles to find it.

My mind immediately segued to an interview Eva Sanchez did on television the other day with Betty Stanford. That was a name I hadn't heard in a long time. They had to do some serious research to find her. As it turned out, they found her living in a nursing home in Kansas City, Missouri. They conducted the interview in a park not far from the home.

"Olisa Carpenter?" Betty asked, shielding the sun from her eyes when she looked at Eva, even though she wore dark shades. They sat on the park bench. Betty's jaws habitually moved in a chewing motion as she scratched her jet-black wig, which became slightly askew. White hair peeked out from underneath.

"The person you should have asked was my husband… God rest his soul. He passed away almost, let me see, about ten years ago now. It's funny to talk about the past to you because my husband and I did-n't talk about it for twenty something years until he was lying on his deathbed. All the chemotherapy and drugs had him lapsing in and out of consciousness when he asked one night, 'Betty, do you think she's okay? Do you think God ever forgave me for turning her away?'

"I wasn't sure who he was talking about until he said, 'little Olisa.' And I comforted him with, 'Yes, honey, I'm sure she's doing fine, just fine.' After hearing those words, he fell back to sleep with a smile. He never asked again after that. He died the next day."

"That must have been tough on you, Betty," Eva said softly.

"Oh it was…but at least Karris's demons had finally been quieted. Praise God he didn't take that turmoil to his grave with him," she added, crossing her heart with her right hand, and then signifying by raising it to the skies. "My only regret is that he is not here with us today to see how his child prodigy turned out. But then again, he just might be…"

Eva rubbed her chin thoughtfully. "Betty, do you think he knew about Olisa?"

"Of course, child. He knew way back then how special she was. God had enriched his life with someone more precious than he had ever encountered before. That's why he was tortured for years by the thought that in turning her away, he had also rejected God."

"Having your people track me down has brought it all to the fore again. When I saw her on the news and realized who it was, I had to grab a chair and sit down before I fainted. And then, sweetheart, I sat down and cried like a little baby. But it was a good thing, because I know my husband's tormented soul has finally made peace with his maker."

"So tell me about their relationship," Eva said, leaning into her.

Betty's chewing motions began again. "The Willis's had been members of our Los Angeles church for as long as I can remember. Stay with me because I'm going back over sixty years. James and Katherine Willis were married by my husband when he was a young man and had just taken over the church after the prior minister died. Karris baptized both of their children: Grace and James, Jr. He presided over the funeral of Grandmother Willis.

"But nothing prepared Karris for that amazingly sweet child of Grace's that landed in his Bible study class." Betty leaned back against the bench with a big smile and clapped her hands in delight. "Oh, we heard she was smart, but they never mentioned the rest. We never thought anything when she was the loudest kid's voice in the choir as she sang every song with a child's innocent gusto. One of those exuberant singers always passed through. But at the age of six, while older 'A' students struggled with two to three lines of a bible passage, she could smoothly recite word for word, pages of the bible. Karris had seen some pretty bright and precocious children in his time, but none were like Olisa. When he asked Grace and her husband—I forget his name…"

Grace never let me hear the end of that one.

"Well, whatever, when my husband asked if they realized what an incredible child they had, he'd quietly say thank you, and no more. It wasn't because he was being modest so much as he seemed to take it for granted in an odd way. Their son was bright too, but Olisa was on another plane."

"Initially, Karris was beside himself with joy at having the opportunity to mentor this child. God had blessed him and dropped the child right in his lap. He truly believed God meant for Olisa to be a part of his life. She made it hard for him to avoid favoritism. But who could blame him? Olisa gobbled up everything he laid out to her with a passion that was hard to imagine coming from a youngster. Her passion was so intense and so deep that Karris always came home from a session with her bone tired, but feeling good. He didn't even come close to satisfying her great appetite. But he didn't mind, he loved it. How often do you get a child who prefers talking about God rather than participating in recess? She asked more profound questions than some of Karris' theology students."

"That must have been a pretty rewarding experience for a man of God.

"It was. Some nights Karris couldn't sleep without thinking about his beloved little scholar. He would just nod his head and smile when she sat at the feet of the deacons and church elders, totally absorbed in their conversations instead of being outside on the playgrounds with the other children. "Betty, I have never seen anything like this child—she's one of a kind," he'd say. "I look into her eyes and she understands, Betty, she really understands!"

At that moment, during the narration, a picture was shown of Olisa standing at the pulpit in a choir robe. Her hair was parted into two long pigtails. But what stood out were the eyes. Even a black and white photograph couldn't mask the intensity.

"Olisa was so remarkable that at the age of ten, my husband occasionally allowed her to take the pulpit and preach the Sunday sermon. Now that was something to see. At first you'd see the smiles—isn't she cute? And then astonishment, because this little girl preached the gospel like an old soul. The smiles would wither away and suddenly she was no longer just a child, but a messenger of God."

"There were times, of course, that my husband had to coach her because like any kid, she might become a little flashy or delight in her own brilliance and get carried away, but that was rare. Olisa genuinely believed that God was her inspiration, and she transfixed the congregation with her sincerity, emoting as if she knew God personally, something that takes some ministers years to be able to accomplish as public speakers. It was unusual to see so much enthusiasm in one so young."

Another photograph showed Olisa sitting with the Reverend Stanford at his desk next to a huge open Bible. He had his arm around her, and they both had big smiles on their faces as she tugged playfully on his goatee.

"We were raising three wonderful boys, but Olisa became the daughter Karris never had. But, it all changed. The problem with a child that gifted is eventual boredom. After awhile, it seemed Olisa began to question everything she had been taught. That girl must have asked a thousand questions a day and wouldn't accept any patented answers. Many of the elders began to get a little uncomfortable with her line of questioning."

"Why was that?" Eva asked as they slowly walked through the park.

"From what I recollect, she wasn't trying to be belligerent or arrogant, but she would challenge their answers with a child's curiosity and a scholar's logic. This just didn't happen with children. Many of the elders viewed it as disrespectful coming from some little kid who didn't have experience like them. Granted, much of it had to do with the fact that they didn't have answers, but they chose to believe she was just turning into a spoiled little brat. No one wanted to admit that she intimidated them."

"Did she exhibit any other odd behaviors?"

"Yes." Betty's jaws moved, as she mulled it over. "There was also a little idle gossip floating around that this child had the sight. At church functions and picnics, they said she would walk up to people and embarrass them on the spot, telling them things about their life that no one could possibly have known. It was hard to get on a little kid about such presumptuousness, so they started scolding her parents, blaming them for spreading vicious rumors that were causing problems in the church. Consequently, they also failed to own up to the fact that all these things turned out to be true. But they needed some scapegoats, so if you can't blame the child then blame the parents."

"Now, on the other hand, some of our congregants weren't put off by this at all and sought Olisa out, begging her to tell them about their lives and their future. They'd pull her aside at a church event, acting as if they were marveling over how big she had grown, but actually interrogating her for as much information as they could get. It got ridiculous after awhile, because they couldn't stop themselves." Betty shook her head at the memory. "They pressed that poor child constantly, and in some cases, with little diplomacy when things she predicted started coming true in their lives. Poor Olisa didn't know what she had gotten herself into. It got a little scary with some folks. I didn't want to believe it, but there it was—this child could see into the future. She was just telling it as if she saw it. Eventually, this created all kinds of rifts in the church."

Another picture showed Olisa lighting a candle at the altar with the Reverend Standford watching.

"Nevertheless, my husband tried to protect Olisa as much as possible. He knew how special she was, and he didn't want to lose her. But the straw that broke the camel's back was when all the testimonials started pouring in from the congregation claiming the child possessed some kind of healing power. Mrs. Rice was the first one, talking about how Olisa laid a hand on her elbow one day and cured her bursitis. Before you knew it, others started making similar assertions about her healing abilities.

"It was getting out of control. C'mon now, a child who had the audacity to challenge church authorities, tell fortunes, and heal people?"

Betty and Eva were now shown standing at the rim of a lake. Ducks dipped their heads in the water searching for fish. Occasionally people drifted by in paddleboats.

"You have to understand… We were basically a very conservative church and not into the shenanigans of the evangelicals or Pentecostal folks. We didn't do all that stomping around hollering or speaking in tongues." Betty stated it like it was an accusation. "We housed a strong middle class constituent and were dependent on their money to keep operating. Olisa had unintentionally offended a few of the old money bags, giving them information about themselves that they weren't too happy to hear. It didn't matter that it was probably true. People don't want to hear the truth unless it's good. The child wasn't a psychologist, she was just honest."

"That hasn't changed," Eva added.

"I'm sure it hasn't. And I haven't even talked about the sermons in which she discussed the visions that came to her in the night, nor how she heard voices in her sleep, Needless to say, this was just a little too much for the long-standing church members. She became a divisive force instead of a unifying one. The worse was that some felt she was spouting things contrary to the traditional Word of God: challenging steadfast church traditions and conventions, testifying that God spoke to her personally everyday. Though most of the ministers in the United States claimed the same thing—this was somehow different. People were uncomfortable with a child saying those things."

The next picture showed Olisa reading to kids not much younger than her in the church's Sunday school.

"They started demanding that some action be taken before this turned into one of those carnival churches, and that included some of our largest contributors. Before you knew it, Karris' ear was bent and twisted every which way like some kinda Gumby doll. There were some veiled threats to Karris's own job security and some not quite so subtle. They knew she was his little prodigy.

"Soon, Karris wrestled with his own internal devils. You see, he was no longer her sole mentor. He heard that her parents took her to other churches, synagogues, temples, Islamic centers, Holy Roller storefront churches, and it was due to her requests, not them. She wanted to see how other people worshipped. I know it hurt Karris's feeling that he was not her only mentor anymore. I hate to say it, but he was a little jealous, and this is what ultimately made him turn his back on her and cave in to the pressures hitting him from all sides. Karris was not one to back down from a fight or to let others influence him. But his own personal needs got in the way this time."

Once again, Betty and Eva were shown sitting on a park bench; this time in a garden populated by roses.

"He didn't sleep at all the night before he talked to the Carpenters. He informed them that he felt Olisa was causing too many problems in the church. But he knew it was just a euphemism; that what he was actually asking that she be exiled from the church, but he didn't know how to say it. I think he would have felt much better if the Carpenters would have cursed him out. But instead, they handled it with so much class it baffled him. They seemed resigned, as if they were expecting it. He said they were more of a comfort to him, assuring him that it was all right and they had already planned to do something about it. They asked him to stay for dinner like he had never said a word."

"So how did he handle it?" Eva asked, concerned etched on her face.

"I found Karris in his study the next morning head down on his desk, an empty bottle of bourbon next to him, and his hand still curled around the glass. He kept his back to me when I came in and started talking as soon as I closed the door. When he turned to face me, his face looked worn, and it was obvious he had been crying.

"Karris was a proud man and always tried to be strong, but this devastated him. He began to question his true loyalties. Was it to God? Or to those who financed his ministry? Or was he jealous of his authority being usurped by a child who had more God given talent than he would ever have? Is that why he failed to stand up to them? Did he lack guts when he knew in his heart the truth about this child?

"You know what really tore him up the most?"

"Please, tell me."

"It was seeing Olisa's face peering from her bedroom window when he left her house. She mouthed the words, I love you, to him and it just tore him up."

Hearing this tore us up, too. Grace was crying, and I was very close. Even Eva looked like she was on the verge of tears. Ms. Sanchez had unearthed memories that we didn't even realize how deeply we had buried.

Betty went on to say, "But it was more than just the words, Eva. It was the look in her eyes—she knew. Knew that everything between them had changed and that they would never see each other again. But in just a look, he remembered nothing but love flowing from her face. Her expression told him all was fine and not to worry—that she understood why he did what he did.

"What chilled me more than anything else that morning was when he finally turned to me, eyes bloodshot, and said, 'Betty, all my life I've been taught to say, get thee behind me Satan! What about Judas? Judas was the one standing behind me tonight. I sold her out, Betty.'

"I jumped all over him for saying such absurd things, but his manic laughter drowned me out. All I could do was hold him tightly until the laughter subsided of its own accord. I can't tell you how relieved I was to hear the welcome sounds of snoring."

"The family never came back to the church. And they moved not too long thereafter to, I think, to Venice. Karris never saw Olisa again."

"So what happened to you guys after that?"

"Us?" Betty took a moment to compose herself as she removed her glasses and wiped her eyes. She put her glasses back on. "We were lucky to make it through the rest of the year. Karris was not the same man after that. He could barely preside over the congregation any more or minister to anyone. He suffered a nervous breakdown. The police brought him home one night because he had been walking down the street stripping off his clothes and reciting the Lord's Prayer, blessing people as he passed by them. Eventually, we left and moved back to our hometown of Kansas City, Missouri so Karris could take time off to heal himself."

"Did he ever go back to the ministry?"

"No. Karris retired, but he continued to work with kids, becoming a director of a program that helped troubled youth. He was great! I can't tell you how many kids benefited from his guidance during the ensuing years. He took each case on as a challenge. I think in each one he saw Olisa. Consequently, no one was ever turned away if he could help it. Her name was never mentioned again in our household, but I know it was never forgotten.

"All those years we waited without one word of exchange. We waited silently for a sign she was okay. I didn't realize until I saw her face on television how much it meant to me. Praise God, she's all right!" Betty gestured triumphantly, raising both fists in the air. "Now, finally, I, too, can lay it to rest. Now the world knows how special she is."

"But Karris knew then…"

Grace's sigh crashed into my subconscious like shattered glass.

"What's wrong, hon?"

"Guess who?"

The crowd parted to let Eva Sanchez through. She boldly strode up to Olisa, hugged her and then wagged a microphone in front of her face like she was bribing her with a lollipop.

"Olisa, How are you? Hello everybody! Do we love her?" Eva asked, goading the crowd and pointing at Olisa as they lustily responded in affirmation. With every bit of media savvy she could muster, she elbowed her way into this impromptu gathering.

"Look how much they love you, Olisa!" Eva wiggled her fingers at people she knew. "We rarely get the chance to actually see you, and I got so excited I had to come up here and say hello. Everyone in the world is trying get in touch with you, and here you are just hanging out with the good citizens of Venice Beach. I think it's wonderful!"

There was an abundance of popcorn explosions, signaling the arrival of more paparazzi.

"People, I must ask that you forgive my intrusion. We, and by that I mean the media, have competed to get an interview with Olisa Carpenter… I guess we just don't have your clout!"

The crowd roared their approval.

"Olisa, it is so beautiful to see the rapport between you and this wonderful community. I suppose we can all learn a lesson from this. This is what it's all about… being with the people. I hope no one minds me saying this, but to be honest, I'm feeling a little selfish… I don't want to leave because I want to be a part of this good feeling, too. Is that all right?"

The sustained applause confirmed her support.

It was a brash move, and might have brought the boo birds out if it had been anyone else crashing the party. But this was Eva Sanchez— the people's reporter. As reporters double parked on Windward Ave, heedless of the tow truck warnings and toted their equipment onto the beach to position themselves as close to Olisa as possible, with one slap Eva had put her rivals in check. No other media darlings would dare step forward at this stage of the game, and some of the paparazzi got put in place real fast when they tried to jostle the wrong people. But no one messed with Eva Sanchez. They loved and trusted her. Moreover, her popularity had grown exponentially with Olisa's.

The Latino population had more than doubled in the last ten years, and they had the L.A. home girl's back. Over the last year, coupled with Sanchez's daring reportage of Olisa, KLSC was solidly number one in Southern California. Eva's involvement in their prime-time programming rocketed KLSC skyward. She single-handedly drew more Latino households than anyone across the country, even outpacing the Spanish-language stations, which was a major accomplishment.

Eva was a fighter and a hands-on kind of person. She didn't mind getting her hands dirty and did all the reportorial grunt work, covering stories in some of the seediest and most ostracized parts of town. She had provided the station a gritty, hip-hop, homegrown, street flavor, that would have been a liability not long ago, but now uniquely made her "a keeping it real" kind of gal, and the public recognized and appreciated it. She was a community advocate, frequently trumpeting causes such as exposing avaricious slumlords or greed stricken retailers who charged insane prices to inner-city residents, exceeding the prices of the same products in such affluent areas as Beverly Hills. It was Eva you saw, not Brevin Hightower, working the weekend shifts talking to drug addicted mothers, teenage runaways, reformed gang bangers, and illegal aliens. Criminal suspects who were Latino, often phoned the station promising to turn themselves in to the police if Eva Sanchez escorted them to the station. It didn't hurt that such support derived from a city boasting the most diverse number of religions in the United States, including a strong Roman Catholic constituent, which coincidentally, is the predominate faith in the Hispanic community, the country's fastest growing ethnic minority.

"Since so many of us are dying to speak with you, Olisa, would you mind if I take my microphone around and let people ask questions, then even more of us could hear you? And I might even ask a few myself."

Olisa smiled. "That's fine."

Sure enough, Eva improvised faster than a jazz musician, setting it up as a special forum in which people asked Olisa anything they wanted with the added draw of appearing on television, too. It had a nostalgic feel, reminding me of the old days of rallies and protests in front of the Venice Pavilion, before the legendary landmark was torn down by yuppie developers. She had turned from being an intruder to a host of this event. I hated to admit it, but damn, it was absolutely brilliant. I could hear her peers collectively sighing.

"Since I have the microphone, may I ask you the first couple of questions, Olisa?"

Olisa nodded, a tranquil smile on her face as she folded her hands in front of her. Someone offered her a chair, but she refused it.

"The archdiocese and the most respected physicians in the world are investigating all the particulars surrounding the recovery of Nick Cavaliere to officially declare if this is truly a miracle…"

"We don't need no stinkin' official word!" someone heckled. "We know what's up! Praise God!"

"Understandably, the court of public opinion has already spoken. But does it frustrate you to know that even though the evidence is on film, medical specialists are still cautioning that before we get hysterical and jump the gun we need to explore the circumstances more closely. The inference is that this might be a sophisticated scam of some type. Do you think it's a power play by some?"

"I don't really care. Miracles occur every day, and they have nothing to do with me," Olisa replied.

"Yes, but shouldn't you defend yourself against all the doubting Thomases out there who still question your abilities?"

"No," replied Olisa firmly. "People have a right to their opinions."

There was thunderous applause and shouts of, "We believe in you, Olisa!"

Olisa immediately corrected them, "I am not the one you should believe in. God is."

"What's your question?" Eva asked a kid holding a basketball in one arm, baggy pants hanging past his knees.

"Man, I just want you to know you're the bomb, you know... I just want to know how it feels... You know what I'm saying? Does it hurt or anything?"

"How does it feel?" Olisa pondered. "It's hard to explain... It's a loving, spiritual energy that is so expansive it fills every fiber of your body. It can make you so physically tense , you want to explode. When someone is healed, I can feel the energy draining from my body. It is such a relief when it ends that I just want to sleep for an eternity. Does that make sense to you?"

"Oh yeah, I hear you... I get feelings like that now and then, too, but it ain't because I healed someone." He grinned sheepishly as his brown face reddened while he self-consciously rubbed his shaved head.

Everyone, including Olisa, laughed heartily.

"I'm not sure if that one will make the news." Eva laughed. "Olisa, I've got to ask you another question."

"Yes?"

"I noticed that you walked on stage barefoot, and I see the same thing today. One e-mail that came in to the station wondered if this was your way of demonstrating solidarity with the hungry and poor people of the world."

"I wish it was that well thought out, Eva, but the fact is, I just don't like wearing shoes. I like feeling the ground under my feet. I think it's a habit I picked up when I visited Cape Verde. Everyone walks around without shoes there."

"Okay. Next. What would you like to ask?"

Eva held the microphone up to a woman with metallic blue hair who giggled nervously.

"When I look at you, I see someone so special and beautiful. How do you see yourself?"

"That's nice, thank you. Um, I see myself as God's servant."

"Kind of like a modern day Jesus?"

"Oh no, Eva! No. I would never even think about such a comparison."

"Well, others do. I can't tell you how many people call, write, fax, and e-mail the station swearing you are the second coming of Christ in a woman's body. Wouldn't you agree you have similar abilities? For example, Jesus healed the sick, Jesus was a preacher, Jesus claimed to be the Son of God sent down to earth to help the needy; Jesus was a prophet, and a spiritual seer who could see into the future."

"I am not Jesus."

"But you do have the gift to see into the future, correct?"

She laughed. "I'd say I'm more psycho than psychic."

"Hardly… There are quite a few people out there who would beg to differ."

Olisa smiled as she brushed back several runaway strands of hair from underneath her scarf.

Meanwhile, I noticed that during the midst of all this, somehow Jon had managed to make his way to the top of the hill. He was standing next to Logan, and they were engaged in a very intense discussion. Jonathan was doing most of the talking. It was evident by the looks on their faces that it was not good. He began to move away, but Jonathan grabbed his arm and said something rapidly in his ear. Logan yanked his arm away and moved to the other side of Olisa. However, the enthusiasm he exhibited earlier while shooting photos had significantly diminished. Jon continued to stand there, with a half smile on his face.

"You seem to be getting a good laugh out of this, sir." Eva spoke to a small diminutive Caucasian man, wearing a very dapper suit and tie. He glaringly stood out among the scantily clad beach crowd. I had spied him earlier, furiously jotting down notes on a pad coupled with occasional spurts of scathing laughter. The sun bore down on his shiny bald spot that served as an island for his muddy reef of hair.

"I just find the fascination with this young woman by the media both amusing and disgusting, Ms. Sanchez. It's not necessarily her fault. I just worry about the numbers of people being lead into a one-way tunnel of darkness."

"And why do you say that?"

"The fact that you have to ask, tells me all I need to know about you. However, I would like to ask Ms. Carpenter a question, if I might. Young lady, it's really not my business, but I'm just curious. What religion are you? Christian, Catholic, Lutheran, Muslim, Buddhist, Zoroastrian?"

His tone was pleasant, but it leaked with condescension. His beady eyes were plastered against his wire-rimmed glasses, and he wore a smug knowing smile on his face that indicated his mind was already made up, regardless of the answer.

"I am none of them and all of them."

One eyebrow partially lifted as he waited patiently for her to finish.

"My God is your God. To me, it doesn't matter if you are a follower of Jesus, Buddha, Muhammad, Yahweh, The Great Spirit, Krishna, or Baha'u'llah—in loving God, we are all one."

The man's arm stiffly flew out, grabbing the microphone.

"Pardon me, Ms. Sanchez, I certainly don't want to exceed my quota for questions, but I must ask, Ms. Carpenter, one more thing: First, I commend you for tolerating such a foolhardy question, surprisingly from Ms. Sanchez, comparing you to Jesus Christ. However, again, forgive me, but, do you believe in our Lord and Savior, Jesus Christ, the Redeemer, who will one day come back to earth to seek judgment on the sins of mankind?" A self-righteous smirk barged its way into his staid smile.

"Careful, Olisa," I whispered as Grace's body stiffened.

The loaded question fueled the intensity in Olisa's eyes.

"We don't have time to wait for Christ's return to earth."

"Excuse me, ma'am? I don't believe I heard you correctly."

"The world we live in is on a course toward self-destruction. Unless we move together as one, we may not be here for Christ to judge. One push of a button can annihilate the human race. Jesus said love thy neighbor as thy self, yet was put to death because of his beliefs, passions, and efforts to promote peace throughout the world. Those who coveted power feared him. His message of love was delivered long ago. We can't just sit back and wait.

"Today we must act. Now is the time to promote global unity. This marks the new age for humanity to begin an era of transformation. We must obliterate all corrupt and harmful political, social, and interpersonal obstacles that prevent us from being free to enjoy our lives to the maximum degree. We cannot wait for the messiah to liberate us, we must do it ourselves."

The resounding applause did nothing to soften the disdain orbiting in his eyes. He trashed the fake smile as he sardonically responded, "Well I do hope you will find it within yourself to one day forgive our dear Lord for moving at such a slow pace. I hope that He will be sure to schedule an appointment with you to help him choose the Day of Judgment," he chuckled with overwrought self-importance. "Hopefully, those who are willing to follow you into the quagmires of hell will make a special note of that," he said, surveying the crowd pitiably.

"I'm not looking for followers. I'm looking for people who are willing to be at war for the hearts and souls of humankind, and who will join me in bringing about peace in the home and on the streets."

He stopped his jittery writing as his eyes fluttered. "Well spoken. You have a very persuasive style about you, Ms. Carpenter. You are good at saying the type of things people want to hear."

"Similar to the man you are associated with?"

The statement buckled his cool. He pretended to ignore it, but the sudden vein jabbing his neck gave him away.

"Satan is also a good speaker," he remarked in a voice that sounded like metal grinding together. "Although I am certainly not trying to infer anything."

"Of course not," Olisa echoed, uncharacteristically annoyed.

"It's just that the bible clearly warns that we ought to beware of false prophets, and it sounds to me like you're trying to preach some new kind of cult religion or something."

"I'm not a prophet, and I'm not preaching religion. I'm just discussing spirituality and love which appears to be a foreign concept to you."

"Touché, Ms. Carpenter, nevertheless, I still would feel more at ease if you would answer, do you believe in the Holy Bible as the only true Word of God?"

"I believe there are many truths to be found in many holy books. Now, it's my turn. Do you truly believe in your heart that God can be confined to any single religion?"

"Yes, ma'am. I do. The Holy Bible tells me all I need to know."

"And I respect your opinion. But I believe denominations, religions, and books are ways to imprison God in tight and neat little boxes that allow us to make sense of it all. It lends power to an ordered script we can follow and a rulebook that we can always reference. But is man so arrogant as to assume he can truly interpret the Almighty? For centuries, the God concept has been developed and sold by men as the correct religion to billions of people through 'divinely' inspired writings. We fight wars because of the varying and contradictory nature of these interpretations; vehemently arguing text and then killing and maiming in the name of God because the other guy didn't follow the prescribed rules. Who is really seeking to be all-powerful? God or us?

"Instead of us being created in God's image, we have created God in ours; specifically to service our needs and to massage our egos. We have created a God who reflects all of our insecurities. We say if you don't show God some respect, his rage will strike you down in a heart-beat. But the true God is not a dictator or an imperialist. God doesn't live to enslave you. God exists simply out of love. It is in acts of love, in acts of compassion, in acts of valuing yourself and your world, that you will find the true nature of God."

The man simply smiled through his clenched teeth as he endured this salvo of words streaming from a woman whose eyes were lit up like Olympic torches. However, his insipid little grin began to look more and more like crumpled paper. It bothered me when he once again whipped out his tiny notepad and scribbled on it as if he were about to issue a parking citation.

"Joseph, who is this man? I know I've seen him before, but I can't place his face."

"Yeah, me too, and it's driving me crazy, Grace."

Olisa's undulant voice swept over the citizens of Venice.

"We praise God's infinite wisdom, yet we turn a blind eye to the possibility that maybe this Supreme Being appeared to us in countless ways and guises throughout the history of our existence. Is it conceivable that this might explain the diverse writings and interpretations? We do the lip service and say that God is everywhere, yet we denounce any religion that claims a vision of God different from our own."

Eva was about to say something, but someone from the crowd cried out, "Olisa, then what is right? Teach us how to discover the truth!"

"My friends, the truth lies somewhere within you. Don't be afraid to question what you have been taught. God is not going to harm you for asking questions and seeking answers. I believe all religions ulti-mately point the way to salvation. God, not man, is the source from which all religions flow. And if they are truly about God, then they all share one universal truth—and that is to love one another and to love ourselves."

Several seconds passed before that man's jarring voice forced my eyes to open. Grace, too, blinked rapidly, both of us seduced by our daughter's distinctive and mellifluous voice.

"You act as if you know God personally."

Olisa walked up to him and gazed unflinchingly into his indignant eyes. Swirls of blotchy red floated to the surface of his doughy face as he tried unsuccessfully to reciprocate her stare.

"I do know God. Just like anyone here can know and speak to God. God resides within you and me. We are all God's children."

She caught him by surprise when she reached out and embraced his thorny little body. The little biscuit-headed man tolerated her hug for about two seconds before edgily backing away. He jammed the pen and pad into the inside pocket of his suit coat, snorting as if he had gotten water up his nose.

"God bless you," she said to his backside as he hurriedly knifed through the crowd, coughing spasmodically.

An errant voice cried, "Hey, man, don't go away mad! Just go away!"

A stray elbow also tagged the man. He fell to one knee briefly, picked himself up and took off running again.

"No, no, that's not the way! We don't treat our friends like that! Violence to those we disagree with will not solve a thing! We can still love even though we may differ."

Fortunately, sanity was restored. If Olisa had not spoken out at that moment, I sensed that biscuit-head might not have made it out of there in one piece.

"I may not have convinced *him* of our birthright as God's descendants, but how about the rest of you? I see heads nodding, but I also sense uncertainty. Why do we make it so complex? It's so very simple. We don't have to wallow in a lifetime of scholarly research to discover the Creator. God is available to all of us the moment we accept the reality of the spirit. That's what makes it so beautiful.

"How often do you take the time out of each day to truly see the world around you? How often do you observe the skies, the trees, the flowers; inhale the perfume of blooming jasmines, listen to the laughter of children, wrap yourself in the emotion of a gospel song, feel the touch of a baby's hand, hear the rhythms of the ocean waves, or meditate in the still of a country night? God is in all these places. Divine inspiration lies in our own backyards. Do you understand? We don't have to be told, it's ours to uncover."

"Amen!"

"The true battleground is not about whose religion is better, but rather whether we can learn to love, respect, and accept our differences. Again, so simple. Yet, for centuries we have made it one of life's greatest puzzles."

"Can't we all just get along?" Eva joked, but Olisa didn't bite.

"Yeah, a desperate, yet innocently coined phrase that a cynical society attacked and tucked away as fodder for late night talk shows, hip comedians, and bullying editorialists spewing elitist values and refusing to see anything valid in such an odd, Pollyannaish concept as love. But it's still the crux to our survival as a civilization."

Eva warmly acknowledged a woman in the audience that was about six feet tall whose prematurely white hair belied her pretty face. She wore a loose T-shirt and sweat pants, and her face was youthful, expressive, and full of vibrancy as she leaned into the mike.

"Hi, Olisa. My name is Beverly Fairchild, and I am the Executive Director of W.I.N.—Women's International Network. We work on behalf of women's rights and causes throughout the world tackling such issues as physical and sexual abuse, genital mutilation practices, incest, and discrimination."

"Ms. Fairchild, you don't have to introduce yourself. I know exactly who you are. It's a pleasure to meet you. I consistently read your magazine and have always admired you and your organization."

"Thank you so much. I am so flattered to hear that, especially since we are so impressed with you and what you've accomplished. Since you're so difficult to catch up with, right here and now I'd love to extend an invitation for you to meet with our group sometime soon!"

"Invitation accepted."

"Wonderful! I will contact your office. However, while I've got the opportunity, I'm curious—how do you view the role of women in the church?"

"It's tough to answer that because there are so many kinds of churches. I find it appalling to still hear that so many of our church leaders continue to struggle with the issue of women taking a prominent position in the church. Lately I've noticed some churches are slowly changing the old rules to accommodate the contemporary woman's desire to seek a more empowered role in the church hierarchy.

"Still, I'm not surprised when the conflicts occur, particularly when you are speaking about the archaic rules established by men of long ago that are steadfastly maintained by the men of today to keep women in their place. Compare the numbers of female and male rabbis, ministers, pastors, etc. and you will see what I mean. How truly egalitarian is it? Can't women be as inspirational as the men? Churches need civil rights movements of their own. That's why I decided a long time ago I don't need an intermediary, a man, or a church to discover my place with God."

"Beautiful… Simply beautiful," Beverly cheered and clapped supportively. "I knew you were the one. The movement desperately needs someone like you. You should have your own church!"

Olisa bowed her head modestly. "No, no, as I said, I don't want to be a part of a structure, only a part of the action."

"My name is Jamal Harris, and we need you, too, sister," announced a light complexioned black man with a firm and possessive articulation on the latter word. He wore an African cap over his closely cropped hair and an open mud cloth vest revealing his bare chest.

"Our black African-American brothers and sisters in the United States are still subjected to the oppressive system of western apartheid fueled by racial hatred and bigotry. We are continually denounced by a white power structure that spouts racist ideologies and methodically attempts to bury us alive in the graveyards of the economy. Where are our reparations? Where are our forty acres and a mule? They may grin in our face and pat us on our backs, but they refuse to recognize the 'original man,' we who proudly hail from the cradle of civilization and whose ancestral makeup reflects the kings and queens of the great continent of Africa.

"And I say this with all due respect, Ms. Carpenter, you are the queen of all queens, my beautiful sister. The organization I represent would *also* love to have a word with you!" he said with a pronounced smile, swiveling his head competitively toward Beverly Fairchild. "And I know, like me, you too are tired of the ongoing discrimination that black African-American people are forced to confront everyday of their lives. We are not taken in by their plastic smiles and artificial hugs!"

Olisa replied, "Yes, I am very tired of the discrimination that we face as African Americans, but my goal is to battle all discrimination."

"I hear what you are saying, sister, but we need to take care of ourselves first before we can help anyone else."

There was scattered applause.

"Yes, you're right, we must help ourselves, and I'm with you all the way, but we can't build a fortress whose walls cast a shadow over our neighbor's land. We are all responsible for each other, and we must all accept the blame if we intend to survive as a human race. We share a symbiotic relationship as human beings. The parts do equal the whole. You can't put a Band-Aid over a bullet hole and expect the bleeding to end. You've got to get to the source and that means withdrawing the bullet. Or to take it one step further—no one gets shot if the gun doesn't exist. Likewise, no one gets killed if enmity is not in our hearts. There can be no vacancy for hatred in the human heart. It must be vanquished, regardless of race or gender. The pot of gold lies at the end of the entire rainbow, *not* at the end of a single color."

Brotha man nodded, but I doubt he was listening. Didn't matter much, the crowd noise would have drowned out any response he would have made.

Eva struggled to regain her reportorial detachment. "Whew, Okay, Olisa, but aren't you concerned that such strong opinions might be perceived in the wrong way? Some might mistakenly see it as arrogance."

"No. I don't concern myself with that. If it's arrogant to ask for racial harmony and peace, then I'm as arrogant as they come."

No sooner had those words departed from her mouth when a figure splintered from the wall of people and plunged at Olisa's feet, attaching himself to her ankles.

"Please help me. I want to hear. I want to know what the world really sounds like, I want to hear your voice, the voice of God," he pleaded in the shortened trombone-like phrasing of the deaf.

Olisa knelt down, cupping both his ears and prayed over him. A few minutes passed before she firmly shouted, "Stand up!" At first there was no reaction except for him wincing as if he were in severe pain.

She lifted his head up so he could see her lips and again commanded him to rise.

"Yes, yes, yes," he cried repeatedly. "Stand up… I can read your lips, and I hear noise, so much noise, but you mean for me to stand… Yes? Yes! Say it again. Please say it again! Yes, yes, yes, yes, oh sweet lady, it sounds so lovely to me," he wept joyfully in her arms, hugging her with all his might. "Oh my God, thank you! Thank you, oh my God!"

But this happy moment only lasted a second before I saw lines riddling Alton's forehead. He quickly forged his way through the crowd, trying to get Olisa's attention. Mainly because there was a stampede of frenzied people barreling straight toward her.

The man's outburst seemed to trigger something. Some of the people looked like the zombies in *Day of the Living Dead* billowing toward Olisa, wailing and crying her name. I saw a man knock a woman over in a wheelchair without even checking to see if she was okay. Someone screamed, "Get the hell out of my way, asshole. I'm next!" Two elderly women beat the tar out of each other with their purses. All anxious to be cured of whatever affliction troubled them. Many had been waiting patiently for just the right time to approach her and now panicked at the thought that they might not get that opportunity.

Matters became even more confusing as the police aggressively entered the fray. Eva looked terrified initially, until she realized she wasn't the target as the crowd literally surged past her in their effort to get near Olisa. No one gave a shit about the other; they climbed over each other's back to get to her, hands sticking out, grabbing, and ripping Olisa's clothes. The next miracle would be getting Olisa out of there unharmed. My heart was starting to palpitate. I couldn't do anything. Grace and I were squeezed so tightly into the logjam of people, all we could do was watch and pray.

But Gumbo was there.

He cleared a path like a lawnmower, flinging people out of his way. Logan wrapped his body around Olisa, and Jon was right behind them, as they made a beeline past us, accompanied by a host of what I found out later were undercover officers who, thankfully, were friends of Gumbo's. Somehow we managed to follow closely behind amid anguished cries and pleas for her to stay and help them. Gumbo looked like the Incredible Hulk as clothes were shredded from his body by hands that sought to find a way to get to Olisa. It was one of the hairiest situations I had ever encountered. Little Oak squeezed her way out of the crowd and caught up to us. We all got out of there safely as we were ushered into an unmarked police van.

"I know who he is!" Grace blurted, as we peered through the rear windows of the squad car and watched the overly enthusiastic adulators grow smaller and smaller as they chased us with outstretched hands. On top of it all, I saw a police cruiser besieged by rocks and bottles and a block away, a news van was being vandalized by gangs of youth.

Thankfully, Gumbo had some buddies on the police force that gave us a ride home; otherwise, we would have had about a thousand uninvited guests following us home for supper. As it was, helicopters buzzed overhead.

Olisa, adrenaline still flowing, sat in the front seat, busily chatting with a male and female police officer. Jonathan sat in the back with Grace and I, staring out the window. The last time I saw him sulking like this, he had barely been passed over for a Rhodes scholarship. Occasionally under his breath I heard, "Stupid. That was so stupid…"

"You figure out who he is?" I finally asked Grace.

"The man who was busy taking all those notes?"

"Yes. The little hall monitor."

"I don't know his name, but I can guess who his boss is," she said.

"Who?" I asked.

"Walter Popcock."

"Walter Popcock... Popcock... you mean Mr. Televangelist himself? Are you sure?"

"I should be. He almost knocked me over trying to get by. That's when I noticed he had on one of those insignias on his lapel... You know, the one with that dumb looking WP logo that I've seen on his television program."

"That dumb looking logo stands for one of the biggest multimillionaires around," I commented. "He just built that mega sized church skyscraper in Orange County on all those acres. He describes his fortress as being only a fingertip away from heaven. So you think the little weasel is reporting to him, huh?"

"Definitely," interjected Jon.

"But why?"

"Because she's the competition," Jon spat.

"Son of a gun!"

CHAPTER 9

Eva's smiling face loomed on the screen. "Thanks for joining us in our search to find out more about the enigma that is Olisa Carpenter. Today we are here at McCabe's Guitar Shop with Kevin Lipsyte, a folk musician from up north in Santa Cruz, California." The camera panned back to show them on a small stage sitting on stools. Kevin let his strawberry blonde hair drop down to his shoulders as he adjusted his San Francisco Giant's baseball cap. He also held an acoustic guitar in his lap.

"Now, Kevin, I wasn't wrong in describing you as a folk musician, was I?"

"No… that's me. I mean, we do all kinds of music, ranging from country to blues." Kevin picked a couple of blues notes on his guitar to accent his point.

"All right! Sounds good. I might have to come by here tonight and listen to you guys play. Do you play any *boleros*? That's the music from my homeland."

Kevin laughed. "If that's what it will take to get you here tonight, we'll add it to our repertoire," he said flirtatiously.

"Then you may see me tonight," she responded in kind. "Okay, Kevin, so tell me, what you know about Olisa Carpenter. You met in Santa Cruz, right?"

"Olisa? Yeah, we met there. She is one of the most out-of-sight women I have ever met in my life. Always courteous, always nice. And those eyes. Oh man… deep. When she looks at you, you feel like you'd been stripped down to your underwear."

Eva laughed. "I might not have said it that way, but I understand."

"She used to frequent George's Coffeehouse and Cafe, usually on Friday nights. The owner, George, was Hungarian. A true jazz aficionado, he offered live music every Friday evening: but not just jazz; he presented, folk, country, classical—you name it. Sometimes he even featured poetry readings. George's was the best. It was a great place to hangout and unwind. I played acoustic guitar and George invited my band to play so many times we became like the unofficial house band."

"So how did you meet Olisa?"

"At George's. If I ever needed a smile, man, all I had to do was look hard enough into the audience, and I'd easily spot her face in the crowd. When I did, she never failed to give me that lift. Afterwards, she always hung around and had something nice to say to us after every show, even if we sounded like falling horse turds." He played a flat note on the guitar, shook his head, and chuckled. "She'd discuss the songs we performed and give you feedback on it, how it affected her and what lyrics had more special meaning to her. Man, she was a bitching gal… We sure missed her when she graduated.

"But sorry if I'm rambling … You said you wanted to know if I could tell you anything special about her?" Eva nodded and he continued, "I guess you mean like magical, spiritual or something like that? The kind of stuff the press is reporting these days, right?"

"That would be good," Eva replied.

"Funny, I didn't think about her that way then… Don't get me wrong, anybody could tell she was different, but I was living in a drug-induced fog in those days before I spent a little bit of time in rehab, you know?"

"Okay, I remember one time after a show; we were invited to an after party at George's new pad tucked away high up in the hills. When I showed up, Olisa and one of her close buddies were already there—an Indian chick with hair down to her ankles. I think her name was Lana or something. She used to dress kind of militant, feathers, earrings, beads, the works… plus, yards of attitude. If I even looked at her cross-eyed, you could feel the arrow in your back. She had a way of making you feel like you were the reincarnation of General Custer without saying a word. Hey, but you know what? That didn't bother me. I understood where she was coming from. The white man literally decimated the Native American population, and culture, man. I got all that from her. When I got a chance to know her, she taught me a lot of things. I was kinda naive about people of different cultures. What do you expect? Hey, I was a white boy from Los Gatos… the only thing ethnic in my family was usually the cover of *National Geographic*."

Eva grinned, but nodded for him to continue.

"Anyway, we were just kicking it at the party, philosophizing, drinking, getting high, partying, you know how it is… Now, here's where it gets a little sketchy… I guess I shouldn't say this on the air," he flicked his nose with his finger, "but like I said, I was getting pretty high. Someone suggested doing a séance. George grabbed some of the lighted candles in the house and placed them on the center of the coffee table in the living room as we all sat cross-legged in a circle holding hands. It was happening… The Indian chick even did this little ceremonial chant; although I was too busy staring at her to remember what she was saying… You know how it is: getting high, getting horny…" Eva shrugged her shoulders.

"Oh, okay, so in the séance, you're supposed to be calling up the dead and all that stuff. About now, I was floating nicely and feeling like one of the dead until the Indian babe started getting real serious, telling everybody that if we really wanted to be in touch with the spirits that we needed to stop bullshitting around and concentrate. She swore that Olisa could actually talk to the dead. I wanted a hit on whatever pipe she was smoking. I think I even cracked a joke about that, and she started cussing at me… Man, she was ticked off. She was really pissing me off as well, because it was affecting the mellow high I was feeling. Made me want to go smoke some more reefer, but I didn't want to be the one to break the chain of hands and hear her dissing me in front of everybody.

"I remembered thinking in my drugged state that Olisa must really be high if she thought she could converse with spirits and all that, but I never saw her take a hit of some smoke, maybe just an occasional sip of wine."

"Tell us what happened next."

"Yeah, well, anyway, she led the discussion on people who were gone from this world and somehow we moved into reminiscing about the great 60's musicians that died young, you know—Janis Joplin, Brian Jones, Otis Redding, Jimi Hendrix, Jim Morrison, Sam Cooke, Tammi Terrell, and so on."

"Some of my favorites."

"Yeah, mine, too. Well, this is about the point things started getting real interesting. We finally all agreed on one name out of the group—Jimi Hendrix. Dude was the man. As far as I'm concerned, every guitar player around has to give him his due…" He noticed Eva rotated her hand to move him along.

"Okay, so the Indian chic…"

"Laura, you mean."

"Yeah, Laura… So Laura, the Indian chick, tells us to say Jimi's name over and over because it helps Olisa focus. Well, the more we chanted Hendrix's name, the more intense it got. I mean super intense."

"Intense in what way?" The expression on Eva's face was intense.

"You know when you hear about the air particles getting thick in some of your horror books—well that stuff is true." Kevin lifted his baseball cap and swept his hand through his hair several times. He was perspiring heavily. "It started getting real icky… I almost couldn't breathe. At first, I thought maybe I was smoking some bad stuff, cause I was feeling all tight and queasy. Then I noticed that Olisa was shaking and everything and in some kind of trance." He shook his body to demonstrate. "Her voice was building in this strange way, like a mantra, man. She said, Jimi if you are in the room with us please let us know. Show your presence. Give us a sign. Don't be afraid, give us a sign."

"Listening to this is starting to frighten me."

"Hey, check this out. That night it had started raining hard, and everyone had already agreed to turn that puppy into a slumber party and crash at George's pad. I'm saying all this to let you know how weird things started getting. All of a sudden, the flames in the fireplace were

popping like gunshots. Then everything got still. It even stopped raining. All of the candles started flickering like go-go dancers. At first I
thought someone had slipped some acid or peyote in my drink, because
candles don't make shadows like that. The more I stared at the flames,
the more they looked like human shapes. It was tripping me out. Plus,
I thought we were headed into the ice age again, man, it was cold in
that house."

"Oooooh!" Eva said, her eyes wide, holding her shoulders and shivering. "We just crossed into Stephen King territory!"

"Yeah, except this (blip) was real. Olisa was into a groove, man, she
kept chanting Jimi's name faster and faster. Suddenly, the phone rang.
I swear we all jumped as if we'd had been goosed. For Christ's sake, you
know we were on edge because it was only the phone, man. We all
laughed nervously—except for George. George's face was so pale it
looked bleached."

"Now this is what's going to trip you out. George had only moved
into the house a couple of days ago, so this was supposed to be a house-
warming party, too. He hadn't even placed an order for the phone to be
connected yet, so he had a big laugh as he watched me, high as a kite,
trying to call my girlfriend on a disconnected phone. He let me spend
about five minutes dicking around with it, oops, sorry about that,
before he showed me I was trying to use a phone that had been ripped
from the wall by the prior tenant."

"George wasn't laughing anymore as the phone rang and rang and
rang. Neither was anyone else. Each ring kept building up like gathering storm clouds. The rings were starting to get so loud I wanted to
crap in my pants. What I remember most is that the one who didn't
seem to be afraid was Olisa. She got up to answer it, but George
jumped up and blocked her path, all bent out of shape and screaming
irrationally at her not to touch the (blip) phone. To this day I don't
know what he would have done if she had taken another step forward.
I had never seen George look that way before. He had a wild crazy look
in his eyes, and he kept staring at the phone as if it was some kind of

monster. Dude's face was so constricted I thought he was having a heart attack."

"That didn't sound good. Tell us something about George."

Kevin paused to play a few notes on his guitar before answering. "George wasn't exactly a young man, he was somewhere in his fifties and he had lived a life. George had traveled all over the world and faced every kind of danger you could think of. His family fled from Hungary during all the war and bloodshed. On a safari, George even survived a mauling by a lion in Africa. George wasn't the type to be easily frightened. But that night he was terrified as the resurrected telephone kept ringing. Olisa smiled at him and sat back down on the floor. She didn't take offense to George's aggression. She seemed to understand."

"That sounds like our girl."

"And I swear that phone rang about another twenty times before finally giving up. Almost immediately, the room filled with heat and I heard the rain slapping the windows again. I looked around, and the only thing that comforted me was that everyone else looked scared shitless, too, except for Olisa and her friend. The Indian chick, uh, Laura, grumbled to Olisa sarcastically about the courage of the white man and how he was the Indian's burden. I heard, 'I warned them not to mess around with spirits unless they meant it—typical!'"

"Periodic chills swept through my body, and it shook involuntarily. But that didn't even bother me... what bothered me was that the nice little high I nurtured had disappeared."

He hesitated as if he were expecting a reaction from Eva. I'm not sure what he expected, because her face had a reporter's detachment. Although I got the feeling she would have loved to have made a crack about that statement.

"Afterwards we all just sacked out in the living room, except for George. He retired to his bedroom without saying goodnight to anyone or trying to make a move on a single woman. And if you knew George, you'd know that was unusual. George made everything an epic event. One night, months later, George and I were having a drink and

I brought it up during a discussion, but his eyes got that funny look in them, and I knew to change the subject. I never brought it up again."

"But I will always wonder who was on the other end of that phone. Yeah, that and the fact that ever since that incident, "Purple Haze" took on a whole new meaning for me." Then interview ended with Kevin playing a few acoustical licks from the song, "Purple Haze."

On the way home, we were trailed by a phalanx of reporters, paparazzi, curiosity seekers, and fans. The police and security were already there clearing an opening through the alley so we could drive through.

Safely tucked inside our house, it was a relief to see Laura, Gumbo and Logan clanging the gate shut and trudging up the walkway as I retired from my window seat to open the door.

"Everybody okay?" I couldn't get the shakiness out of my voice.

"Yeah, Unc, we're fine," Gumbo replied smothering me in a generous hug. How 'bout y'all? Where's Olisa."

"She's relaxing in our bed—"

I didn't have a chance to finish before Grace cried, "Jonathan, no!"

Jonathan rushed Logan the second he stepped inside the house. Laura had to jump out of the way.

"Hey!" Logan cried defenselessly as I saw two pair of feet sink over the couch. Jonathan's hands were fastened around his neck. Unlike me, Gumbo was on it quickly, prying Jonathan's fingers loose and yanking him off Logan. Bewildered, Logan gradually sat up, vigorously rubbing his neck and accepting my outstretched hand as he warily rose to his feet.

"What was that all about, man?" Logan asked, never dropping his eyes from Jonathan's as he calmly brushed his clothes and bent down to pick up his black Kangol hat and camera. He swiftly inspected the camera; its strap was broken. He rolled it around a couple of times in his hands. Olisa told me that Logan had witnessed the aftermath of the genocidal massacre of more than 1, 000, 000 ethnic Tutsis in Rwanda. It would take more than this to fluster him.

I wish I could have said the same thing about my son who grunted and cursed as he futilely did pull-ups on Gumbo's locked forearms.

"Let go, Gumbo, I'm serious, man…"

"Soon as you cool down, cuz."

"All right, all right, I'm cool." He threw his hands up in the air, Gumbo's arms still wrapped around his chest.

The second Gumbo relaxed, Jonathan slipped out of his arms and charged Logan once again, and once again found himself sandwiched in Gumbo's arms.

"We can dance all night, cuz. Ain't you tired yet? I know I am."

"All right, Gumbo. This time I'm definitely fine. You can let go, I'm through with that punk ass bastard."

Gumbo slowly unfolded his arms as Jon held them straight up a little longer as if to prove he was under his own control before letting them dissolve to his sides.

"You guys need to chill out! Don't you know Olisa is trying to sleep in there?" Laura pointed to our bedroom. "Fighting is not going to do it. We're all about family here, so try to find a way to work this out!" Laura admonished.

"Tell him to work it out, Laura. Not me! Jon's the one with the problem."

"Want to know my problem, Lo? My problem is you! That's what the fuck my problem is!" Gumbo gave Jon a reminder tap on the arm as Jon inched forward.

"Jon, I'm telling you, man, don't walk up on me no more," Logan warned as Gumbo hastily stepped between them. "I took it the first time, but I'm not your whipping boy… but that's all right… I'm leaving right now, out of respect for your family." He nodded at Grace and I, who were standing side by side in shock. "So you don't have to worry about me. Just don't walk up on me, again, okay?"

Jonathan shook his finger at Logan. "Nigga, you don't tell me what I can do and what I can't do! Come on, Gumbo, back off me, I'm not going after the little chump," he barked, shoving Gumbo's hands.

"Just get to stepping, Lo, and take your shit with you. It's over! Understand? Send me your bill. I'll pay you what I owe you. Here, I probably got enough money in my pocket to cover your ass right now!" Jon uttered condescendingly, fumbling inside his jacket and drawing out a huge wad of bills. "Here you go! Take what I got. I'm sure this will more than enough cover your expenses!" He flung it toward Logan.

Logan swatted the bundle away. "No! Keep your damn money, man. I told you before, it ain't about the money!"

"What's it's all about then… getting my sister killed or trying to screw her?"

Logan's face was more leveled by that comment then Jonathan's necktie tackle. "Man, what are you saying? I tried to protect Olisa."

"Did you do something with my sister, man?"

Logan shook his head and waved him off as he turned and walked toward the door.

"Don't turn your back on me, Lo! Look at me when I'm talking to you!"

"Ok, Jonathan, that's enough," Grace said firmly, closing her eyes. "You've stated your piece. I can't even believe your father and I let it go on this long. No guest has ever been treated like this in our home." She turned and grabbed Logan by the elbow before he was able to walk out the door. "I am so sorry, Logan. Please forgive us."

"Ma'am, it's okay…"

"Guest? Mom, he's not a guest. He's an employee. I hired him to do a job! You don't need to apologize to him! You saw it. He almost got Olisa killed! He had absolutely no right sneaking her out to the beach behind our backs! Who the hell does he think he is? He knows what a security risk it is!"

"You got it all wrong, Jonathan, I swear I didn't…"

"I don't want to hear it, Lo," he argued, waving his hands and glaring out the window. When he turned back to face him, a new expression appeared on his face.

"You know what, baby? Mom's right, I apologize for losing my cool. My bad. Some situations don't always work out the way you want.

You know what I'm saying? But that doesn't prevent us from acting like professionals, right?" Jonathan walked around the house and bent over to pick up the loose bills strewn about the floor. He gathered the bills, and neatly folded them, placing them back in his pocket.

"Seriously, send me your bill. You put too much time and energy into this. We'll chalk it up to a bad day. You know what I mean? I still want to work with you… you know. I'm still a consultant at RPM. We have another video coming up, and I'll tell you what—the job is yours! I may get stupid now and then, but I'm not a fool. I meant it when I said you're a great photographer. I'll give you a call real soon, okay?"

"No, not okay."

I thought to myself, uh, oh.

Olisa emerged from our bedroom into the living room, eyes hard. "What exactly is going on here? Jonathan, why are you going off on Logan?" She walked up to him, her arms tightly folded.

"Going off on Logan?" Jon asked incredulously, his arms outstretched. "I know I didn't hear you right. This is the guy that damn near got you killed, and you think I'm going off on him?! Am I missing something here? There was a mob scene out there today, Olisa. We don't know how many people may have gotten hurt. You could have been hurt," he argued, pointing his forefinger at her. "We had no way of preparing for something like that on such short notice. We're lucky we made it home in one piece."

"But we did, Jonathan."

Jonathan rolled his eyes in frustration. "Oli, those people were ready to tear you into souvenir pieces."

"They wouldn't have harmed me."

"How do you know that, Oli?" Jon asked, circling her. "Some of these folks aren't thinking with clear heads. And don't even think about going out there without notifying someone first! Logan had no business bringing you to the beach without sufficient planning and protection. Do you think all the alarms and all the security we've got around here is for decor! All I'm saying is, he should have talked to me first!"

Point made, he stepped back and planted himself against the living room wall.

"Is that what this is all about, Jonathan? Talking to you first?"

"Olisa, please… You make it sound like I'm wrong to try and protect my big sister when I see her life may be in jeopardy. We are family and a team. That's my responsibility. Get real! In my business I've seen what can happen to…"

Olisa waved him off, marching up to him, hands on hip.

"Jon, you are my brother, and I love you, but this is my life. I don't have to talk to you first. Do you understand?"

He didn't say anything. Instead, he crossed his arms in a snit. Olisa pushed his arms down and grabbed him by the shoulders. She tried to make contact with his restlessly roving eyes. He tried to pull away from her, but she held firm. Finally, he looked her solidly in the eyes and said, "Olisa, I understand, but you can't run around doing impromptu interviews. You're tossing all our work down the drain. I had you set up with Susan Blair on channel 7 for an exclusive one on one interview?"

"Who is Susan Blair?" she asked, releasing him from her grip. He looked relieved.

"The superstar diva of the major networks, that's all. Put it this way. It doesn't get any better than Susan Blair. The president of the free world is on a waiting list to meet with her. She is the number one news anchor. What do you think her reaction is going to be when she finds out that a wannabe like Eva Sanchez got you first? I'll be lucky if her people even take my phone call!"

"Oh, they'll take it."

"Is that right, Logan?" Jon was once again intercepted before he could get halfway to Logan by Gumbo. Jon comically stood on tiptoes and peered over Gumbo's huge shoulder to make his point to Logan.

"Scuse the hell out of me!" Jon continued. "Now you profess to know what Susan Blair's going to do! When did you become the network president?"

Olisa sighed in exasperation. "Jonathan, stop… Please."

"It's okay, Olisa. Yes, I do know, Jon. Susan Blair has a reputation for acting huffy, but she's not about to risk losing an interview on one of the hottest news stories to date, especially with the opportunity to upstage Eva Sanchez. I guarantee you she'll do the interview."

"Oh, well now that you've given us your guarantee, I guess I can get some sleep!" Jonathan threw his hands up. "By the way, almighty Kreskin, did you happen to peek into your crystal ball before we got mobbed today?"

Gumbo moved away as Olisa got back in Jon's face. "Jon, it wasn't Logan's idea. I'm the one who called and begged him to see the sunrise with me. And he's the one that argued with me to stay home or at least let someone know where we are. So I called Laura. I told Logan I was going to the beach whether he joined me or not. So don't blame him. Blame me," she punctuated by tapping her finger to her chest. "I'm the one who misread the situation. Thank God he was there when things got out of hand."

Jonathan self-consciously rubbed the back of his smooth head as he released a heavy sigh. "Hey, man, I'm sorry… I…"

"Don't even sweat it, man, I understand. If it was my sister, I might have reacted the same way."

"Are you guys all right?" Peter asked blowing in through the open door, briefcase in hand and tie flapping over his shoulder. "Olisa, I was worried…"

"I'm fine, Peter," she assured him, patting his shoulders as they embraced.

"Good. Man, I had to park about five blocks away from here. It's a zoo out there! The traffic is bumper-to-bumper on Lincoln Boulevard I'd have gotten here faster if I had just gotten out the car and walked. Plus, the adventures of our gal Olisa are all over the tube, with easy to follow aerial shots of where you live. The neighbors must love you guys."

"What? Is that why they haven't spoken to us for the past couple of weeks?" I remarked sarcastically.

"Not at all, Mr. Carpenter, once security let me pass, one of your neighbors emphatically asked me to be sure to pass along a sexually explicit two word phrase that shows how deeply he feels for you."

"Don't bother telling me, I can already feel the love."

"Absolutely, Mr. Carpenter. On another note, get the champagne glasses out people! Jon doesn't even know about this. You mind, Jon?"

"It's on you," Jon said tiredly, massaging his forehead with one hand.

Peter clapped his hands excitedly. "Okay, first, I want everyone to take a seat at the dining room table so I can properly make the announcement."

"Peter, just tell us. I've got a major headache, and I'm just not into games right now."

"Jon, give me a minute, and I'll get rid of that headache real quick. C'mon everybody, just humor me," Peter cajoled.

We all reluctantly pulled up chairs at the table and took a seat.

"Olisa, your friend, Ms. Moss, called today."

"Cecilia Moss?" she exclaimed. "How is she? Is she ready for another reading?"

"I forgot to ask," Peter laughed loudly, "but that's not the reason she called. OC, are you aware of how much your friend is worth, monetarily speaking, of course."

"No… We never really talk about that. I know her late husband did well in retail or something."

"Yeah, he did pretty well… Ryan Moss initially made a fortune in California real estate during the 60's and then parlayed some of that money into a virgin idea that led to him owning the world's oldest, largest, and fastest growing health food store chain; along with Moss' airport gift shops, Moss' exquisite mail order catalog, and all its subsidiaries. Oh, and a few hotels here and there. When he died of a heart attack a few years ago, Cecilia became a major stockholder in Moss Enterprises."

"So basically what you're telling us is that the Malibu Lady is loaded," I deadpanned.

"To put it lightly, Sir Carpenter. She notified the office this morning that it's her seventy-fifth birthday, and she's decided she wants to become the philanthropist she has always dreamed about. She wants to be involved in some good works before she finally takes leave of this planet and can't think of a better thing to do than donate fifty million dollars to the growth of O.L.I.S.A., Inc."

I don't know what else he said because the chairs screeched loudly on the dining room's hardwood floors as everyone jumped up screaming. Even Olisa bounced up and down, clapping her hands.

"Petey boy, you were right." Jonathan laughed. "You just turned my headache into a footnote."

"She donated $50 million dollars?" I reiterated, still unable to get past that figure.

Peter laughed loudly. "I repeat, for the hard of hearing—50 million dollars, Mr. C. She said the money is to be distributed in whatever way Olisa sees fit, including building a center for the company. But that's not all… She plans to campaign on our behalf to some of her rich society gal pals to get them to contribute as well. She insisted that I tell Olisa how much she loves her and that she has complete faith in what she's doing and will donate more if necessary!"

"I don't believe it… That is so wonderful of her! I'm going to call her tonight!"

"Mercy me," Grace gasped.

"Yeah, you do that, Olisa." Jonathan beamed while pacing the room. "People believe in you, girl. They are sending whatever they can, a quarter, a dollar, cookies in foil… it's remarkable! And we're just getting started. O.L.I.S.A. Inc. has officially become a multimillion dollar company tonight."

"Which means we can start allocating funds to organizations that need our help right away, yes?" Olisa asked anxiously. She was fired up.

"For sure, Olisa. But not until we make sure all things are in place first." We need to meet and review and sort through all the information pouring in, and then we get to do the fun part and make decisions on where the monies should be allocated. Do you see now what I've been trying to tell you?" Jonathan's eyes glowed and his energy flooded back. He was all business again.

"Do you see what's happening, Olisa? I know you love hanging out with your friends at the beach, but you have more worlds to conquer than being on display at the boardwalk. You're going to help millions of people in your life before we're through. Wait until you see what happens when we set up a website! It's going to blow your mind, baby! Are you listening to your little brother? I keep telling you, let me take care of things. Let me take care of you. The only thing I ask is that you stay focused. We can't let anything or anybody ruin things for us now!" Jonathan kept his eyes trained on Olisa, but it was fairly obvious whom he was referring to.

"Congratulations, Olisa." Logan pecked her on the cheek. "*Ciao*, everyone."

Olisa stepped in front of him, grabbing his hand before he reached for the door. "Wait, Logan… why are you leaving? You're a part of this celebration, too. Is it because of what Jon said? I'm sure he didn't mean it the way it sounded."

"No, Olisa, I think that's exactly the way he meant it. Ask him."

She glanced sideways, but Jonathan averted her eyes.

"See… But, it's okay, Olisa. This goes back… It isn't the first time your brother and I have had discussions…"

The glare from Jonathan's eyes could have lit the logs in the fireplace.

"I'm not sure what you're intimating and I'm not sure I really care, but if Jon's forcing you to go…"

"No, that's not it, Olisa," Logan interjected as he played with her fingers. "I'm not leaving because of Jon…"

Jonathan thoughtfully rubbed his thumb back and forth across his bottom lip.

"Then why?"

"Because of you…"

"Me? What did I do?"

Logan shook his head and chuckled softly as he gazed into her unyielding eyes. Nervously he clasped her hands.

"Can we talk somewhere else?" he hinted, self-consciously.

"No. Say what you have to say here. We've come this far."

About that point we should have given them some privacy, but no one moved.

"Okay," Logan sighed, "I'm all messed up behind you. But it's even deeper than that. I don't fit into the game plan. You don't need distractions or conflicts in your life right now. The public is making enough demands on you as it is. You need a clear head so you can concentrate on the future."

"Is that you talking or my brother?"

"It doesn't matter," he defended. "What matters is you helping others."

"And what do you need, Logan? At least give me that courtesy before you take off—or should I wait until you consult with Jonathan, first?" Despite the unusual chill in her voice, her rapidly pooling eyes betrayed her.

"No, I think I can speak for myself, Olisa." His fingers wrestled with her rigid ones and then interlocked. "I need you."

Olisa chewed on her bottom lip and slowly swallowed. She tried to drop her eyes, but Logan wouldn't let her. He gently lifted her chin so he could hold her eyes in his. He had a lot more to say, and I don't think he gave a damn who was in the room.

"When that crowd started coming at you, I didn't know if they wanted to hug you, kidnap you, or kiss you to death. All I knew is I didn't want them to get near you. For the first time in my self-centered life, I didn't care what happened to me as long as you were safe. And unless you know me, you'll never understand how significant that is."

"Does anyone really know you?" Olisa asked, softly.

"I think you do."

He gently caressed her face as a tear rolled down his thumb and slashed across his wrist.

About this point, I was wishing I could fade into the walls. And I'm sure that my fellow spectators felt the same way. However, we just stood there like backdrop. No one dared to move or even cough. It was like, to do so would break the spell that had somehow involved us all.

"Olisa, I'm not used to this, feel kind of funny, you know… all mush mouth…"

"Good. I like it."

He smiled. "Do you? Yeah, I'm glad, but it doesn't work for a photojournalist. I'm not supposed to let my emotions stand in the way of a job. I've been to places where I've shared a cup of coffee with the devil. You do your job. You live and die for the big prize winning shots. Nothing has ever held priority over my craft, until I met you. The first time I laid eyes on you at my opening, I was undone. It's an understatement now because the world has begun to see it. But I knew you were something special. And, I'm not talking about the God person… I'm referring to the woman. In you I saw *my* miracle."

She wouldn't look at him as he held her hands close to his chest.

"It's like I told you. It's never been about the money; it's about you. Maybe I'm being too presumptuous, but all I want is to be close to you tonight, tomorrow, and every day thereafter. Now do you see why I must go? Mentally it's impossible for me to just be your photographer. I want more. See? I'm being selfish. But I guess I picked the wrong person and the wrong time because this thing is much bigger than us…"

She turned away from him, folding her arms protectively. He moved behind her, gently caressing her shoulders.

"I'm sorry, Olisa, I shouldn't have said all that. I didn't mean to embarrass you in front of everyone."

"Oh, don't worry about us. We…" Grace never finished, because I clamped my hand over her mouth. But it didn't matter.

Logan didn't blink when he said, "It's just that I've never felt this way before about any woman."

"And what way is that?" she asked softly, turning to him as he pulled her close.

"How can you ask when you already know?"

"Because my own emotions are in the way. I can't tell if it's something I'm feeling or something I want. Sometimes a girl just needs to hear the words for herself."

We didn't get to hear the words. Olisa touched his lips with her finger and led him past us, through the kitchen, and out into the courtyard. It seemed like the air was sucked out of the living room. Suddenly it got very cold and very empty when Grace closed the door behind them.

They say, "The hits just keep on coming," and so do the guests on Eva's Special Edition that claim to know Olisa. The worst part is, there I was again, sitting in the den, and watching this piece of flotsam they call a TV news show. Although, I had to admit, "ole boy" was dressed to the nines in his tailored Italian suit. He looked familiar to me.

"Our studio guest this evening is, Donald Harris, a financial analyst and C.P.A. out of Hancock Park." They both sat on plush sofas, facing the camera as she leaned over and shook his hand. "Welcome to our show, Donald."

"Thank you for having me, Eva," he grunted importantly as he adjusted his glasses.

"So are you handling Olisa's finances, sir?"

He chuckled. "I wish, judging from what I heard recently."

Eva folded her hands and studied him. "We talked earlier. So I want you to be brutally honest and tell us about your association with Olisa."

He quickly rubbed his hands and grunted again. "Absolutely. I didn't really know Olisa, personally. She wasn't part of our crowd. But she did go out with my partner. One date, and it changed his whole life."

"Just his?"

"No. Mine too. I still think about it and that was almost twenty years ago. Bruce Walker and I were high school running buddies. Man, we partied hard, until he met Olisa. The best part is, and you said be honest…"

"That's right."

"It all happened because he lost a bet with some of the fellas. Been so long I can't even remember how he lost. All I know is we railroaded him into asking Olisa Carpenter to be his homecoming date. And since he lost the bet, the rule was he had to accept the dare. In those days, Bruce was the man. Every girl's breath contained the words—Bruce Walker—'Oh, girl he's so fine!' When I ran with him, his leftovers were other guy's trophies."

Eva sat back in her chair. "So now I'm curious. What did Bruce Walker look like?"

"Oh, he was a pretty boy: honey complexion, green eyes, curly brown hair… upper middle class, bourgeoisie. His father had a very successful dental practice and was President of the Black Dental Association. Bruce's mother was a gorgeous, high class, fashion designer and owned two boutiques. One was located in Leimert Park and the other in Fox Hills. Bruce was one of the few blacks that came from an old money background, aristocrats, where politeness was a state of being."

"Was that the same for you?"

"Uh, uh. That wasn't the case with me. My father started out with nothing and worked his behind off starting out as a janitor. He eventually became wealthy from all the maintenance services he owned. We were a family of "bean counters." Our money could disappear tomorrow. So we weren't old hands at living the lifestyle, and I guess as a result I tried harder to be a part of the bourgeoisie crowd, acting out how I thought rich kids should act, which meant basically my head had a habit of being up my ass." He covered his hands over his mouth.

Eva patted his arm. "It's okay. I've heard worse. Go on."

He adjusted his glasses, which kept sliding down to the bridge of his nose. "I loved being one of the chosen few. Didn't hang out with anyone who wasn't in the best social clubs." He jokingly wiggled his head in a haughty gesture. "We were the webe's not wannabe's; the style makers not fashion violators. In a nutshell, we fancied ourselves the I in 'it.' I guess that also meant I didn't think I had to have feelings."

"Bruce did have a conscience and felt kind of bad that we forced him to play this game with Olisa—but a dare was a dare—you couldn't turn it down… you had to follow through."

Eva folded her hands on her knee as she crossed her legs. "Why did you pick on Olisa?"

"I don't know… Ignorance, I guess," Donald replied, pulling on his earlobe. "Nothing to analyze. Typical high school jive. I did a lot of things I am embarrassed about in high school. But hey, that's a part of growing up—right? We were immature. So? Get over it. The drums said she was a space cadet. She had a pretty face, but her hair floated all over her head, and she wore these flower child, beatnik outfits straight out of the sixties. That girl was capable of wearing anything. We used to call her time traveler because of all the bizarre outfits—mixed up, dated stuff. In retrospect, she was probably ahead of her time, she was doing sixties stuff before it came back in vogue. And she hung out with the outcasts… low class, 'po' folk, political groups waving signs about nothing. They said she was either some kind of Jesus freak or voodoo child. People say they saw her talking to herself, wandering around in a serious daze as if she were on another planet. To be honest, I pegged her as a druggie."

"Guess it's true, you can't judge a book by its cover."

"For real," he said, shaking his head. "You know what the real trip was—she didn't get it. Most babes had a cardiac arrest if Bruce even glanced in their direction. My partners and I sat their nudging each other, figuring she'd either stumble all over herself or take off running when Bruce strolled over and sat next to her, rubbing shoulders during lunch. Man, were we in for a big shock. She greeted him like it was an everyday thing. Tripped us out. Smiling and talking to him not because of who he was, but like it was nice to have company during lunch. I'm thinking, this girl has definitely lost touch with reality. Girl, don't you know that's Bruce Walker!"

"Shame on her." Eva grinned sarcastically.

"Bruce comes back about a half hour later, looking all hang dog like he just lost a tennis match. I ask what's wrong and he says,

'Donnie, she turned me down. Says it isn't really her kind of thing, but thank you.' He's got this pitiful look on his face, and we're all busting up, figuring he's messing with us, and about to break up any minute—but he's dead serious."

Donnie cocked his head and demonstrated how he looked at him. "I panic for a second, and tell him to shine it. That he's officially off the hook, and this chick lives somewhere in fantasyland, so let's move on. I quickly change the subject and ask who he seriously plans to ask to homecoming. He gets real quiet, sulky, and looks me dead in the eyes and says—her. He sees I'm about to (blip) on myself and walks away, leaving me hanging. I think I yelled out something sarcastic like what she do, put a mojo on your ass? He didn't say a word, ignoring me and a fine honey who caught up with him.

"Before the week was out, Bruce was laying down a heavy duty rap on Olisa, trying to get next to her every chance he got: sitting with her and her friends during lunch, walking her to class, meeting her after school. By the way, her friends seemed just as amazed as we were. He was doing all this stuff. At first I thought, oh, this is an ego thing. He's doing this because he's never been turned down before, especially by someone like Olisa. He's just wants to prove a point. But I knew that wasn't really Bruce's style. It didn't happen often, but he'd been rejected before. He'd just move on. This time he was serious. And it was starting to get ridiculous—to the point of obsession."

"Why do you think Bruce was obsessed with her?"

Donald held his glasses to his nose and thought about it for a second. "On the QT, he took me aside and told me she was really a trip to talk to, and he really enjoyed it. That I'd be surprised if I took the time to get to know her. Said he had never shared so much about himself with anyone in his life as he did with her. That looking into her eyes was like being in the land of enchantment. He had never known beauty like hers."

"Wow. That's beautiful."

"Maybe to you. Remember, we're young and stupid. I'm staring at him like—bro , are you all right? Were you hit on the head? Did she cut one of your hairs or steal an article of clothing behind your back? What's up, homey? What kind of spell did she put on you? He'd just look at me like I was lost. The more he talked about her, the more it got under my skin. Although, I did gain a new respect for her, I said to him, No, Bruce, my man. We all underestimated her. She's smarter than you think, bro, because she did what the other gals couldn't do to you. She's playing you!"

"You didn't."

"I did. Now why did I have to go and say that? He went off on me, telling me I was close-minded. Bruce had never talked to 'me' like that. We were partners. I'm serious. I really did start to wonder if she had hexed him or something. My boy was going through some major changes right in front of my eyes, getting more quiet and introverted. Even worse, I kept getting the impression that I was being measured under a microscope, that he was assessing me and all his other friends."

"Well, eventually his wish, or curse as I called it, came through. A couple of weeks later, she accepted his invitation to go to homecoming. Can't tell you how irritating it was to seem him acting all humble and grateful when she finally said yes."

Eva eyed him quizzically. "So you really had a problem with this."

Donald returned her stare. "Yes, but no matter how disgusting it was, Bruce was still my "boy" and I apologized, and he did, too. I just made an extra effort not to say how I really felt about her in front of him anymore. Homecoming night we double dated. Hey, I must admit, Olisa looked pretty damn good that night—don't get me wrong, she still wore her typical odd ensemble, but on her it worked—long flowing gold chiffon gown, cape, scarf—kind of a gypsy look—loose frizzy hair flowing from underneath the cap, but somehow sister girl managed to pull it off. This may sound stupid, cause I'm definitely not a poet, but in hindsight I'd even describe her as being radiant. I also never realized how flawless her skin was. Of course I'd never been that physically close to her before, either, as we sat in Bruce's Mercedes."

Homecoming night. After he described the way Olisa looked, it all came roaring back to me. I always wondered about that night, because this guy, Bruce, didn't seem like the type to date her, even though he was nice. Of course, Olisa didn't tell me anything about that night. This was getting even more interesting. I turned the volume up.

"Bruce said when he went to pick her up, her parents were very cool and about as down to earth as you could get. Although, her father still gave him the eagle eye. The flip side of the coin was her mother seemed delighted with the prospect of her going out."

"I'm delighted to hear this story." Eva leaning toward Donald with her elbows on her swinging knees and hands folded under her chin. "Tell us what it was like to be out on a double date with Olisa." An anticipatory grin creased her lips.

"I don't know what I was expecting of Olisa, but she certainly poked a hole in all my theories. I thought she'd be real quiet, shy, withdrawn, maybe even a little intimidated."

"And?"

"Wishful thinking. You couldn't shut her up. And I don't mean that in a derogatory way, because she was very gregarious. It was as if Audrey Hepburn had jumped into the car. This was a completely new experience for her. She was giddily excited, asking a million questions, giggling and laughing, doing some sisterly bonding with my date. Not reserved, but open with her emotions. Bruce and even my damn date loved it, but I was sickened by it. If anything, I'm the one who came off introverted that night."

"Why?"

"It's cause I was in shock that's why. We all had our noses in the air and pictured ourselves as pseudo-intellectuals, though that night I rapidly became aware that I didn't know what the word truly represented. If Olisa had shown ego, she'd have swooped past us in that department. But she was much more gracious than that."

"Even then, huh?"

"Yes. And Bruce was definitely right about one thing. Her eyes are her most striking feature: deep, dreamy, mesmerizing… A couple of times when she looked at me, I started getting a little uncomfortable. It was as if she knew what you were thinking. Like she could get inside your head any time she wanted to. It was kind of creepy or maybe just my overactive imagination inspired by the wine I had brought along for the ride."

Eva playfully slapped his shoulder. "So she finally won you over, right?"

"Wrong. Having said all that, I remained fiercely and stupidly defiant, determined to make her realize how lucky she was to be associated with us instead of vice-versa. Kind of like a person obstinately pursuing a useless argument. I wish someone had lynched my ego Homecoming night."

Eva directly eyed the camera and shook her head. "Men."

Donald shrugged his shoulders. "I know…what can I say? Anyway, whenever she was separated from Bruce, I made a supreme effort to whisper in her ear, like a megaphone, how much of a privilege it was for her to hang out with us. I'd say, don't you know how popular my boy is? See all these women checking him out? Did you know you're not ordinarily his type?"

Eva gasped. "I can't believe you said that!"

Donald looked embarrassed, shrugging his shoulders again. "Yep. And she took it, too. Everything I dished out. Never seeming affected by my big mouth or cruel remarks, so of course, I couldn't stop myself until I saw some pain in her eyes. To this day, I don't understand why she made me so angry or why I wanted to hurt her. I was acting like a parasite trying to tear her insides apart. Her calm demeanor hollered at me like a bully, and for some ignorant reason I wanted to break her. The more alcohol I drank, the more nasty I got, finally playing my trump card and exposing our horrid little secret, supposedly under the auspices that it was for her own good. I let her know that Bruce only asked her out because he lost a bet."

"That must have crushed her. How did she react?"

"Instead of seeing the anticipated pain on her face, I got only a pathetic smile. She said, 'Thank you, Donnie, but I know that.'

"How did you know? Didn't that piss you off?

"'No. He told me the truth a long time ago. That's when we became friends, and I accepted his invitation to go out. If he doesn't want to go out again, that's okay, I'm having a great time tonight.

"I was speechless. I backed off after that. She beat me at my own game.

"But ironically, it didn't end there; she held my arm and said, 'How about you? All the things you've shared with me about your life are nice sketches, but they're superficial. The only way to create a true painting of your life, one that has color, and vibrancy, and one that you'll enjoy is to open up your heart.'"

"Ho, ho…now I've got to ask, how did you react?"

"I'm sure I had a dumbfounded look on my face. I asked what she meant by I don't enjoy it. She slowly scrutinized my face, probing my eyes."

"'I look at you and see you have everything you want, ' she says, 'except what really matters. You're a good-looking guy, great athlete, you have plenty of friends, girls are attracted to you, I see all that… but you're still not happy.'"

"Well now, I'm really pissed, so I say, yeah, okay, you tell me what would make me happy."

"'Oh, I'd guess you want your father to be a little less busy, be around a little more to appreciate what you've accomplished in school instead of expecting it. I think that might help.'"

"Uh, oh," inserted Eva.

"Uh, huh. Tell me about it. That (blip)…oops, sorry…screwed me up. And although she said she was guessing, she knew she was right. My only question was how she could she have known? I didn't even discuss these types of things with Bruce. It was all part of the facade."

"Why do you say that?"

"My father was never around, always on the road. When I told him about my grades and victories, they were never enough. His story was always better, his life was always tougher, and he assumed I'd always do well, constantly reminding me how he made everything easier for me.

So how did she know? Ultimately, it didn't matter. I was already torn up for the rest of the night."

"Wow." Eva eased back in her chair, folding her hands in her lap. She pointed at the camera sarcastically. "Dr. Phil, eat your heart out!"

All Donald could do was grin and nod his head as he stared at the floor. Eva turned serious again. "So Mr. Harris, we know how you felt that night. How did it affect the rest of your life?"

Donald cupped the back of his neck with his hands as he stared at the ceiling.

"I guess, in retrospect, that night permanently changed me. I finally got it. I understood where Bruce was coming from. I knew why he was so attracted to her. I understood why he thought he was in love with her. In fact, before the night was over, I was jealous of Bruce and wished I had met her first. I wanted to know more about her and scoop her up like a ball with jumping jacks."

"As it turned out, there was no 'love connection' between them. Bruce did ask her out again, too. She turned him down. Said she wasn't ready for a relationship, right now. They ended up good friends. But because of her, Bruce gained a whole new perspective about life. Probably much better than what he would have gotten out of most relationships. He changed, too, or maybe the person he truly was finally arrived. He distanced himself from the old cliques and made a point of meeting new people."

"Do you ever see Bruce anymore?"

"We still keep in touch from time to time. He's married now… got two boys. He's a chiropractor with his own practice in Seattle."

"I see."

"Turns out Olisa was good for me, too. And I say this with all due respect to my wife and family. I love them, but in one night, Olisa helped me to become a better man. Perhaps if I had been more courageous, something might have happened, but I was too in awe of her after that. Besides, I'm not even sure if she would have had me. It doesn't matter. She was one of the best things that ever happened to me. I'm really glad I got the chance to know her."

"We're getting a chance to know her, too. Donald, thank you so much for your honesty. We're pleased that you could share your Olisa story with us this evening." Eva warmly shook his hand, and then smiled broadly at the camera.

CHAPTER 10

"This is just infatuation, right? She can't really be in love with him?"

"Sure she can," Grace, replied matter-of-factly as she carefully laid her head against the rapidly vibrating car window.

"Man, I just can't believe it," Jonathan stated from the back seats. "Why now?"

"Why not now? Name me a better time." I swerved the Pathfinder to the right and drove up the steep dirt road, idling the car until Gumbo's red van popped into the corner of my rear mirror. The suns blinding glare obscured the already indecipherable letters on the sign.

"You know what I mean… things are finally coming together big time and now we've got a distraction we don't need."

"Correction—you don't need. I think Olisa's fine about it."

"Yeah, I know… That's what I'm talking about. How is she going to find the time to have a relationship with all this shit going on?"

"Jonathan, please…"

"Sorry, Mom… It just, baffles me. We're just getting started."

"Love has a way of finding time whether you're ready or not," Grace commented, frowning at the window. "With all the women you've dated, haven't you ever fallen in love?"

Jonathan gave it about two seconds of reflection. "No… okay, maybe I shouldn't have answered so quickly… yeah, I guess once. I thought I was in love when I was in college. She dropped me for a football jock. Man. That cut me to the bone. I promised myself I'd never be anybody's plaything ever again. It's definitely not fun to let somebody jack up your feelings that way."

"But that's you, Jon. That's your experience… not everyone acts or thinks the same way. Next time, the love bug might hit you. And I might even see some grandkids."

"Not for the kid right now, Mom. I love going out with different women. My career is priority. My baby is this business. But who knows? One day you might see those grandchilluns you're looking for."

"Thank goodness."

"I don't get it, Jonathan, you're the one that hired him! So relax and let it go. Your sister's a big girl. She can handle it. There are worse things to worry about… Like am I headed in the right direction?" I asked looking around for signs.

"I didn't know they had met. I brought him in to be her photographer, not her lover. The guy's definitely got talent, but I really don't know him. He comes in and out of town. When he calls, I hire him. But for all I know he could be a serial rapist or a killer."

"Come on now, you been reading too much Stephen King."

"Okay, but I'm telling you, the guy's a player. Don't think this is the first woman he's messed around with that he photographed. He's a dog."

"You should know," I chuckled.

"Now you're getting it."

"Joseph, you need to wash these windows," Grace fussed. She briskly brushed the inside window with her hand to no avail. The dust was thickly caking on the outside.

"What difference does it make, Grace? We're in the mountains, driving on a dirt road, and you're worried about whether the windows are clean?"

The windows may have been dirty, but they weren't messed up enough to prevent me from seeing a huge shadowy character bounding and weaving his way through the trees. Do angels need exercise?

"Whatever."

"Honey, it ain't like it's the first time she's been gone. At least she's here, where we can see her any time, instead of another country!"

"You're right. You're right," she admitted resignedly. "I should be more thankful. This is the best thing for her. I'm just being a mom."

"And one of the best."

"I'm afraid, Joseph. I can't shake this feeling of dread… like last night was the last time we'll see her at home… am I making sense?"

"Yeah," I said, drumming the steering wheel. "I got it, too." I closely examined my set of directions, which seemed in direct opposition to the street signs. I might as well have asked the coyote I saw sprinting through the shrubbery for directions. "It's going to be all right," I muttered unconvincingly.

The last few days had been excruciating. How often does a parent hustle their child out of the house because it's no longer safe for them?

We had no choice.

The last couple of weeks, invaders from all over Los Angeles County besieged our little walk street, some from as far away as "Merry Ole England," begging for a peek at the "Good Witch of Venice." I felt like we had been conquered by the neighboring country the way complete strangers settled into our community, hung out in the streets, camped out in yards, passed in herds down the street, hassling the neighbors with question after question.

When all was said and done, the police offered little in the way of advice except for us to get her out of here so they could maintain better control and ease the neighborhood congestion. The local crowds, let alone the steady steam of visitors and transients who now stretched the path of the boardwalk to our house overburdened them.

It was building too fast for comfort, and the police admitted they didn't want to assume responsibility for whatever happened. They knew they could be outmanned. I could have fashioned a nice case about how they were being paid to protect us, but this had already shaped up as a highly unusual situation. I didn't want my family tested any further on how well they could handle it. Their argument, and a fairly good one at that, is that the officers couldn't stop and I.D. every single person as a suspect without turning it into a police state. Junior, who was visiting that particular day, snidely remarked, "It already is—what about racial profiling?"

Still, we listened to them.

Potentially it was too dangerous to take chances. There weren't many moments in the day when we didn't hear the crunch of footsteps, a camera snap, the whirring of a video, or an obscure voice shouting her name. These sounds had become as much a part of our ecological habitat as the birds in the trees and the police helicopters in the sky.

Luckily, Nick Cavaliere phoned expressing concern, urging us to get Olisa out of there, and, I think, feeling a little guilty that he may have been the prime motivator for this havoc. He had called upon a few friends and found the perfect hideaway for Olisa on the southernmost slopes of the Santa Monica Mountains, off Pacific Coast Highway, near Will Rogers Park. A retreat that was hard for just anybody to get to and perfect for screening intruders. It was one of several houses owned by an enormously wealthy real estate developer currently in Saudi Arabia. Malmud welcomed her to stay there, rent free, for as long as she'd like, although we had already agreed that she was never to stay in one place too long.

The house had been vacant for months after he chased away the former tenants who claimed they were import/exporters but turned out to be major drug dealers. He hadn't planned to sell the house for a while anyway. Nick cautioned that it might be run down because no one had inhabited it for months.

I wish our house were that run down.

The house sat in the uppermost section of the mountains and was camouflaged by the trees nestling it. It took a second or two for me to register we were parked in front of the entrance. It was a gorgeous Spanish hacienda style ranch house with a low red tiled roof made of stone and concrete. The walls encircling it were around six feet high. Yeah, it was a little worn, a little run down, begging for a paint job and no one had taken care of the grounds consisting of about an acre, but it wasn't a bad deal—that's for sure! The only access to the house was to drive in from the road so it was fairly easy to secure, and that's what we needed. But Nick knew that, having been one to have experienced the glow of fame before and dealing with it now with his own resurgence and career offers tumbling in by the pounds.

As we stepped out of the car, Gumbo's van slipped in behind us.

"Where's Olisa?" Jonathan quickly asked Gumbo after noticing only Little Oak and Logan climbing out of the van after him.

"You know, Oli... a sunny day, a fall breeze, a chance for some space and solitude. She made us stop the van so she could get out and walk the rest of the way," said Logan.

"By herself?"

"I thought you'd be happy I wasn't with her. She's got Free with her."

Jonathan pretended to ignore Logan as he tried to spot Olisa from the crest of the hill.

Meanwhile, the front door was locked so we paraded around the walls toward the back of the house.

There behind the house, actively working on the hillside alongside his crew, was Nick Cavaliere. I could also see people working inside the house, cleaning, gardening, painting, the works. Nick was absorbing all the costs himself, having already refused our offers to recompense him. As he put it, it was something he had to do.

He looked even better than the last time I saw him. Tanned, trimmed and shaved, the cleft chin stood out in his structured face like a beacon. He was vibrant and full of energy as he labored with the crew, pulling up weeds. His egregious spirit was contagious as he laughed and cracked jokes. It was obvious this man luxuriated in his second chance.

The Latino crew seemed absolutely in awe of him—in a way that transcended his stardom. They knew his history and rebirth, like most of us knew, but this was different.

"Hey, what are you doing standing there? Come on over." Nick got off his knees and wiped his hands on his pants as he greeted us with hugs and handshakes. "It's so noisy out here I can't hear a thing. How are you? Where's Olisa?" Every movement in his body, every muscle, sinew, seemed manufactured to provide him with the greatest pleasure.

"She's on her way."

"Good, good," he said, patting my shoulder.

"You guys are hard at it."

"You better know it. Got the best crew in the world working here. Most of who are friends and relatives of my housekeeper, Estella. The majority of people you see are from El Salvador, although we have a few Guatemalans in the mix. I love them, man. They are the best. See the older man over there painting the wood trim? That's Oscar. He was a doctor in El Salvador before he fled here during the revolution. Guy over there owned a couple of stores in El Salvador before they were burned to the ground. It's sad, but it didn't stop them. It's amazing how resourceful people can be when pushed. So what do you think about this place?"

"I think it is beautiful, Nick." The black cloud had finally lifted from Grace's voice.

"Let me show you around," he said, escorting her by the arm as we followed.

"This house was actually built at the turn of the century… reminiscent of Spanish colonial revival. Did you see the stone tower in front? The building was formerly a hunting lodge before Malmud renovated it. Right now he's visiting family in Iran and doesn't plan to be back for a while. Anyway, as you can see, it's made almost entirely of stone, indigenous stone. They actually blasted the mountain to get the rocks and carted them here on horse-drawn wagons."

"Man, I love it… What ingenuity," Jonathan replied, shaking his head and marveling at the large U-shaped courtyard we passed through.

"The walls have a natural-finish exterior and over there is an atrium, garden room, pond, outdoor and indoor fireplace, hardwood floors andskylight on the stone stairwells. Give us a couple of more days, and we'll have it up to par. I think Olisa will be pretty pleased with the place, however long she decides to stay. As you see, access is not easy. Therefore, she'll be in good shape. She's welcome to move in tonight."

"I'll let her know, but do you mind if Grace and I move in with her?" I joked.

"Seriously, you can." He laughed. "It's spacious enough. It's got four bedrooms, three bathrooms…"

"Shoot, I wish. Unfortunately, we've got to stay at the pad, just to make sure we don't get any uninvited roommates. Luckily, my nephew and his wife, along with additional security, have consented to stay here with her, which helps us breathe a little easier."

"Very good."

"You know how much we appreciate it," I added, placing a hand on his shoulder as we exchanged eye contact.

"Please… I'm the one who's grateful," he stated as we retraced our steps back to the hillside behind the house."

"It's about time she got here, there's Free…" Jonathan pointed.

Free popped into view: dashing around the side of the building, tail whipping furiously as he crazily sprinted in circles, barking excitedly. Abruptly, his fur bristled, and he began baring his teeth as he slowly backed up with a low growl.

"What's wrong, boy? Where's Olisa?" Free seemed grateful to see me as he darted to my side, bumping against my leg and leaning against me protectively.

"Why are you panting so hard?"

His only response was the warm pee I felt on my leg as he relieved himself.

"Free, what the hell is wrong with you? You have hundreds of damn trees out here and you choose my leg? He's never done that before, Grace, can you believe this?" Free looked at me like, I'm sorry, I don't know what got into me.

"There's your answer, Joseph," Grace answered softly.

I looked up and there stood Olisa in the distance, her back turned toward us. Her hands shielded her eyes from the glare of the sun. Five feet to her right was the reason for Free's anxiety. It had actually been in front of my eyes the whole time, playing tricks on them with the suns assistance. It was well camouflaged against the trees—a huge buck deer. A magnificent specimen. His antlers endowed him with the grace of royalty. He stood rigidly at attention, deliberating his next move. Olisa made no furtive move as she calmly watched him.

Finally, he took a couple of reluctant steps toward her, body shaking, prickling with nervousness. Calmly, she reached out and caressed his stiff upright head, which gradually lowered as he moved even closer.

"Whoa, careful, Olisa," Jonathan whispered.

"Too late now," I whispered back.

It was one of the most awe-inspiring visions I have ever been blessed to see. A wild creature like that compelled to trust her despite all the potential harm human beings hold for it. It looked like something out of a fairy tale as we watched Olisa tenderly stroking his muscular physique. He didn't bolt until he heard the jarring click of Logan's camera. With a leap and a kick, he disappeared into the trees, leaving us breathless.

"Apparently all of God's creatures find it easy to share a kinship with you," Nick teasingly yelled as the two approached each other and embraced. Suddenly, I heard a curt scream and noticed an elderly woman sinking to her knees, clutching her chest. I thought the poor woman was having a heart attack. She murmured incoherently in Spanish, or at least incoherent to me, because it started a chain reaction and other men and women quickly followed, displaying the sign of the cross against their chest.

They recognized Olisa. They slowly began moving forward, abandoning their rakes, shovels, and brushes, greeting her one by one with hugs, handshakes, and praises. It was an unexpected reception, and Olisa was totally unprepared for this demonstration of adoration. They gathered at her feet as she sat on the grass. Moments later, she was conversing with all of them in Spanish.

Except for a young man who worked feverishly on the hillside, about twenty yards away, as if his life depended on it. He tore at the weeds as if he were ensconced in battle, gathering the piles and throwing them into trash bags purposefully. His wiry brown muscles glistened in the sun as he shook his head like a wet dog, beads of perspiration flying everywhere. He showed little interest in what was going on. Occasionally, he glanced at the circle of figures, but then worked more determinedly than before. I wondered if he was an ex-con or something who wanted to make a good impression or just someone who was desperate to receive his full wages. The kid had a street tough look to him so I doubted he was a brown noser.

Nick walked over to him, reassuringly placing his arm around him and gesturing to the gathering, but it didn't seem to have an effect. The young man politely declined and continued to work.

I found myself caught up in watching him and began to notice that his rapidly moving lips indicated he was talking to himself.

So my boy was just crazy, that's all.

Yet, he looked real familiar to me. Maybe he was one of the homeless youngsters that sometimes came around the restaurant soliciting food. Oftentimes, we'd fix up a plate for them of whatever we had in excess after the restaurant closed.

Shortly, an elderly woman departed from the circle, an irritated expression on her face. She stomped up to this heavily scarred young man. I couldn't hear what she was saying, but it was evident by her gestures that she scolded him. Now and then, she whipped her finger in his face and pointed at Olisa. He kept his head down, intermittently nodding, but his face was devoid of expression. Frustrated, she returned to the group and sat down on the grass with the workers clustered around Olisa.

"I told Maria Elena not to bring him," said a Latino man with a rancher's hat. His skin was as brown as mine was, and his face looked as if it had weathered many storms, physically and emotionally. He had just left one of the portable outhouses as he adjusted his belt buckle and glared at the lone worker.

"Yeah?"

"She wouldn't listen to me, but she never listens to anyone. She's even more bullheaded than me."

"Why didn't you want him to come?"

"He's not Salvadoran, like us. He's Mexican… You know… They're very different from us," he remarked, saying the word Mexican like it was a curse word that explained all I needed to know. "I can look at him and tell he's no good… That guy. He's a gang banger. However, my sister always finds a way to see something that no one else can see. I guess that's good, her seeing the best in people… But still… This guy. I can tell he's a troublemaker. Oh, but Maria Elena felt so sorry for him. She said, 'Miguel, that young boy needs help. Look at his face, he doesn't know whether it's day or night. We must help him.' She went right over and brought him inside the house. This stranger… I've never seen her do anything like that. Stray cats, yes. But some bad kid? She saw a homeless boy who needed help. I saw a wounded mountain lion. And when he gets better—look out!"

"She gave him food, and now he stays in our house! A complete stranger! We don't know anything about him. Maria Elena, she's a good person… But he can't be trusted. I just know he's going to steal us blind when he gets a chance. We don't know who he is. He never talks about himself. She tells me, we have to give him time Miguel, but I don't care… I don't want him around! Maybe now she will see what I've been saying," he said, pulling the lip of his hat tightly down over his forehead.

"Look at how he acts, *Señor*. He's in the presence of a holy woman and the very famous man she healed; a man who was kind enough to allow us to work here and he shows no manners and no *respeto*. And he's the one that begged to come along when he heard we were going to do some work for *Señor* Cavaliere. It's the first time I saw some kind of life in him. But I ask, why does he refuse to come over and show his respect? He might as well spit in God's eye."

I thought, the day ain't over yet.

Suddenly, the man's sister reemerged from the circle of people on the grass, clutching Olisa's hand and towing her toward the youth. Everyone else followed closely behind them. This was going to be interesting. But that's when it hit me. I couldn't believe it took me so long.

It had been so out of context. Recognition hit me like an errant fastball before Olisa said, "Hello, Chato."

His hands froze, and his body straightened up as if he had been identified in a police lineup. Tears chased the dirt down the sides of his cheeks. Besides being out of context, I didn't recognize him because his tattoos had been obliterated. However, the bruises and scars remained, the final remnants of his past as one of the most terrifying gang bangers around. The facial arrogance that once commanded fear had been transformed into a haunted, contrite expression that seemed unable to deal with this developing scenario.

"I didn't know you were here. Why are you over here by yourself? You should have come over and said hi. After all, you and I share a special bond."

His eyes blinked, but that's all.

"Because he's crazy, look at him, he shows no gratitude or appreciation. *Señorita* Olisa, please forgive him. You should be ashamed, boy. Have you no honor?"

"No, *por favor, Señor*, no criticisms, no put downs. This is what he's encountered his whole life. He can't help what's going on in his head. He's confused enough already."

Chato's head stayed rigid as he bent over, mechanically pulling weeds. However, his eyes, even though they steadfastly remained straightforward, projected a deep sadness.

"Won't you look at me?" she asked tenderly.

"I can't."

"Why?"

"Because they're right, I don't deserve to," he lamented, his body now trembling involuntarily.

"That's not true. Why would you say something like that, Ernesto?"

Hearing his given name triggered something inside of him. For the first time, albeit reluctantly, his eyes met hers. His face mirrored so much inner turmoil, I found myself cringing.

"That day, when you saved my life," he said shakily, struggling to speak, "should have been the happiest day of my life, you know what I'm saying? For about a day it was, you know. I thought I would be one of those Jesus dudes running all crazy down the streets. You know, preaching the gospel or something... But as soon as the lights, cameras and all the people were gone, I became scared to death. I had changed. My head was all weird... different... I didn't want nobody around me, dude. I don't mean you, ma'am. That's just how I speak. You know? Because I didn't know what to do. I was scared. I tried to be like those kids on the Brady Bunch, you know, all good and stuff... but it wasn't working. It's like I kept hearing this yelling in my ear saying that ain't you, *vato*... But the only friends I know is my homies, you know... But I think they're kind of afraid of me... They didn't know how to act around me... And I didn't know how to act around them, either.

"Things had changed, you know... I was different, but I don't know what that means. Seems like I started hating myself more than before. I didn't belong anywhere, you know... Then I just started tripping, wandering around. I figured if I could just get rid of these tattoos, it might be better. So I headed down to Mexico and got them all taken off, but still, nothing changed. It didn't wash away the stuff in my head. All the shit I done. I was still the same person. I couldn't change even though you gave me a new life. I even thought about going back and gang banging and stuff... But that wasn't me no more. I just missed being around my posse—that was my family. Until *Señora* Rivera took me in, I had no place to go... I guess that's why I'm here."

He weakly pulled at some weeds.

"Ernesto, you think you have to try and be a good person. You already are. Before you were catering to the anger and fear within yourself. Your religion was hurting others and destroying your world. Now you are reckoning with the God of love, the God that truly exists inside of you, and it's a new emotion for you to deal with. It's one that requires you to accept that whatever ruled your past is gone. Now you must learn to love Ernesto again."

"Yeah, but I did some bad things, Olisa. The kind of things that would make you and all the people here hate me."

"We're not here to judge you, honey. Don't beat yourself up trying to renounce the things you did in the past. We can't do anything about that. However, remember the past, so you can avoid making the same mistakes again. You must let the knowledge you gained enable you to harvest your future. I don't love you for what you were, I only love you for what you can be. Look into my eyes and you will see God's face just like I see it in yours."

She cupped his face in her hands, and he fell into her embrace, his shoulders heaving, his sobs muffled. Signings of the cross-swept through the workers, as she softly said, "Ernesto, you can change your life. There is a famous quote by St. Augustine that goes like this: 'The key to immortality is living a life worth remembering.'"

"But how do I do that?" Ernesto questioned as he withdrew from her arms.

"Haven't you figured that out? That's why you are here. To be with us… To work with us and help us achieve our goals." She held him by his shoulders. "Ernesto Padilla, you and I are connected, you're not going anywhere. You are staying right here. We've got work to do."

"You serious?"

Not as serious as the pained expression on my son's face. Jonathan looked like he was in the middle of a strained bowel movement. But he wasn't going to say anything at this point. Whenever Olisa spoke this firmly, it was useless to try to change her mind.

"Of course I am. God led you here. This is not a coincidence. You are here for a purpose. You are family."

Ernesto grinned like a little boy getting a shiny new bike for Christmas.

So caught up was he in the moment, that he failed to notice the new level of respect accorded to him by people who moments ago were ready to give him the same goodbye party as Joan of Arc.

CHAPTER 11

"You want the door closed, little brother?"

"Even though I live for the sound of a bustling restaurant, it might be a good idea, Wilma. Thanks," I said while clearing paper off my desk for Peter and Jon to sit their plates of food.

"Thanks for hooking us up with lunch, Aunt Wilma!" Jonathan yelled.

"Yeah, the food looks great," added Peter.

Wilma smiled. "Anything for my growing boys. Enjoy guys!" Wilma closed the door to my office. Finally, we could talk without yelling.

"Jonathan, I haven't seen figure skaters perform faster turnarounds than you," I teased as I immediately added some hot sauce on my short ribs.

"Okay… Okay, I admit it, the kid is great. He works his butt off. He's been with us, what, a month? I still have to tell him to slow down and take a break. I've never seen anyone so happy to get a second chance. Living in the house with Olisa has been the best thing in the world for him. I guess considering where he's coming from, it makes sense."

"Yeah, but the best part was watching him come into his own at the Santa Monica Civic," Peter ruminated as he scooped up a forkful of jambalaya. "Did you see the expression on his face after they gave him a standing ovation?"

"Like he had died and gone to heaven," I recounted.

"Hey, not bad for a guy who was supposed to be helping out with security," added Jon. "Of course, Olisa never informed me she was going to introduce him to the audience."

"It was spontaneous."

"I guess so, Dad, but Ernesto walked up and handled the microphone like a champ."

Peter nodded his head in agreement.

"But that's what was so great about it, Jon… His impromptu speech was so impassioned… The way he reached out to the audience and asked them to be his friends and support now that his life had swerved in another direction. Anybody with half a heart could relate to his sincerity."

Well the *Los Angeles Times* certainly did. Check this out," Jonathan said reading the newspaper to us:

PRODIGAL SON RETURNS! Notorious former gang banger, Ernesto 'Chato' Padilla, who hundreds claim was healed by Olisa Carpenter, surprised everyone when he appeared at the standing room only crowd at the Santa Monica Civic Auditorium that featured another Universal Concert for Spiritual Healing—sponsored by the O.L.I.S.A. Inc. group. Padilla, who disappeared after the alleged healing, has been sought after by the police, press, and medical community, for months. His reemergence completely shatters the rumors that he died shortly after the stabbing that some blatantly declared a hoax, and his sudden disappearance as clear proof of it. Padilla described the incident in detail and his life for the first time since July 4th *weekend to ardent, primarily young, and supportive attendees that were there to see touted miracle worker, Olisa Carpenter. Carpenter, among other alleged acts of healing, has been largely recognized for healing acclaimed actor, Nicholas Cavaliere.*

In a moving speech, Ernesto spoke earnestly to the audience about the adversity he faced in his life. Born in a very poor section of East Los Angeles, Padilla was a victim of domestic violence by an alcoholic father who was an itinerant laborer. His father continually walked in and out of their life, stranding his mother with three children to raise. One night Padilla's father returned in a drunken rage killing his mother, two siblings, and then finally himself. Ernesto escaped death because he had snuck out the window earlier that evening to play with his friends. He ended up living with his grandmother in the Venice/Oakwood area.

Padilla, who was especially close to his mother, couldn't deal with it and found himself drawn to trouble like ugly to a blowfish. He talked about being kicked out of schools, gang life, drug dealing, attempted suicide, and the rebirth that came from "God's saving hand through Olisa." Padilla concluded his speech by making a passionate plea for a major truce among all the gangs in the city. His heartfelt story and requests for peace brought down the house with the force of a spiritual axe as the audience rewarded him with a rousing ovation...

Jonathan slapped the newspaper down. "Not bad, huh?"

"Not at all, Jon," I stated, "and the best part is Olisa didn't even have to perform a miracle last night."

"Who needs to when you have a living miracle standing in front of you," Peter said, in between sips of lemonade.

"Yeah, but they still don't want to give her any credit. C'mon, 'alleged acts of healing?' They are still looking for loopholes... It kills me."

"So what, Jon. She doesn't need the press to validate her, son, as long as she's helping others, right? The people know what's going on."

"It's true, Jon. You hired me to do public relations for you, but my impact hardly matters. Word of mouth and the healing of Nick Cavaliere has generated the kind of publicity money can't buy. I've been more caught up in control issues and handling the tremendous number of requests, than a direct public relations push. Look, the upcoming concert for the Staples Center was sold out the second the tickets were posted. They camped out in sleeping bags. The Staples Center is begging us to commit to some more nights. The truth is we need to search for larger venues. Right now the Rose Bowl is on the table, but it's starting to look tiny in relation to the demands."

Jonathan cupped his hands behind his head as he took in what Peter was saying.

"Remember when you had to scramble for musical groups? You'll never have to worry about that again. We've been getting calls worldwide from entertainment agents, begging to get their clients booked on any future concerts we organize. They know being associated with

Olisa's 'for a good cause' banner is the best exposure they can find. I'm talking A-list musicians, celebrities, actors, comedians, and politicians who have committed to giving all proceeds to the cause. Everyone wants to be a part of the Universal Healing revue now."

"Incredible," I said while rereading sections of the article as I scooped a forkful of macaroni and cheese. "Well, it makes sense. Ever since the word got out that her family owns the Soul of Venice, we have a waiting list for the next two years. Our lines are longer than the AMC Theaters. We've had to hire extra personnel just to turn people away. Seriously, when they do get in, they are either hoping to catch a glimpse of Olisa or want to know if there are healing ingredients in the food."

"And what do you tell them, Pops?"

"I joke it's a trade secret, and I leave it at that."

"Man, thank goodness, you act like getting rich is some kind of social disease or something."

"Let's just say, I don't have your talent for pushing the envelope. Seeing money pour into the restaurant because of my daughter's spiritual finesse wasn't exactly how I had imagined it."

"What difference does it make, Dad. Money is money! I could have done it for you a long time ago if you had listened to me."

"Not to change the subject, gentlemen, but, Olisa asked me to bring something up to you, Jon."

"She couldn't do it herself, Peter?"

"She thought you'd handle it better if it came from me."

"Uh-huh."

"Well, first of all, she appreciates the fact that you're giving her protection and she loves her mountain retreat. She can hike, have solitude, meditate…"

"Peter, I don't need the icing. What's up?" he asked, slowly tapping his glass of lemonade with a fork.

"All right, all right… The isolation is driving her crazy. She wants to be more involved. This is not what she was expecting. She's starved to get out, socialize, be more active, and commune with people."

"Is that all? Peter, you know as well as I do that we're about to go national with concert dates booked across the country. She's about to get stupid busy. She'll be begging to hole back up in the mountains. Plus, I could schedule her enough interviews per day to last into two more millenniums. It's a done deal. Tell her to relax."

Peter chomped down on a spicy hot andouille sausage. He quickly downed his mug of lemonade. "Whew," he said, wiping his forehead. "That was good!" He paused for a second to gather his thoughts. "Okay, Jon, she's willing to do the interview scheduled with Susan Blair, but after that she says no more. She finds interviews a waste of time and doesn't want the spotlight focused on her."

"She should have thought about that before she jumped out there and healed Ernesto!" he argued, tapping his glass again with the fork.

"Jon, you know that's not right."

"Yeah, I know, Dad, but when is Olisa going to realize she lost her privacy on Independence Day? The public owns it now. I'm just trying to keep this from being a paparazzi hoe-down, but everyone's shitting on me."

"C'mon, Jon, we all appreciate the effort you've put into this."

"I hope so. I've got a fairly good idea of how hard it is to be under the microscope after working with celebrities in the music biz."

"No one's challenging your expertise, Jon," Peter assured him.

"Then what's really making her antsy? Am I moving too slowly for her on the donations? Is that it? Tell you what, we can start donating major monies to whatever institutions or charities she selects right now, if she wants, Peter. I don't care, all I've been trying to do as her liaison and her controller so she doesn't have to shoulder the financial burdens."

"She knows that, Jon."

"Well then what is it, Peter? She confides in you. What's going on?" He tapped a little faster on the glass of lemonade.

"Again, Jon, she wants to be actively involved. Yes, she would love to get those donations out to people. As you already know, Olisa's primary motive is to help people, and she doesn't want her efforts to be regaled as a bunch of 'superficial movie star sanctioned pabulum.'"

"Oh, now I see… So she saw the editorial in the *New York Times* last week by Theo Balanis."

Peter nodded.

"Tell her don't pay Theo Balanis and his editorial diatribe any mind. Balanis makes love to cobra pussy, so excuse me, but who cares what he thinks? Obviously, he's going to be skeptical because he didn't eyewitness the events. He calls her "the preacher's answer to David Copperfield." I'm sorry, Pops, but to hell with him. Theo Balanis just wants another Pulitzer Prize on his mantle.

"So how do you really feel, Jon?" Peter chuckled. "She knows that, bro. She just wants to stay as far away form the trappings of show biz as possible. The concerts are ok, but we all know they are only spokes in the wheel. Bottom line—she sees her true impact as being among the people."

I grabbed his hand. "Jon, you're about to shatter your glass of lemonade the way you keep banging that fork against it."

"Yeah, sorry," he said, halting his drumming for a few seconds before resuming, this time, adding a knife to the drum roll. "So Dad, what's your hit on this?"

"Why do you even bother asking me? I want to ship her away to Siberia. Olisa's knows what she wants, trust her… her instincts are usually on the money, anyway."

"All right, Peter, it's obvious my wealth of knowledge and experience don't seem to mean anything. One more time—what does she want to do?"

"Well, funny you should ask. She'd like to run something past you and see what you think."

"I'm honored… What is it?"

"It's an idea that Ernesto came up with."

"Ernesto? Great! What pearls of wisdom did Ernesto offer? Everything you wanted to know about gangbanging, but were afraid to ask?"

"Close… But keep an open mind, because from the mouth of babes…"

The camera shot a close up on Eva's face and then pulled away to show her seated in the studio in a very fashionable business suit. Success had been good to her, and she looked particularly good this evening as she flashed that award-winning smile.

"Good evening and Happy Holidays! I'm Eva Sanchez, and this is Special Edition, December 1st. The holidays arrived early this year." Every time the camera captured her from another angle, she smoothly turned to face it, never missing a beat in her narration. She was now the polished professional and fluidity was her middle name. She emoted sincerity as she went on to say, "Usually, when the word drive-by is mentioned, you think of gunfire. You think of the innocent lives that were stolen away simply because they happened to be in the wrong place. You think of the sickening turf battles that occur as routinely as the seasons. You think of the aftermath of bloodied bodies in the streets.

"This evening I am relieved to say that the word drive-by can also connote something positive. Tonight, we are going to investigate the flurry of drive-bys that are starting to appear with some frequency in the City of Angels. It's the kind that is quickly finding favor in other metropolitan areas as well and growing in popularity like a hit record. This kind of drive-by doesn't leave a trail of tears or alarming statistics. Tonight we will explore one of the most outstanding, innovative, and successful programs I have ever had the pleasure of reporting.

"This holiday season there is an excitement, intensity, and spirit in the city that I have never seen before. Olisa Carpenter's brother, Jonathan Carpenter, was the first to forewarn us to be ready for the drive-bys as you remember on this program, and its hit like *El Niño*." A picture of Olisa and Jon flashed on the TV screen as she continued with her report.

"'Drive-by Blessings!' And by that I mean packages containing generous amounts of food, books, and sometimes even cash, have been mysteriously left in the most impoverished areas of the city: on the doorsteps of churches, schools, rehabilitation centers, skid row, housing projects, women's shelters, clinics, and homes to the joy of its recipients. Sometimes at the risk of their own lives, these individuals have dropped off this material and then quickly disappeared. Let's hear what Eunice Carter had to say about this phenomenon."

I thought to myself, Sista, couldn't you have at least fixed yourself up a little bit before you let the cameras catch you? Eunice was cloaked in a beige robe and wearing a scarf that ballooned out like a covered wagon because of the curlers inside. Only half her teeth were showing. I shook my head, embarrassed, but still happy for her as I listened to what she had to say.

"Hey, at first, I didn't know what to think… I was up getting a drink of water around 3:00 AM in the morning, and I see carloads of people stop in front of my house in the middle of the night. So I yell out the window a warning that they had better watch out cause I'm about to put a bullet up their… you know what. However, they yell back, 'God bless you ' and now I'm stumped. By now my two youngest boys are up. Then these people started lining up boxes on the porch and speed off."

"For a second I wondered if it was a bomb or something, but my boys had already dashed out the house, ignoring all my screaming and started pouring through the boxes. Praise God! There was enough food in those boxes to feed everybody in Carson, plus gift certificates to a grocery store and clothing store! I also found a note that said, 'One Love inspires the Spirit to Awaken—We love you! After all I've been through… It just made me feel so good. God bless, you Olisa!'"

"Ms. Carter, who you may remember lost her son, Aaron, a football star at Carson High School to a drive-by last year." Sadly, Aaron Carter's picture appeared on the screen. He was suited up in his football uniform. He held his football helmet in the crook of his arm and displayed a charming smile. "Aaron had just received a football scholarship to Notre Dame before he was viciously gunned down by an unconscionable group of hoods, because one of their girlfriends flirted with him. After all the Carter family has been through this year, we certainly wish them the best."

The camera cut to Eva's smiling visage at the studio desk. "And I'm getting daily reports that hundreds of gifts like these are being dropped off throughout L.A. County. It's also been reported that these drive-by blessings have inspired copycats in other cities to do the same thing. No one knows when the next one will occur or where, but the anticipation is high and people are buzzing throughout the city. And maybe for the first time that this reporter is aware, the 'City of Angels' is finally living up to its name. It's refreshing to broadcast something positive and that's what we plan to do this evening. As Jonathan Carpenter said, the focus of the Olisa Group is 'Don't wait for government intervention when you can create your own miracles!' Here are some more interviews we've gathered from some of the people hit by drive-bys."

I didn't have to hear anymore, particularly since I knew every location that was targeted. It certainly didn't stop there. In the coming days, Olisa was seen in dungarees accompanied by taggers and gang members, cleaning graffiti off the walls throughout the city. It was something she used to do prior to becoming famous, but now it was an event, shadowed by the camera and she hated it, but Jon insisted it was for the greater good.

Ernesto, who had risen to legendary fame, recruited many of the gang members, who oftentimes were rivals in the worse sense. Considered an "Untouchable," he could pretty much approach any group because of how he came to his notoriety. Once they realized who he was, they found a way to work together and honored the truce. No matter what you thought of these little hoodlums, interestingly, spiritual things awed many of them.

For instance, working with Olisa, I was blown out to observe how many Latino gang members wore crucifixes and rosaries around their necks. I also saw religious icons like the face of Christ ringed with a crown of thorns, Christ's figure nailed to the cross on their arms, tattoos of the Virgin of Guadalupe, or the Madonna with baby. I was told these all served as a form of protection and comfort. I found it ironic how strongly religion played a part in lives that were in contrast to peace.

However, the more I thought about it, the more I saw it wasn't that different from the mainstream. After all, isn't God's name invoked in a huddle when we ask for strength to go out and kick our opponent's ass?

Somehow, the gap between a supposedly civil culture in which we played healthy sports such as football, soccer, basketball, and boxing, and indulged in religious wars in which we prayed for God's strength suddenly lessened the gap between gangs and us.

Jon got what he wanted—powerful visuals: a beautiful, vulnerable looking woman, working with some of the most fearsome looking cats in the city. The same dudes who might have shot you for looking at them cross-eyed, now scrubbed walls as if it was a prized Lexus. Again, the images were so powerful that not only did it motivate you to go out and find a wall with graffiti on it, but it made you want to go find you a gang member to help you clean it!

Olisa was nowhere to be found, yet seen everywhere, thanks to Logan's photographs, and Jonathan supplying the prized visuals to the press who gobbled them up. There were shots of her talking to junkies on the street, homeless people, teenage runaways, youth groups, and so on. Nothing could be publicly planned, because it would have been too crazy. Once the word spread that there was an Olisa sighting, the people came in droves and we had to get her out of there.

The money continued to pour in from all over the world. The daily cash amounts were so overwhelming it made me shudder. However, the maelstrom of attention Olisa was receiving was even scarier. Jonathan had done his job too well, and I urged him to pull back, because a nerve had been touched in the public's psyche. He had hot-wired an engine that we knew nothing about. Olisa couldn't step out in the public without it causing chaos. Everyone wanted to get next to the healer. But all weren't necessarily sincere.

Deep in thought, Olisa watched a woman named Sonia meticulously paint her hands with henna on a tabletop in the large courtyard. The ancient style of Indian adornment known as *mehndi* was popular with Olisa ages before Hollywood celebrities became smitten with it. Her feet already stained with a striking henna tattoo.

Before the fame, Olisa would have driven down to Little India in Artesia on Pioneer Boulevard and hung out in Sonia's shop, doing lunch, buying music, shopping for spices, and art. But that was then.

Since it was next to impossible for her to spontaneously leave her mountain retreat for fear of the crowds, Jonathan indulged Olisa's whim by generously flying Sonia up by helicopter to the Canyon retreat. Olisa was ecstatic. She loved socializing with Sonia and always found the application of *mendhi* art on her body as meditative.

Meditation was certainly not on Jonathan's mind as Grace and I angrily watched him pace around in the courtyard from our lounge chairs. Gumbo and Laura were also there. Laura sat next to Olisa and fiddled with a crossword puzzle. Gumbo sat point at the end of the long rectangular tabletop, rummaging through a bowl of mixed raw vegetables.

"Ouch!" Jonathan cried, after accidentally kicking over a planter of orchids. At least, I assumed it was an accident.

"Olisa, you absolutely cannot do it," Jonathan yelled. "I mean, come on, you're not really serious, are you?" He lowered his voice in an attempt to sound reasonable.

"I'm very serious, Jon. I want to do this. I'm going to accept Walter Popcock's invitation to attend his church service and meet with him."

"Oli, this guy doesn't want to make friends, he wants to castigate you in front of his congregation in the worst possible way. You've been getting all the press lately, and believe me, he's not very happy about that. He doesn't just want to cripple you, he wants to bring you down. He's the 'Crusader for God's Law.' You've heard the radio show, you know the hype."

"Yes, but something inside of me is urging me to go."

Jon squatted down next to Olisa, urgency in his voice.

"OC, ordinarily I'd understand, but this is Popcock—a sanctimonious piece of vulture feces. He can't be trusted. I can't even believe you're considering it."

"Jon, what can he do to me?"

"I don't know, that's why I'm worried. He's got something up. It has all the makings of an ambush."

"God will protect me."

"Olisa, I'm not even sure God would venture there without body-guards."

"I'll be fine."

Jon stood back up. He threw his hands up and gazed at the sky in exasperation. He looked back at Olisa.

"Olisa, don't you get it? The man wants a piece of you! You don't need him. *We* don't need him. Besides, I thought you made it a policy not to affiliate too closely with any single group or denomination?"

"Jon, somehow this is different."

"Oli, the man hates you. Do you think you're going to win him over? You can't convert someone like him. That's like asking the devil to trade in his horns for a halo."

"Hmmmm," was Olisa's only response as she watched Sonia.

Sonia didn't appear to be bothered by any of this. She continued to paint decorative birds on Olisa's hand.

Jonathan took a quick breath and was ready for round two with Olisa. "He hasn't come out and said it yet, but he's about two broadcasts away from naming you the antichrist on his radio show."

"I've heard."

"So why go into the enemy's camp?"

"It's not a war."

"To him it is."

"This may be a historical moment, but I agree with Jon," I chipped in.

Olisa glanced at Grace, who solemnly nodded her head in agreement.

"Hey, OC, just remember, security's going to be difficult once we're inside his fortress, you know?" Alton munched on carrots plastered with so much dip they looked like ice cream cones.

"Forget it, guys."

"Forget what, Laura?" Jon asked, irritated.

"Can't you see that she's going to see Popcock no matter what you say?"

"How do you figure?"

"Look at her, she's already splashing on the war paint," Laura teased. "She's getting ready to do battle."

Jonathan's shoulders dropped. "Is that true?"

"*I'm* not the one preparing for battle," she stated matter-of-factly as she admired Sonia's handiwork.

I handed Jonathan a portion of the newspaper in my lap and leaned back in my lounge chair while I checked out the latest football scores. Eventually, I heard a sigh as he retreated into his chair and immersed himself in the newspaper.

Anaheim.

Knotts Berry Farm.

Disneyland.

The Glass Cathedral.

The Glass Cathedral, bastion of Walter Popcock and associates, was as notable and as entertaining as all the others located in its home base in Anaheim. I didn't even want to guess how many millions it took to build this fairy tale castle. I kept expecting to see a miniature golf course surrounding it. Still, the physical makeup of the church was both awe inspiring and intimidating, much like its maker, but in many ways just as hollow. We were allowed in by church people who greeted us as if they were used car salespeople ready to make a deal and just as ready to spit on our backs if we walked away without closure.

"Good morning, Mr. and Mrs. Carpenter. It's a pleasure meeting you. Right this way, Mr. Lee. Hi, Ms. Nelson, how are you today?"

They knew who we were. Each staff member politely greeted us by name and discussed pleasantries and anecdotes with each one of us like we were reunited high school friends. Ordinarily, I would have been flattered.

Instead, I was scared shitless.

We were the visitors on their home court. I imagined them studying our bios and reviewing videotapes of us during their church meetings until it was emblazoned in their brains. They had to know everything about us before they could do battle. And they expected to win, but I couldn't figure out their game plan.

SOUL EYES

I couldn't see Popcock verbally attacking Olisa at a church service he invited her to; that wouldn't look right in front of his congregation and could prove disastrous. So what was he planning? We agreed to take a wait-and-see attitude until he played his hand.

Meanwhile, the crowds outside the gates were building and waited eagerly to enter the church as if it were judgment day. Popcock's ubiquitous legions proudly displayed the P's on their lapels as they finally opened the church doors and ushered people to their seats. There were so many rows in the church, it looked like an indoor coliseum. However, there weren't enough to seat the hundreds of dejected people forced to remain outside. Before the church doors quickly closed, I heard people chanting Olisa's name.

A conservatively dressed sycophant whose offset smile never disappeared gave us the grand tour of the institution. However, her effusive hospitality was overcompensation for the patronizing expression in her eyes that said, "I was like you once—adrift in a secular wilderness until I found my salvation in Walter Popcock and the Glass Cathedral."

Soon we were escorted to the executive boardroom that was so gigantic you expected Jesus Christ to show up and take a meeting.

It was not hard to spot the impeccably dressed Walter Popcock among the elders with his helmet of shocking white hair. Right there beside him was old biscuit-head whose eyes targeted us like a sharpshooter. He whispered something in Popcock's ear, and Popcock responded by gesturing in broad sweeping motions for us to join him inside.

Popcock was slight of build and far more low key than the magnanimous figure that filled the television screen. He shook each of our hands, clasping them long enough to give you the impression he was trying to suck the energy from your body. When he got to Olisa's he held on to her hands as he sustained eye contact with her. The way he subtly sized her up was more like a snow leopard than the kind and wise grandfatherly image he conveyed on television.

"Olisa, what a pleasure to finally meet you. I am so delighted you decided to honor us by being here. I think you have already met my trusted associate, Arthur Furhman?"

Furhman, otherwise known as "Biscuit-Head," nodded affirmatively as he struggled to maintain his smile. "I trust we have treated you and your family well, thus far?" he asked, still not releasing her hands.

"Yes. Everyone has been very kind. Thank you for inviting us."

"No, thank you. It's not everyday we get such an esteemed celebrity to grace us in our worship of Christ, our Lord," he offered with a tinge of possessiveness. "I pray we won't disappoint you."

"I'm sure you won't."

"Praise God!" He emoted with a paternal stroke of her arm. "And here I had this impression you felt uncomfortable worshipping inside a church."

"I believe you can worship God anywhere as long as your heart is true. I love the church and what it represents. It's those who defile the purity of God's love that I am opposed to."

"Amen," Popcock said with his carnivorous grin as he continued his unabashed study of her. "I would love to continue this discussion, but I must attend to the good work of saving souls. Perhaps, if you are still willing, you might spend some more time with us after the service."

I hated the way he phrased that.

"We shall see," Olisa responded.

I suspect Olisa didn't fail to hear the caustic remark layered under his honey-toned voice as he scurried away with his entourage. Old biscuit-head couldn't resist turning around and giving us the same look a black widow spider gives her mate before the final kiss.

Next, we were escorted to seats near the front of the stage as phantom whispers accosted our movement through the congregation. The stage looked like an island as it loomed among the sea of onlookers. Consequently, for something that supposedly was not publicly announced, I was stunned at the number of media present. Popcock was known for eschewing any media not closely identified with his "controlled" environment, particularly since the press had not always smiled upon his many extravagances. Eva Sanchez, Theo Balanis, and many other media elite attended.

This was definitely an ambush. Whatever Popcock was planning bore no goodwill toward Olisa. The climate had been set for her downfall.

Furthermore, the press recognized a potential skirmish when they saw one. I'm sure that they were equally surprised that Olisa chose to visit the lair of the same person that lustily denounced her over the airwaves. The old fox wasn't about to surrender his crown or his money to some pretentious godchild.

The little ditty I used to read to Olisa when she was a child kept ringing in my head: "Run, run, as fast as you can, you can't catch me I'm the gingerbread man." According to the fable, the nice and encouraging old fox swallowed him up in one gulp.

"The Lord is my light and my salvation; whom shall I fear?" Popcock asked, addressing his congregation with the fervor of a coach at a pep rally. "The Lord is the strength of my life; of whom shall I be afraid? Though a host should encamp against me, my heart shall not fear; though war should rise against me, in this will I be confident. The Lord is my strength and my shield!" declared Popcock, reciting from Psalms as he excoriated the enemies of the church and railed against those who defied the true Word of God.

The demure man offstage had transformed into a fiery crusader, extolling the virtues of all those who fight the good fight for God, emphasizing "we against them," "righteousness against evil," "believers against nonbelievers." A hailstorm of amens zinged the air.

I was aware of his popularity, but I usually only allowed him about thirty seconds of channel surfing time. This was the first time I listened to an entire sermon, and I had to give him his props. He truly was an amazing speaker and perfectly suited for television where the attention span is less than a commercial break. I might have even found it inspiring if he wasn't spewing all his underlying vitriol at my daughter.

"Who is this King of Glory? The Lord God almighty. *He* is the *only* King of Glory!" In a grand flourish, he dramatically raised his hand toward the ceiling of the church as the majority of his congregants did likewise, raising their faces heavenwards. My eyes also searched the skies, but my vision of heaven was intercepted by the Letter "P" floating blatantly among the painted clouds in the ceiling.

Pausing, he surveyed the audience as he wiped the perspiration from his face with his silk handkerchief. "My friends, we have come a long way, haven't we? However, we have so much further to go. It won't be long, because God is on *our* side as long as we believe and continue to do His good works. And that, my brothers and sisters, will happen as long as we give to this ministry our time and our resources to help the unenlightened escape from perverse darkness to divine light!

"In this evil society of ours, we are easy prey to all those new age books, and gurus who talk like they know God. Brothers and sisters, they've even convinced some of you to trace their footsteps all the way into the ungodly fires of hell. Friends, what you need to do is follow the pathway to the bible. Its message has remained unchanged for centuries and is far more relevant than *today's* gurus who might not be here *tomorrow*. When Jesus Christ reappears in all His glory, He is gonna run these heretics out of town like a pack of wayward mongrels! The bible says beware of false prophets. You better pay attention people, because if you want redemption and if you want salvation, then look no further than right here in this holy book! *This* is where it begins, and *this* is where it will end! Thank you Jesus!"

He smiled like a proud grandfather as his devotees leaped to their feet yelling rabidly. It was no coincidence after the applause died down that he then chose to bestow his attention upon us.

"Brothers and sisters, I have been informed that God has sent us some new friends here today to sit among our family. I ask you to please welcome our visitors with open arms."

You've been informed! It was your invitation!

"One of them has recently been all over the news of late. They've been calling her names like the High Priestess and Good Witch of Venice, which personally, I think is unflattering for such a lovely lady. Her name is Olisa Carpenter, and I know she's not expecting this, but

Ms Carpenter, would you please honor me by joining me on stage for the benediction?" His hands were outstretched, but his smile was as inviting as a piranha's.

Olisa took a moment to gather her strength before slowly rising and proceeding up to the stage. I had to dig deep to keep from yanking her down as she scooted past me. She grabbed my hand and Grace's hand, squeezing them reassuringly. I held my breath as she sauntered up the steps. She looked absolutely beautiful with her thick mane of rippling hair flowing defiantly behind her. Her henna stained hands and feet sported the full *mehndi*, and she wore a brightly colored sari adorned with jewelry. I'm sure Popcock likened her to a savage walking among his "civilized" minions. It probably didn't help when Little Oak, dressed in full Native American regalia, stood to hug her when she reached the end of the row.

He extended a hand to assist her onto the stage, but I noticed instead of giving her a good old fellowship hug, he held her hand and petted it. Old "biscuit-head" must have forewarned him about the deleterious effects of one of those hugs.

"Olisa, thank you for coming. We are glad to have you with us, particularly with all the controversy you've had to endure."

Controversy?

"Because here we accept all of God's children…"

How generous of you!

"And the one thing that can never be debated is your depth of courage. Seeing you stand up to those misdirected souls. God bless you! That's something not even the liberal media moguls can fake!"

Implying what? I could feel the anger coursing through my body.

"Reverend Popcock! Reverend Popcock!" wheezed an anxious voice from the congregation.

"I'm sorry, Olisa." Popcock bounded down the ornate stairway in the direction of the unseen plea. As he stood in the middle of the congregation, he cocked his head with his face, contorting empathetically as he spoke to an individual consumed by the audience. The person wasn't even visible on the gigantic video monitors sprinkled throughout the church like scoreboards at a Laker's game.

"What can I do for you, young man?"

"I need healing, Reverend Popcock. "

"Son, that's something only God can grant."

"I don't doubt it, sir, but they say she can, Reverend. I mean, I'm not trying to be disrespectful, but that's why I came here today."

Popcock released a heavy sigh. "I guess we should be grateful for whatever brings God's children our way. What's your name young man?"

"Rodney, sir… Rodney Isaac."

"Rodney, I don't think anyone here would disagree with you that Olisa Carpenter is, indeed, an extraordinary person… But aren't we asking a little much of her?" He said it with the intimacy of two old chums hanging out. Olisa appeared surprisingly unaffected as she listened.

"But I saw her on television healing that actor. She's the answer to my prayers."

"But Rodney, I hate being a doubting Thomas, but you know television does not always reflect reality."

"Yes, sir, but this is different. Everyone says she has the gift."

"Rodney, far be it from me to dissuade someone with so much faith that a miracle can't happen here today. The bible tells us that miracles have existed for centuries. But I would be remiss if I didn't caution you that there are no guarantees that Ms. Carpenter can heal your affliction as they keep telling us." He looked back at the stage. "Am I right, Ms. Carpenter?"

"You are right, Reverend Popcock, there are no guarantees."

Popcock turned back around with a complacent smile. "See, but I can guarantee you one thing, that as long as you put your faith in Jesus Christ, you will be rewarded with eternal happiness."

The audience punctuated it with an "amen."

"I understand, Reverend Popcock, but I just can't go on like this anymore. I saw what she could do. Please let her try."

"All right, son," he sighed wearily. "If Olisa is willing, I will back away."

Olisa nodded and smiled.

"Then come on up, son. I'm sure some of the ushers will lend you a helping hand."

As the ushers converged on him, I spied an enormous being standing unobtrusively against the wall next to a stained glass window to the left of the stage. Intensely, he watched the proceedings from the protective abyss of his black shades. The sunlight streaking through the stain glass windows made his already obscured figure fade in and out.

After an interminable amount of time, Rodney Isaac finally made it on the stage. He was a young African-American man, in his early twenties: gaunt, crippled, and aided by a walker. He slowly and agonizingly clanked across the stage accompanied by a very solemn Walter Popcock.

Isaac ended his trek, standing unsteadily in front of Olisa.

"Ms. Carpenter, please help me," he pleaded, his eyes lowered deferentially. "Please…"

"Only the Creator can, Rodney."

She lovingly cradled his face in her hands as they stood silently in meditation, all the while his legs trembling mightily. That's when I saw something so jarring the entire church gasped in one breath.

And it wasn't a miracle.

Olisa forcefully shoved him backwards, screaming disdainfully, "What is this? How dare you make a mockery of the church! Don't you have any respect for God or the people here or yourself? What you are doing is despicable!"

Isaac tumbled painfully to the ground, followed by the walker, which crashed loudly against his prostrate body. The amplified stage made it sound even worse. Terrified and disoriented, he laid passively on the ground as Olisa glared down at him.

Secretly, I always feared that another Mama Willis disaster might occur again. Well, the nightmare had finally arrived, and she was unraveling.

The Reverend Popcock was as shocked as all of us, but then a subtle smile escaped his lips and reappeared in his eyes. This was better than he ever imagined. I'm sure he wanted to do a "River Dance," but he restrained himself as he kneeled down beside Isaac protectively holding him in his arms.

"Don't take your frustrations out on this poor young man, Olisa! It's not his fault. Everyone knows you did what you could with the best of intentions. However, the truth is, Rodney Isaac placed his faith on hearsay. Only God is omnipotent."

Popcock closed his eyes as he clumsily flicked his hands out for both Olisa and Isaac to grasp while he served as the symbolic bridge. He prayed, "Dear God, let this good woman join me now in guiding those who have strayed back to the path of righteousness…"

However, it was evident Olisa had other things on her mind.

"I'm still waiting for the truth, Rodney."

Up to this point, Isaac had been avoiding eye contact with her. Reluctantly, he looked up and gazed into Olisa's eyes.

Popcock's tone changed as rapidly as his eyes flipped open. "Olisa, don't do this to yourself. This is a live broadcast that is being captured around the world."

Ignoring him, once again she firmly repeated, "Rodney."

At first I thought it was only fear I saw in Isaac's eyes, but there was more to it than that. The look on his face reminded me of a John who suddenly realizes he propositioned an undercover officer instead of a prostitute.

"Get up, Rodney. Do you hear me? I said get up! "

"Enough, Olisa. Need I remind you that you are in the House of the Lord. I will not allow this man to suffer any further degradation."

But Rodney was already on his feet, shaking tremendously, but not because he needed a walker.

Popcock's face became ashen.

Shouts of "It's a miracle!" peppered the air.

"No!" Olisa shouted, quickly dousing the building adulation. "No! This is not God's work!"

The irritation in her face yielded to compassion as she reached for his hand. "Why, Rodney? Why come here and deceive God and others who welcome you with their embrace? Especially when the real truth is you're not disabled, you're an addict!"

"My God, have you no shame, woman?" Popcock remarked curtly, possessively locking his arms around Isaac. "First you give this man false hopes, then knock him to the ground and chastise him? In the history of this church, I have never felt the need to ask someone to leave, but today I'm afraid I must…"

"No, reverend!" Isaac uttered as he wrestled away from Popcock's grasp and crumpled to the ground on his knees clutching Olisa's hands. Tears fell steadily from his eyes as he struggled to speak. "I'm sorry… I can't lie to you…"

He held her hands like a man afraid to drown if he let go. "You know don't you?" he stuttered. "I can see it in your eyes. You know that I ain't nothing more than a broke down smack user."

"What I know is that you've been crying for help for a long time."

"What? What is going on here?" Popcock demanded.

"They said you were a fake! But it's not true. Oh my God, it's not true."

"They who?" Popcock asked defensively, his eyes morphing into granite.

"They said God would reward me in heaven if I exposed her in your church for being a fraud. They told me I was doing a good thing."

"Who told you?" Popcock grilled him again.

"I don't know who those men were. All I know is they said they were friends of yours."

Popcock huffed, "Come now. That's ludicrous!"

"That's what they said, Reverend. I'm sure they were lying now. I was just hanging out by the video store, begging for change when two guys showed up in this big stretch limousine, decked out in some serious threads and flashing a wad of hundred dollar bills. They slapped down five $100 dollar bills in my hand and promised me $500 more if I acted like I was crippled. They convinced me Olisa was some kind of witch and that the media and her were in bed with the devil. They said this was my one chance in life to be a hero if I helped them put an end to this evil. They even gave me a walker. What was I supposed to do? I ain't no rich man. I live in a halfway house, so I jumped all over it!"

"Please, turn those cameras off!" Popcock screamed. His eyes had a worrisome expression as they darted from camera to camera. He acted as if this was the first time he noticed them. "This is reprehensible!" he barked self-righteously. "No viewer should be subjected to this abomination of all that the church represents. Do you have any idea what these men looked like?"

"Not really. I just remember them giving me money. I don't care about them or their money any more. I just want to apologize to Olisa and the congregation and to God for being so wrong. Please have mercy on me."

"We all forgive you and love you," she said tenderly as she pulled him to his feet.

The word "amen" undulated through the congregation.

"You really do have the gift, don't you?" he asked admiringly.

But that was a rhetorical question as he closed his eyes and embraced Olisa with great élan. Murmuring rolled through the congregation like an undercurrent. Popcock's eyes volleyed to ol' "Biscuit-Head" who quietly scampered offstage. Soon, turbulence erupted in the audience as Popcock's flunkies seeped in, confiscating cameras and hustling recalcitrant press out of the church.

It was far too late for all of that. They couldn't impede the dozens of people who had already gotten up on stage, nor the ones that formed a line that cascaded from the top of the stage to the bottom of the auditorium. A tone had been set by Isaac's embrace of Olisa. They all wanted to hug her, touch her, and have their spiritual moment with her. It didn't matter how long it would take, they weren't going to leave until they felt her caress. Olisa did her best to oblige them. She hugged them, mothered them, and even cradled adults like children. Olisa remained on stage for almost two hours, giving and receiving love without a strain showing on her face. And the filmmakers and photographers who escaped the disconcerted ushers had these scenes broadcast on networks throughout the country and world

Eva Sanchez interviewed many of the recipients of Olisa's hugs. One of who said, "After seeing her in person, I believe she was sent here on a mission from God. I've never been around anyone who has exuded so much love. It was like looking into God's eyes."

I almost felt a tinge of sympathy for Walter Popcock who stood forlorn on the corner of the stage, groping for words. He tried to improvise, even tried to muster a high-minded smile, but he had lost control. He always preached the Glass Cathedral was God's House, but the pouty expression on his face made you think God punished him and sent him to his room.

After the service, an impossibly more dour than usual Furhman escorted us to the exit, where an enormous crowd assembled at the gates roaring for Olisa as we strained to hear what the vermin had to say.

"Reverend Popcock asked me to extend his apologies to you. He had planned to spend more time with you, but, unfortunately, fell ill after the sermon."

What a surprise.

"Oh, I'm sorry to hear that. Is there anything I can do?" Olisa asked.

Furhman paused for a second then said, "No, no, I'm sure he'll be fine. He just needs a little rest. He's been keeping a pretty hectic schedule, plus, experiencing that disturbing scenario in which that poor misguided man, so desperate that he'd concoct a lie like that…"

Yeah, that poor misguided man…

"God bless him, though. He'll be in our prayers, as will you and your family," Furhman pronounced, in a very hollow tone.

What? As hostages?

He signaled for security to escort us to our limousine. He bid us a pleasant goodbye, but his eyes tracked us like a California condor.

CHAPTER 12

Olisa never received another invitation from the Glass Cathedral. Nor was there ever another face-to-face meeting between Popcock and Olisa. His image and credibility suffered a public flogging as he continued to deny to the media any association with the "phantom" men who attempted to frame Olisa at the Glass Cathedral. Popcock's foiled plan and nationwide humiliation consumed him and transformed him into a character as obsessive and pathetic as Captain Ahab. He excoriated Olisa every chance he got in his weekly radio and television broadcasts.

"I truly hate to think like this, but sometimes, friends, you must, in the perilous and never-ending battle for men's souls. Has it ever occurred to you that in all the recent and embittered attacks on my character by the liberal media that no one has brought up the possibility that maybe, just maybe, some of Olisa's more radical devotees, in collusion with my enemies in the press, might have set this whole thing up to make me look bad? Why is it that no one ever discusses this issue? Now I'm not saying Olisa is not a good person—she is—and I think she means well. But the truth of the matter is that those people surrounding her, the ones the press refers to as her disciples, are certainly not the kind of disciples I'm familiar with. These folks kind of scare me. They're a little unsavory and possibly a lot dangerous."

"Do you hear what I'm saying, people? One of her followers, at least the one we know about, has a criminal record as long as a yardstick. He is a notorious gang banger known for his reign of terror in the Venice and Mar Vista areas. The head of her organization, Mr. Jonathan Carpenter and his music business cronies, have shoveled more filth, depravity, and violent thoughts into our young people's minds than can ever be accounted for. They have unscrupulously promoted some of the most debase artists and entertainers in modern times, whose sexually explicit and angry lyrics continue to corrupt our youth. And many of these purveyors of the evil running rampant in our contemporary society, have unashamedly brought their perverse recitations to their so-called universal healing concerts. They talk out the corner of their mouths about God, and then go out and make millions for Satan!

"One of her best friends is a man that loves his own gender a little too much, if you know what I'm saying. Apparently, he planned on marrying one of his boyfriends until he died of an aneurysm. It's always sad to hear about anyone dying in such a horrible way, but the bible says God condemns homosexuality. Obviously, this is God's way of meting out punishment to all who defy His laws.

"And I don't think anyone can fault the Indians, I'm sorry, Native Americans, for being angry after suffering so much abuse in the history of this nation, but it's over now. We can't pay for what our ancestors did eternally. It's time to move forward. Hey, you know I've got issues with some of those folks in Washington, but they have at least tried to correct those wrongs. The Indians now own land, oil wells, and casinos! They've got the equal opportunity to gamble and make money just like any other sinner. Be that as it may, Olisa's best friend, apparently, hasn't heard that the Indian Wars with the States are over. She speaks on college campuses and reservations, lambasting Christianity, while turning right around and indulging in pagan rituals. It's kind of hard to fit into society when you're going into those sweat lodges doing God knows what, isn't it? Correct me if I'm wrong, but I've got a feeling they ain't singing Jesus' praise in there.

"And let me tell you brothers and sisters, this person they've been calling a holy woman, Olisa Carpenter, has sometimes been seen in those pagan centers too. Yet, Ms. Carpenter tells us she doesn't like to be confined to worshipping within a church structure, but she can spend time lying against those musty walls… hmmm… Kind of interesting, don't you think?

"Furthermore, they've got this lewd photographer, some claim is her boyfriend, out there shooting propaganda for them. His recent photographic retrospective of children around the world lashed out and blamed the United States for not helping these malnourished children. The United States has done more to help more people than any country I know. We're at the height of patriotism, yet this person dares to insult the greatest country in the world!

"Do you understand what I'm saying, America? These people say they're trying to unite us in some kind of ambiguous cause, yet it seems to me they're hell-bent on tearing this country apart. We're supposed to herald a photographer who tries to shame his country the same way they've tried to humiliate me? The same man whose tribute to women of the third world was really nothing but a porno exhibit, showcasing naked breasts. However, if you were aware of his lifestyle over the years, you wouldn't be too surprised.

"You see friends, I've been doing a little research, and maybe I sound like a foolish old man spouting things off the wall, but that's all right, because I'm proud to say at least I'm a fool for Christ—not the devil!

"Now their whole deal is to try to pass this woman off as some kind of miracle worker. There may be some truth to that, but, be forewarned, cause if you read your bible carefully you'll see that Revelations tells us that one day the antichrist will appear in the guise of someone very powerful, someone we'd never suspect. In addition, I may not be quoting the holy book verbatim, but I can tell you this much, I've never heard any tales about Jesus Christ returning as a woman. Have you? So who is Olisa Carpenter?

"Now they talk about her in all these saintly terms, but wasn't she once referred to as a witch? Seems like a lot of us forgot about that with all this stuff they've been force-feeding us. I didn't forget, brothers and sisters, because I've dedicated my life to rooting out the Prince of Darkness. The devil was once an angel, too, before he was cast down from heaven. His knowledge of the Scriptures is second to none, and he knows God. You can bet he uses that to his advantage when he builds detours to turn us away from the right path. He can perform miracles, too. Just remember, when the Rapture, the Tribulation, the second coming of Christ in judgment is here, only those who accept Jesus Christ as their personal savior will find a seat in His heavenly palace.

I'd had enough of Popcock's tirades masked as sermons as I switched the radio station to the soothing sounds of jazz. I only wished Popcock's personal vendetta could have ended just as easily with the flip of a channel. In the weeks to come, he campaigned for support from some of the most powerful churches across the country, including several prominent black church leaders. Leaders whose envy exceeded their capacity to view the good. Some didn't mind going to bed with the same man who initially abstained from participating with other white churches in offering an apology to the black descendants of slaves for many of the injustices incurred and ignored by the Christian Church.

Except now they were united in one unholy alliance—to circumvent Olisa's movement. Olisa had not only upstaged them, she had usurped them of their power, prestige, and influence in the community. She snatched up territory faster than a drug dealer. They were intent on stopping her before they were completely shorn of their sanctimonious authority.

Sadly, they didn't see that by attacking Olisa they were laying down paint on the wrong canvas. The person they perceived as a detriment to their aims was the same person whose sole purpose in life was to weave a spiritual quilt among all people in an effort to eliminate racism, sexism, and any other obstacles that got in love's way. Unfortunately, I suppose it was difficult for these groundskeepers of glory to focus upon something so simple and pure.

"Once you commit to ridding yourself of all self-absorption and hatred, then you begin to discover how much easier it is to feel compassion toward others. I feel nothing but love toward the Rev. Popcock," Olisa was quoted as saying in a *New York Times* interview with Theo Balanis in response to the vicious and personal attacks mounted by Walter Popcock.

"But you must admit, Olisa," Balanis commented, "some of the things he says are libelous, scathing, and defamatory attacks on your character."

"It doesn't bother me. I know who I am. Does he know himself?"

That's what I loved about my girl. She could be more diplomatic than a politician, but it all came from the heart. It would take more than rabid statements from Popcock to rock Olisa's equilibrium. But Grace and I were still worried about her. No matter what she said to the press, the pressure and the strain taxed her, especially with the upcoming tour Jonathan had planned for her. She was constantly on edge and irritable—very uncharacteristic of Olisa. Sometimes she would just withdraw and speak to no one for days. If she had been a singer, they would have called her a diva.

The one person who seemed to be able to bring her out of those moods was Logan. He was a comforting presence to her, mostly, though I am embarrassed to say, because he paid more attention to the woman in her, not the goddess. It made her happy. It took her mind off the pressures. For that I will always have a warm feeling about Logan.

Jonathan managed to tolerate the relationship, but still viewed Logan as a wandering Romeo who would one day get bored and walk out of her life searching for a new creative high. I didn't care what Jonathan said about Logan, both Grace and I had a good feeling about him. Grace always smiled when she'd watch the two of them take long walks through the hills, hand in hand. I think she remembered *us* in *them*.

Grace and I also agreed that this tour thing was no good. In fact, Grace spoke of constantly having premonitions about it. It was already overwhelming dealing with the enormous attention at home, let alone confronting the road issues. There was a torrent of emotions out there and not all good. Olisa was greatly loved, and revered and she had amazingly built a bridge between the "haves and have nots." But, there was also a freaky amount of hate, suspicion, and skepticism out there, much of it fueled by Popcock and his cohorts.

We were at fault, too. We took the ball and ran with it under the banner that we were going to change the world. I wonder, in retrospect, if things may have gone differently if we had tried harder to downplay

Olisa's gifts. But that, unfortunately, we'll never know. Fate has a funny way of intruding upon your life, one way or the other.

The first time Olisa indicated she was burned and disenchanted with the whole process was while the two of us sat on the couch watching a heated debate on NBC. It was an in studio televised panel hosted by the number one news anchor, Susan Blair. The discussion involved noted personalities, Beverly Fairchild, founder and president of W.I.N, seated in the center; Hakeem Woodson, activist and poet, seated to the left of Fairchild; and to her right, Richard K. Martin, author of *God and the South Will Rise Again!*

The discussion was already underway by the time we had tuned in. Susan Blair was the real life Murphy Brown in terms of attitude and looks. She was in her mid forties, shoulder length blonde hair and she was very elegant. She could also be as gruff as she could be charming. Rumor had it that she was really ticked off that she ended up interviewing Olisa after the little upstart—Eva Sanchez. However, that's what the public was craving, and that ultimately was her meal ticket. That is one of the reasons she decided to host discussions revolving around Olisa. The other is that Eva Sanchez wasn't conducting panel discussions, nor did she have her own show, yet…

"You really believe that God has blond hair and blue eyes?" Susan asked, leaning forward on the long table with a smirk as she faced the panel.

"Well, ma'am," the elderly man drawled, "I grew up seeing pictures of Christ not only in my bible, but in the stain glass windows of my church in Arkansas. That's all I've ever known. I've gotta believe that God inspired the artists who created them. Yes indeed, I mean, maybe his hair was black instead of blond, and maybe his eyes were brown instead of blue, but there is no doubt in my mind that he must have been a Caucasian man."

"Okay, so let's hypothesize for a moment. What if he wasn't. Would you still cling to your beliefs as steadfastly that Jesus is Lord?" Susan clasped her hands together and waited for the response. Her coolly analytical blue eyes gave no indication of what she was really thinking as she waited a response.

"I can't really answer that, Ms. Blair."

"Why not?"

"That's because he doesn't have an answer, Susan!" snapped Hakeem Woodson.

"I'm not going to answer that question, Mr. Woodson, because that's a fantasy question. I'm talking about reality."

"Then you better reread your bible, Mr. Martin, because there is nowhere in the bible that discusses Jesus being fair skinned. Jesus was described as having dark olive skin and hair like lamb's wool. How do you explain that?"

"I don't choose to, Mr. Woodson, because that's what you and those other revisionists say."

Incensed, the black man shook his head. "No, the only revisionists I've seen in history, sir, are white authors like yourself who persist in reinventing history by making all gods and heroes in their image. It's manifest destiny, except, instead of leg irons, we are enslaved by psychological chains. We're expected to pray to a Jesus who is the same color as the slave master. But what do you expect? It took two hundred years and DNA to prove to you that 'your' great President Thomas Jefferson, was responsible for all those mulatto babies running around the plantation hollering, 'Where's my daddy?'"

"Sir, I think you're not only digressing but being overly emotional." His eyes blinked rapidly as a thin smile pierced his lips.

"Yeah… well, you know how we are. But thank God we are so damn emotional, because it inspired us to fight for our inherent rights and to search for the truth instead of accepting myths like the blue-eyed Jesus!"

"I'm not going to respond to that, sir, especially since the truth speaks for itself," Martin replied patronizingly. His smile disappeared as fast as his blinking eyes.

"Let's talk about the truth. Mr. Martin, both Joseph and Mary had Hamitic ancestors, which means they were of African descent, which also means they were black, not white. My advice to you is to read books like *What Color was Jesus,* by William Mosley, or *The Black Lineage of Christ Jesus* and *The Black Presence in the Bible* both by Walter McCray, and…"

"The only thing I need to read, sir, is the good old fashion King James Bible, not some leftist fairy tales written yesterday!" He pulled out his pocket Bible and placed it authoritatively on the table.

Susan quickly intervened. "Gentlemen, I think Beverly has something to contribute to this conversation."

A frowning Beverly Fairchild jumped in, "I sure do. And I think both of you have narrowed this discussion of 'Religion's Place in Our Society Today' to competing male egos on Western Christianity."

"Beverly, I'm not a Christian. I'm just trying to point out to this man the hypocrisy of his beliefs and how self-serving they really are. Personally, I'm a Muslim."

"Oh Lord," Martin smirked, rolling his eyes. "So you're one of those terrorist folks that want to kill all the white devils. Now I get it."

Hakeem pounded his fist on the table. "Once again, Mr. Martin, your ignorance stands out more markedly than that confederate flag on your lapel. First, let's get something straight: I'm an orthodox practitioner. I'm not of the Nation. Furthermore, I don't believe that W. Fard Muhammad was Allah incarnate or that Elijah Muhammad was a divine messenger of God. Secondly, if you knew anything about the Koran you'd realize that color has no bearing on those who are the true followers of the Islamic faith. We are all equals in Allah's eyes."

Martin leaned forward on the table and glared at Hakeem. "That's good to know when y'all follow him to hell! Cause it says in Psalms 2:12 'Blessed are all they that put their trust in Him!" he shouted, accidentally spitting on Beverly's hand in the process.

Beverly wiped her hand in disgust. "And it's the emphasis on Him that is the crux of your problem, gentlemen." She flipped her hair defiantly.

"Excuse me, young lady?"

"What that means, Mr. Martin, is that God is a great deal younger in age than the Goddess."

Both men stared at her as if she had grown a third eye.

"You might want to explain that, Beverly." Susan looked amused.

"Before there was Christianity, before we evolved into a patriarchal society, many of the ancient religions were matriarchies and worshipped the Goddess. It wasn't until centuries later, that western civilization took over with its male dominated societies and started devouring all the scriptures concerning the Goddess and revising their sacred histories. Libraries were set on fire, and record keeping priestesses were slaughtered. God was made in the image of man and women were tossed aside."

"My goodness, if this isn't about the biggest bunch of I don't know what—"

"If you don't mind, I'd like to finish, Mr. Martin," Beverly flatly stated.

"Sure, whatever."

"Look at Eve. She was considered inferior, unclean and couldn't exist without Adam's rib. Western religion validated women's persecution. Goddess worship was soon belittled as a cult of people who practiced black magic…"

"Ain't it?" Martin grumbled.

Fairchild shook her head in exasperation. "A woman's position in western religion is one that is inherently devalued. The patriarchal emphasis in western religion is the main reason why our society is so screwed up. And if my memory serves me correct, it took till the year 2000 for the AME church to elect the first female bishop in the denomination's history, who happened to be African American, and it was gender, not race that was at issue here."

Hakeem shifted in his seat as Martin shot him a self-satisfied glance, but Beverly Fairchild rapidly deflected it.

"We need to shift gears and begin to focus on a matriarchy again, a system that encompasses tolerance, sympathy, and love. When a child is ill, it searches for its mother. Our society needs to be mothered. I see us emerging toward a Goddess movement out of necessity, and people like Olisa Carpenter are accelerating it. She is not only the most amazing person I've ever seen in my lifetime, but the embodiment of the earth mother."

"Who I might add is African American," snipped Hakeem.

"And who they also call a witch," bit back Richard Martin.

"This is man's way of discrediting her, because if she had been a man she would have been called a prophet!"

"Oh, that's hogwash, woman!"

Susan Blair tried to regain order as the argument continued to spiral.

I turned to Olisa and said, "I may not have your psychic abilities, but I can feel you thinking. What's up?"

Olisa laid her head on my shoulder. "Dad, now I truly know what Ghandi meant."

"About what?"

"He said, 'Everyone is eager to garland my photos and statues, but nobody wants to follow my advice'."

"Yeah…"

"Why don't they get it, Dad? Why are they wasting time arguing over color, over gender, over politics, over religion? They're focusing on everything but love. Is it me? Have I been sending out the wrong message?"

"No, Olisa, it's certainly not you. You're about as right as anyone can be. However, no one said it would be easy. People don't share the same prescription lenses."

I wrapped my arm around her and playfully wiped the frown off her face just like I used to do when she was a youngster.

"Dad, can I just disappear for awhile, do you think that would be okay?"

"Honey, I think you can stop this bus and get off any time you want."

She sighed and laid her head on my shoulder. We fell into a deep and comforting silence as we watched the low flames dancing in the fireplace. I knew it was bullshit and so did she. But it sure sounded good.

Of course, I didn't realize how serious she was until the next day. Grace, Olisa, and I were sitting outside in the patio having breakfast Sunday morning when we heard Jon pull up in his car. Five minutes later, he came traipsing into the patio with a little extra hitch in his stride, obviously in a good mood.

"Hey, family. Is it a beautiful day or what?" he said, rubbing his hand and giving Grace and Olisa a wet one on the cheek. "I might have to join you for your walk today, Olisa. I need to get rid of some of this fat. Look at this." He lifted his T-shirt and clasped the fleshy handles of his stomach.

Olisa smiled as she idly stirred her fruit salad.

"So, what are we eating?" he asked, serving himself some bacon, eggs, and pancakes from various platters. "Oh man, see, this is why I get fat."

"How was the drive?" Grace asked as she handed him the syrup.

"Too nice to be working. I didn't run into any traffic."

"That's good."

"After we get through eating, Olisa, let's meet. I have some great stuff I want you to see. Are you going to be at the meeting tomorrow? I mean you don't have to. I just think it'd be good if some of our new staff got a chance to meet you before we hit the road."

"Jonathan, I can't do it anymore."

"What?!"

"No more shows. After the Shrine, that's it," Olisa remarked softly.

It was like the Twilight Zone. Jonathan instantly aged from thirty-three to seventy-three.

"What do you mean?"

"Jon, I'm wiped out. I just can't do it anymore. I told you when we first discussed the idea that I might feel this way one day."

"Yeah, I understand, but you can't quit right now. We're just getting going. Saving the world takes a lot more work."

"No, Jonathan. The organization can continue without my active participation. It's not working out anymore."

"Not working out anymore? It's working beyond belief! We're making so much money Bill Gates is looking over his shoulder. Not working? We're building you a headquarters in Malibu, Olisa! That means it's working! Superbly, I might add! You're doing exactly what you always wanted to do—making an impact on the world by helping people!"

"And we can continue to do that. We can take that money and do the things we're supposed to with it. You don't need me anymore. God will provide from here on."

"Forget that. We need you, Olisa. Otherwise, we might as well close shop. It's not God that they see, it's you!"

"Are you listening to yourself, Jon? Your reaction is exactly what I'm talking about. It's not me. It's God working through me."

"Okay, okay, I know that, come on, I was so discombobulated by what you said, my words got all twisted up, and I apologize. But try and understand. We need you to continue to do the Lord's work. You are the symbol. You know what I'm saying? You can't quit! Everything's finally in place. Why are you trying to ruin everything?"

"Wait a minute, Jonathan, did you hear anything that your sister said? She just said she is burned out and needs to break away!" I argued.

"I got it! Okay? She can do that. You know what? Let's forget about talking business today. I'm flexible. Besides, I was thinking about spending the day with this new honey I met anyway. Might even bring her up here so she can enjoy the outdoors. Huh? That would be a good thing. Sure, Olisa can take some time to herself. I'm down with that. We're all a little tired and maybe I've been pushing everybody too hard. Sure. That's all she needs is to revitalize, and get her energy back so we can start up again."

"Jonathan, you're still not listening. Olisa wants it to end. Are you more concerned about her or yourself?" I asked him.

"You had something to do with this, didn't you?"

"Jonathan!" Grace scolded.

Some of the edge left his eyes.

"Dad had nothing to do with it, Jon, except for listening to me cry the blues."

"But I bet he didn't try very hard to talk you out of it!"

"You got that right! You see, my investment in her supersedes all the other crap because it's about her welfare, not mine."

"Oh, so what you're saying is I don't care about her?" he asked, eyes smoldering.

"Jon, why don't we take that walk you were mentioning earlier," she cooed, gently tugging on his arm.

"That's an excellent idea," Grace agreed. "Why don't you do that? It will give you a chance to really talk. Right, Joseph?"

I just kind of grunted my assent as Jonathan thumped his napkin down and locked eyes with me one last time before ambling away. I watched as several security figures followed behind them at a safe distance.

"Maybe everything is going to work out after all," Grace sighed.

"Maybe," I replied as I watched a tall figure silently interweaving between the trees like the legendary Bigfoot. Except I don't ever remember Bigfoot wearing shades.

"Things have changed," Jonathan proclaimed as he marched into the boardroom of his Century City Office a couple of days later, eyes red, and jaws attacking his gum. There were about twelve people present including Peter, Gumbo, Logan, Grace, and myself. The others were executives Jon previously hired to help run the corporation. He dramatically slapped some papers down on the table and surveyed the room, his eyes eventually resting on Peter. "Petey, you better cancel the ten city tour, we're not going to need it."

There was a chorus of groans in the room.

"What?" Peter yelled, his body snapping to attention like a switchblade. "You're shittin' me, right? Do you know how long it took me to arrange some of these deals? Jonathan, I can't just *cancel.*"

"I know, Peter, I know, and I'm sorry. Olisa abruptly changed her mind. Basically, she's disturbed by all the attention focused on her."

"Okay, so what are we doing?"

"She wants us to divert more attention toward the fund-raisers and charities. C'mon, are you really all that surprised? You guys talk all the time."

Peter nodded his head while thoughtfully tapping his pen on his notepad. His eyebrow suddenly arched. "So let me get this right. If Olisa has refused to do any more shows, then why aren't you on your knees clinging to a toilet bowl instead of looking like you're holding the winning lotto ticket?"

Jonathan chuckled. "Let's just say, Mr. Kaplan, that I was a little taken aback at first, but I managed to recover. Olisa and I worked out a little compromise. Savannah…"

"Yes, sir." Savannah, his longtime assistant, pushed her laptop computer aside and bounced to her feet as she passed out paperwork. Cute, brilliant, and very efficient, I always thought she would have been the perfect wife for Jon. Except that she was physically too heavy for his taste, which is probably why he hired her, no distractions. I suspected she secretly carried the torch for him, but being the consummate professional, you'd never hear it from her. Nevertheless, no one was more loyal to him than Savannah. She was a homemaker without the sex. If he said the sun was purple, she'd go out and buy purple sunglasses. She attended to his every need, fastidiously arranging his schedule from his work life, to his dating life, to how much underwear he needed when he traveled.

"Olisa promised to do one more concert, my choice, after the Shrine Auditorium this weekend. Take a good look at the literature Savannah is handing out. It's a retrospective of all the marches in Washington D.C. over the past forty years, all the way back to Dr. Martin Luther King. You getting it now? That's right, baby! OC is going to Washington!"

"Washington?" we gasped.

"That's right, Washington, D.C., the State Capitol. Can't you see it? A unity march to the steps of the Lincoln memorial. Black-white, rich-poor, young-old, male-female, gay-straight, anyone and everyone together, hand in hand."

His eyes flashed with the grandeur of his inner epic.

"The way I see it, why do an off Broadway production when the greater stage awaits you! Olisa's fame has risen above it all, anyway. Every show Peter scheduled has sold out the instant the public received word Olisa was coming to town. Look, it's not often that the venue itself considers canceling. But the Shrine Auditorium feels it's ill prepared for the turbulence that might ensue because of the endless deluge for tickets and added shows.

"The Shrine people see a potential disaster. I see a sign. If this is going to be our last one, than let's do it right! We can accomplish everything we want in this one march. The million man march, the million mom march, the million youth march, the Gatekeepers, civil rights protests, those organizations were all just simply hors d'oeuvres; we are the entree."

"And baby, believe it or not, we are going to provide food for every single person. Don't shake your heads. That's right, we're going to feed the masses. Just like the *Sermon on the Mount*! And they'll be feted by the world's top musical groups and speakers who have been clamoring for a spot on our board for months. Savannah, get a hold of Junior. Tell him he's going to be our musical director, and I need him to pull together all the musicians."

"Okay, Mr. Carpenter." Savannah quickly jotted down notes.

"And make sure he balances the more commercial music with some of that world music that Olisa is crazy about. You know, shit with that natural, traditional feel to it: Indian, Native American, Japanese, African, Irish, Mexican folk music. Just give me a mish-mosh of stuff. Tell him I trust him, he knows what to do!"

"Yes, sir."

"Logan, I need you to put together a camera crew. We're going to turn this into a documentary. You know, the making of, the Universal Healing Concert in the State Capitol. I'm sure we can get Nick Cavaliere to narrate."

"All right, I got it," Logan said, tugging on his goatee as he camped out in the corner of the room. "Anyone in particular?"

"Yeah, the best crew you can buy. This isn't a student film. We're talking about history. I want every scene to be pure gold. You got me?"

"Yes, sir."

"Spare no expense. We're going all out."

Mainly because what they were going to get back in return was a mere fraction of the output. My hands were clammy.

"Sir, I've got Junior on the phone," Savannah yelled. "He said he'll do it as long as he can debut the song he wrote for Olisa. He said it's a killer."

Jonathan laughed. "Tell Uncle Junior he can do whatever he wants. He's the musical director. He's got carte blanche on this one." He stomped around the room pumped up as if a caffeine-loaded dart had shot him. "Peter, as usual, you'll handle all the public relations arrangements and info.

"Aye, aye."

"Folks, this is going to be a monster! And we've got sixty days to pull it together."

"Sixty days! You're going to give us that much time? We'll be bored stiff! Peter added sarcastically, his head thunking down on the table.

"Peter, Peter, Peter… What are you worrying about? This is destiny we're talking about! You can't stand in fate's way. It's like turning on the faucet, let the water flow!"

"Unless the Department of Water turns it off first."

"Now I know I'm not hearing negatives out of you, Peter. You, more than anybody else here knows this was all built on a positive foundation.

"I know that, Jonathan, but how in the world are we going to pull this off in such a short period of time? Isn't the grand opening for the new corporate headquarters around the same time?"

"Yes, and according to my calculations, it's scheduled to open exactly one week after the concert. How do you like that for perfect timing?"

"Jon, that's impossible!"

"As my father always says, nothing is impossible, Peter!" Jonathan retorted. "This is it, man. We've got to dig deep now so we can all reach the Promised Land. Olisa will finally get everything she wants."

"Olisa?" I blurted out. I couldn't stop the sarcasm from tumbling out, even though the ice was starting to thaw between Jon and I.

"Yes, Olisa!" Jon refused to look my way, and it was probably good, because I knew we were headed toward another face off.

"The Universal Healing Concert is going to be the greatest statement on racial harmony and peace on this planet! It will be the penultimate event! No one has to feel alienated because of color or gender, and no one has to worry about obtaining tickets. They aren't going to be turned away at the door because they weren't celebrities or didn't dress right. Everyone who has a heart is invited to this extravaganza. Huh? C'mon, y'all, talk to me, what do you think?"

"What about security, man? It's going to be mad," Gumbo pointed out, folding his arms nervously as he leaned back in his seat.

"Don't worry about security, big fella. We've got the A Team in our corner on this one. Name your favorite: the FBI, Secret Service, CIA, Army. Doesn't really matter, they'll all be there. I've already talked to some of the big boys from Washington. It's going to run smoothly, you'll see. It's destiny, baby!"

A feeling of dread surged through me and my hands wouldn't stop shaking. Grace's eyes were languid. She was not one to unmask any family grievances in front of strangers. She would air her feelings privately with Jon. But she already knew it was a futile exercise.

"Jonathan, you may be right about all of this, and it may turn out to be one of the greatest marches in history, but it's also going to be one of the greatest migraines, too," Peter grumbled.

"Give me some love, brother! You know it's all going to work out fine." Jonathan laughed, clinching Peter in a playful bear hug. "All right, everybody. We've got very little time and a lot of work. Let's do this!"

CHAPTER 13

Both Grace and I were surprised that Olisa agreed to do a phone interview with Eva Sanchez shortly after her appearance at the Shrine Auditorium. Usually, she was too exhausted to want to do anything but rest, but I guessed it was one of her concessions to Jonathan, knowing it was only going to be temporary now. Still, I could tell it was a struggle for her to stay alert as Eva's voiced blasted from the speakerphone as we rode in the limousine back to her house in the Santa Monica Mountains.

"Olisa, thanks for granting me this interview. You must be exhausted."

"Yes, I am, but I'm also energized by all the love I received this evening."

"They do love you, Olisa, they really do!"

"And I love them. But as good as it feels, I don't want to be the only beneficiary. We've got to spread the love worldwide if we're going to heal a world."

"Well, you certainly gave it your best effort this evening, devoting a large portion to touching and hugging your fans."

"God's fans. Yes. I try and hug as many people as I can, even though I know my cousin, who's in charge of security, wants to hang me. It's just something I have to do." She sighed. "I really miss the days when I could just intermingle with people without being noticed."

Olisa, I can't imagine you ever not being noticed. You are such a striking woman."

"Thank you, Eva, but this is Venice Beach we're talking about. It's easy for me to get lost in the shuffle. There are plenty of distractions."

Eva laughed. "True. Well, the word is your hugs go a long way. I've interviewed people who swear that after hugging you, days later they find illnesses have disappeared from family members and friends they come into contact with."

"I don't know, I think people underestimate their innate ability to be healers. But thank you."

There was a pause on the line. "There are people who vehemently oppose everything you are doing. They accuse you of being blasphemous. They claim you ridicule biblical stories and say things that are inflammatory and anti-Christian. How do you respond to that?"

"I have never denounced anyone's religion. What I argue is that faith in God should not be measured by beliefs in Bible stories or by memorizing all the truths from any religion. I encourage people to explore the true nature of God and not allow themselves to be dependent on someone else's work. I'm not sure what else I can say."

"I think you've said a great deal. I would suspect there will always be those who disagree."

"Yes."

"On another note, I also understand that you are planning one last concert that will take you to the steps of the White House door."

"Yes."

"Why only one more?"

"Because there's too much attention on me and not enough on God."

"But can you really step out of the spotlight, Olisa?"

"I must. The message is getting lost in all the sensationalism. It's not about me. I'm just an instrument of the Creator."

"I understand, Olisa, and I truly hope you can, but you're beyond being a superstar. You're an icon. For example, tonight at the Shrine Auditorium there were thousands outside of the building, holding up traffic, waiting for the end of the show, and trying to sneak one peek at you. At least they were relatively peaceful except for a sketchy report that has yet to be substantiated about a minor skirmish that occurred. It's rumored there were blows exchanged between your security people and some hecklers."

"I don't know, this is the first time I've heard about it," Olisa replied, looking at me for confirmation.

I could only shrug my shoulders. I hadn't heard anything.

"Well, we only have a few seconds left… as always, Olisa, good luck. This is an incredible undertaking. People are already speculating that this will be one of the greatest events in the new millennium. Please keep us apprised of your progress."

"I will."

A frown creased Olisa's forehead when we arrived at her haven.

Little Oak greeted us at the door with a smile, but it quickly faded when she saw Olisa's face. "Everything all right?"

"Laura, has Alton gotten back yet?"

"Not yet. But he just called. Said he was on the way, but had to tie up some loose ends. Why? What's going on?"

"Uh, nothing… I guess I'm just being paranoid."

"Your paranoia is about as frivolous as dialing 911."

"No, no, really, I'm probably just tired. Everything is fine. I'll see him tomorrow."

"That's right," I agreed. "All things can wait until tomorrow, kid. Get some rest before I dip a pen into those ink bags growing under your eyes."

"Sure."

She gave me a kiss then retired to her room. However, the distress remained on her face. Whatever bothered her had something to do with this so-called minor skirmish. It was the first time I had heard about it too. Gumbo was surprised to find Laura, Grace, and me waiting for him when he pulled up. He said the much-ballyhooed skirmish was no big deal. Just a bunch of hecklers they tossed out. Nothing out of the ordinary.

Later that night I pretended to read, but nervously kept pulling back the curtains and staring out the window into the pitch-blackness of the mountains. Periodically, I'd see security wandering about like specters in the night. A couple of them nodded reassuringly to me that everything was fine. The anxiousness in my stomach told me different.

In those rare prescient moments, I truly appreciated the blessing and curse that haunted Olisa her entire life.

"You too, huh?"

"What do you mean, you too? Wilma asked haughtily.

"Well let's see," I said, examining the draft of the new menu. "The cover art with platters of food on clouds is a nice touch. Okay, let's see… 'Seafood Gumbo. You'll know you've made it to the Promised Land when you taste this aromatic combination of crab, shrimp, chicken, and sausage, accompanied by a bed of rice. Especially suggested for an entire party because there's enough here to feed the masses.'"

Wilma grinned sheepishly. "Okay, I…"

"Hold on, let me read this. 'Holy Fried Chicken! After you take a bite of this scrumptious treat, you'll be ready for your heavenly rest… and don't forget to order the Sweet Low, Sweet Chocolate Cake?' Should I stop here or do you want me to keep going?"

Wilma laughed. "Well, Joe, we did name this 'The Soul of Venice.' Don't you think it's about time it lives up to its name?"

"Hey, I'm down with that, but don't you think you're laying it on just a little thick?"

"Not at all. They'll love it. They already think the foods been blessed. Just the other day this woman, must have just come from a holiness service, jumped up during the Sunday brunch and started dancing all over the restaurant."

"No she didn't."

"Yes she did, honey. That church lady started doing a big butt dance just like this."

Wilma snatched off her apron and started waving it in the air. She mimicked the woman, dancing throughout the office, bumping the files, cabinets, chairs, and desk with her butt while screaming out, "Hallelujahs and praise the Holy Ghosts." The look on her face had me falling out laughing. Before long, we were leaning on each other, tears streaming down our faces, and on the ground in hysterics.

One of the bus boys burst into the office, seemingly worried. Five other workers stuck their heads in the door, also concerned.

"What's all the noise! Is everything all right! Oh…" he said when he saw us sitting on the floor, still giddy with laughter and holding our sides.

"Everything is okay, Geraldo. Wilma just told me a funny story."

"Oh, you must have told 'El Jefe' about that lady!"

"You got it, Geraldo."

"Yeah, she was so funny. Some of our customers checked to see if they ordered the same thing."

That got us to giggling again. Geraldo, too.

"Okay, have fun," he said with a wave as he shut the door.

"Thanks for checking, Geraldo," Wilma yelled.

After he closed the door, I heard him laughing with some of the other workers.

After a momentary rest, I could finally talk again. "So you're going to add to this fervor?" I asked, holding my jaw, which ached from laughing.

"Damn right. See, you been away too long. That's the only thing that can be added. Not enough room to add any more people. And I've got a list of executives ready to play *Let's Make A Deal* with you. All you've got to do is say yes, and you'll have a string of restaurants world-wide. You think I'm kidding."

"No I don't." I rubbed the bridge of my nose. "Wilma, there was a time I'd have been all over news like that. Now…"

"You don't even have to go there," she said sympathetically.

Just then, the office door flew open with such velocity that Wilma and I jumped like the Holy Ghost had entered the room.

"Alton!"

"Hey, y'all. Sorry, I didn't mean to scare you. It's just that… Unc., we got to go!"

He was breathing hard and the look on his face made my stomach drop.

"Gumbo, what's wrong? Where's Olisa?"

"She's fine, Uncle Joe. It's Ernesto. They got him."

"They've got him? Who's got him?"

Alton knew he was talking too fast. He took a deep breath. "The police. They arrested him."

"What?!"

"Yeah. They picked him up at the Century City office. There were blacks-and-whites all over the place. They had so many guns drawn, I thought I was at the Alamo."

"What did they arrest him for?"

"Murder. Said he killed two people."

"Lord have mercy," Wilma cried.

"Gumbo, was Olisa there?" My voice dropped.

"Yep. They paraded him past her in handcuffs. Jonathan and Logan tried their best to talk her out of going down to the county jail, but…"

"Shit! Okay, I'm ready."

"Good, we can leave in my car."

"I really didn't think it was any big deal, Unc. I mean, yeah, I was kinda pissed off at Ernesto for losing his cool at that time, but I thought he had calmed down. I just can't believe it," Gumbo kept repeating as he drove the Ford Explorer down Olympic Blvd., past Century City. Fortunately, the traffic was pretty light even though it was four in the afternoon. Thus far, we were making all the lights.

"Gumbo, what happened?"

"During the show, two *ese's* started heckling Ernesto for no reason. Calling him every name in the book, in Spanish and English. I mean they wouldn't let up. It's not like we hadn't encountered hecklers before; except these dudes had it in for Ernesto. I thought they were from some rival gang he fought within his past, but Ernesto said he had never seen these cats before."

"How did Ernesto handle it, did he go off on them or what?"

"It wasn't like that Uncle Joe. Ernesto just laughed at them and tried to ignore it. I'm not even sure I could have been as cool as he was with the kind of stuff they were dishing out, challenging his manhood and all that. We even sent Ernesto to another section, but those chumps followed, still bagging on him. Finally, we threw their butts out of the auditorium."

Gumbo suddenly screeched to a halt at the light.

"Slow down, you trying to give me a heart attack? You almost ran that light."

"I'm sorry, Unc. I'm just hyped."

"I understand. We all are. But you don't need to get a ticket or get arrested."

"Okay, I'm cool." He wiped his sweaty forehead.

"Were these cats drunk or high?"

"I don't think so, my guys told me they didn't smell any alcohol on them, and they didn't really look high either."

"So then what?"

"Ernesto was posted alone at one of the exits when the concert was over and one of the guys walked over and bitch slapped him."

"So that's what started it."

"Yes and no. Ernesto still didn't throw down on him; at least that's what one of the witnesses told me. It wasn't until dude threatened to do the same thing to Olisa that he finally lost it. Before we could get to him, he stole on one of them and dropped him on his ass. To be honest, at the time, I was kind of happy he did, because you should have heard the kind of shit those punks were laying down. Anyway, the worst part is, when Ernesto knocked dude down he threatened to kill him if he came anywhere near Olisa. And he said this in front of a whole lot of people."

"Great…"

"C'mon, old man! Don't you know how to make a right turn?" Gumbo barked at the car poking along ahead of him. "But you know what was weird? Those punks backed away looking all happy, like they had knocked him on *his* ass. I didn't see 'em again after that."

"Did Ernesto try to follow them?"

"Not with us holding him. It didn't take much restraint. He felt horrible afterwards for losing his cool. I mean, I really didn't have to get on him. He beat himself up more than I ever could."

I stared out the window. Damn. I was afraid of that. The traffic was starting to build up. "You hear anything about a police report?"

"Yo, I got one of my buddies in the department to check it out for me. Here's the odd part. The police report says, they found Gary Mejia and Richard Alvarez around 5:00 A.M., dead, face down in a Culver City alley. Somebody shot them execution style in the back of the head. The police found the gun with Ernesto's fingerprints all over it a few blocks away in a trash bin."

"That doesn't sound right to me."

"Sounds like a bullshit setup to me, Uncle Joe. I mean, Ernesto and I have gotten kinda tight after all this. I've learned he's a pretty smart dude. If he was going to do something like that, I can't see him being that stupid about it."

"Gumbo, anyone can be stupid when they are in a rage."

"Yeah, but in my heart, I just don't believe it, Uncle Joe."

"Me neither, man, of course, at first, I didn't believe O.J. did it either." I let out a big sigh. "Were you guys with Ernesto all night?"

Gumbo swallowed hard. "No. After things calmed down, Ernesto told me he needed to chill… said he wanted to go take a walk on the beach. I told him it was fine with me. It was stupid. I should have gone with him."

"It's not your fault, Gumbo. You made the right decision."

Gumbo's lip stopped trembling as he gripped the steering wheel harder.

"Did he get a chance to say anything to you before he got arrested?"

He tilted his head from side to side as his neck cracked loudly. "Not really… except when they were carting him away. He kinda laughed and said, 'At least I know now what happened to my automatic. I thought my grandmother found it and tossed it away with all the others. Trip, huh, *Vato*?' I didn't know what to say as they shoved him into the police car."

It was bumper-to-bumper traffic as we approached the county jail. News helicopters buzzed like gigantic mutant wasps in the sky. We were just a few blocks away and reporters and camera operators were leaping out of their vehicles and racing down the streets past the stalled cars toward the jail.

"Guess Olisa must already be here," I muttered as I motioned Gumbo to pull into one of the parking lots.

We never got inside the jail, even though we tried every gimmick we could think of. Too much of a madhouse. The police wouldn't let anyone outside the department inside. We finally reached Jonathan on his cell phone and learned that he had hired an attorney, gotten in and out safely, and they were already headed back by helicopter to the Santa Monica Mountains. We climbed back into Gumbo's van, relieved that the way out of downtown Los Angeles was much easier than on the way in.

I was relieved that we didn't have any road rage incidents as I watched two men jump out of their cars and square off after a collision that occurred when they tried to do a Lewis and Clark and find exits out of the traffic that didn't exist. I made Gumbo go over the story again as we drove up Sunset Boulevard on our way to the Santa Monica Mountains.

At the house, we found a very sullen Olisa sitting on a chair in the living room. She was deep inside her head and not speaking to anyone. We walked around her, discussing the problem among ourselves like she was a statue.

"How ignorant can you be?" Jonathan barked as he stomped around the living room wringing his hands. "Nobody needs this shit right now. I knew we shouldn't have let Ernesto join us. You can take the gang banger out of the city, but you can't take the city out of the gang banger. That's just the way it is…"

"Ernesto didn't do it," Olisa interrupted, her voice somber.

"Then who did, Olisa?" Jon asked. "I don't mean to sound like a cop, but who else has the motivation?"

"I don't know."

"Look, Sis. I know you love Ernesto. Maybe at another time he could have changed. But there's too much pressure here. Chato got smacked and he lost it. You don't do that to a dude with his history… the old ways kicked in. He couldn't help himself, you know?"

Olisa just stared at the floor, her hands clasped to her head.

"You can't be with him every minute, honey. He's a young kid. It's tough. I mean. Look, it was *his* gun."

"That doesn't mean he pulled the trigger, Jon." She embedded her fingers in her thick hair.

"Okay, but even if someone else did it, or even one of his homies as a vendetta, why are only his fingerprints on the gun?"

"I don't know. I just know he's innocent."

"How Olisa? How do you know that?"

"Because he told me he is!" She repeatedly ran her fingers through her hair.

"All right. All right." This time Jon measured his words more carefully. He plopped down on the couch. "It's going to work itself out. Hey, innocent till proven guilty, right? I'll take care of everything. I'll have Sheldon Silver, the 'old gray wolf' on this. He's one of the best lawyers in the city. If anybody can get this kid off, Shel can."

Olisa made no comment as she got up and walked away. Grace immediately followed behind her into her bedroom and held the door open while I walked in. She then closed it.

"Mom, I couldn't even touch him," Olisa said as she sat on the bed and unconsciously stroked her cheekbone with her fingers. I stood by the door. Grace sat down on the bed with Olisa. "All I could do is stare through the glass partition while we talked on the phone. Yeah, he walked out there at first, all macho, the violent gang banger back in his body. But I understand. He was in jail; he had to be Chato again. Until he saw me. Then he dropped his head, barely talked. It was awkward, but I had to ask, 'Ernesto, did you kill them?'"

Grace reached out and held Olisa's hand. I don't know what else to say, except that when they locked eyes, it was a mother-daughter type of understanding.

"All it took was the gaze from those brown orphan eyes, and I had my answer. There was no way he could have done it. He mentioned being at the beach, smoking a joint, and falling asleep in the sand. The next thing he knew, the sun woke him up."

Grace nodded her head in support.

"I immediately assured him that we would find a way to get him out. But he didn't seem to care. He said the only thing that mattered to him was that I believed him." Olisa stopped talking while she reflected on her conversation with Ernesto. I felt like I should say something, but I really couldn't think of anything to say. I would be just talking to fill the void. So the room remained silent until Olisa spoke again.

"Just before his time was up he said to me, 'Olisa, this may not be so bad, you know? I've done some really stupid things in my life. I've hurt people, Olisa, really bad. I don't know if I ever killed anyone, but whatever I did, I did to prove I was the man. You know? And all that stuff was like ignorant, man, you know? Then you came and changed my life, and now I don't think that way no more. But I never paid for my past crimes, either. Maybe this is payback time. Maybe I deserve to be in here, you know what I'm sayin'? How do you say it? It's all come back full circle? So you know, don't worry. It's all good. They was gonna catch up with me sooner or later, yeah?'"

"But you have changed, Ernesto, I told him. In the process, you've changed many lives in so many good ways with the drive-by blessings and initiating the truce between the gangs. I love you Ernesto, and I love what you've become. Ernesto is the one who's living, Chato died a long time ago."

"Yes, he did," Grace echoed, still supportively holding Olisa's hand.

"Right about then the guards came to lead him away. I thought he might freak, but all he did was smile. He seemed at peace with himself. I was the one who couldn't stop crying."

I must have been feeling sadomasochistic because once again, I decided to listen to one of the Reverend Popcock's weekly radio broadcast while I drove to the restaurant.

"How about it? You believe me now?" Popcock implored from the speaker. "Are you starting to see what I've been talking about? Uh-huh. All may not be what we perceive it to be. They say this gal can do miracles. Is that really the case? Or are we all victims of mass suggestion? Has peer pressure convinced us that we have seen a miracle when one may not have really existed? Talk to me people!"

"Okay, kiss my ass!" I barked at the radio.

"Don't we just love it when a magician, or master illusionist they call 'em nowadays, works their magic on us with a sleight of hand? We love to be fooled. We love to pretend it's all magic. Yet, we know for a fact that if we're allowed to go backstage, we might find out how they do it. Doesn't that mean it wasn't truly magic, but a well-crafted trick?"

This man is unbelievable! I thought as I rolled over a curb to make a right turn. Thank goodness no one was standing there.

"Well get hard-core and ask yourself, friends—have I been duped by an elaborate hoax? Nick Cavaliere is one of the finest actors of our generation. When he stood up from that wheelchair everyone yelled, it's a miracle! But did we ever wonder if this man just pulled off his greatest acting job? Maybe he was cured months ago. Now I'm not saying that's the way it was folks, but you've got to ask tougher questions. You can't just accept things at face value.

"What we 'do' know is that this character, Chato, was arrested for a brutal double murder. That's what we know. And maybe we need to find a way to get backstage at Olisa's camp and find out what other magic tricks they've got in their little back pockets."

I decided to cancel my doctor's appointment later that afternoon. After listening to Popcock, I was sure my blood pressure had soared sky high. I didn't want my doctor to see it, so I rescheduled for the following week.

Although Popcock's voice will always be the one rattling my eardrums, he was only the catalyst. The media also became a partner in what I called the "Crucifixion Plot." Ever since Ernesto was arrested, the news hounds no longer hesitated to probe into our lives with a vengeance. The arrest made it safe to go after Olisa, who up to this point was inviolable. The gates were open for anything scandalous. They were all competing to outdo the other. I couldn't really blame them. It wasn't exactly like we had discouraged the publicity.

I guess that's the price you pay for getting too big. It was time to put Olisa in her place. Some relished it, mainly because she never followed media protocol. Of course, the tabloids didn't care, they made up their own headlines. One linked her with a recent mass cult-suicide of 200 people who believed that an alien vessel would restore them to life and they would all become Gods in the afterlife. The connection to Olisa? One corpse was found clutching a magazine to her breast with Olisa's face on the cover.

Nevertheless, Olisa met with whomever she wanted and for however long she wanted regardless of their status in the hierarchy. It used to frustrate the hell out of Jonathan because he was aware of how vicious the press could be if they felt they were being snubbed.

For example, Theo Balanis, one of the most respected investigative reporters in the nation, got only a thirty-minute interview with Olisa. He was constantly peeved whenever he saw local street reporter turned celebrity anchor, Eva Sanchez, flashing that "stay bright" smile in her interviews with Olisa. He had been looking for an opportunity to skewer Olisa ever since, but knew that she was virtually an untouchable in many people's eyes. When things started unraveling around her inner circle, he couldn't believe his luck, particularly after receiving an anonymous phone tip while researching information for a feature article on corruption in the record business.

When I returned from the men's room, Jonathan was pacing back and forth in his humongous office. I thought he was talking to himself until I realized he was wearing a headset.

"La Tisha, why do I feel like I'm having such a hard time communicating? English is your native tongue, right? Yeah, I'm being a smart-ass, because I'm busy. Something unexpected came up, and I need to take care of it, okay? No. You fucking calm down. I know we've been planning this for weeks, but it's not happening tonight. Look, I'll have Savannah messenger the tickets, take one of your girlfriends, find a boyfriend, I don't give a shit. Later!"

He ripped off the headset and flipped it across the room. He still clutched the papers stiffly in his other hand as if he had rigor mortis.

He stared at the fireplace in his office as if he wanted to toss the papers in it. But first he'd have to light it. I don't think he wanted to bother with it. His face was so pale his skin looked discolored.

He shook the papers at me. "Dad, can you believe how these assholes are trying to fuck me after all I've done for them? What bullshit!"

"That's why I rushed over here. I noticed you made the newspapers today for all the wrong reasons." He motioned for me to sit down. His leather couch was so plush, it hugged me gratefully when I sat down. It was going to be difficult getting back up.

"I'm the only representative for RPM who made the papers, and I don't even work there anymore!" he yelled at the ceiling. He threw the papers down on a mahogany desk that was about as wide as a landing strip. He sat down behind it and eased back into his black leather recliner, laying his feet on the ottoman. He rested his hands behind his head as he stared at the ceiling. There was a dour expression on his face.

"Yeah, I noticed. I'm reading the *Los Angeles Times* this morning and I come across this five-page article by our friend, Theo Balanis, that's the first of a three part series about corruption in the record business. And your picture is prominently displayed as one of the key suspects who have been offering kickbacks to programmers to add songs to the radio play lists."

"Dad, tell me something I don't know." The way he looked at me, you would have thought I wrote it.

"Jon, I'm just worried. They're saying RPM and other record companies pay independent consultants like yourself millions of dollars to dangle money, audio equipment, prostitutes, luxury cars, exotic vacations, and leased houses to station personnel."

"Pops, the deal is that RPM records confessed to the existence of kickbacks in the company when they realized that the criminal investigation was headed for their doorstep," he said averting my gaze.

"So you already knew about this."

"Oh yeah. Everyone associated with the industry knew about it. The investigation about payola scandals has been going on for over a year. There will probably be a subpoena at my door any day now." He stood up again with his back to me. He distractedly traced his fingers along an elaborate wooden frame that housed a magnificent painting of Paul Robeson presiding on the wall.

"Jon, why didn't you say anything?" He seemed irritated that I broke his concentration. For a second, it looked like he wanted to smash his fist through the painting. "Like what? RPM didn't sweat it because they seemed to be focused on the big guys, not the little folks. That is, until a tip was made to both the fraud section of the Justice Department and the criminal investigation unit of the Internal Revenue Service to expand the probe to independents like RPM Records. A partner of mine over there, Luther Simon, told me they fully cooperated with the government investigation to avoid being hit with a payola offense. That way, they could receive a more lenient sentence."

"This is unbelievable."

"Tell me about it. I'm sure you read that promotion chief, Jalisa Miller, paid a $100, 000 fine and received two years on probation. Her brother, Patrick Miller was fined $250, 000 and received a two year probation for some kind of tax violation related to bribery."

The whole thing confounded me. All I could do was shake my head. Jonathan's hands quivered as he lit up a cigar and eased back in his chair.

"Luther says everyone in the Urban Music division is shittin' because they know executives are being convicted left and right and all they have to do is follow the trail of the money to the program directors for each station. And that shouldn't be too difficult, considering Miller and Miller rolled over on everybody to protect themselves. Moreover, there's a lot of talk that it would never have happened if I hadn't been such high profile because of my sister."

"So they're pissed off at you."

"Yeah, me, the one they begged to stay on as a consultant. You know how it is. Someone's got to be the scapegoat, so they rolled over on me. Figured I can afford it." He plopped back down again in his chair, hands once again behind his head.

I hated to ask. "So what are you going to do?"

"My attorney, Sheldon, told me to blow it off and concentrate on the march. He said it's going to take a long time before they actually get to me, if they ever do. He suspects that the worse that will happen to me is I'll have to pay a fine and/or get a couple of years probation."

"That's not bad."

"What? I did what they paid me to do. I can cause a little grief to some of the folks there if I talk, too. But hopefully, we won't have to go there." After he said that, there was a half smile on his face that seemed to buttress his emotions.

"But, forget all that… You know what's really a pisser? Knowing that Popcock's ass is behind this in some way."

"No doubt."

"That son-of-a-bitch will do anything within his power to stop us from going to Washington. But I've got something for his hypocritical ass." He literally cackled at the thought of it.

"Just think. All eyes will be on Olisa. Our girl will be a goddess for modern times. And we can be proud because we helped to put her there."

I wanted to comment, but my insides were too queasy. Jonathan slapped his hands on the desktop with finality, and with a determined look, pushed himself up from his leather chair. His smile was a little strained. "You want to get some breakfast, Pop?" Without waiting for an answer, he nonchalantly grabbed his car keys and extended a hand to me. I was kind of glad he did that, because his couch didn't want to let me go.

And that was it. He was fine.

I did agree with Jonathan on one issue. Popcock was behind this. I was especially convinced after seeing his Grandpa Walton act on the *Larry King Show*. He, of course, was horrified by the disturbing reports about fraudulence, bribery, prostitution, and other evils invading the Olisa Carpenter camp.

But I had gotten used to Popcock. He didn't bother me anymore. Like someone wearing a KKK hood, I knew where he stood. What was more worrisome to me was that my son never refuted the reports leveled at him about his scandalous activities at RPM records. A day later, he appeared almost apathetic to it; justifying it in conversation with, "Hey, I'm a promoter and I sell records. The public buys what they like, if they hear it. If you've got to wax a few palms to get folks to play it, I don't understand what the big deal is."

"Because it's against the law, Jon! You told me yourself, it's only legal if you disclose the amount you paid to listeners."

"Yeah, but that's bull, Pops! The listeners could care less about all that. Our society's foundation is based on capitalism. Whoever has the most dollars wins. If I pay you more than someone else to get you to play my song, hey, get over it! That's what capitalism is all about in this land of free enterprise."

"It's against the law, Jon."

"So was Prohibition. But hey, why are we even debating this? Thank God I've got more than enough money to fight this. Let's not worry about it. This ain't nothing. Besides, they may be paying *me* to drop the whole thing before it's over." This statement tickled him.

Power does corrupt. It may be an old cliché but for me it was fact. It caused me many sleepless nights, and many door-slamming arguments. Mainly because I dared to question who I should really be afraid of.

I was half-asleep when Beverly Fairchild, former model turned activist, appeared as a talking head on the screen. I used the sofa arms to pull myself up from my slouched position as I glanced at my watch. It was two-thirty in the morning.

"If she were a man, would you have been as quick to judge her, Mr. Sorenson?" she asked with a perky flip of the hair.

I pressed the info on the remote control. It was the *Chase Sorenson Show.* I had never watched his half-hour program before, but I knew about his politics. He was cloned from the same factory that produced the Biscuit-Heads and Walter Popcocks of the world. And speaking of factories, the small studio audience that attended his show, no matter what the age, looked like they had all been manufactured at "Wonder Bread."

"I don't think that would have anything to do with it," said another talking head, a jowly man who spoke as if he had a grapefruit stuck in his throat. He sat behind his talk show desk and tugged on his bowtie.

"Sure it does," Beverly fired back from her chair to the side of his desk. "All of this has been blown out of proportion. Why should Olisa's character be tainted because some of the people around her have gotten into trouble? Ernesto Padilla has yet to go to court, and likewise, her brother is being investigated and nothing has been proven yet."

A sprinkling of boos and catcalls from the audience could be heard.

Sorenson sneered. "You forgot to mention the uncle who has been in rehab several times, or her best friend who had her own battles with alcohol."

"You mean the one who was physically and sexually abused as a child?"

Sorenson's only response was to roll his eyes.

"The same one who has devoted much of her life to helping young women find a purpose in their life? Or the uncle who has performed free concerts to assist the homeless? That one? If you're going to tell a story, Mr. Sorenson, try telling it in its entirety."

"Hmmph… Whatever… But come on now, Ms. Fairchild. Surely, you're not so naive as to believe that she's not responsible in some way for their actions. After all, they do work for her."

"Yeah!" Someone shouted, as the audience cheered.

Fairchild was oblivious to the hostile crowd. She knew what she was up against, and she was ready to do battle as she locked eyes with Sorenson. "Oh, so in other words, if a disgruntled employee marches through the office shooting half a dozen employees, this is the supervisor's responsibility? Do you know how ridiculous that sounds?!"

"But how can you ignore the fact that there's a criminal element around her?" Sorenson jiggled his newspaper at her.

"Conservative talk show hosts like yourself, along with your crony the Reverend Popcock, have been trying to tear her down since her rise to national prominence. You can't handle the idea that a beautiful and powerful African-American woman has made such an impact on the world. You can't control her, and it drives you crazy! The only way you can empower yourself is to discredit her and nail her to the cross."

She was met with a loud barrage of boos. Sorenson milked it with a dramatic pause before rising to his feet with righteous indignation.

"That is utterly reprehensible, Ms. Fairchild! I'm appalled that you'd stoop so low as to squeeze the race and gender card into this discussion. Why don't you top it off by addressing your lady goddess as Jesus Christ while you're at it?"

The boo birds rose to their feet, too, screaming and yelling at Fairchild. Beverly was cool, though. She folded her hands with a grin and waited for Sorenson and the audience to take a seat before she calmly asked, "Are you absolutely sure she's not, Mr. Sorenson? You can sneer as much as you want, but maybe God came back as a black woman so he could challenge people to look beyond gender and ethnicity. If it were true, would you still accept Jesus as your savior?"

"I would if there was a kernel of truth to it. But, Beverly, who is being ridiculous now?"

"Yeah! Come on! Get real!"

"All those people who continue to ban women from assuming an active role in church leadership, like the group you're affiliated with, Mr. Sorenson," Beverly replied facetiously.

"Incredible, just incredible," Sorenson grumbled, shaking his head and looking bemusedly at his devotees. Everyone around this woman is being investigated for something, and yet people persist in following her."

Boos and hisses filtered the air again.

"I read a poll about a year ago that said 80% of Americans believe in miracles. In Olisa, people have found a breath of fresh air and a sense of hope. They are not going to give up on her that easy. We don't need more corrupt politicians, police officers, sport figures, or supposed men of God who fall down on their knees, braying tears for their sins. We need more Olisa Carpenters. To me, Olisa is the balm for healing a cynical society that has somehow lost its innocence."

"She's not Jesus Christ!" someone yelled. I turned off the tube. I didn't need to hear the response.

The night air was chilly and breezy, but it felt good to me as I wrapped my jacket tighter, sat, and admired the full moon. It lit the patio up like a night sun. That's when I saw a shadow leaning against the wall in the corner, studying the luminescent orb just as intently. He noticed me about the same time and walked lightly toward me. When the moonlight unveiled his presence, I was relieved to see Logan's handsome face. While I bunched my jacket to stay warm, he wore only a T-shirt. I felt old.

"Mr. Carpenter, I didn't know you were out here. I was getting ready to go home until I saw this moon. It's beautiful isn't it?"

"Yes it is. I was going to write a little in my diary, but I got hypnotized."

"That's pretty cool that you keep a diary. I do, too. It used to come in pretty handy during my travels."

"I bet."

"Yeah, I can remember camping out in the African veldt listening to the earthshaking roar of the lions contrasting with the silence of the moon. There was a natural symmetry to it all that was just awesome, man… talk about a moon. You ever been to Africa?"

"No, never have. But I'd sure like to go one day."

"You'd love it. The night sky can be spectacular. Africa is imbued with this fascinating and ancient aura that encapsulates the entire continent. Yet, there is a dangerous edge that tops it all off. You've got to do it."

"I will, although I think I can live without the 'dangerous edge' part. I've got enough of that now."

"Yeah, I hear you." He chuckled.

We both gazed at the moon a little longer.

"The way you're grunting, you've either got a sore throat or something to say."

"Um, yeah I do, Mr. Carpenter. You got a minute? I don't want to intrude."

"Pull up a chair, man. I'll give you all the time you want if you stop calling me Mr. Carpenter. I remember when you and I were Joseph and Logan."

"I'm just a little nervous," he said, clearing his throat again and pulling a lawn chair toward him.

"Been there. Just tell me what's going on and we'll wing it."

"Okay… Cool." he hesitantly sat down. "Joseph, you probably know how I feel about Olisa."

"I've got an idea."

"I love her. I really do."

"Judging by the way you look at each other, I'm not surprised. But, why does it seem like you are?"

He thought about it for a second. "I'm sure Jon has already told you a little bit about my background. My history with women…"

"I'd say he's broadcast it a couple of times."

"I'm sure. I can't say I've been real successful at maintaining lasting relationships. The love of my life has always been a camera. The women in my life have been more like mistresses then girlfriends. And I never ever thought that would change, until I met your daughter."

I remained as motionless as the moon.

"The first time I saw Olisa at my show, it was all over. I fell so hard I'm still bouncing off the mat. I've shot thousands of images in my life, but none more beautiful than her. I mean, I feel kind of weird telling you, her father, all this stuff, but I wanted you to know."

"I always like hearing good things about my daughter."

"Mr. Carp… I mean, Joseph. I feel like Olisa's my soulmate. Does that sound corny? I didn't know love could do that to you."

"Remind me to tell you about me and Grace one day." I laughed.

"Good, I'd love to hear about it. Your family is great. I envy the bond you guys have for each other."

"Thank you, but like any couple we have our arguments."

"Yeah, but it looks like you manage to work them out."

"We try."

"That's something you can't take for granted. I never had that. My family is originally from Jamaica. My father was a hustler and a prime time womanizer. They came to New York the year I was born. He disappeared when I was around three years old, and we didn't see him again for about a year. Said he had been looking for work, though we never saw a dime."

He let out a chuckle, even thought his face was impassive.

"Those early years, I remember us spending most of our lives like the fugitive, man, moving from city to city. My mother claimed she was trying to find better jobs. The reality was, she was running away from him. He should have found work as a private investigator, because he always seemed to find us. I was twelve years old when he was fatally shot by the police in an attempted armed robbery at a liquor store."

"I'm sorry to hear that."

"I wasn't," he said quickly, practically stepping on my words. "I was scared to death of him. If the cops hadn't killed him, I would have." He drew in a deep breath. "He used to beat the hell out of my mother, and I've wrestled with that guilt ever since." He scratched behind his ear as his mouth twisted into a wry grin. He suddenly rubbed his lips with his fingers and the smile disappeared like it had been Etch-A-Sketched. "My mother raised me in the best way she could, man, but it wasn't easy. Eventually, she settled down and got married to a good man, but me, I couldn't stop running. I was always daydreaming in school. Wishing I could escape to all these exotic places I saw in the pages of encyclopedias. Man, I spent so much time in detention in high school that they should have made a nameplate for me."

He chuckled again, but this time I joined him, and a real smile evolved from his lips. "So after all that, how the hell did you end up in photography?" I asked.

"Luckily, this one art teacher saw something in me that no one else did. She became like a mentor to me. She recognized how much I loved pictures and turned me on to photography. Man, that did it for me. It opened up a whole new world. I was so into it I even finished high school. Photography helped me to make sense of the world. I guess that's why I have this thing about people being abused in my work. Plus, it took me to all those places I had once only dreamed about. Photography was the only thing I felt I had a grip on, and the only thing I could trust to never fail me. I loved women, but I couldn't even spell commitment, let alone act upon it. There was too much world to see out there. Then I met Olisa, and all I wanted to do was share her world."

"Logan, that's great, but shouldn't you be discussing this with Olisa?"

"I have. But she insisted that I talk to you about something that's come up."

"What?"

He got quiet again.

I waited.

He rubbed his hands together and gazed at the moon as if he were waiting for a cue card to come to his rescue. He sighed, then his gaze shifted to me.

"There's this woman who had been kind of showing up lately wherever I've been shooting. I'd see her at the concerts and sometimes in Century City in the mall area. I couldn't help but notice her because she's real attractive and always smiling," he said it like it was painful.

"… And always alone. One day she finally approached me and struck up a conversation. Said her name was Barbara Redding and that she was an aspiring photographer. She mentioned she knew all about my work and had attended all my shows. I never recalled seeing her at any of them. But she was familiar with my work. She could rattle off all the pieces I did, plus titles. I'm ashamed to say I was impressed and flattered. I guess I needed the attention."

"We all do. But it sounds more like she was hittin' on you."

"Yeah, I guess so."

"And what about you?"

"No, but it was a hell of a test. I did talk to her, but it was just shop. I swear, nothing happened, sir. I mean, it's been difficult sometimes. I get lonely knowing I have to share Olisa with the world… but I'm okay with that. I love her, you know?"

"Yeah, I know… And?"

He rubbed his hands on his knees and took a deep breath. "Well, I did something stupid. I agreed to go to a bar with her and have a drink. I know you're looking at me funny but that's all it was going to be. She knew where I stood with Olisa. You know Olisa means the world to me?"

"Yeah, you told me. You love her." I gave him a look that said, "Whatever you say next will determine the state of our relationship."

"Okay, I know it doesn't sound right, but I'm not lying to you. We were just going to talk film. I missed that. It's something I used to do all the time with my friends, male and female. I needed to find out what was happening in the world. Hang out a little, you know? I've been feeling real claustrophobic lately. I figured no one really knows who I am so I could probably get away with it, you know?"

"Yeah, I know." My eyes were still glued to his.

"I know you know… well, we were just talking, and then before I could react, she flung her arms around me and started kissing me. I damn near fell off barstool. When I pushed her away, she gave me a hard slap in the face and stormed away, yelling loud enough for anyone to hear that, 'I'm tired of being treated like your personal whore.'"

I closed my eyes.

"That's when I saw the guy concealing his camera follow behind her out the door. I thought I was going to die. I charged after them, but by the time I reached the streets, their sports car screeched around the corner."

"They got you."

"Got me good."

"So what you're really telling me is, we can look forward to seeing you on someone's front pages."

"Guaranteed. I just don't know whose."

"Uh-huh."

"I'm sorry for causing you more grief. I didn't expect everything to get this convoluted."

I rested a hand on his shoulder. "Welcome to my world, Lo. Olisa knows?"

"Oh yeah, I told her right away."

"She believe you?"

"Yes."

"Then so do I."

He heaved a sigh of relief. "She said I should just go and talk to you and you'd understand."

"I do, although I expect you'll make better decisions in the future."

He hung his head. "Definitely."

"By the way, was Olisa okay with it all?"

"Yeah... a little too okay. I mean she could have shown at least a hint of jealousy..."

I laughed. "I imagine Olisa doesn't do jealousy well. Too forgiving."

"Yeah, no kidding." He grinned. "Joseph, I know I shouldn't ask, but would you mind talking to everyone else about this? I'm..."

"I understand. No problem. I'll let them all know what's going on."

"Thanks... And Jonathan, too? You know him and me."

"Yep. Don't worry about it. I'll take care of it."

He looked like he still wanted to crawl inside a hole.

"It was so stupid. I really do love Olisa. You believe me don't you?"

"Son, you wouldn't have gotten past 'the woman was really attractive' if I didn't believe you. Now, tell me some more about those gorgeous African skies."

Damn, those tabloid magazines don't waste time! Within a couple of days, *Idol Gossip* magazine featured Logan's picture on its front cover and was available in every newsstand and grocery store throughout the country. They set him up like a tea party. The headline read, "PSYCHIC HOLY WOMAN, OLISA CARPENTER, SHOULD HAVE

SEEN IT COMING!" In the foreground, the picture portrays a distraught woman whose face is partially buried in her hands rushing out the building. In the background, a stunned Logan holds the side of his face. Under the photograph is the caption: "Lover's Quarrel—Mystery girl-on-the-side of celebrated photographer, Logan Matthew, has breakdown crying out—I'm so sick of this! I'm tired of his lies! I'm tired of being used! I'm no longer going to play his whore!"

In all of the compromising photos strewn throughout the magazine, remarkably, her face is never clearly shown. I speculated she was a call girl who got paid very well to do her high performance job on Logan. And the stories accompanying each picture read like trashy romance novels. They made up stories wherever they deemed necessary. In order to be in all the places they claim he was rendezvousing with her, he had to be able to split in two like an amoebae. It was evident to me that many of the shots were gleaned from some of Olisa's concerts and then graphically treated through the computer to look like he was somewhere else. By always standing close to him, she made it easy for a photographer lying in wait to snipe shots of them talking. They were then scanned into the computer to produce "graphic whoopee."

Surprisingly, Jonathan handled it better than I would have suspected. Naturally, his first response was the requisite "I'm going to beat his ass down," but after cooling off, he pretty much agreed with the rest of us that it smelled like a setup. I think he was more disgruntled that Logan didn't recognize that everyone closely associated with Olisa was a target and a potential weapon to be utilized by her adversaries to discredit the movement. Still, he was happy to drop the issue. He was much too preoccupied with promoting the Universal Healing Concert and March in Washington to waste the energy on another scandal, particularly after dealing with one of his own.

CHAPTER 14

With less than two weeks remaining before the big event, Grace and I planned to stay one more night at Olisa's before returning home to Venice. As the march neared, we consciously spent more family time with Olisa. She needed us, and we needed to be near her. It had been almost a month since we had been home. There were security people posted at the house and around the walk street, but Grace was still anxious to get back and check everything out.

That evening, Grace went into Olisa's bedroom to see how she was feeling. She had complained earlier about headaches. About a second later, Grace screamed out my name and I sped into the room. Olisa was violently thrashing in the bed, still asleep, but eyes wide open, stricken with terror.

"Joseph, help me!" Grace cried out as she struggled to hold her, but it was futile. Olisa's arms flailed about like a broken helicopter blade. Finally, we subdued her but her head continued to swing from side to side. Suddenly, her body went still. She was awake, but her eyes darted around wildly, looking disoriented.

"Honey, are you all right?" Grace brushed her hair back and wiped her wet forehead. "My God, you are burning up! Joseph, feel how hot she is... hurry, dampen one of the wash towels and give it to me! She feels like she's got a fever."

When I returned with a cold washcloth, Olisa's eyes were more lucid.

"How's my girl? I thought you were trying out for a martial arts movie."

"Daddy..." She smiled faintly.

"The dreams again, Olisa?" Grace asked, her face taut. She stroked her face tenderly with the cloth.

Olisa nodded as she hugged Grace's hand to her face. "We were sitting in front of the fireplace and Daddy fed a log into the fire when it burst into flames. The sparks leaped onto the curtains, and before I knew it, the whole house was on fire. I ran outside, but the flames chased me, jumping onto my clothes, my hair. I could feel the heat even though I knew it was dream."

"Okay honey, don't talk about it anymore. You're perspiring again. Let me get you some more clothes, you're soaked."

Grace left and I took over her role, wiping Olisa's forehead.

"I've been having these dreams nightly, Daddy. Tonight was the worse. It's like the minute I shut my eyes they start up again. What's it all mean?"

"I don't know, sweetness. You either missed your calling as a fireman or you're just under too much stress."

She smiled again as she squeezed my hand. She held it until Grace came back with a change of clothes.

Olisa's phobia about fires was nothing new. She had been that way since childhood. Nothing else frightened her: snakes, spiders, heights, enclosed spaces—nothing. But she constantly had nightmares about fire. The first time I really noticed it was when she was about four years old. One morning she happily pranced into the kitchen waiting for Mommy to find her some clothes. I accidentally left the burner on after cooking bacon, and a small grease fire erupted like a geyser in the pan. Man, you would have thought it was raining fire and brimstone the way she bolted out the kitchen!

At first I cracked up because the flames had already died out, until I peeped out the kitchen curtains and saw her running down the street butt naked and howling at the top of her miniature lungs. I chased her for almost two blocks, pajamas and robe flying behind me, before I caught up with her. She was in hysterics and wrestling to get free. She wanted to run some more. People gaped at me like "That poor child, what in the world did you do to her to make her that way?"

It took me forever to coax her to come back inside the house. Everyone has a boogeyman. Hers was made of fire. Lighting a match too closely could be a traumatic event for her. Even candles scared her. During Halloween, the pumpkins that grinned savagely at her with their glowing teeth unnerved her. We were assured she would outgrow this paranoia, but it never happened. Fire dreams tormented her like an Achilles heel.

Mama Willis theorized that the ghost of her late husband, Reverend Willis, who perished in a church fire, was trying to communicate with her. She was constantly in Olisa's ear telling her to look for the hidden message beyond the fiery dreams.

The phone jolted me out of my reverie. As I picked up the receiver, I turned to see Olisa sitting up rigidly in bed intently watching me. Grace tried to get her to relax, but she resisted. The expectation in her eyes made me nervous.

It was my mother-in-law, Katherine Willis. I could barely make out what she was saying. She was hysterical!

"Slow down Katherine. I can't understand you. Please, slow down!"

"Joseph? Oh Joseph! Is that you? Praise God!" Then there was panic again. "Where's Grace? Is Grace there? Please tell me she's there, Joseph! Please don't tell me she's in that house!"

"She's right here, Katherine, with Olisa."

"Thank you, thank you , Lord… Jonathan, too?"

"Jonathan's at his office, I talked to him not long ago. What is going on? You're scaring me!"

In the background I could hear Papa Willis yelling, "Are they all right, Kath? Goddamn it. Tell me something, shit. Who are you talking to? Is that Joseph? Ask him, where's the kids!"

"They're fine, Papa," she yelled off the line. "Thank you, Jesus. Let me talk to Grace, let me hear her voice."

But Grace had already snatched the phone.

"Mama, what is wrong with you? Joseph already told you. I'm fine… we're all fine. No, I don't know anything." Grace's eyes ballooned, and she began gesturing at the television.

"Joseph, quick! Turn on the TV. Hurry!"

I fumbled with the remote control. Emerging from the black screen was an aerial shot of a house swarmed by angry flames. Although the firemen were still running around frantically battling the flames, trying to contain them so that didn't spread to the other homes on the walk street. It looked like they pretty much had it under control. It was only one house on a walk street.

The remote control fell out of my hands as I heard Grace gasp. The camera panned the gathering crowd as I recognized many of the faces. There was Fred and Nancy Schafer, talking to Wesley Guillory. Oh, behind them were Cedrick and David, slowly shaking their heads, their faces contorted in disbelief as they watched our house burning. I heard a newscaster say something about a pipe bomb as I snatched my car keys, but it gets all kind of fuzzy after that.

The next day we got to share our plight with the whole world as a battalion of cameras observed Grace and I sifting through the ashes for salvageable belongings. Reporters shouted from behind the ropes protecting our privacy, begging for an interview. The firefighters did the best they could do. The exterior of the house was still fairly intact, but the interior damage was irreplaceable. There was a surreal sheen in the hazy air as ashes occasionally floated above the ground. I discovered a pair of dress shoes I had never taken out of the box—untouched in what used to be my closet. My eyes burned.

At least our family was there. The Willis's, Peter, Laura on her hands and knees sorting through the rubble for valuables, although apparently thieves had picked off what they could, despite the police presence. Gumbo grimly interrogated the security officers assigned last night and even the police chief as to what steps the department intended to take. Wilma was there supplying food and making sure we all had a bite to eat. And a solemn Jonathan continued to field calls on his cellular phone as he paced through the damage.

Olisa tearfully pleaded to come, but we couldn't allow it no matter how insistent she was. Logan stayed with her, and I was told later it turned into quite a wrestling match, but he prevailed. We didn't want it to become more of a circus than it already was. Too many nuts out there. Too dangerous. That was verified when the police lieutenant handed us a note left in our mailbox written in bold cryptic letters:

TO THE PARENTS OF OLISA CARPENTER—THE NIG- GER WITCH. IF YOU CAN'T READ THIS LETTER, THEN SMELL IT. THIS IS YOUR FIRST AND LAST WARNING, NIG- GERS! NO ONE GOT HURT THIS TIME. NEXT TIME, WE CAN'T BE RESPONSIBLE FOR WHOSE BLACK ASS GETS BLOWN AWAY! FOLLOW THIS ADVICE—DO NOT GO TO WASHINGTON! KEEP YOUR CHICKEN FRIED, WATERMEL- ON EATING ASS AT HOME AND EVERYTHING WILL BE FINE. IF YOU INSIST ON GOING TO WASHINGTON, THEN THE TRUE MESSENGERS OF GOD WILL SEND THAT COCK- SUCKING BLACK BITCH TO HER ETERNAL REST IN PICK- ANINNY HEAVEN! AND ALL THE REST OF YOU FAT LIPPED DARKIES WILL BE RIGHT BEHIND HER IF YOU FUCK WITH US! THERE IS ONLY ONE GOD AND HE IS THE WHITE LIGHT! NOT A GODDAMN INK SPOT. HAIL TO THE TRUE MESSENGERS OF GOD!!

As the anger seared my insides, I felt compelled to not only rip the letter to shreds, but to scream at all those ignorant idiots out there star- ing at our tragedy like it's some bizarre form of theater. I wanted to call out the coward who I'm sure was in the audience, watching and grin- ning, and I wasn't going to stop until he materialized. That's what I felt like doing. Instead, I simply handed the letter over to the police who assured me that not only would they look into it but that they would also contact the FBI.

This wasn't the first death threat we had received. There were many. They started coming shortly after Nick Cavaliere was healed. They have been as regular as those addressed to "resident." However, this was the first time someone acted on it.

The worse part is, we had no idea who planted the bomb. Like I told the police repeatedly and then the FBI, I'm sure Popcock had something to do with it, but I had no proof. Though he sometimes acted like a virulent strain of Rush Limbaugh in his public tirades, he had no history of violent acts despite his mouthing off. Can't arrest someone for that. But my gut told me he had everything to do with it.

My gaze fell on Grace, alone, sitting cross-legged in the charred divan, completely oblivious to the crocodile snapping photographers pressed against the ropes. I huddled next to her, shielding her from their penetrating stares like a veil. She surprised me with a smile so warm that it lulled me into her aura of intimacy. We were alone in our living room one more time. An entire stack of photo albums stuffed inside a footlocker had been preserved. Giddy laughter sprang forth as we perused the photos that had now become our most valued possessions on earth. Soon the whole family surrounded us as we passed the books around and all of us were caught up in this lunacy.

"Look at this." Grace held up a sepia toned photograph. "Grandfather Willis managed to survive this fire."

"Ain't that something," Papa Willis said, his eyes moist as he looked over Grace's shoulder. "Ain't that something?"

There he was, the Reverend Odis Willis, dressed to the nines, arm in arm with his pretty young bride, Mama Willis, displaying a smile a yard wide. They proudly stood in front of their new church, ready to tackle a future they believed was filled with promise. I held Grace even closer to me as warm tears rolled down my cheeks. In that blurred moment, I remember being so grateful to have my family and friends around to love. Damn the material things, they were replaceable... but not family.

Nick Cavaliere phoned me a day later. His voice, choked with guilt. "Joseph, I-I-I don't know what to say to you. I'm so very sorry about what happened... I wanted to be there with you guys... I..."

"Nick, stop acting like you set the bomb. I know that. But if you had showed up, it would have made it more crazy than it already was."

"That's what Lena told me. Still, I feel so bad."

"Stop, if it wasn't for you we wouldn't be sitting in this house right now. We'd have been scrambling around."

"I guess, but if it wasn't for me you might not be in this predicament right now, either."

"Nick, if it hadn't been you, I guarantee you it would have been someone else," I snapped tersely. "You're starting to sound like an insecure actor."

"Can't help it. It's in my blood." His mood finally lifted.

"No. It was that last movie you did before the accident. That was an absolute piece of shit. Makes me think you faked the whole thing so you could go into hiding."

This time I heard that full-throated laugh he was famous for.

"Okay, you found me out. Just don't mention it to Theo Balanis."

"Depends on how much he's willing to shell out."

"I knew from the first time I met you, you were only in it for the money."

We both laughed.

"Joe, can I be frank with you for a minute?"

"You can be Ted, Shirley, or Zachariah if you want. I know how you actors like to change their names."

"Seriously, Joe."

"All right, go ahead."

It seemed like forever before he spoke again. "You can't let her go to Washington, Joe. You just can't."

What was I supposed to say?

"Are you listening? I'm afraid for her, for you, and Grace. No matter what they tell you, no matter how much security you may have been promised. They can't protect her. Look what just happened."

"It's different now, Nick. We've got the big guns in on this," I declared with pomposity.

"So did Kennedy... So did King... So did Sadat... So did Indira Gandhi... You get what I'm saying?"

"Uh-huh." I was getting irritated. I didn't need this pressure right now.

"Screw the march, man! Please forgive me for saying this, but there are bastards out there who don't give two pennies about offing your daughter. They'll approach it with a sense of duty and kill her for the glory of God!"

"You don't think I know that, Nick? You don't think that shit fucks with me every goddamn day?! But how the hell am I going to stop her? Her mindis made up. She's more determined now than ever before. The fire pissed her off. She refuses to let a bunch of assholes stop her from doing God's work."

"I think we all know this is more than just a bunch of assholes."

"I know that, Nick, but she's a grown woman, who makes grownup decisions. You know, I'm sorry, too, but what's with all this sudden concern about her going to Washington? Huh?"

"I just think when all is said and done, no matter how big the event, the world is not ready for Olisa. Why sacrifice her to the wolves for nothing?"

"Uh-huh… But you were ready, huh, Nick? And now that you're healed, fuck everybody else. Is that the mentality you're talking about?"

"Yeah, you're right. I am a great example of how selfish a person can be." His voice rose barely above a whisper. "That's why I say, don't let her do it, because she will not be truly appreciated. In the end, we're all in it for ourselves. We believe in God because we're afraid hell may actually exist."

I felt like a jerk for what I had said, but I couldn't stop myself.

"Do you realize what this is doing to me and to Grace? I doubt it. How could you?" I felt the vein sticking out of my forehead. It always does when I'm screaming.

"You're right, my friend, I could not possibly know how you feel in these extraordinary circumstances," Nick whispered. "But I have three grownup children of my own, and I know how *I'd* feel. I'd do anything I could to stop them."

"You'd have to kidnap, Olisa."

"I'm willing to do that if you are."

Does he have shit for brains? He was dead serious. I just sat there holding the phone, speechless and suddenly very tired.

"Joseph, I have had a very long and prosperous career, and I've been very fortunate because I've worked with a very loyal and remarkable film crew that has been with me throughout the majority my career. They trust me and I trust them…"

Why we segued to the "Lifetime Achievement Awards" I had no idea.

"… And some of these guys I worked with, particularly in my action films, are absolute geniuses. Hands down, the best in the business regarding special effects."

"Great."

"They are great," he continued ignoring my indifferent tone. "Consummate professionals. Man, these guys could do anything. If you asked them to blow up a building, they could do it with you standing right in the middle. Remember what I said about trust? Any stunt can be inherently dangerous, but I rarely used a stunt double because I trusted them. That's why people believed it when I walked out of a burning building—because I did, thanks to them."

"I see."

"Do you? Mark Baylor, who is head of that special production unit is a very close friend of mine. I could call him any time and he'd be there if I needed him. He's willing to work independently if necessary, but only as a special favor to me."

"Yeah?"

"Yeah."

The silence on the line was torturous.

"Listen, Nick, I just heard a beep. I better answer that. It's probably the FBI. They have some questions they still want to ask me."

"Sure, Joseph. You take care of that. Joe, please let me know if there is anything I can do. Don't wait too long, okay? Call me."

"Oh yeah, absolutely. I'll be in contact. Gotta go." I quickly hung up the phone. I was hyperventilating. Just then, Grace passed by on her way to the kitchen.

"Joseph, are you all right?" she asked, alarmed, rushing to my side.

"Oh yeah, I'm fine. Water just went down the wrong way that's all. Nothing to worry about."

"Okay… you look like you were having a heart attack or something."

"Old iron heart? Naw. Everything's fine. I was just trying to get a little attention from you."

"Well, you got it. I'm going to check on the food. You sure you're okay?"

"I'm sure," I lied again.

She kissed me on the forehead and reticently went back into the kitchen.

I don't know why Nick freaked me out. He's a good guy. All he was trying to do was help. My nerves were just frayed. I'll call him after all this is over with and apologize, I told myself. It's just stress. The household has been frazzled and we're all starting to bite each other's head off.

Maybe I felt guilt deep down inside. Maybe in some weird way, I had a little resentment that all we've ever focused on is trying to protect Olisa our entire lives. I felt like a heretic for even thinking that. She was my daughter. But sometimes I wondered if we shouldn't have been more selfish. We were all targets now. In some ways, she was more protected than us. I thought about an interview I saw on cable recently conducted by a young brother named Jason Collier. His program was called *Meet the People*. The program entailed him traveling throughout Los Angeles County each week and hooking up with interesting people to interview on a variety of topics, ranging from drugs to knitting quilts. This week his topic revolved around Olisa and the upcoming march. Ironically, the interview was held on the Board Walk at Venice Beach.

Collier, with his hair in intricately designed cornrow, wore a dark Gray Nike warm-up. He stood poised with his microphone next to a short stocky black man, who wore a tank top and shorts. The man was truly distracted as his eyes kept darting around with all the goings on at the beach.

"Hey, everybody, I'm Jason Collier, and I'm here with Dimitri Quarles. Dimitri was recently released from SoleDad Prison. What they lock you up for, brotha?"

"I was, uh, incarcerated for carjacking and armed robbery."

"Well, I'm sure you're happy to be out on this beautiful sunny day."

"I sure am, Mr. Collie," he said, lasciviously eying a voluptuous girl who skated by.

"Uh, Collier."

"Exactly, Mr. Collie," Dimitri said, clapping his hands excitedly. "I just want you to know, Mr. Collie, that I'm happy to be on your show."

"We're pleased to have you," Jason remarked, scratching his head. "Listen, why don't you just call me Jason."

"All right, Jace, " he said, clapping the very slender Jason, a little too hard on the back, causing him to bobble his microphone.

"Okay, so moving on. I understand you've met Olisa Carpenter before?"

"Yeah, yeah, that's right."

"So are you going to the march?"

"Hell yeah! I would love to participate in the march and support the sista, if I can find a way to get there."

"So, Dimitri, what can you tell us about your experience with Olisa? Dimitri?"

Dimitri had to wrestle his eyes away from a couple of female body builders that passed by. "Okay, yeah…I've never seen anybody like her before in my lifetime!"

"You are talking about, Olisa, right?" Jason interjected.

Dimitri looked at him like he was crazy. "Of course, man! A holy woman? Yeah, I used to know her back in the day. Well, I don't mean really knew her. I just saw her hanging out all the time in the Venice hood. She was always involved in all these good works programs. You know, charities, that kind of shit."

"And let me tell you something, all that shit they say about her, it's true. She did all that shit back then. It just wasn't all over the news and shit, like what you do. Everybody knew she was different. Know what

I mean? None of my homies fucked with her. She was always nice, but, like Cameo sings, 'She's strange.'"

"Can you elaborate on that a little?"

"Huh?"

"Explain it to us."

"Oh, okay… Well you know all that stuff they talking about on July the 4th. That ain't nothing. I saw her take on Pookie Taylor."

"And who is Pookie Taylor?"

Dimitri looked at Jason like he must have been crazy for not knowing who Pookie was.

"He was the baddest muthafucka… Oops, can I say that? That's right. This is cable! Anyway, muthafucka pretty much controlled all the shit going down on the Westside. You could travel 100 miles away and all you had to say was that you know Pookie and you were covered, deal that? Cause nobody messed with my boy, Pookie—except Olisa. You don't believe me, check this." Dimitri started gesturing with his hands like he was in a hip-hop groove. The music we could faintly hear in the background due to being near the roller bladding area must have influenced him.

"Some of Pookie's boys were thumping on this dude who was trying to get by without paying his respects. Boy didn't have no money, so they had his ass surrounded. I remember thinkin' they was about to turn him into a punching bag until I sees this skinny ass chick with wild flying hair come walking up and stepped in front of dude."

Jason pointed to a spot on the Boardwalk. "Well, I'm not surprised, because she proved that right over there."

"Oh yeah? They were even talking about that in the joint. So, she gets all up in Pookie's face and starts talking all this crazy shit. I mean in Pookie's face, man! Righteously dressin' his ass down… Preaching the shit to him like no minister I've even seen. All this shit about him not respecting himself or the neighborhood or God. It ain't like Pookie had never had anyone preach to him before, but not with their finger all in his face like that. I was like, whoa, man. What the fuck is he going to do to her! I got scared."

"She's an amazing woman," Jason remarked.

"Fo sho. Now, the whole neighborhood was gathering around them and I'm thinking, if she had a chance to walk away she done fucked up. Now it's going to be all about his manhood. Ain't nobody gonna embarrass him in his hood. Even dude who was about to get jumped was trying to restrain her, but she wasn't going for it. I'm like, oh shit, oh shit, cause Pookie is an equal opportunity muthafucka, he'll slap a bitch down and try to fuck her in broad daylight. Muthafucka don't know about conscious."

"But he fucked me up on this one. She said her piece to him, and turned her back on him and walked away. And Pookie didn't do did-ley-squat! You know what I'm sayin'? He walked away, too. Nobody said shit to him about it either, except for me. He kind of respected me, and I had to be careful, too, depending on his moods. And as I caught up to him, I was hoping he wouldn't try to take the shit out on me."

"So what did you say?"

"I said to him, 'Hey Pookie, why you let her get away with that? Was her shit that good?' He turned slowly toward me and I got real scared, not from him, but because I saw something in his eyes I never seen before. Fear! The muthafucka looked like he seen a ghost. He says, 'Yeah, she talked some good garbage, but that ain't why I didn't do nothin'.'"

"Now, I'm all messed up. Then he says, 'Did you see that big black muthafucka floating behind her? That's why I didn't do nothin'. And he stares at me real hard. Then looks around all crazy and shit like he's worried about somebody following him. I'm looking at him like maybe this is a joke, but I see he's as serious as an Al Sharpton perm. So I says my goodbyes, and I take my ass on out of there. Mainly cause I value my life."

"What a trip, man," Jason said to the camera. "So what happened to Pookie Taylor?"

"Never saw Pookie again after that, either. Last thing I heard he moved out to West Covina or something. Tell you the truth, I don't even know if he's around anymore. Somebody told me they found him in the streets with a knife in his back cause he owed money on some drug deal. Cold shit, ain't it?"

"Yes, it is." Jason said solemnly. He then gave Dimitri a brotherly handshake, and winced a little because Dimitri obviously has a strong grip. "So Dimitri, I hope to see you in Washington." While the theme for the show played and before they could turn off the audio, Dimitri yelled, "Hey, Mr. Collie, you know any way I can hitch a ride to D.C.?"

To say tensions were festering about a week before the grand event was about the greatest understatement ever made. A slamming door evidenced this as Olisa tore past us, her face hidden.

"What in the world!" Grace exclaimed.

Next thing I knew, Olisa whistled for Free, and I saw them treading up the crest of the hill.

Once again, the front door opened as Peter and Logan walked in with hangdog looks on their faces.

"Anybody want to tell us what's going on," I asked, looking from one to the other.

Neither seemed particularly anxious to begin. Peter finally spoke up.

"I guess I'm partly to blame for the whole thing."

"Pete, it's not your fault. You thought she already knew about it. I didn't know either. This was Jonathan's deal."

"Logan, what was Jonathan's deal?" I was afraid of the answer.

Logan smirked, glancing at Peter.

"This one's on me, Joseph. Usually, I don't bring business matters up to Olisa. One, because Jonathan has repeatedly asked me not to, and two, because it makes sense. She doesn't need to be bothered by extraneous day-to-day details… but this is something I assumed Jonathan had already confirmed with her."

Arms now folded, my eyes widened as I waited for Peter to continue.

"So, this morning I innocently asked Olisa which colors she preferred I use so I could complete her on-line shopping site."

"What on-line shopping site?"

Peter and Logan both appeared stunned by my admission.

"You didn't know either, huh?" Logan just shook his head.

"Ever since Olisa announced this would be her last event, Jonathan has been planning a major launch of Olisa's Universal Healing Products to coincide with the march." Peter winced when he saw our reaction.

"He's what?" Grace and I asked simultaneously.

"Greeting cards, posters, cosmetics, soaps, protein powders, tableware… it's a long list. His slogan is 'All designed to bring out the Goddess in your universe!'"

"Oh, no," Grace groaned, bowing her head.

"That's about the reaction Olisa had, multiplied by ten."

"I don't believe Jonathan. He didn't consult with anyone?" I could barely see, I was so angry.

"No Joseph," Peter corrected. "He consulted with people. Major companies and major suits."

"He just didn't consult with us," Logan added as he peered out the front window. He spotted Olisa sitting on the hill with Free. "I'll be back." Logan hurriedly walked out the still open front door.

"Anyway, Olisa demanded that I drive her to Malibu so she could be a part of the tour."

"Tour?"

Peter self-consciously rubbed his face. "Yes, Joseph, as you do know, the Olisa Inc. building is finished."

"Surprising, ain't it?"

"So Jonathan was giving a kind of pre-tour to some of the executives before it officially opens in two weeks."

"What a guy my son is."

"Joseph don't," Grace chided.

"Well, that guy wasn't too happy to see Olisa standing next to me in the lobby while conducting his tour. He played it off, but you should have seen the look he gave me, like I had shot him in the back."

"He's a piece of work," I huffed.

"Jonathan being Jonathan, though, recouped fast. He immediately flashed that winning smile and wrapped Olisa into his arms and told her, 'You spoiled my surprise. I wanted to make a private presentation to you. But that's okay. I want you to meet some people.' He then introduced her to the people who were already oohing and aahing as… How did he put it? That's right, as 'the one who makes this gorgeous new building pale in comparison like a light bulb to the sun.'"

"Nice, but why do I think Olisa was unimpressed?!"

"Because you know your daughter pretty well, Mr. C. But man, what a scene watching twenty-five suits rushing her like she was selling hot stocks. Olisa tried to be nice but she was just too angry. She tried to hint to Jon that they needed to be alone and talk, but he was too into his flow. Finally she yelled, 'Jonathan if you don't get these people out of here, now!'"

"'Okay, honey, ' Jon said, still trying to smooth things over. 'My goodness, what has Peter been telling you? Let me talk with my associates for a bit and then we'll talk all day if you want.' And she said, 'No, Jonathan. I'm not waiting. Apparently, there has been far too much talk without me present. The bottom line is, I am not going to let you do this. You are betraying God, me, and deceiving the people who have placed their faith in what we are doing!'"

"Deceive is a good word."

"Joseph, please," Grace admonished me again.

"Jonathan's amazing, though," Peter recounted. "Nothing fazes him when he's in his zone. He said, 'Hold on, Olisa. Don't make up your mind until you talk to Frank Pelligrino and Cheryl Roberts.'" Frank and Cheryl were VP's of sales at one of the largest fortune 500 companies in the nation, and he called them over to give Olisa a quick synopsis about what they planned to do with the products.

"Olisa was furious! She slapped Jonathan's hand off her shoulder and yelled at him again to get them away from her. This time I think Jon got the message. He said, 'Olisa, what are you doing? These people are here because they are devoted to you.' That's when Olisa cut him off. 'No, Jon, they're here to make a buck. I'm just a good excuse… I mean it, Jon, get them out!'"

"Frank and Cheryl didn't become top executives for nothing, and they ushered the people out of the building. Jonathan was irate. He said, 'Olisa, what is wrong with you? Do you know those people represent the fruits of entrepreneurs across this country? I flew many of them here. They're here on your behalf. Everything they do will benefit you. Let me do my job! This is how an organization is run!'"

"'Jonathan, don't you see? she said. 'It will never be over. Money begets money. That's all you're talking about.'"

"'No it's not,' Jon argued. Look how many people we're going to help here. This is not a bad thing. It's all good. Wait till I show you all the ideas and products we've come up with: oils, perfumes, soaps, paints, floor wash, candles… check it out, let me show you a prototype.'"

"I don't know if I want to hear the rest," Grace said with a distressed look on her face as she looked out the window at the empty dirt road leading to the house.

"Well, I do, keep going."

"All right," Peter said, hesitantly. "Well, Jonathan went and grabbed a candle out of his briefcase that was a miniature image of Olisa and handed it to her saying, 'Don't you see it Olisa? Olisa Inc. products for those seeking a little magic healing in their lives. What do you think?'"

"Oh no," both Grace and I gasped.

"Yeah, Olisa held that candle, and all she did was stare at Jon in disbelief.

"Jonathan's eyes were so wide it made mine hurt. 'This is where you need me, sis,' he stressed. 'I'm going to make it all right, Olisa. We're going to change the world, baby. And we can do it without you taxing yourself to heal another soul after the concert.'"

"I think I can fill in the rest. Olisa broke that candle over her knee."

"No Mr. C, although she may have wanted to. She just handed the candle back to Jon. I think what broke was her heart, because all that rage dissolved into tears. 'No, Jon, no,' she whispered. 'This is not the way. This is a bastardization of everything we've accomplished. I feared this would happen from the very beginning, and here we are. Don't fool yourself. You're not helping people. You're helping you. You are forming a new bible that dictates what people need for their lives.'"

"'No, Olisa, that's not true,' Jonathan fought back. 'I'm not harming anyone. I'm making them feel good! This is making them happy! If you're uncomfortable about me using stuff with your image on them, we can easily change that. I see what you're saying. That's a good point. Look, I'll commission some of the best artists in the country, and we'll design new images: ones with rainbows, stars, suns, moons, oceans, that kind of stuff. Give it an environmental focus... you know. That makes sense. See, we need your input. That was stupid on my part. I should have gone to you from the beginning. I was just afraid you were going to shoot it down, that's why I didn't tell you. I wanted you to see the results.'"

"What did Olisa say?" Grace's voice was clogged with emotion. So much that I could tell Peter felt guilty about continuing. But I nodded for him to go on.

"She said, 'Congratulations, Jon. You are now God.' Jon looked at her oddly. 'I mean it,' she said, patting him on the shoulder. 'How does it feel to be God. To fashion a world in your own image?'"

"'C'mon, Olisa, you know that's not true.'"

"'It's not? Name one time you mentioned God in your entire explanation.'"

"You could tell it was killing Jon not to be able to challenge her on that one. But he was speechless."

"'Jon, you are guided by an enormous spirit,' Olisa stated, 'but not one that I want to live by. You are consumed by the spirit of greed. It's clawing at you, choking you, and eating you up.'"

"Jon acted like he hadn't heard a thing. He started right back in with the sales pitch like a man possessed. This time Olisa wasn't listening. She let him rant for a minute and then sealed it up with, 'Jon, it's over.'"

"Jon tumbled backwards like he had been shot. 'Olisa, what do you mean it's over? Anything can be worked out. Like for instance…'"

"No, Jon. I told you one day, it might all have to end when I got tired of it. This is that day. All I ever wanted was to help people, to heal them because I have been blessed with special gifts, and to find a way to help them be at peace with each other. You convinced me that I could use my gifts to uplift society in that way, but things have changed. I will not be a part of a system that will tyrannize them or prey upon their spiritual weaknesses."

"See, you're still not getting it, Olisa. What I'm trying to do…"

"No, you're not getting it," she retorted. "True spiritual healing comes from inside. It doesn't come from the purchase of a store product. It comes from here, she emphasized, planting her hand to his chest. Buying products is easy… it's safe… it allows you to go home and feel good about yourself. It's cosmetic healing without all the work, but it doesn't teach you compassion."

"That's when she walked away. All I could do was follow while he angrily trailed us shouting. 'No, no! It's too late now. You can't quit on me! It doesn't work that way, Sis. See, we've got people to answer to now. It's way beyond I want to do something else in my life. Do you fucking know how much I've invested into all of this? There are some very important people involved in this I didn't tell you about. They're not going to take this information too lightly. Do you hear what I'm saying? You can't quit on me, Olisa. We're in this together, baby! Who's betraying who now, huh? It's not over, Olisa. Do you hear me?'"

I could barely look at Grace's tearstained face. We were completely at a loss for words.

Meanwhile, a car hauled ass up the road, waves of dust spewing from under the tires. We didn't have to guess who it was. Jon was driving so recklessly that a security guard had to dive into some shrubbery to get out of the way. Jonathan sprinted into the house like a posse was on his ass. If the front door hadn't been open, I believe he would have crashed through it.

"Where's Olisa?" He was breathing hard, perspiration breaking out on his forehead.

"Hi, Jonathan. How are you? Why don't you sit down and have some tea?"

"Dad, I'm not in the mood. I just need to speak with Olisa. Oh my, is that my pal over there?" he said derisively. "I'm sure he couldn't wait to tell you what happened. He likes to do that. I think it makes him feel good."

"You know it's not like that, Jon."

"Really? So break it down for me, sweetie, what's it like?"

"Jon, why don't you sit down and relax so we can have a civil conversation. Olisa just took a short walk, she'll be back."

"Can't, Mom. I'll just go look for her."

"No, Jonathan, I think you should," Grace stressed more firmly.

I understood her concern. There were huge bags under Jon's sleep deprived eyes. There was also a frenzied, crazed look in them. One fueled by fear. The person standing before me was a stranger. Not our son.

"What?" he asked, realizing we were all gawking at him. "What did he tell you? I'm fine!"

Just then, Logan walked in from the rear.

"Oh, maybe it was pretty boy that told you something." He started to walk up on Lo, but I moved in front of him. He locked eyes with me for a second, but then backed up against the bookcase behind him. He angrily folded his arms. "So what'd you tell them, Lo? Did you tell them how you turned my sister against me? You've known her for six months, and I find it kind of funny that she doesn't trust me anymore."

"I didn't have to say anything to her, Jon. You did that all by your lonesome."

"Fuck you, man, and fuck you," he raged, pointing at Peter. "At least I thought I could trust you, Peter, but I see now."

"I've never given you any reason to doubt me, Jon. But I'm not so sure about you. You gave me the impression that Olisa knew all about the merchandising campaign."

"Oh yeah, sure, we're supposed to believe the guy whose ancestors killed Christ!"

Peter's tried to smile, but couldn't, as he made a better decision and walked out the door.

Grace slowly walked up to Jon who glared defiantly and whacked him hard across the face.

"Jonathan, how could you be so cruel and insensitive to anyone, let alone Peter. You know he's family!"

Jonathan clinched his jaw, trying desperately to maintain a stone face, but it soon crumbled as his body wobbled and he fell into Grace's waiting arms. A little boy's voice I hadn't heard in years trickled from his lips.

"Mama, I'm sorry, I'm really sorry. I didn't mean it. I promise, I'll go apologize to Peter. Don't worry, I'll make it up to him. I'm just feeling a lot of pressure right now. You guys just don't know."

"Then tell us, son. There's no way we can help you unless we know what going on," I felt like my eyes were on the verge of welling up, too.

"You guys can't help me. Only Olisa can. If she doesn't go to Washington in a couple of days, that's my ass. They're going to kill me."

"What?" Grace pulled back as she cupped her hands to his face. "Jon, who's going to kill you? My God, who are you in business with?"

He clapped his hands to his head as if it were about to burst. "I'm hooked up with all kinds of people, Mom. That's all you need to know." He began wringing his hands and pacing about the room. "When Olisa told me she'd do one more event, I hustled around to get some fast backing. I didn't have time to check resumes, I just went to some big money people I knew about through some contacts in the record biz. We had one shot, I wanted to make sure we reaped the max on the whole thing."

"So pay them back."

"It's not that easy, Dad."

"Why not? With all the money that's in Olisa Inc.?"

"These people are expecting to get twenty times what they paid out. But, I had it all worked out. They were just loans, not a partnership. They were going to get paid back easily."

"And they never would have left you alone," Grace added.

"Maybe, but I'm telling you, I had it all planned. I could have paid the loans back and still accomplished our mission to help people. It would have worked out." Jonathan started bawling again. "I'm so sorry… I just did what I thought was right. I got in over my head and tried to move to fast… I wasn't trying to hurt anyone. Please believe me. If I could just talk to my sister, I know she'd understand."

A voice that sounded like a gentle breeze said, "I know you tried your best, Jonathan. And that's why I'm not going to let you down."

Olisa stepped into the living room and stood stoically beside me.

Hearing Olisa's voice made all the swelling in Jon's face practically disappear, he was so relieved and buoyed by her words. He grabbed Olisa so tightly I thought I'd have to use the "jaws of life" to spring her loose. She said, "Everything is fine here. I need you to go to Peter."

He held her a minute longer searching her eyes one last time and then he was gone.

And so was Olisa. She left the room before we had a chance to talk with her. But I saw her eyes when Jon hugged her and it will haunt me for the rest of my life. They were disconnected from reality, yet, resolute, they spoke of love, of self-sacrifice and something that filled me with dread. Grace noticed it, too

It was obvious she had been having premonitions. She also had the look of someone prepared to die.

CHAPTER 15

Unable to fall asleep, around midnight I decided to take a walk and stretch a little bit. I was too tight.

"Mr. Carpenter, I don't think it's a real good idea for you to walk out there alone. I'd be happy to accompany you."

"I've got it covered, Melvin. I just need some fresh air. I'll make it short."

"Okay, Mr. Carpenter."

Actually, I don't think Melvin was real excited about escorting me anyway. It was a little creepy walking on one of the mountain trails as crickets chirped. I slapped my neck as the mosquitoes treated me like I was a fast food restaurant on two legs. As I shined my flashlight on the path, grotesque shadows leaped wildly about me. When the incessant sounds of the crickets died, I knew I was no longer alone.

It was him.

He receded into one of the giant shadows, and I might have missed him if not for the gleaming polar cap of hair and golden trumpet hanging loosely at his side.

"You're here."

"You knew I would be," he said in that voice.

The light of the flashlight made all the shadows dance at my feet as I jiggled it nervously.

"It's that time isn't it?"

Silence.

"You're getting ready to take her away, aren't you?"

Still nothing.

"Well, I won't let you. We need her in our life more than you do."

I gazed into his shadowy essence, and I felt him taking me in as well.

"That's it? No answer? All my life I've prepared to be there if my daughter was in trouble. And here I stand, utterly helpless. Don't you understand? She needs me. Don't let me be powerless. I'm begging you with all my heart. Please give me a solution. Tell me what I can do."

"There's nothing I can tell you, Joseph."

My shoulders sagged with exasperation. "Oh, that's good. Thanks for the advice. I'll tell you what. I'm not going to sit back and let my daughter be murdered. I'm going to do something. To hell with destiny. If this is my fate, then let it be. But I guarantee you, I'll play a part in how it ends."

"That's what you should do, Joseph," he rumbled in a detached voice layered with emotional overtones.

Once again, I heard the crickets and the pesky mosquitoes.

He was gone.

I walked back to the house and was zapped in the eyes by the criss-crossing flashlights of the security patrol.

The second I laid in bed, Grace rolled over and said, "I saw her tonight, Joseph. She appeared at the foot of our bed."

"No doubt," I said. "I guess its old home week again."

"You too?"

We kept each other company talking all night. And when the morning sun flashed us, I still wasn't tired. That's why I had no problem answering the bedside phone on the first ring.

I knew who it was. He was returning my call. I nodded at Grace as she watched me with anticipation. Her head fell back into the pillows as she briefly closed her eyes and breathed deeply. I saw her mouth moving and realized she was saying a prayer. This was it. We agreed there would be no turning back.

With three days left to go before the D.C. march it was like a tomb inside the house. There was still a security team watching the premises for trespassers, but the rest of our family, Jonathan, Peter, Wilma, Alton, and Little Oak had already flown to Washington. Logan was still around, but he was at home packing and tying up some loose ends in his studio. The only ones left in the house were Grace, Olisa, and me.

Our flight, which included Logan, was scheduled for tomorrow afternoon.

The atmosphere surrounding us was tense, oppressive. We knew what lay ahead of us, and we dealt with it the best way we could. Olisa spent most of her time alone in her room meditating. Grace read a lot, and I wrote in my diary. We took several long quiet walks together, always accompanied by security.

At around 5:00 P.M. I took a call from Jonathan checking in. His voice was barely audible.

"Hey, Dad. How's it going?"

"Hey, man, hanging in. How about you? How's the weather?"

"Great. About 70 degrees… Got a nice little breeze."

"All right. Make sure it stays that way."

"I'll do my best. Um, look, everything's arranged."

"Perfect. So what time can Olisa check out the building?"

"She needs to be there 8:00 P.M. sharp. The door will be unlocked. If she's not there by that time, Savannah has instructions to lock it up by 8:15."

"I'll let her know. She's very excited. She didn't really get a chance to thoroughly check it out last time."

"Yeah, I know. Dad?"

"Yeah?"

"Is she absolutely sure about this?"

"Yeah, it's something she needs to do. You agree?"

There was a long pause. "Yes."

"Good."

"Dad?"

"Yeah, partner?"

"Do me a favor. Tell her how much I love her, okay?"

"You got it. Although I suspect she knows, but I'll relay it anyway."

"Thank you. I'll see you guys in Washington. Be safe."

"You, too. Bye, Son."

I still held the phone to my ear, even though it had clicked minutes ago. It was Grace who gently took it out of my hand and placed it in the cradle.

It was about 7:45 in the evening when we made it to the O.L.I.S.A., Inc. building in Malibu. We were escorted by a fleet of police and security officers. As I turned to go uphill, I noticed Danielle Cavaliere cruising onto the highway, but he never looked my way as he turned in the opposite direction.

The office was tucked in an isolated area off Highway 1 not far from the Pepperdine Campus. The building's backside faced the hills peppered, with expensive houses. You had to park the car and walk up steps to the modest, but elegant three-story structure. We parked on the lower level, which meant we had to walk up a small grade to get to the building as the caravan of cars followed suit.

"Why aren't we driving all the way up to the building, Mr. Carpenter?"

"My son told me they had been doing a little resurfacing, so he wanted to make sure no cars parked on the grounds before next week's opening, Officer McKay."

"Makes sense to me," he said, signaling the other cars to park.

Grace and I watched Logan help Olisa out of the car. "Come on, old lady, how are you going to make it up the hill if you can't even get out of the car."

Olisa smiled crookedly as she paused before accepting his hand. When she got out the car, she kissed him on the cheek. "Thank you, kind sir," she intoned softly.

"You are certainly welcome beautiful lady."

"Almost 8:00," I hated to interject.

It took a bit before they finally wrestled their eyes away from each other.

Olisa then walked over to us, her spirit rising, and said, "Oh, it's such a wonderful night. And I'm here with the people I love most in the world. It can't get better than this. This is going to be the nicest walk I've had in awhile. Look at that building. A whole new beginning."

"Yes it is." I struggled to let go of her.

"Olisa, be sure to smile. I'm going to take your picture when you're at the top of the hill."

"Wait a minute," Officer McKay said, frowning. "We're all going up there, right?"

"Would you mind if I take a few minutes on my own, officer?" asked Olisa sweetly. "I just want to get a feel for the place."

"I understand. But I really think we ought to check it out first. You never know."

"No one knows about this place, officer." I glanced at my watch. "We haven't released the address yet."

"What about the construction crew? People talk, you know? No, I don't think we should take a chance. We'll accompany you, and then leave you alone, okay?"

"Sarge, look what we got coming our way!"

"Oh, shit! Who the hell invited them?!"

Barreling up the road like NASCAR racers were several news vans. Reporters hanging out the windows like college kids on summer break in Palm Springs. In the distance, you could hear the whirring sound of an approaching helicopter.

"I thought you said, no one knows about this address? What's that?"

I shook my head. "Looks like someone tipped them off. You were right, people can't keep their mouths shut."

"Olisa, looks like you're going to get a little time to yourself, try to make the best of it, while we try to control the hounds."

"Thanks, officer," Olisa said, waving as she headed up the slope to the building.

After she reached the top, before opening the door, Olisa turned and gave us a beatific smile as Logan snapped the picture. A second later a flurry of cameras were going off behind us as the officers worked diligently to keep the clamoring paparazzi corralled.

Ten minutes had gone by since she had been in the building, and it was 8:13. One of the paparazzi broke through the human barrier of officers and started racing up the hill, but Logan tripped him as he went flying headfirst into the brush. He poked his head out and started cursing, but no one could hear what he said over the two horrible explosions that were so loud it sounded like the apocalypse had arrived.

Grace and I fell face down into the dirt then clung to each other. When I dared to look up, the O.L.I.S.A. Inc., building had converted into a giant bonfire. All around us, reporters and camera operators darted and skirted every which way, many toward the fire. Cell phones were whipped out and glued to their ears as they babbled excitedly. It was only seconds before the faint sounds of sirens penetrated the air. I could hear them, even over our own mournful wails. Outlined in the blaze I saw Logan on his knees, his camera dangling from his neck, as he convulsed with tears. Everything was vague after that, because I was doing the same thing.

My daughter, Olisa, my heart and my soul, was gone. To imagine never seeing her again, was a pain far too unbearable.

Eva Sanchez tearfully announced on the evening news, "No one, not even the extraordinarily gifted Olisa Carpenter, could have survived such a catastrophic fire. Our hearts go out to her family. I don't think anyone could deny that she was truly an angel sent down from heaven to make this a better place for all of us. She was our one true hope, and now it's back on our shoulders again. Remember, she gave us the answers: love and forgiveness. That's how we can heal the world. I'm told that the march will go on as a memorial to Olisa Carpenter. She will be missed. If you can't be there, at least be there in spirit. Thank you and goodnight. God bless you."

Not long after that news report, the most important call of my life came in on the direct line. I pounced on it like a cur to scraps. My in-laws, my parents, and my sisters had all joined us in the house. I don't think anyone breathed, even as I fell to my knees in tears cradling the phone.

Needless to say, we never made our scheduled flight to Washington. Instead, Cecilia Moss, the Malibu Lady, chartered a private jet for us. Nick and Lena Cavaliere joined us on the flight.

Grace and I didn't want to go, but we had to do it. It was for Olisa, and I'm glad we went. In many ways, it helped to soothe the pain. We all participated in the Unity march, arm in arm: Grace, Jonathan, Little Oak, Gumbo, Logan, Peter, Nick and Lena Cavaliere, Cecilia Moss, James and Catherine Willis, Uncle Junior, and my parents and sisters.

The President spoke and so did many world leaders whose hearts she touched; poets, and motivational speakers, including Beverly Fairchild, who in a particularly eloquent speech said, "For all of you that thought you had it together, think again. Because if Christ had come back to earth as a woman, we proved with Olisa Carpenter that we aren't ready because she's the closest thing to Christ we may ever see in our life-time. Maybe next time we'll be able to see past gender, race, physiolog-ical and philosophical differences, and straight to the heart."

Olisa would have loved it. Loved seeing the millions of people, of all ethnicity's and religions who showed up in her honor, with their heartfelt and sincere pledges to devote their lives to bringing peace and harmony into the world.

Of course, the top international musical groups performed with a vehemence that many of them never matched again in their own con-certs. It was the most uplifting and incredible thing I had ever seen short of Olisa's miracles. Man, it would have lifted her heart so high. I could envision seeing her dancing joyously and unabashedly to the outpour-ing of eclectic music that rocked the nation's capital.

And Uncle Junior finally did it. Accompanying himself on a twelve string acoustic guitar, he sang his newly written composition, "A Song for Olisa." It had them crying from D.C. to Moscow.

Jonathan broke us up again in a moving tribute to his sister. "… Olisa, retained a childhood innocence we adults lost years ago. A yearn-ing, a hunger, a zest for living that if it could have been bottled would have set us free. I'm truly going to miss her."

Grace and I were so proud of Jonathan and the way he gallantly stood on that stage and faced the audience. Even more so when he scrapped the merchandising campaign. In fact, he went so far as to make sure the street vendors hawking products illegally with her image on them were unceremoniously removed from the event.

Did Olisa's existence and death ultimately change the world? That's something that I've pondered for quite some time. The Memorial March was one of the most spectacular events ever. The mood and ambiance of the ceremony lasted for quite awhile, coloring, at least in philosophy, the future direction of international politics and legislation for at least a decade.

Olisa touched countless individuals both literally and figuratively in ways that significantly changed their lives. Even Eva Sanchez eventually admitted in a televised interview that she lost her objectivity when she went home and hugged her mother who suffered from stomach cancer. Ironically, the next day in her scheduled medical exam, the doctor was stunned to announce that all the tumors had completely disappeared and she had a healthy prognosis. Olisa had embraced Eva for the first time the day before.

I can't begin to say how many people sold their souls to publishers for lousy book deals in an effort to capitalize on their shared and in many cases, imagined experiences with Olisa. The only one we endorsed was a beautifully written book by our other son, Peter Kaplan, who lovingly wrote about his friendship with Olisa. There were hundreds of book proposals received by book publishers covering every angle. I'm not including all the competing television movies and feature films that were either directly about her or a similar character. After Uncle Junior's "Song to Olisa" stayed on top of the charts for months, record companies tried to duplicate the effort commercially. Naturally, they lost sight of the significance behind the song and the fact that Uncle Junior donated the majority of his profits to the O. C. Scholarship fund.

But what can you say? Olisa always warned us to be prepared for this.

A religious group known as the Olisians was formed who compiled all of her speeches and interviews over the years and used them for worship like they were the gospels. Never acknowledging that this is exactly what she preached against. It didn't help that one radical faction of the Olisians claimed in a vision that Olisa came to their leader Alison Favreau and ordered the cult to commit mass suicide because once again the world was not listening. Fortunately, the rest of the devotees weren't real high on this. They ousted Favreau as leader for about ten other reasons as well, including the fact that she thought she was the reincarnation of Joan of Arc.

Yes, the world changed—good and bad. At least I never heard the apocalyptic blast of the trumpet. Not yet, anyway.

There was another good change. Alton and Laura had a child a year later. They named her after Olisa. She's called Little O or Oli. To date, I haven't been notified as to whether she has any extraordinary powers, but she sure is damn cute.

The Soul of Venice is still around. In fact, Wilma and I have opened up two more locations in Oakland and San Diego, and the lines are just as long as the one in Venice. And we have special days each month in which we serve dinners to the homeless.

After the Universal Healing and Unity March, Jonathan also personally transformed. He devoted himself to carrying out Olisa's dreams and making them a reality. All of his energies went into operating O.L.I.S.A., Inc. the way it was intended. He reconstituted the institution and turned it into a truly philanthropic organization. It was renamed Olisa's Institute For Healing And Social Change, and millions of dollars were donated to charities and social organizations dedicated to erasing racism, violence, poverty, and pandemic diseases such as A.I.D.S.

Apparently, Jonathan wasn't the only one committed to change. There was a major upheaval in the Glass Cathedral. Some of the loyalists in the Walter Popcock camp elected to turn over a new leaf a day after the march. Given complete anonymity and reduced sentences, they confessed to being paid by people in Popcock's employ to discredit Olisa and her associates by any means necessary; including revealing information on who actually planted the bomb in the Carpenter's Venice home.

They also stated that the two young men, former gang members and drug dealers, who were found dead in a Culver City alley had been paid cash by Popcock's organization to taunt Ernesto Padilla and goad him into fighting. Consequently, there was a hit placed on these same men. The damning evidence came when a handwritten note by Popcock was given to one of the conspirators. It read, "After they do their job, please be sure to dump out the garbage, so it doesn't stink up the place!"

Walter Popcock and his henchmen, featuring the irrepressible Mr. Furhman (a.k.a. Biscuit-Head) are now facing trial as co-conspirators to first-degree murder, amongst the other eleven accounts including extortion, bribery, and the imminent possibility of federal indictment for defrauding his parishioners over $180 million dollars! Many believe he was responsible for bombing the O.L.I.S.A., Inc. building, which would tie him to Olisa's death, but no evidence has been found to support that.

By the way, it now appears that one of the main witnesses against him was his wife of twenty-five years who, while rummaging through his personals, found out that not only was he having an affair with the musical director of his television show, but that her three year old son is his. Moreover, during the process, she decided to rummage a little more and found some additional items she could turn over to the state as evidence proving that not only was Walter Popcock able to move people to Christ through his television and radio shows, but that he could move money from their pockets to his ministry, too. I'm reminded that "Love is a many splendored thing" as his ministry is currently being dismantled.

Ernesto Padilla was immediately set free from jail and Grace, Gumbo, Little Oak, and I were there to greet him for a bittersweet reunion. Unfortunately, I was unable to revel in imagining Popcock and Biscuit-Head in prison garb. We became victims of another tragedy only two weeks later. Jonathan was found severely beaten and left to die in a vacant lot in Venice. Someone sprayed his car with bullet holes and left a note in his lapel that read, "We never forget." Many of the locals had used the lot as a dog park, and someone found Jon in the morning. He had already lapsed into a coma.

CHAPTER 16

Grace squeezed my clammy hand as we confronted a sea of flashing lights that gradually merged into one harsh glare. The tension in the air was stifling, making my head pound so much it felt like a percussionist got trapped inside.

Meanwhile, security attached themselves to us like a piece of lint. But I didn't mind. There were still some crazies floating around out there.

We were instructed to make all our statements short and sweet. Then proceed to get the hell out of there. A real stretch, I thought facetiously. Like I want to be here. All I could think about was how they had beat Jonathan down. They had tried to kill him! For all we knew, as we stood awaiting the start of our press conference, he could be dead. But we had been advised to do it, forced I maintain, because the questions refused to go away. Our son was near death, in a coma and we had to talk to these imbeciles just to secure a degree of privacy. One of the organizers signaled to us that they were ready to start.

"Mr. and Mrs. Carpenter, once again I offer you my deepest sympathies for your loss, which turned out to be ours as well. Olisa's impact on our society during the short time she shared with us could never be measured."

We both nodded in appreciation.

"That's why I ask you to please forgive me for asking this, but if I don't, then I'm not doing my job. Is there any possibility that Olisa Carpenter is still alive? As you well know, her body was never found. Many people refuse to believe that she has truly left us. It seems like we were just getting to know her."

I closed my eyes, took a deep breath, and then exhaled slowly.

"Eva, nothing would bring us greater joy, but let it go. Grace and I were there. Olisa is dead. And we are going to have to live with that final vision every day of our lives. Our only comfort is knowing she has finally found peace of mind."

Of course, it wasn't enough. They wanted, needed more.

Dissonant voices roared at me. The press was anxious. Obnoxious. Bullying. Asking sugar coated questions, but looking for hard-core answers.

We endured their screams. Watched them vie for attention. Ducked when they volleyed grating interrogatives. They climbed over each other like crabs in a barrel as they fielded ego-spawned inquiries before the bright lights.

"Please folks. One question at a time."

"Mr. and Mrs. Carpenter, who was Olisa Carpenter?"

A shrill laugh escaped my mouth. Stay calm, be focused, I told myself. Grace's soothing touch prevented me from jumping off my rickety bridge of sanity.

"Who was Olisa, you ask. Who was Olisa Carpenter?" I echoed sharply. "Are you referring to before or after the media intrusion?"

Whoever asked the question chose not to elaborate.

"You still don't get it, do you? To you, she was a phenomenon, a spectacle for the modern age, a 'freak of nature' as one of you so eloquently quipped…"

Grace gently tugged my coat sleeve.

"To us, she was a gifted, beautiful girl, who grew up to be an even more incredible woman. She was our daughter. Do you understand? Our daughter. And I will never be able to convey to you how much we love her and miss her."

I wanted to say more, but my throat felt like it was populated by wads of cotton as I labored to breathe. My heart beat fast, and I was beginning to hyperventilate as anxiety swirled through me like a centrifugal force, causing my body to shake involuntarily. If not for Grace's warm and caressing hand, I would have met the floor headfirst.

It was so difficult to disguise the bitterness ravaging my body. These people made our lives impossible. Somehow, I had to transcend it. That's what she would have wanted. I struggled to compose myself as tears ran mercifully down my cheeks.

Sliding protectively in front of me, Grace took over, addressing the press in a voice that was as calm as mine was frantic.

"Olisa was one of the most wonderful, compassionate, and caring people the world has ever known. We were richly blessed to have her be a part of our lives. And maybe, somehow, now that she's gone, maybe, there is still hope that the love she tried to deliver us will still find a home in our hearts."

No one said a word.

But, somebody left the gate open, because the silence was soon jarred by first one question, followed by an onslaught of others.

"That's it," I said, hugging Grace and waving my free hand tiredly. "I'm sorry we can't answer all of your questions, but right now our son is in desperate need of our attention. We ask that you please keep us in your prayers. Thank you, and peace."

I knew our words were in danger of being swept away as soon as we backed away from the podium.

Pandemonium broke out and we were quickly sandwiched by a wall of bodyguards herding us back inside the hospital.

In that moment, all of life fragmented as rabid photographers and jabbing microphones assaulted us from all sides. Fortunately, security blocked the press from going any further. We rounded the corner and walked down the narrow white Spartan corridors. Our police escort halted at the door to Jonathan's room. I knocked three times on the door, and the crack in the door grew larger as it slowly opened. Two behemoth security guards eased out the door, bellies rubbing against us as we squeezed in like alley cats through a gap in the fence.

"Thank you, gentlemen. We'll be okay now."

"Are you sure, sir? It's no problem if you want us to stay inside with you."

"No thanks, Vince. You and the crew get some coffee or something. It's all right. We got it covered. Thanks."

"Call us if you need us, Joseph. We've always got a couple of people posted outside your door."

"Sounds good."

"Ma'am."

"Goodnight, gentlemen. Thank you so much. God bless you."

The second I closed that door and heard the lock click under its own accord, I regretted it. In the room, I felt it… a presence.

My chest instantly constricted and my breath shortened as though invisible fingers began to close around my throat. I froze, unsure of whether to fight or flee.

I didn't even realize how hard I had gripped Grace's wrist until she winced. Even so, that wasn't why she sank to her knees, it was in reverence to the giant figure looming over our son. It wasn't long before I followed her lead, head bowed.

It was Him.

He didn't stir or flinch as we entered the room. He seemed to be only focused on Jonathan as he took off his dark glasses and gazed down at him. The angel's massive hands swarmed over his face.

He had never been the one to fear.

Soon Jonathan's body violently flip-flopped, and the air in the room transformed into a living breathing entity as a powerful earsplitting sound assailed our ears.

Then it was over and the air quieted.

Dispassionately, he covered his eyes with his shades, turned and studied us for a long moment then passed by us.

No, correction, through us.

It felt like a sudden gust of warm Santa Ana winds, but the hairs on our arms bristled as if an electrical storm hovered overhead.

I spun around, but in a blink, he was gone.

And we were alone.

Alone with our hysterical tears…

Tears of unbridled joy. An elation that left us hugging and laughing and unable to fathom whatever in our lives could have caused us such sadness.

Until Jonathan groaned, "Oh, God…"

Confused as I was, I didn't know if he meant it as an expression or if he really meant…

Regardless, we rushed to the table, ignoring the jungle of irritating wires and intravenous cords that had been keeping Jon alive and hugged him, the table, and each other in our jubilation.

At that moment I remembered thinking, "I thought he wasn't supposed to intervene?" An answer ripped through my conscious mind; *I shouldn't, but it doesn't mean I can't, Joseph Carpenter. Nothing is impossible.*

Just then, hospital personnel and security burst protectively into the room as clarity began to emerge from the murkiness of Jonathan's eyes. He groggily asked, "What happened?"

"What happened?" I yelled repeatedly, looking at Grace as both of us giggled like little kids sharing a secret. We were on a high that'd make a drug addict envious.

"The question is what hasn't happened, boy?"

But we had to step aside as wide-eyed doctors and nurses rushed to his bedside shocked to find him sitting up and smiling.

"Dare I say, it's a miracle?"

We let the doctors have their time to examine him and let him rest for a couple of hours. The next time we saw him, he had improved so rapidly he was kicked back and intently reading the newspaper.

"Man, I've been missing out on all kind of fun stuff."

"That's what happens when your lazy behind won't get out of bed," I said smiling.

"I see. So what else is new?"

"Even with sleep you're still pushy," Grace said kissing him on his forehead as she sat on the bed with her arm around him. "Be patient, there's time to talk."

Jon widened his eyes anxiously as I asked personnel to give us some time alone with our son. They willingly obliged as we waited for them to leave the room. That's when we gave Jonathan an update on everything that occurred while he was in a coma.

"So where's Logan?"

"Logan? He's down in Mexico right now. Said he's always wanted to spend time there because the area is rich for his photography." I watched the door as I spoke.

"Is that right?"

"Yes, said he may never come back. Got an opportunity to get a house on several acres in a very remote area. Logan plans to build a huge photography studio there. The best part is, he even took Free with him."

"Yeah? That's cool... it really is."

"Oh yeah, Grace, show him that article you've been saving."

Grace went and retrieved a newspaper lying among a stack of papers. She removed the paper clip on one of the pages toward the end and pointed to the article circled in red for him to read. Jonathan's face brightened as he read the Mexican paper.

He was far more fluent in Spanish than I am. The only thing I know is that we found a small article that was particularly interesting. My Spanish was a little rusty, but I noticed the word *milagro* sprinkled throughout the story. The best I could make of it was that this miracle happened in a small town hospital in which three AIDS patients who were on their deathbeds were miraculously cured overnight. No explanation. The doctors were completely baffled. The locals were on their hands and knees testifying that they had witnessed a *milagro* or miracle! They swore they saw the Dark Virgin of Guadalupe visiting the patient's bedsides the night they were cured. She was brown skinned and wearing a multicolored robe.

"I knew there was a reason I had to come back to the living!" He laughed slapping the paper enthusiastically. "Some things never change!" He began reading the article again.

"No they don't." I laughed heartily.

"So when are we going to take a Mexican vacation?"

"In time," Grace said with a note of caution, hugging him with one arm and holding my hand with the other. "We just have to be patient. Let things die down a little. Go on with our lives. The right time will present itself."

"Man, that sounds familiar," Jonathan teased.

Damn, it felt good to laugh again.

ABOUT THE AUTHOR

Wayne L. Wilson was born and raised in Los Angeles, California. He received a Master of Arts in Education, with a specialization in Sociology and Anthropology, from the University of California, Los Angeles. Prior to establishing a career in writing, Wilson co-owned and operated an international publishing company, specializing in innovative multicultural designs for fifteen years. Wilson has written ten published books targeted toward children and young adults. His short stories and essays have been published in commercial and literary magazines. Wilson is also a screenwriter and a member of the Writers Guild of America. Presently, Wayne lives in Santa Monica, California with his daughter.

Excerpt from

LIFE IS NEVER AS IT SEEMS

BY

J. J. MICHAEL

Release Date: August 2005

CHAPTER ONE

Spring of 1967

Reverend Perlie Johnson of Mount Olive Baptist Church eased his aching body onto the purple seat cushion of the old African wooden chair. He breathed a sigh of relief that at last he could sit down. The chair, with its detailed Egyptian carvings on the back, wasn't the type of chair you would ordinarily find at a church pulpit. It stood out and was a bit much for most traditional Baptist churches. However, it supported Reverend Johnson's heavy frame and aching back. At sixty-seven, Rev, as he was called by his congregation, didn't care what others thought of him.

He was drained of energy, for the Holy Spirit had descended on him. It wasn't the first time this had happened in his forty years of preaching. This Sunday morning he felt tired and old. Maybe, he thought, it was time to retire from the only thing that he loved and knew how to do—preach. The problem was who would take his place?

God had not granted him the gift of a son, and he was not about to turn his church over to any of the up and coming young ministers who thought they knew everything. No, somehow he had to find the way to go on until God was ready for him to stop.

He had been wrestling all week with how to get a message across to his congregation. It all started with a conversation he had had earlier in the week with his right-hand man, Deacon Willie Coleman.

"Rev, you heard about all that mess going on at Howard U?" Deacon Coleman asked.

"You mean those militants or Black Panthers, whatever they call themselves, stirring up the young people on the campuses across the country?" Rev replied.

"Yeah, they're the ones," Coleman confirmed.

"They're at Howard, uh."

"Yeah, they're the ones that closed down the administration building."

"What's wrong with the president and deans over there, letting those rabble-rousers on the campus? They're a bad influence on the young people, teaching bigotry, hate and separatism. We got to do something."

"I don't know how much you can do, or anyone else for that matter," the deacon replied. "This movement is strong. It could turn out to be a pretty nasty fight. Do you want the church to be involved in that type of battle? You never know what side people will take."

"You got a point there, Coleman. The least I can do is start right here with our church family. We have to make sure our members, and especially the young people, are not involved in any of these goings-on. If they are, I want them to get out!" Reverend raised his voice. "The only cause they need to serve is the Lord's! That damn war in Vietnam isn't helping this country any. Our young boys are being sent over to some foreign country to be killed, maimed and hooked on drugs. What's this country coming to?"

"I don't know, Rev. Things haven't been right since Kennedy was assassinated."

"I tell you it's nothing but the devil taking over the minds of our young folks. Look at how they're dressing. Any young woman with any respect for herself would not go prancing around in those skirts that stop at least ten inches above the knee. If she bends over, you would see what God gave her. They better not try and wear any of that mess around here. Thank God my granddaughter Lindy is not involved or influenced by any of that mess."

Deacon Coleman could see how riled up his minister was. "Now, Rev, the movement has some good points. It is giving our kids a sense of their roots, self-esteem, and taking pride in how they look," the deacon said, readying himself for a challenge as he looked the Reverend dead in the eye.

"I don't mind them taking pride in themselves, but they cross the line when they foster violence, anti-white messages, and disrespect what we worked for all these years. That's all I am saying. These Black Power people are wearing those loud-colored African dashiki shirts, and if that isn't bad enough, look how they are wearing their hair. It is a disgrace to the Negro race."

"We are not called Negroes anymore, Rev. We are black folks," Deacon Coleman pointed out. "Don't you listen to the Godfather of Soul, James Brown? 'Say it loud, we're black and we're proud!'" He laughed. He liked to taunt his old friend.

"Black? Man, there is not a black spot on me, or you for that matter. We are colored folks, Negroes, and don't you forget that," Reverend Johnson chided him.

After that conversation, Rev went into prayer and asked God to show him or tell him what to do. During the week, he worked on changing his sermon, but the words he wanted wouldn't come. On Sunday morning, he proceeded with his original sermon, "Getting Your House in Order," when midway through the message, he felt the Holy Spirit rise up in him. He always knew when it happened. He would get hot, hotter than normal. Even his voice changed. Then the words would just pour out of him. Rev came from behind the pulpit and stared out at the congregation. They knew the Spirit was upon him. They had witnessed this many times.

"We got to get order in our houses," he began. "God's house is in order. God didn't put us in a disorderly world. We create our own disorder. I think there is a lesson here for us to learn. When we have children, we have to have our houses in order. Why are we letting our daughters, our women, flaunt themselves in an ungodly manner? They're not living a Christian life."

Several people hollered, "Amen, Rev. Come on, preach the word!"

"Our women have been dressing like harlots, wearing dresses and skirts that only have a yard of material. And pants that don't cover the area that don't need to be seen! What do they call them? Yeah, *hot pants*!" Rev's voice screeched as he said the last two words.

"They cover their faces with cakes of makeup that make them look like Jezebels…"

The congregation was silent.

"You know that they are up to no good when they put on their Jezebel costume. Because that it exactly what it is, a costume. They're doing the devil's work, enticing the men to fall and sin. All that makeup, that nakedness, and that big hair is the work of Satan. We can't let Satan into this house. No, sir. We have to keep order in this house. Satan is trying to confuse us by making women think they should wear the pants. Next thing you know, the men will be wearing dresses."

He paused, and the congregation laughed. Rev knew humor would lighten the mood.

"Satan is at work here," he went on. "Strike him down, Father. Send him back where he belongs—to Hell."

"Amen!" screamed the congregation in unison, as if someone had held up a cue card.

"Don't come into this Lord's house dressed like harlots. Get right with God." Rev held the Bible up at the congregation. "Put on some decent clothes to worship in the House of the Lord, and going to school and work. Jesus ran those money-baggers out of the church. He'll run you out, too."

Some of the sisters of the church stood waving their hands in agreement with the minister.

"We're not going to sit by and do nothing and let this church, city and country go to Hell. I am here to tell old Satan: Get back. We are Christians, and we are going to fight you, Satan. We are not giving up on our Christian sisters and brothers without a battle. So get back, devil."

Rev stopped for a moment as if he were listening to someone speaking to him. By now the church members were on their feet urging the minister on. Finally Rev Johnson turned and strutted back and forth across the dais. He was speaking so fast the congregation could hardly understand what he was saying.

"The Holy Spirit is telling me this morning that you young people need to show some respect and appreciation for your elders instead of giving them backlash. Your parents work hard for you every day so that you can go to school and college to help raise up our Negro race. And what do you do? Drop out of school, and get involved with drugs and the wrong crowd. Talking about 'they're my friends.' Friends? Let me tell you who they really are—demons! You called them friends. Child, they want your soul. They frequent those places you hang out at—you know what I'm talking about—wearing disguises, the big hair, short dresses and dashikis. What do they do? They give you cigarettes, sex, marijuana, and alcohol, promising you a good time. What do you give them? Your soul. That's right, your soul.

"You think you know everything. We old folks, as you call us, don't know anything. You know it all. You think we weren't young once. The devil, he's just laughing, as he sets that trap for you. Then when you are down, whom do you blame? You point the finger at your parents, the government and the church. Don't fall into that trap. Save yourselves. Get right with God. Obey your mother and father. Honor your mother and father. It's called God Power."

Rev stopped and wiped his forehead then leaned on the podium for support. "I'm tired, children. I'm tired now. You know what you need to do to get right with God. God doesn't like his children not obeying. He will punish you. It all starts in the home and church. We old folks have to see that there is togetherness and order in the home. Obedience starts in the home and church. When order is seen in the home, it will reflect itself in the community. Don't let these fast-talking, slick devil workers pull the wool over your eyes. Walk with the Holy Spirit. Talk with the Holy Spirit, and see with the Holy Spirit. Won't you join the church today? Let the Holy Spirit move you today. Remember, say it loud: God Power!"

"God Power!" shouted the congregation. They clapped their hands, held them up to receive the Holy Spirit and shouted as the Spirit took over. The organist struck the keys to "We are Soldiers in the Army, We Got to Fight," and the gospel and young people's choir began to sing.

Several visitors came forward and joined the church. Reverend Johnson smiled to himself as he thought of how he could still arouse the Holy Spirit in himself and others. At least 700 or more people, from what he could tell, were packed into the church; even the balcony was full. He silently thanked the Holy Spirit. If someone didn't like his sermon or wanted to complain, he would tell them to complain to the Holy Spirit, for it wasn't his words that Sunday morning, but the words of God.

Silently, he thanked his grandfather and father. Both had been southern Baptist preachers from Virginia. He had been ordained into the ministry by both of them. The difference between him and them was that he went on to divinity school. Rev soon found out that he learned more from watching his father and grandfather than from the school.

He could hear his father saying, "Boy, you got to make them shout, cry, and call on the Lord. Fall down on one knee and look up to the heavens, and pray as if the devil was after you," Papa John would chuckle.

Rev recalled watching his father strut back and forth across the pulpit, mesmerizing the worshippers with his heartbreaking stories. Then he would call on Jesus Christ and the Holy Spirit. "Get control of them early and always keep them in the palm of your hand," Papa had told him. "Moreover, whatever you do, invoke the power of the Holy Spirit." It always worked.

As he made his way to his chair, Rev took the white linen handkerchief from the pocket of his robe and wiped away the beads of sweat that had formed on his brow and nose. His grayish white hair was almost plastered to his skull. He wore his hair long to cover the thinning around the top of his skull. He ran his hands through his hair to make sure every strand was in place.

Rev shifted his weight on the chair to lean on his side, to get a better view of the Sunday school children as they marched down the center aisle of the church, until they all stood in front of the dais. The podium blocked part of his view of the congregation, which he thought was good. He didn't have to stare into their faces after he gave the word. Sometimes the extremely severe message was targeted at a particular member or members. Rev could then retreat and study their reaction by sneaking a look around the podium.

He barely heard the young people reciting their poems. His mind kept drifting in and out. He wiped the sweat from his brow again and reached for a glass of water. He was exhausted from preaching for over an hour, and the weather was unbearable. One would think that it was already August in DC. It was near 90 degrees, and it was only May. The sweat kept pouring down the Rev's face. Another hot Sunday like today and he was not going to make it. He made a mental note to tell his daughter Margaret to set the air conditioning at a lower temperature next Sunday if it was still hot. One could never tell about the weather in DC. It was as fickle as their football team, the Redskins.

Rev remembered when the church didn't have air-conditioning, and they had to suffer through those long hot days. He wasn't going to do that anymore. Through the years they had raised funds and renovated the church, bought the property next to the church, and built a parsonage, all thanks to the efforts of Margaret. She chaired the committee that was responsible for the renovation and restoration of the church. It took several years to complete the project. Many board members opposed the restoration of the church that included the building of the parsonage, saying it cost too much. Margaret fought them tooth and nail until she got every penny she needed to do the job.

Coming up 16th Street going north toward Silver Spring, one couldn't help but notice the large gray brick structure with the well-kept lawn and the large sign that read: The House of the Lord, Mt. Olive Baptist Church, Pastor Perlie Johnson. The interior décor was just as beautiful as the exterior. Rev's dream had come true.

It seemed like only yesterday that he was a young man attending Howard University Divinity School. He had left southern Virginia after that awful thing had happened with his beloved Amanda, and his father had passed. Rev felt a slight pain in his chest. After all these years, he still felt something whenever he thought about those years. He tried to forget that time in his life. He had told the founding members of the church that he was reborn the day he left out of Virginia. He brought his mother and baby daughter with him. It was rumored that his wife had run off with another man—a white man. But he never talked about his past, and they never asked.

He worked nights at the main post office sorting mail. It was a good job for a Negro man. During the day he attended school. Rev dreamed about having a big church on 16th Street, the Gold Coast and spiritual corridor of Washington, DC. He knew that previously closed doors of Washington society would open to him. He found people in DC to be very cliquish. Nevertheless, he knew that money, time, and having the right skin color would win out.

Rev figured he had a lot to be grateful for. The church was getting ready to celebrate its fortieth anniversary. It was thriving, and more and more people were joining every week. Margaret's health was better; the spells had subsided. Rev prayed everyday that God would relieve her of her misery, or at least let him get some rest from it. His only granddaughter had just graduated from Howard and was getting ready to go to medical school in the fall. *Yea, God is good,* he thought.

Reverend Johnson looked to his right at the young people's choir. He could not see the face of his granddaughter, but her brownish blond hair could not be missed. Rev closed his eyes and remembered the first day he had looked at her in the hospital crib.

She had startled him when she opened her eyes. The violet blue eyes of his wife Amanda stared back at him. As the years passed, Lindy grew to look more and more like her grandmother. What worried Rev was that she also acted a lot like her grandmother, and this was not good.

Rev's watery eyes caught those of Deaconess Walker. He quickly looked away, as he didn't want to lock eyes with that woman. She had become a pain in his side. They used to have fun together until she got too serious, and he had to drop her. She was talking about leaving her husband, his good friend Deacon Walker, so that they could be together.

Rev knew that he couldn't afford a scandal like that. The church folks of Mount Olive Baptist Church would run him out of there, even if he had founded the church. Rev could see the headlines in the *Washington Post* talking about the senior pastor of Mt. Olive Baptist Church expelled from the church for adultery. No way was he going to let that happen to him. Besides, he had had to let her go anyway. Lately, it had been difficult getting the old boy to perform. After all, he was in his late sixties.

He caught a glimpse of Miriam Williams; she had recently joined the church, a widow from North Carolina. She was soft-spoken, not a bad looking woman. Her striking feature was her body. She was hippy with big legs, something he'd always found attractive in a woman. Maybe it wasn't too late for him to settle down.

He had almost remarried years ago, soon after he had moved to Washington. Julia Palmer was her name. He thought about how she kept pressing him to get married. Julia was a good woman and would have been a good mother for Margaret, though he doubted whether Margaret thought so.

But Julia had given him an ultimatum to marry her or she would leave. Just when he had almost given in, he'd had that damn dream again. It had started soon after he left Virginia.

He would wake up in a sweat, with tears running down his face. At first, he couldn't remember the details, just a sketchy outline of the events. Eventually, he began to remember bits and pieces of the dream.

He would barely lay his head on the pillow before he would hear this buzzing sound, and bells. After many years, Rev realized that the sounds were bells—faintly, but nevertheless bells. As the buzzing sound got louder and the bells dimmer, he felt as though he was being sucked out of his body. He was in complete darkness. Fear gripped him, and then these horrible, grotesque faces appeared in front of him. Rev could not see their bodies, but he sensed that they were trying to pull him down. Just when he thought they were going to engulf him, Rev felt another presence, a light, in the distance.

Instantaneously, he started moving toward the light. He could still feel the power of the others trying to get him. Whenever the fear gripped him, Rev moved back toward them. The bells got loud again, and he felt this feeling of love, and he tried again to move toward the presence. The presence was Amanda. Her arms were stretched out reaching out for him. She was standing at the gateway to a city called Shamballa. Rev tried calling to her, but no words came out of his mouth. He woke up frightened out of his wits...

He had the dream one night that he and Julia spent together. He felt her shaking him.

"Perlie, Perlie wake up, you're dreaming."

He'd opened his eyes and stared at her. She had a troubled look on her face. He felt tears running down his face. His chest was heaving. After a few seconds, he was able to speak.

"I was dreaming. It's OK; I'm all right, go back to sleep. I had better leave now before it gets light. I don't want Margaret looking for me."

Although he had the dream quite frequently, he and Julia never talked about it again. She knew it was the same dream, because he always tossed around in the bed and screamed out the name Amanda.

Julia suspected that something terrible had happened to him or his wife before he came to Washington. She tried to get him to talk about it, but Perlie would give her a cold stare. She felt him drifting away from her. Was it the dream coming between them, or was he still in love with his wife? Julia begged him to go get help, but he was too proud to see a psychiatrist.

"What would my congregation and my daughter think about me seeing a shrink? No," he would tell her. "It was just a dream."

After the dream, he would be withdrawn for days. Julia couldn't get him to go anywhere. He would stay cooped up in his office or the church. He didn't have time for her. Julia decided to give him an ultimatum. Get help so they could move on, hopefully to get married, or she was leaving. She never heard from him again. Julia decided the best thing to do was to move back to Florida to care for her aging parents. Many years later, Rev heard that she had married her high school sweetheart.

All he had left of Amanda was that dream, until the suitcase came. It came with a letter informing him she had died of malaria in Africa. Her body, as she wished, was buried there. All her belongings were in that one battered suitcase.

He took the old suitcase and put it up in the attic. It was months before he opened it. When he lifted up the lid of the suitcase, he could smell her. His eyes watered and his heart ached. Rev quickly looked through the things. He pulled out a Bible that was marked with writing all through it. Amanda had neatly filled in the family genealogy, hers and his. His remorse turned to anger; he tore the pages out, and then felt badly that he had desecrated the Bible.

He moaned as he read the title of the second book, *The Book of Life*, by Two Adepts. Two adepts of the devil, he thought. The book brought back old hurtful memories to him. Amanda had changed after she had started reading it and going to those meetings with the white folks. They'd acted as if Amanda was one of them. When he'd asked her about them, she would clam up.

Papa John told me that I had to put my foot down, Rev thought ruefully. He had raised me to be a man and not to be led around by the apron strings of a pretty woman. Those white folks were putting ideas in her head, making her think that she was better than the rest of us because she looked like them.

Rev had found two pieces of her jewelry: the ring he had given her on the day they got married, and the gold heart-shaped pendant he'd given her when Margaret was born. He put the jewelry in his pocket and tossed the books back into the suitcase. Rev squeezed the suitcase under some other junk in the attic. He vowed to throw it away one day, but for right now he decided it was best left alone.

When Margaret turned sixteen, he gave her Amanda's ring. She never wore it. On Lindy's sixteenth birthday, he gave her the gold pendant. She never took it off. It was like having Amanda back, and that was what worried him. The though of her and all those old memories made Rev want to scream. *Why, Amanda, why did you do it?* It was over. Let it die.

The Sunday school children finished their program, to the joy of all. Rev wiped away the sweat now mixed with tears.

SOUL EYES

2005 Publication Schedule

January

A Heart's Awakening
Veronica Parker
$9.95
1-58571-143-8

Falling
Natalie Dunbar
$9.95
1-58571-121-7

February

Echoes of Yesterday
Beverly Clark
$9.95
1-58571-131-4

A Love of Her Own
Cheris F. Hodges
$9.95
1-58571-136-5

Higher Ground
Leah Latimer
$19.95
1-58571-157-8

March

Misconceptions
Pamela Leigh Starr
$9.95
1-58571-117-9

I'll Paint a Sun
A.J. Garrotto
$9.95
1-58571-165-9

Peace Be Still
Colette Haywood
$12.95
1-58571-129-2

April

Intentional Mistakes
Michele Sudler
$9.95
1-58571-152-7

Conquering Dr. Wexler's Heart
Kimberley White
$9.95
1-58571-126-8

Song in the Park
Martin Brant
$15.95
1-58571-125-X

May

The Color Line
Lizzette Grayson Carter
$9.95
1-58571-163-2

Unconditional
A.C. Arthur
$9.95
1-58571-142-X

Last Train to Memphis
Elsa Cook
$12.95
1-58571-146-2

June

Angel's Paradise
Janice Angelique
$9.95
1-58571-107-1

Suddenly You
Crystal Hubbard
$9.95
1-58571-158-6

Matters of Life and
    Death
Lesego Malepe, Ph.D.
$15.95
1-58571-124-1

2005 Publication Schedule (continued)

July

Class Reunion
Irma Jenkins/John
  Brown
$12.95
1-58571-123-3

Wild Ravens
Altonya Washington
$9.95
1-58571-164-0

August

Path of Thorns
Annetta P. Lee
$9.95
1-58571-145-4

Timeless Devotion
Bella McFarland
$9.95
1-58571-148-9

Life Is Never As It Seems
J.J. Michael
$12.95
1-58571-153-5

September

Beyond Rapture
Beverly Clark
$9.95
1-58571-131-4

Blood Lust
J. M. Jeffries
$9.95
1-58571-138-1

Rough on Rats and
  Tough on Cats
Chris Parker
$12.95
1-58571-154-3

October

A Will to Love
Angie Daniels
$9.95
1-58571-141-1

Taken by You
Dorothy Elizabeth Love
$9.95
1-58571-162-4

Soul Eyes
Wayne L. Wilson
$12.95
1-58571-147-0

November

A Drummer's Beat to
  Mend
Kei Swanson
$9.95
1-58571-171-3

Sweet Reprecussions
Kimberley White
$9.95
1-58571-159-4

Red Polka Dot in a
  World of Plaid
Varian Johnson
$12.95
1-58571-140-3

December

Hand in Glove
Andrea Jackson
$9.95
1-58571-166-7

Blaze
Barbara Keaton
$9.95
1-58571-172-1

Across
Carol Payne
$12.95
1-58571-149-7

Other Genesis Press, Inc. Titles

Acquisitions	Kimberley White	$8.95
A Dangerous Deception	J.M. Jeffries	$8.95
A Dangerous Love	J.M. Jeffries	$8.95
A Dangerous Obsession	J.M. Jeffries	$8.95
After the Vows (Summer Anthology)	Leslie Esdaile T.T. Henderson Jacqueline Thomas	$10.95
Again My Love	Kayla Perrin	$10.95
Against the Wind	Gwynne Forster	$8.95
A Lark on the Wing	Phyliss Hamilton	$8.95
A Lighter Shade of Brown	Vicki Andrews	$8.95
All I Ask	Barbara Keaton	$8.95
A Love to Cherish	Beverly Clark	$8.95
Ambrosia	T.T. Henderson	$8.95
And Then Came You	Dorothy Elizabeth Love	$8.95
Angel's Paradise	Janice Angelique	$8.95
A Risk of Rain	Dar Tomlinson	$8.95
At Last	Lisa G. Riley	$8.95
Best of Friends	Natalie Dunbar	$8.95
Bound by Love	Beverly Clark	$8.95
Breeze	Robin Hampton Allen	$10.95
Brown Sugar Diaries & Other Sexy Tales	Delores Bundy & Cole Riley	$10.95
By Design	Barbara Keaton	$8.95
Cajun Heat	Charlene Berry	$8.95
Careless Whispers	Rochelle Alers	$8.95
Caught in a Trap	Andre Michelle	$8.95
Chances	Pamela Leigh Starr	$8.95
Dark Embrace	Crystal Wilson Harris	$8.95
Dark Storm Rising	Chinelu Moore	$10.95
Designer Passion	Dar Tomlinson	$8.95
Ebony Butterfly II	Delilah Dawson	$14.95

Erotic Anthology	Assorted	$8.95
Eve's Prescription	Edwina Martin Arnold	$8.95
Everlastin' Love	Gay G. Gunn	$8.95
Fate	Pamela Leigh Starr	$8.95
Forbidden Quest	Dar Tomlinson	$10.95
Fragment in the Sand	Annetta P. Lee	$8.95
From the Ashes	Kathleen Suzanne	$8.95
	Jeanne Sumerix	
Gentle Yearning	Rochelle Alers	$10.95
Glory of Love	Sinclair LeBeau	$10.95
Hart & Soul	Angie Daniels	$8.95
Heartbeat	Stephanie Bedwell-Grime	$8.95
I'll Be Your Shelter	Giselle Carmichael	$8.95
Illusions	Pamela Leigh Starr	$8.95
Indiscretions	Donna Hill	$8.95
Interlude	Donna Hill	$8.95
Intimate Intentions	Angie Daniels	$8.95
Just an Affair	Eugenia O'Neal	$8.95
Kiss or Keep	Debra Phillips	$8.95
Love Always	Mildred E. Riley	$10.95
Love Unveiled	Gloria Greene	$10.95
Love's Deception	Charlene Berry	$10.95
Mae's Promise	Melody Walcott	$8.95
Meant to Be	Jeanne Sumerix	$8.95
Midnight Clear	Leslie Esdaile	$10.95
(Anthology)	Gwynne Forster	
	Carmen Green	
	Monica Jackson	
Midnight Magic	Gwynne Forster	$8.95
Midnight Peril	Vicki Andrews	$10.95
My Buffalo Soldier	Barbara B. K. Reeves	$8.95
Naked Soul	Gwynne Forster	$8.95
No Regrets	Mildred E. Riley	$8.95
Nowhere to Run	Gay G. Gunn	$10.95

Object of His Desire	A. C. Arthur	$8.95
One Day at a Time	Bella McFarland	$8.95
Passion	T.T. Henderson	$10.95
Past Promises	Jahmel West	$8.95
Path of Fire	T.T. Henderson	$8.95
Picture Perfect	Reon Carter	$8.95
Pride & Joi	Gay G. Gunn	$8.95
Quiet Storm	Donna Hill	$8.95
Reckless Surrender	Rochelle Alers	$8.95
Rendezvous with Fate	Jeanne Sumerix	$8.95
Revelations	Cheris F. Hodges	$8.95
Rivers of the Soul	Leslie Esdaile	$8.95
Rooms of the Heart	Donna Hill	$8.95
Shades of Brown	Denise Becker	$8.95
Shades of Desire	Monica White	$8.95
Sin	Crystal Rhodes	$8.95
So Amazing	Sinclair LeBeau	$8.95
Somebody's Someone	Sinclair LeBeau	$8.95
Someone to Love	Alicia Wiggins	$8.95
Soul to Soul	Donna Hill	$8.95
Still Waters Run Deep	Leslie Esdaile	$8.95
Subtle Secrets	Wanda Y. Thomas	$8.95
Sweet Tomorrows	Kimberly White	$8.95
The Color of Trouble	Dyanne Davis	$8.95
The Price of Love	Sinclair LeBeau	$8.95
The Reluctant Captive	Joyce Jackson	$8.95
The Missing Link	Charlyne Dickerson	$8.95
Three Wishes	Seressia Glass	$8.95
Tomorrow's Promise	Leslie Esdaile	$8.95
Truly Inseperable	Wanda Y. Thomas	$8.95
Twist of Fate	Beverly Clark	$8.95
Unbreak My Heart	Dar Tomlinson	$8.95
Unconditional Love	Alicia Wiggins	$8.95
When Dreams A Float	Dorothy Elizabeth Love	$8.95

Whispers in the Night	Dorothy Elizabeth Love	$8.95
Whispers in the Sand	LaFlorya Gauthier	$10.95
Yesterday is Gone	Beverly Clark	$8.95
Yesterday's Dreams, Tomorrow's Promises	Reon Laudat	$8.95
Your Precious Love	Sinclair LeBeau	$8.95